The Mercy Carver Series

Dark Shadows
Book 1

Jana Petken

Cover design by Novel Design Studios

Also available from Jana Petken:

Multi Award Winning, Best Seller *The Guardian of Secrets*

Screenplay, *The Guardian of Secrets*

Audio book and CD *The Guardian of Secrets*

The Mercy Carver Series: *#1 Best Seller Blood Moon*

Multi Award Winning, Flock Trilogy *The Errant Flock*

The Scattered Flock

Swearing Allegiance: The Carmody Saga

Summer 2017 *Flock: The Gathering of The Damned*

Acknowledgements

Many thanks to Shellie Hurrle, editor

Final edits, Caro Powney

My publicist, Nick Wale.

Bob Martin

and

Rena, my wonderful mother, gone but not forgotten

Author's note

Hi, this story is set in England and in Virginia in the years 1842 and 1860. To be true to the story and the authenticity of the characters, the spelling is in both UK English and American English. I hope you enjoy it.

Amazon Reviews

"What an absolutely superb book. I say this should be a TV series, not because there are so many cliffhanging moments, but because there are so many "Oh Nooooooo! That's not what you should be doing," moments.

Jana Petken grabs the reader by the scruff of his neck and drags him/her straight into the action. She pulls no punches in her writing, you'd better believe that!

Everything's flowing along nicely when without warning the author throws another spanner in the works, leaving the reader with no choice but to hang on tight as she bounces you from pillar to post, from safe streets to brothels, from England to America and from promises to betrayal."

"Trust me, once you sink your teeth into this well-written and mindboggling historical romance, you'll be as keen as I am to see what happens next! On to Blood Moon, Book 2..."

Award Winner Readers' Favorite 5 ***

"Ohhh, long sigh. That is what I did when I finished reading Dark Shadows, the first book in the Mercy Carver series by author Jana Petken. A stunning work of historical fiction, the book is heartbreaking and ultimately a story of redemption.

I enjoyed Dark Shadows to no end. Author Jana Petken has done a wonderful job at creating a lovely and sympathetic character in Mercy Carver; she's a character that the reader will truly feel connected to, and will hope for the very best for her. Jana Petken has also written with an authenticity and real knowledge for the time period and that adds to the very realistic feeling of the book. Dark Shadows would be enjoyed by anyone who loves historical fiction, action, adventure, or just a great work of fiction. I am happy to highly recommend Dark Shadows."

Prologue

London, 1842

All those who saw Joan Carver lying in bed in that softly lit bedroom knew she was dying. No one would say the word *death* out loud. The word was frowned upon, yet it was a constant, a consistent force that took family members, neighbours, and friends on a daily basis in this poor Elephant and Castle district that stood one mile from the South end of London Bridge and fell under the purview of Southwark Borough Council.

The Southwark Elephant and Castle area had an elegant side to it. There were grand houses, theatres, and gardens, and plans to build a new church were well underway, but there was also the overpopulated, poorer streets where large families, widows, and those without employment lived. The houses provided for them were commonly known as almshouses. They were usually free of rent and were, to all intents and purposes, Christian charity homes. But the houses were small, cramped, and in most cases in dire need of repair. Walls crumbled, and every day the sound of hammers and men cursing filled the streets.

Thomas and Joan Carver had been married for just over a year. Thomas had fallen in love with his wife long before she was of an age to notice his affections. They had played in the street together as children: hopscotch, tag, and marbles. He had grown into manhood loving her with a passion that was all-consuming. He had often declared that she was his soulmate, sent to earth in order to spend her entire life being loved by him. He called her an angel and a gift from God.

They lived at 32 Gaylord Street, in a rented, two storey, back-to-back house. It contained one bedroom, a narrow stairway leading off through a door from the one other room they called the parlour; it was furnished with an open fireplace with hooks and fireplace hangars for cooking pots to hang from, a small pantry, one wooden armchair, a small table, and four chairs. Thomas Carver prided himself on being able to pay his rent on time every week, but he was one of the very few in his street who could afford to do so.

Men took whatever jobs they could find for a measly wage, and on a Friday, drowned their woes in beer, taking home an even lighter wage packet to their wives and children. Jobs were scarcer for lower-class women, who fought for domestic service positions in grand houses. This type of work, no matter how menial, was the pinnacle of success for most girls.

Entire families without gainful employment and not on the waiting lists for almshouses were tossed out of their rented homes and forced to enter the world of disease-ridden, hard-labour workhouses. Once there, they were given beds and barely enough food to sustain them, but husbands and wives were separated, as were the fit and the infirm, the old and the young. It was a fate worse than death for some families, but for others, life in the workhouse was a better prospect than slow starvation, plague, and long chronic illnesses leading to the inevitable journey to the local graveyard.

Disease was rife in the Elephant and Castle area. Large families lived in cramped conditions. Sanitary waste gathered in cess pits beneath homes, while horse manure and urine soaked the streets above, causing putrid smells to consume the air. Tonnes of raw sewage dumped straight into the River Thames was eventually carried up the river by the tide. It was a dire situation, and one that plagued these poor Londoners, for tuberculosis, typhoid, influenza, scarlet fever, diphtheria and cholera affected one or more family members in every household in every street. Illness and death became a game of chance in which luck and only luck determined who would remain healthy or who would fall to a, most often, fatal illness.

Thomas Carver was indeed lucky, for, at the age of sixteen, he had managed to procure highly sought after work on the London and Croydon Railway line. This line had been followed by the London and Brighton Railway and the South Eastern Railway lines, and these additional lines had generated new job opportunities. Thomas had a solid and secure job, and he was recognised as being a naturally talented engineer, yet he'd felt compelled to take on a second job at night, delivering coal to the local publicans and hoteliers. And somewhere along the way, Joan was left alone, pregnant, and desperately unhappy.

The local midwife had arrived at dawn on this dull October day. She had also been present the previous day but had left for a few hours rest, promising to come back at a moment's notice. As Thomas had the wherewithal to pay she eventually called the doctor in, and both were of the same mind regarding Joan's prognosis, making this morning particularly painful, for the very same doctor and midwife had delivered Joan seventeen years earlier.

Thomas paced up and down his parlour, cursing under his breath for not spending that precious time with Joan because of ambition and greed. He found himself thinking about their last quarrel, Joan's tearful face, and her arms around his neck as she pleaded with him to spare her a thought and a moment of his time.

"Money will not bring us the 'appiness we seek," Joan had stated. "'appiness comes when we are together. Whether we are dressed in new clothes or rags makes not an ounce of difference. Thomas, I need you in my bed at night, not the extra sixpence you make heaving sacks of coal."

Joan had been right all along, he thought, for his happiness was complete only when she was by his side.

As Thomas paced in the small hallway, deep in thought, the house was being steadily filled up with family members. His mother and mother-in-law were with Joan in the bedroom. His father and father-in-law sat in the parlour, along with two of Joan's male cousins and Thomas's brother. Thomas was joined in the tiny hallway by three female cousins, who were beginning to get in the way of his pacing.

A growing number of friends and men Thomas worked with had also joined the small group of close neighbours already outside number 32. They came to sympathise, to pray, and to comfort the Carver family. Joan had already gone in their minds, for they knew they would never again see her alive. She would not walk down the street with her bright smile, lightening the moods of those she met along the way. She would never again make her customary broth for sick neighbours or enrich lives with her kindness, exquisite beauty, and graceful countenance rarely seen on these poor streets.

The crowd continued to grow, not only to listen to the doctor's pronouncement of death, which would surely come but hopefully to hear and cheer the news that Joan had somehow managed to deliver a living, healthy baby that even now fought bravely to leave the womb before its mother took her last breath.

Some of the women living in Joan and Thomas's street had brought an assortment of baked goods and anything else they could spare from their measly pantries. The men, sensing that young Thomas would appreciate a drop of gin, had dutifully chipped in to buy him a bottle.

As the morning wore on, Thomas, a mild-mannered man transformed into a frightening mess of jumbled and unpredictable reactions. His wife's screams of "Mercy, God, 'ave mercy" were like daggers slicing into his heart, and he silently cursed God, his Son, and all his angels. Thomas no longer paced, but rather stepped in time in the now-crowded hallway, filled to the brim with the presence of yet more family members. He wasn't in the mood to talk and told those present to stop asking questions. He drank a cupful of gin and told his three female cousins, who were chatting among themselves, to shut up and go outside. Finally, he came to stand inches from the closed bedroom door.

"Where the blazes is God?" he inadvertently said out loud.

His sister-in-law, Lizzie, was praying, and she gasped at his foul language.

Thomas's face was creased and filled with rage as he turned to stand nose to nose with her. "Shut up! Shut up right now, you! Who are you praying to, eh?" he shouted. "There is no bloody God, and if there were, I'd call him a cruel and 'eartless bastard for what he's putting my poor Joan through!"

He turned from Lizzie, and his hands caressed the bedroom door. Tears ran unabated down his face. He knocked on the door. "Let me in," he sobbed.

It was scandalous for any man to behave like this in front of other men toughened by life's troubles, but Thomas was past caring about what was right and what was wrong in the eyes of old women and men he could knock down with one punch. He needed to see Joan, to hold her and to comfort her. If she was going to leave the world with him alone in it, he wanted to say goodbye in his own way. He had every right to be with her until her last breath.

He'd made up his mind. He looked at the grieving faces and saw their silent warnings. *Don't you dare go into that bedroom*, they were saying with their eyes.

Bugger off the lot of you, Thomas thought dismissively before turning the doorknob and opening the door.

As he entered the room, he breathed in the rancid smell that hung in the air. Then his bright, tear-filled eyes saw the blood. He stood motionless.

Thomas's mother and mother-in-law left the room immediately, unable to witness Thomas's reaction to the horror of seeing his young wife dying.

The doctor and midwife stopped what they were doing and helplessly watched as Thomas gulped for air between throaty sobs.

Thomas tiptoed closer to the bed. His whole body shook with grief and disbelief. He hadn't expected Joan to look *this* bad, so pitiful and shrivelled. She looked like an old woman.

"That's not my Joan!" he said to the doctor dazedly. "That's not my beautiful wife."

Blood loss had turned the frayed white cotton sheets bright red. Joan's raging fever had stranded her in some distant world, parted from reality, and without conscious knowledge that she had to push a baby out of her. Her clammy skin, high temperature, and rolling, glazed eyes were clear signs that she had already succumbed to childbed fever, an all too frequent infection that occurred when a baby was too large for a young and malnourished body. Joan was like a small, fragile bird, in size, with narrow hips and a feather's weight.

She was whimpering one word that was barely audible: "Mercy, mercy, mercy," over and over until it sounded like a soft, hypnotic lullaby to Thomas's ears. Thomas couldn't take his eyes off her thighs. Her legs were wide open, and drops of lumpy blood were bursting out of her birth canal in quick succession. He cried, and then he got on his knees and begged the doctor to save her.

The doctor tried to pick Thomas up, glaring at him with both anger and pity.

"Get up, for God's sake. I've seen men lose their wives more times than I can count, and their babies. But you're behaving like a demented fool!" he whispered ferociously. "Get up off the floor and get out of here. I'll not be disturbed like this."

There was no response from Thomas.

"Thomas Carver, you get up from that floor and let me do my job!"

Thomas wrapped his arms around the doctor's legs.

The doctor spoke to the midwife, standing with her hands at her throat in shock. "Get someone to bloody well take him away, right now."

Thomas's brother, John, and his father, Tom, appeared and physically dragged him by his shirt collar across the floor and then outside to the landing.

Thomas, gaining his senses now, was also filling with a rage he never knew existed in him.

On the landing, the doctor begged Thomas to calm down, ordering everyone present to restrain him from entering the bedroom again. "I can't have you in there, Thomas. I have to get this baby out, and you're getting in my way. If Joan doesn't deliver soon, she'll die with it still inside her!"

His statement shocked family members, neighbours, friends, and even Thomas into silence. The word *death* had finally been spoken aloud.

Thomas heard and lost all reason. His already mangled thoughts were now joined by images of blood pouring down his wife's open legs, her sweaty hair sticking to her head, her fevered eyes wide but unseeing, and her open mouth asking for mercy in a voice he didn't recognise.

Getting up off the floor, before his friends could react, he grabbed the doctor by the throat. Walking backwards, he pulled the doctor towards the front door, threatening to kill him. He bumped into friends and neighbours in the crowded hallway, barely noticing their presence but finding the strength to knock aside anyone who barred his way. This was a new Thomas, a stranger to family, neighbours, and workmates who had never seen this side of his character. The quiet, gentle man had turned into a raging bulldog, intent on killing the doctor who was trying to save his wife's life.

Outside the house, Thomas was finally pulled off the doctor and forcibly pinned to the ground by his father, father-in-law, and neighbour.

Tom, Thomas's father, had seen his wife lose three infants. Looking embarrassed, he leant into Thomas's ear. "You've turned Joan's last 'ours or minutes into a bloody sideshow! Get up, ya' stupid git and behave like a man," he hissed. "You're a bleedin' disgrace. Carver men don't cry. You're giving me a right showing up in front of the whole bloody street, d'you 'ear me?"

"I can't lose 'er, Pop," Thomas wept.

"Joan won't be the first to lose a babe or her life giving birth. You're old enough to know that, so get a grip of yourself, for Christ's sake. I brought you up to be a man, not a weeping woman."

Whilst Tom Carver spoke to his son; the doctor crawled on all fours until he managed to get to his feet some distance away from Thomas who'd been very close to choking the life out of him. He was still coughing and holding his reddened neck as he rushed past neighbours who watched in horror. Fearing for his life, he muttered, "Crazy bugger."

Thomas was held by his arms on the dusty ground until the doctor disappeared from sight. He was then freed but continued to sit where he was, crying, apologising, and now deaf to his father's continued insistence that he should get back on his feet and make amends to everyone present.

Another local midwife was sent for immediately. Thomas calmed himself and walked back inside his house, apologising to everyone he passed. Minnie Fowler from next door told him that her husband had gone for the best and most popular midwife in the area. "She's delivered 'undreds of babies, and a lot of 'em 'ave lived," she said proudly.

Thomas nodded in appreciation and went back to Joan's bedside, ignoring numerous pleas not to. "No one will keep me away from my Joan," he told everyone quite calmly. "I'll be there for 'er, 'olding 'er 'and until an 'ealthy baby comes out of 'er and she falls into a peaceful sleep."

As he closed the door behind him, he told himself not to lose hope. Losing hope earlier had caused him to go mad. He would cling to it. He would pray. He would kill anyone who mentioned the word *death* again.

Joan's wailing now sounded like the dying cries of a wounded animal. She arched her back to a breaking point. Her body was wracked with spasms that almost lifted her in the air.

The mothers were with her again. Joan's mother, Sylvie, made the sign of the cross. Thomas's mother, Grace, eventually ran from the room, unable to watch the ugliness of it all.

Mercy; that pitiful word continued to fall off Joan's tongue as though no other word existed in her mind.

Sylvie tried in vain to stem the blood flowing freely between her daughter's legs, whilst urging her to push the baby out at the same time.

Joan tilted her head back on the pillow and stared up at the ceiling. "Oh God, have mercy! Show mercy to this child! Please, mercy…mercy for my baby!"

She suddenly stopped speaking and moving. Silence filled the room. Her breathing slowed to a soft, panting breathlessness, and she closed her eyes, unconscious now to her world of pain.

Thomas left the room of his own accord; he was not strong enough to watch his wife's suffering, after all.

In the hallway, he slid down the wall and once again cried openly in front of the men he worked with. He covered his face and prayed between sobs.

A large-framed midwife with a ruddy face, warts, and heavy chin trotted into the house with a determined expression, but one which also lacked emotion. She suddenly stopped when she saw the multitude of men in the hallway and stared at all the faces in turn. Her hands then went to her hips and rested there, clenched, as though they were ready to do battle.

"Right, who's the father here? Who's the 'usband that's being a sissy, by all accounts?" she demanded to know.

The crowd parted, and Thomas looked up at her for the first time. Wiping his teary eyes, he said, "I'm Thomas Carver. Will you save my wife, please? Save her. She can always have another baby…just save her."

"I'll try my best, boy. That's all I can do."

"Please. She's young, and she's got her whole life ahead of 'er. I can live with the death of a child but not 'ers…never 'ers."

The midwife rolled up her sleeves with impatience. Her eyes flashed Thomas a warning. "You pull yourself together. That's enough of that sort of talk. From what I've been told, your wife is in a very bad way, and you sitting 'ere on the floor like a bloody moody schoolboy won't change that. Now, go and get yourself a stiff drink and wait as any other man does in your situation. You have to be strong. I can't be doing with 'ysterical fathers-to-be. Do you 'ear me?"

Thomas nodded his head.

"Thomas, I need you to stay out 'ere. If it's God's will, she'll deliver and live, but be ready for the worst." Her voice then grew harsh as she turned her attention to the other men present. She pointed to the bedroom. "Right, you lot. No one, and I mean no one, goes in there. No matter what you 'ear from that room, keep *'im* out." Then, she walked past them and went into the bedroom, closing the door behind her.

Thomas finally stood up, straightened his back, and asked for a shot of gin. No more crying, he told himself and no more making an arse of himself in front of his mates either. He'd gone from hope to despair to hope, and then back to despair so many times these last two days he was bloody dizzy. But he had a gut feeling about this midwife. She seemed to know her stuff.

He needed a drink to settle his nerves. He'd gone off his rocker earlier on, and he'd be the first to admit it.

Joan lost blood every month, and he was overreacting. She was just losing a bit more than usual, that was all.

He shut out all the whispers, noises, and pitiful expressions, and thought about Joan; not as she was now, but as a bright-eyed beauty, the greatest gift a man could receive. He pictured every memory and relived them. Her soft, sweet laughter rang in his ears. Her strong character that had put him in his place more than once made her even more desirable. Her eternal optimism and brave acceptance of poverty were noble and pure, unlike his insatiable ambitions and need for more money. He had quite simply married the perfect woman, and he'd make sure she knew that when this was all over.

He leant against the wall and drank the tot of gin in one quick gulp. Hands intermittently patted his shoulders. He drank another couple of tots. Then he awoke from his dreams to face a grief-stricken road again. His Joan was lost to him. She wasn't going to live. He was kidding himself. He could see by every expression on every face that this was the truth of it. His seventeen-year-old bride of a year was going to leave him alone and take every bit of meaning from his life. He would not be able to live without her.

After a prolonged silence, a piercing scream penetrated the closed bedroom door. Thomas stood in silence, to attention, and as still as a statue as he waited and prayed.

In the crowded hallway and street outside, one could hear a pin drop. The silence was unbearable.

Then the sound of a baby crying loud and vigorously filled listening ears until every person was clapping and crying and patting Thomas on the back.

Silence again. All eyes stared at the closed bedroom door. Thomas slid once again down the wall onto the floor. His legs wouldn't hold him upright another second. It seemed like an eternity, but only minutes passed until the bedroom door finally opened.

The midwife marched out of the bedroom, holding a baby swathed in bloodied sheeting in her arms. She showed the infant to Thomas. "You have an 'ealthy daughter, young Thomas Carver," she said.

Thomas gazed lovingly into the tiny, perfect face. He opened his mouth to speak, but instead, he stopped himself and looked deep into the midwife's unfathomable eyes. "And my wife? 'Ow is she? Can I see 'er?" he whispered hopefully.

The midwife lowered her eyes. They were no longer hard or passive but filled with emotion. She focused on the baby's tiny face, refusing to look Thomas in the eye. "I'm sorry. I'm really sorry, son. I did everything I could…everything. She was just too weak when I got to 'er, and she 'ad already lost too much blood. She was very brave, though, you 'ave to know that. She fought 'ard and got your daughter into the world. She saw 'er just before she took 'er last breath."

Thomas's chin sat on his chest. He was afraid to look at her sorrowful eyes but did hear the midwife's words, "She smiled, Thomas. Your Joan smiled. 'ad she lingered a day or two more, she would have faced terrible suffering, and death would have taken 'er in any case. Believe me; this is for the best. She's at rest and at peace."

Thomas sat on the edge of the bed next to Joan. He was alone, silent, and lost in grief. He stared into Joan's small, oval-shaped face as though looking at her for the first time. A grey pallor, chapped lips, and pain were still deeply etched in her expression, even in death, but she looked better than the last time he'd seen her.

He stroked her wet skin and then looked at the bloodstained sheets. The smell of stale sweat, blood, and death hung in the air. He found it difficult to imagine that the stench belonged to his sweet wife, who always smelled of freshly cut flowers.

He leant in closer and kissed her full lips. Then he lifted the top half of her body until it came to rest on his chest. He rocked her back and forth and stroked her damp black hair, still shimmering like diamonds.

"I love you, my Joanie. You're the only woman I've ever loved or ever will love." The tears rolled down his face. Every now and then he sniffed loudly and wiped his runny nose. He twisted her long, curly tendrils around his fingers, just as he always did. He lifted her face to his and kissed her again, this time on the forehead. Eventually, he let go of her and laid her down on the bed.

He knew what he had to do. She was his soulmate. He thought for a moment. A small smile lifted the corner of his mouth. She might still be here, watching him, waiting for him; he turned around, thinking he might see her shadowy figure beckoning him. There was nothing but emptiness and silence in the room. "Wait for me, Joan," he whispered into the air.

He looked at her a moment longer and then opened a bedside drawer. After lifting out a thick piece of cloth, he unrolled it until it revealed a long dagger. It had a pearl and silver hilt and a long, curved blade. It had been passed down to him by his father, who had been given it by his father. He looked at it, turning it over in his hand. It was probably the most expensive possession he owned, never to be sold or pawned. It was meant to be passed down to his eldest son when one came along, and it was supposed to travel down the Carver line.

All that meant nothing to him now. His younger brother could have it, for this particular Carver line would end with him, here and now.

He laid the dagger on the bed beside Joan. Bending over her, he kissed her forehead, lips, and cheeks for the last time. He held her hand, kissed that too, and then laid her arm by her side for a moment until he got himself into position.

The Bible was on top of the bedside table. He picked it up and grunted, still hating God, his minions, and the world he was leaving.

Lying on his belly face down, he placed the Bible on the pillow. He measured the line and distance from the Bible to the base of his neck, near the small hollow under his Adam's apple. Then he picked up the dagger and sat it atop the Bible's hardcover surface, pointing it upwards until its blade tip caressed the hollow in his throat at a perfect angle. Grabbing Joan's limp hand, he curled it around the pearl hilt. His hand covered hers, holding the blade steady.

"I'm coming with you, my darling girl," he said. "I don't want to stay 'ere without you. Will you forgive me for doing this when you see me in a minute or two?"

Closing his eyes, he concentrated. He was not thinking about courage or fear, nor regret or indecision. No, it was imperative that he focus on the dagger's pearl hilt, not the long blade. His neck needed to make contact with that hilt with one quick thrust downwards, for he might not have the courage or maybe even the means to push the blade into his neck a second time. The very thought of that gave him the determination he needed. He wanted to die almost instantly, without screaming out or languishing there for minutes, choking on his own blood. If Joan were watching, she wouldn't want to see that.

Looking at his wife, he tightened his grip on her hand, took a deep breath, and with one swift push of his head downwards felt the blade pierce his skin. He tried to push it all the way through his throat, but it slipped sideways and came out at the side of his neck, having severed his carotid artery. He coughed silently, and his eyes widened. Blood spurted forcibly from his open mouth, and he drew his last breath.

The discovery of Thomas's dead body was only the beginning of what was to become a nightmarish and unforgettable afternoon for all concerned.

After staring at the blade sticking out of the side of Thomas's neck, all four grandparents' eyes began to wander in a daze. No one spoke. Each was alone in a world he or she could not begin to understand. So profound was the shock that not one single tear fell. There was only a macabrely hypnotic fascination in that room where once a young couple had loved and laughed.

Blood was splattered on the walls. It was on Joan's face and hair. Thomas lay partially face down but twisted towards Joan at an awkward angle, his head impaled in mid-air by the dagger, the hilt of which still rested on top of the Bible and the point protruding from the side of his throat.

Joan's small hand rested beneath Thomas's long, fat fingers. She looked peaceful and serene. Finally, the Jennings' and Carvers left the room, closing the door behind them.

When the commotion outside died down, Thomas's father asked everyone to leave the family in peace. Brothers and sisters were also encouraged to go home. Only Joan's and Thomas's parents would remain.

The undertaker, accompanied by two men in his employ, and a local copper had been and then left in quick succession. The copper had asked questions, and the answers had been precise and clear: Thomas had been alone in the bedroom with his dead wife, as was his right. He had killed himself and been found slumped in death next to her body.

Tom, their spokesman, summed it up by saying, "My son chose to die with his wife. What other answer to your questions can be given when we 'ave none to give?"

Two sets of grandparents and the local vicar sat in stony silence in the Carvers' parlour. Both men had teacups half-filled with medicinal brandy in their trembling hands.

The women lifted cups of hot tea to their lips between intermittent sobs. The vicar held his Bible to his chest but was at a loss to find any suitable words of comfort. Thus, he murmured prayers that no one wanted to hear.

The baby, for a time forgotten, was being rocked back and forth, sleeping contentedly in Sylvie Jennings' arms. A wet nurse had been requested and was due to arrive any minute.

The curtains had been drawn, and the vicar was still being ignored by everyone else in the room.

After a while, it became evident that decisions now had to be made. One set of questioning eyes looked at another. Funeral arrangements and the baby's future should be discussed. All four grandparents were intimately involved, as the vicar reminded them after he'd experienced what he believed to be the longest silence in his career. "The baby must be placed in an orphanage, for there can be no other future for a sinner's child," the vicar's voice rang out clearly and with a tone of authority.

This statement brought life hurtling back into all four grandparents. They shouted a vehement "No!" in unison.

"This baby's going nowhere, Reverend. 'Ow dare you even bloody suggest such a thing? My Thomas had flaws like the rest of us, but he was no sinner!" Tom hissed, trying not to raise his voice or lose his temper.

The baby would go home to the Carvers' house for the time being, all four grandparents agreed. It was also decided there and then that the best course of action would be to take equal responsibility for the child for the foreseeable future.

"What shall we call 'er?" Sylvie Jennings asked the others. "Thomas and Joan never mentioned a name for the infant. They wanted to wait until they saw the babe. Did they say anything to you? " she asked Grace.

Grace Carver shook her head. "No. They were sure a name would just come to them as soon as the child was born and its gender known. We could call her Joan?"

"No!" Sylvie shouted. "Not Joan. I couldn't bear that. I couldn't live with that name. There is…there was only one Joan, and she's gone. My girl, my Joanie's gone…she's gone…"

Joan's father, Walter, cried. He'd said nothing since the sight of Thomas lying dead next to his daughter. He gulped down the last of his brandy, unable to contain his emotions any longer. Pain had slowly seeped into his veins and had rushed through his body like a tidal wave.

"Dear God, my little girl, my Joan…my Joanie, asking for mercy. Christ Almighty that word will stick to me like bloody shite forever! That's all she asked for, Reverend!" he shouted now, turning his anguish towards the vicar. "What bloody mercy did she get, eh? She was dying, and in so much pain I wanted to shoot 'er myself, just to put 'er out of 'er misery. God forgive me, but I did," he sobbed. "Mercy, that's all my Joan asked for, wasn't it? That's all she wanted. That's the only bloody word that came out 'er mouth the whole time she was in agony. She didn't call 'er old dad's name or 'er husband's. She didn't scream for 'er mum either. Bloody mercy, that's all she said. So where was your God, Reverend? Where was 'is blasted mercy, eh? Answer me that?

"They were just a young couple starting up. They had their 'ole lives to get through together. I'm sick and tired of seeing youngsters dying of plague and starvation whilst you sit in people's houses, claiming that God is merciful. You and your Bible and your bloody mumbo-jumbo prayers. Look at you. What words can you say from that blasted book that can ease our suffering, eh? Put the babe in an orphanage? Is that the best you and your God can come up with? Jesus Christ…go on, get out! And take your merciful God with you before I blaspheme further."

"That's enough!" Grace half sobbed, half shouted. "Enough of the cursing, you! Your Joan's at peace now and so is my Thomas. They've gone from us, but this is no time to blame God or anyone else. We 'ave to think about a proper send-off for the two of them; a decent burial. And we need to think about the well-being of this baby. That's all that should concern us now." Grace turned to the vicar. "Reverend Smith, please stay. Walter didn't mean it. 'E's just upset and…"

"Bloody right I'm upset," Walter butted in. "But you're right, love. We need to get this sorted."

The vicar nodded and tentatively relaxed his tense muscles.

Tom poured some more brandy into the cup. The bottle was almost empty. He looked at Walter, still reeling. "'Ere, Walter, we may as well finish it off."

Walter nodded, "I'm grateful Tom. This'll calm me down or send me into a drunken stupor. I don't care, which comes first."

Tom Carver looked at the two women and decided that, for once, the women could have their way. He shrugged. He didn't truly care what the infant was called. "You two decide on a name between you. Call the babe whatever you deem fit. I don't care one way or the other."

"Well, you should, Tom. She's our granddaughter, and she needs a name…a nice name," Grace admonished him.

"Mercy," Sylvie sobbed, staring at the newborn baby. "We should call 'er Mercy. It's a fitting name, and the last word my Joan ever spoke. Mercy Carver, that's what we'll call 'er." She looked at the other faces.

"Are you off your head?" Walter said in a raised voice. "'Ave we not heard that blasted word enough today? Don't be so bloody stupid. Mercy's a rotten name. She'll be laughed at 'er whole life. Mercy? Don't you think it's bad enough that her father stuck a dagger through 'is neck and left 'er? What's folk going to think? Jesus Christ!"

Walter and Tom shook their heads. The vicar crossed himself and stared at the Bible on his lap.

Sylvie, usually as quiet as a mouse, spoke up again. "Now you two listen to me," she said, wagging her finger at the men. "This baby is alive against all the odds. Another minute and she would have died inside 'er dead mother. It's only by God's grace that she made it into the world in time," she sobbed again. "My Joan got 'er wish. She got mercy. Walter, Tom, don't you see? She delivered an 'ealthy child. Grace, what do you think?"

"God saved this baby; that's merciful enough for me. It's a good name, fitting and beautiful. I'm with you, Sylvie."

The two men shrugged, defeated and drunk on brandy. Their wives had spoken.

Chapter One

London, 1860

Mercy Carver strolled sedately down the street, pensive and distracted. Someone called her name, and she waved back absently without looking up to see who had greeted her. It was her eighteenth birthday, a day that under any other circumstances would have been celebrated with all the pomp and ceremony the family could muster. Not today, though. This was not a time for happy reunions. She had been adamant with her remaining grandparents, Sylvie Jennings and Tom Carver, that she wanted nothing to do with any birthday party they might be planning.

Mercy's lacklustre enthusiasm with regard to this milestone year and anything her grandparents had to say about it was like a heavy weight on her shoulders. Her grandparents were selfish and cruel, as far as she was concerned. Their secret deal four years earlier to marry her off to the grocer, Mr Black or Big Joe, as the community called him, would now have to be honoured. This day heralded the end of her dreams for a better life and the beginning of a dismal future that she would rather not face or even think about. Her life was ruined.

This morning's walk to the dressmaker felt like a walk to the gallows, she thought, with her being the condemned prisoner facing death. This was to be her final fitting for a wedding gown she didn't want to wear in a ceremony that would bind her for life to a man she already detested. She would rather face the gallows.

Her thoughts had clarity. She had tried the wedding dress on three times already, but on all the previous occasions her grandma had been with her, gushing over her beauty, how expensive the dress must be, and how generous Big Joe was for buying it.

Mercy was now convinced that her grandparents had not cared one little bit about what she thought or what she wanted from life when they callously made the deal with the old grocer. When she turned fourteen, she had been dreaming of grand adventures and travel to other lands. Her grandparents, on the other hand, were signing her life away for profit, and they hadn't even bothered to tell her what they'd done to her. Their love for her was, therefore, nothing more than a selfish commitment to material gain.

As she walked, she took a closer look at the familiar ugly buildings around her and realised just how boring her life had been so far. It had not been at all interesting. She had played in the street, gone to school, and then left school at the age of thirteen, expecting and intending to begin her search for employment like every other girl she knew.

The girls she'd gone to school with were either in domestic service or worse, had been kicked out by their parents and sent into the workhouse. Why her grandparents continued to imprison her at home, teaching her to sew, cook, and clean house every day like *that* was her job had been a mystery, for it made no sense at all.

Her grandparents, both sets, had always struggled to make ends meet. Grandpa Carver had been laid off work because of bad lungs. He now sat all day, staring out of the window, watching everyone else coming and going. Yet, the food was still put on the table, and she, Mercy, was still being clothed. Grandma Jennings had never worked a day in her life, and her husband, Grandpa Jennings, had long since died of consumption, along with Grandma Carver.

Mercy picked up her pace again as her anger grew. Disgust still lay heavily on her heart, even after all this time. She felt the same rush of fury and despair every time she thought about *that* day…the day she finally found out why she was excluded from employment, from going out with other girls, from talking to boys her own age, and from having even the smallest of freedoms, like walking to the grocer's or visiting a relative alone. On *that* day, she found out why.

Her grandparents had sat her down shortly after her sixteenth birthday. They had made it clear, in unwavering tones and without emotion, that a deal had been struck with Big Joe, and that it involved her marrying him when she turned eighteen. The pact had been documented and signed by all parties when she'd entered her fourteenth year. They had shown her the papers with pride written all over their faces!

She remembered Grandpa Carver's exact words now: "Ow the bloody 'ell do you think we've managed to put food on the table these last two years, eh? Did you imagine we'd just been lucky enough to feed and clothe you with no money coming in?"

Mercy had cried for a week. She had found no consolation in the fact that her grandparents' only stipulation at that time was that Big Joe would have to wait until Mercy's eighteenth birthday before putting a ring on her finger. Clever, Mercy, thought now, for in the deal was Big Joe's promise of money every week and cheap food right up until the wedding day. He had agreed to the terms even though he would have to wait four years. He'd taken care of her family, and her family in return had sold her into an arranged marriage. Yes, very clever on her grandparents' part, for they could have married her off much sooner had it not been for the ongoing funds and free food.

Mercy hated Big Joe. He was leery and old, and his saggy pot belly wasn't hidden well enough under his dirty grey apron that should be white. He had dirty teeth, and hair that was thinning. His bald patch was sprinkled with freckles and had horrible dark moles that she could never bear to look at, never mind touch. He was at least forty-five, and why everyone called him Big Joe, she'd never know, for she towered above him in height.

Since the truth had come out, she'd been forced to go to his shop every day, and she'd been threatened not to be offish with him. Her grandma told her she had to flirt and make him want her. She was also told that the way to a man's heart was not through his belly, as most women thought. No, Grandma Jennings had added, the way to snare a man was to make him want your legs open every day of the week!

Mercy shivered with revulsion. Joe had the disgusting habit of dribbling at the mouth when he saw her. On her dutiful social outings with him, her grandma in tow, he made sure whispers in her ear with his wet tongue were understood. "I'll be 'aving my fill of you in no time, Mercy. You just make sure you keep that cunt of yours nice and tight for me. Don't let another man's cock in there 'cos if you're not a virgin when I sign those marriage papers there'll be 'ell to pay."

She had no one to talk to, nowhere to run to, and nobody to escape with. She was Big Joe's property, and everyone knew it. No boys came near her, no girls wanted to befriend her, and her grandparents refused to talk any more about it.

She walked on. She would try on the wedding dress for the final time, and then she'd forget about him and her wedding. Today was her day, and she was going to make the most of it.

Mercy had often thought about what her life would have been like had she grown up with a mother and father. She had never mourned them, never known them, and never missed them. The only thing she could honestly say she missed was the actual experience of having parents, instead of grandfathers who had been overly tough with her and grandmothers who were too weak to argue with their husbands. She was not allowed to cry or to have a moan, even when she'd fallen down and cut her knee or her elbow. Tears were forbidden lest she got a good thrashing.

She now lived in an almshouse with her grandma because Sylvie Jennings was a widow. Grandpa Carver lived with them as an unemployable invalid. Big Joe had made sure they'd gotten to the top of the housing list. She hated the house and her lumpy mattress that stood in the pantry by day and lay on the kitchen floor at night. But as much as she hated that mattress and floor, the thought of living in Big Joe's house was even more abhorrent to her.

Mercy covered her nose and grunted in disgust. She remembered her granny telling her that in 1848, Parliament had established the Metropolitan Commission of Sewers. She'd also said that the commission ordered a survey of the antiquated sewage systems and had drawn up plans to clear the cesspits. A fat lot of good that had done, Mercy thought. They'd made the air even smellier instead of better.

She had grown up with the smell of shit and pee. One of her greatest ambitions was to walk in the countryside, miles from London and its suburbs. To breathe clean air and lie in a field of newly-cut grass would be a wonderful thing, she'd often thought.

Mercy wiped her brow with her hankie, complaining to herself as she did so. The heat was beginning to settle in the air, and that made the stinking sewers and cesspits even more unbearable than usual. Last year, London's summer had been even hotter and had lasted just as long as this year, which added to Londoners' many years of ongoing misery. The stink of overflowing sewage in the River Thames and many of its urban tributaries was something they had learned to live with. Mercy and her grandma never went out without large handkerchiefs in their pockets or bags to cover their mouths and noses with if they had a good distance to walk. The warmth in the summer air encouraged bacteria to thrive. In the previous year, a lot of people had become sick. Even work in the great House of Commons had been affected; so she'd heard from just about everyone who'd been to the other side of the river.

"This is why you shouldn't disobey your grandpa and me by going across London Bridge. The centre of London is the best place to be if you want to make yourself sick," Grandma Jennings often told her.

As she passed St Mary's Church, Mercy thought about the life she had dreamed of. She had known from a very young age exactly what she wanted to do when she was grown up. She was going to be an explorer, an archaeologist maybe, and she would write about her travels and about all the treasures she would find along the way.

Walking and looking at buildings, graveyards, parks, and shops were her favourite pastimes, but she had done that so often in this small area that the sight of them no longer gave her any satisfaction. Nothing seemed to change. The streets and the houses in them were always the same, day after day, year after year. The park and its trees changed colour with the seasons, but it was still the same park and the same trees. The people she saw were the same faces she saw every day, and her small world was suffocating her.

As she walked along the street towards the more elegant part of Southwark, she began to dream about all the possibilities and opportunities central London could bring her, were she free to choose. She could, for instance, live in the attic of a grand house and work in the kitchen, or if she was lucky and did well at her job, serve tea upstairs. She could clean rooms in one of the larger hotels, where she would meet new people. She would have a half day off every week and would walk down unknown streets, through new parks. She would visit museums and have tea in quaint little tearooms, and her curiosity would be appeased. She would write about her experiences in a journal, learn about the world and the unusual people in it, and save money in order to travel even farther afield. But her loyalty to the grandparents who had brought her up without question convinced her that they were much more important than her own selfish ambitions. Fate had therefore dictated that she, Mercy Carver, would never have what she wanted out of life, apart from today.

Chapter Two

Mercy looked into a shop through its window and saw her own image staring back. She pushed her nose against the glass and cupped a hand at the side of each eye, thus blocking out the sun's reflection. She was at the local pawn shop, which specialised in clocks and pocket watches. She had to know what time it was. Timing and her best performance in dramatics were going to be her keys to success today.

Mercy had told a fib this morning. Her grandma was beside herself, knowing that the wedding dress had to be picked up and that she just wasn't well enough to go to the shop to get it. Mercy calmed her down by saying that she'd get Mrs McCallum to go with her. Mrs McCallum lived just around the corner and would be quite happy to have a walk with her and see the dress.

But Mercy had no intention of going to Mrs McCallum's or anyone else's house. It was a big lie, the first she'd ever told. If she was to spend her whole life in the Elephant and Castle, be married off to Big Joe, have children, and grow old before her time without having truly lived, she deserved this day and was not ashamed of the lie she had told. Her conscience was clear. She felt no guilt gnawing at her, nor would she feel remorse when the day was over.

She had left her grandma's house earlier than she was supposed to, to buy some time for her well-guarded, secret adventure, as she, Mercy Carver, was going to walk across London Bridge for the very first time in her life. She would do it on her own and savour every sight she saw on the way. She was going to look down into the murky water instead of staring at it from a distance, see the great ships and boats at close quarters, and have her first cup of tea in central London.

Ten thirty, the grandmother clock inside the pawn shop said. Perfect, Mercy thought. The dress shop was only two streets away now, and the women were expecting her anytime this morning.

Mercy straightened and studied herself in a mirror that stood six feet tall. She couldn't quite believe what she saw. The woman staring back at her was a stranger to her. Her white dress was beautifully cut, just on the shoulder, and made of the finest cotton with embroidered satin panels and trimmed with lace and pale pink ribbon edging. Her corset had given her a tiny waist that had been measured at a very respectable, twenty-one inches. The gown's skirt ballooned outwards right down to the floor, giving her a body shape that was completely new to her. Her breasts were lifted, full and rather revealing, she thought, feeling slightly shy and uncomfortable at the sight of them. She also looked tall, so much taller than before, but the little pointed shoes with curved heels had a lot do with that.

Under her veil, soft curls cascaded down her back to just above her waist. Her small oval face with slightly pointed chin, perfect cheekbones, and huge emerald green twinkling eyes were further enhanced by perfect, pink bow lips.

Mercy saw a woman staring back at her in the mirror. There was an iridescent light emanating from her eyes…not because of the gown, the marriage, or the wedding, but because she was just about to put her plan into motion.

"I should have cut your 'air," Agnes, the stylist said, interrupting Mercy's thoughts. "It's far too long. Long is not in fashion this year, especially with this gown."

"Nonsense. When hair is like silk and 'angs naturally curly like that, it should be left just as it is," Doreen, the dressmaker said. "It might not be fashionable, but I would sell my soul for that texture and colour. It is, after all, a woman's crowning glory,"

Doreen, standing slightly behind Mercy, studied her in the mirror. "You're a very lucky girl, Mercy. Big Joe was very kind to pay for all of this. 'E might be well off, but let me tell you, the veil by itself cost 'im a small fortune. 'E's the best match in the area, so be thankful that you'll be well looked after. 'E's got no children from that sickly wife 'e used to 'ave. Blimey, she could scarce stand up straight most of the time, never mind bear 'im a child. 'E'll leave everything to you; don't forget that either. If you give 'im what 'e wants every night, you'll tire 'im out in no time. 'E'll be dead soon enough with 'is big fat belly and all the nightly jumping and 'umping about the bed with you. You take it from me, if you constantly let 'im have 'is way, 'e'll not be long for this world."

"That's a terrible thing to say," Agnes scolded Doreen whilst trying to look serious.

"I'm just saying as 'ow it is, Agnes." Doreen played with the veil, spreading it out and measuring its long train. "You mark my words, Mercy. You'll be a rich widow in no time. I'll tell you right now if I didn't know who you were or where you came from, I'd think you were a bloody duchess or a real lady. You're beautiful, but you also 'ave grace and posture, just like your mother 'ad and talk nice and proper too. It's a natural gift and not every woman 'as it, especially around your neck of the woods. You've got all the attributes men want, and they'll be your weapons, so use them well, and they'll take you a long way."

Mercy sighed. "What I want is to get employment and not have to marry an old man. What's the point of having looks if all they've got me is a horrible old, fat, balding man for my trouble? I hate him!" she sobbed loudly. "I'm dreading it. I feel like I'm about to go to prison without having committed a single crime."

The two women looked at each other. Mercy was aware of the pity in their eyes, and that was exactly what she wanted to see. It was time to perform.

"If only I could have one day, just one day to taste freedom in a gown like this. If I could just do one thing with my life today, it would see me through all the horrible years to come with that filthy old git who sticks his wet, slobbering tongue in my ear every time I'm with him. He makes me want to puke! I swear I'll end up killing myself. I'll be just like my da'. Without hope..."

Mercy's tears and wretched sobs stopped the two women in their tracks.

The girl was right, Doreen was thinking. Big Joe was a lecherous old git and had a different woman paid for in coin almost every night of the week. Removing the veil, she got a better look at Mercy's anguished face. She sighed. She'd been paid to make Mercy look like a princess, and that's what she'd done, and done it well. She couldn't say anything that would help the girl. Life with Big Joe would be bloody rotten, and that was the truth of it. He'd set his sights on Mercy when she was just a young girl; everybody knew that. Now the time had come to marry her he'd make sure she was never out alone again. He'd work her hard in his shop all day, and he'd have his way with her whenever it took his fancy. Doreen screwed up her face in disgust behind Mercy's back. Personally, she'd rather eat rats than marry that bloody dog of a man!

Mercy took one more look at herself in the mirror. She was not vain, but she was well aware that she looked every bit like a sophisticated woman. Soft pink rouge had been painted on her full bow lips and cheeks, and black kohl now defined her eyebrows and lifted the corners of her eyelids, making her eyes appear twice their size. The effect was subtle, but it had changed her girlish face into something beautiful and elegant. She sniffed into the handkerchief Doreen had just given her.

"I had hoped to get the chance to wear a gown like this more than once in my life," she said. "But living in the Elephant and Castle won't give me any opportunity at all, ever. My Grandma Jennings says Big Joe always works and goes out to a man's club at night, and I'm not to nag him about it. I bet I'll just spend all my life alone and miserable. I should kill myself right now!"

Doreen turned Mercy from the mirror and held her by the arms. She wore a shocked, frightened expression. Tears welled up, making her remove her eyeglasses. "Now you listen to me, girl. I knew your father and your mother. I was at their bloody wedding. I've never seen a couple so much in love…they made me right jealous, so they did. What your father did; kill 'imself, was a terrible waste of a life, and I'll not 'ave his daughter in 'ere threatening to do the same thing. Now I don't know what I can say to 'elp you. I don't know what I can do to make you feel better. But if I ever 'ear you mention killing yourself again, I'll give you a right good slapping. Do you 'ear me?"

"Yes, I'm sorry," Mercy sobbed again. "But if I could just go into London, across that bridge, just once, I'd have the memory of it and would be satisfied with that. But how can I go to London in my old rags if I want to have a cup of tea and go inside St Paul's Cathedral? I saved some pennies. I have them. It took me almost a year, but I have enough for an outing and maybe even a short carriage ride after I've had a scone and tea. That's always been my dream. Just once…if I could do it just once, I'd never complain again about anything."

"I understand, Mercy, really I do," Doreen told her, softening her tone. "I would love to tell you to grab every opportunity that comes your way and go after your dreams, but you're betrothed, and there's nought you, me, or Agnes 'ere can do about it. You're too beautiful for your own good, that's the truth. If you'd been brought up on the other side of the river, you would have found an even better 'usband; an aristocrat, maybe."

"Do you really think so?"

"I know so," Doreen told her.

Mercy seized the chance. Now she would test the waters.

"What if I could just wear this for a short while? It may be my only chance. You did say you would love to tell me to grab opportunities, even though you can't. Doreen, I promise I won't get it dirty. No one will know except for us three. Can I please? I'll be back in three or four hours to carry the dress home in its box. Please?"

Doreen and Agnes looked horrified and shook their heads. Fumbling with panic, Doreen began to undo the tiny buttons on the back of the gown, just in case Mercy was thinking about bolting out the door with the dress on.

Mercy cried and tried again. "After today my life is over. I'm just going to *have* to kill myself. If I can't have one good memory, what's the point of living?"

"Mercy, you'll get us into a bother talking like this. Big Joe and your family will 'ave our 'ides."

"But not if they're none the wiser. They would never have to know," Mercy rushed in. "Who the bleedin' hell do we know that goes into London from this side of the river? If I could just see St Paul's Cathedral and say a prayer maybe…to help me through this…"

"Right, that's enough, Mercy Carver," Doreen interrupted her. She wagged her finger an inch from Mercy's face. "Get that dress off you right now and don't you dare move."

Doreen gave Agnes a sly look and nodded towards the back room. They walked towards it, whispering, and then disappeared inside, leaving Mercy alone. Mercy sighed. Her plan hadn't worked. Now she'd have to go to London in rags with pretty hair. She was going to look stupid.

Doreen came back out alone. "We've discussed it, Mercy. We can't allow you to wear a wedding dress on the streets of London, and you're a fool to think we would. Sorry, but it will come back with its 'em covered in mud and 'orse muck, and we'll get shot for allowing it to 'appen. But…" She stopped speaking just as Agnes appeared carrying a burgundy gown.

"This was made for a young lady from Knightsbridge."

Mercy's eyes opened wide. "What…?"

"No, don't ask questions. I may be in Southwark, but I'm quite well known for my work and designs in the 'ighest quarters. I get clients who 'ave titles, but not many people know that, so don't spread it around. I could close up this shop tomorrow and live a comfortable life, but I'm planning on moving to the country. I want a nice cottage where I'll dress the gentry and feed my face on scones and butter. I'll be respected and asked to attend dinner parties and local balls. I'll find myself in with country society and marry a nice man. I've got big plans, Mercy, and so should you.

"Do you imagine you'd be 'ere if you were marrying a man who didn't 'ave Big Joe's money and position? God Almighty, folk from these parts would never be able to afford my gowns, not in a month of Sundays. The only reason I'm 'ere is that my 'ome is upstairs and the rent for this building is cheap. Now this dress 'ere was ordered, but the girl is pregnant. She fell for a baby just a couple of months after she got married and told me to keep the dress. She didn't ask for anything in return, so the gown is mine. She was about the same size as you. Would this do for your big adventure?"

Mercy stared into the faces of the smiling women. She didn't know whether to laugh or cry with joy. She grinned and nodded her head, unable to speak.

Doreen smiled and held Mercy's hands. "Now let's find you a bonnet. You 'ave your day, Mercy Carver. You bloody well deserve it, and you'll never get another chance because that old man you're marrying will never let you out of his sight."

Chapter Three

Mercy walked gracefully down to the end of the street. She stood for a moment to get her bearings. This was the point where junctions and wider roads started to emerge. These were the roads that led to the bridge and where the new tram lines began.

Her shoes were pinching just a little, but that wouldn't deter her from her quest, it would just force her to walk a bit slower. Doreen had told her to walk with her head high, chest out, and waist in. She also added that it wouldn't do any harm if she were to swing her hips a bit too.

Her burgundy puff-sleeved gown had a small delicate collar with black velvet piping. It was fastened with black velvet buttons, running in a neat line to her waist, and matching the black velvet shawl that Doreen had insisted she take with her. Her bonnet, a gift from the dressmaker, was also burgundy, trimmed in black with black feather plumes at its crown and black velvet ribbon tied in a large bow under her chin. She carried a small pink and black silk purse and parasol to match. *Mercy, you look like a lady; you do, indeed*, she thought as she moved closer to the bridge.

Mercy's heart quickened; there it was! She stopped at an embankment, the furthest she'd ever walked, and cautiously looked around her in all directions. Southwark Cathedral was just ahead on her left, and London Bridge with its five magnificent arches was straight in front of her.

She crossed the busy road junction and felt her heartbeat quicken. There was a lot of work going on in the side streets and on the busy main roads. One could easily believe that London's entire working population were congregated here, digging and shovelling dirt. They were working on the new sewage system, she determined now. She'd heard that some politicians and lords had succumbed to cholera. That was what probably urged the government to get a move on and fix London's stink, she thought, disgusted that it had taken a high-class person to die before they sorted the problem.

Mercy took her first step onto the bridge. She attempted to blend in, but she noticed that the bridge's traffic consisted of heavily laden carts filled with flour sacks and vegetables, coal wagons, tradesmen carrying pots and pans, and just a few plainly dressed men and women who probably worked on the other side of the bridge. Every now and then a horse-drawn omnibus would pass. She had heard the noise from their passengers before she saw them. They were filled to capacity, and most children sat on their parents' laps. She'd seen these multi-person transport carriages before but only from a distance; they didn't come all the way to the Elephant and Castle, just as far as Southwark Cathedral.

Mercy could well understand now why there were no grand carriages or gentry in sight, for with every step she took, the stink got worse. She also knew she should have the sense to get to the other side as quickly as possible, but she couldn't prevent herself from stopping every few feet to look down at the water in the Thames as well as all around her at the comings and goings of others.

Her grandparents had been right about something, she admitted now. It seemed to her that every person in England had come here to this river and had left their shite behind.

Carts and omnibuses continued to pass her in both directions. People bumped into her, and some didn't even say sorry. Men tipped their caps to her when she passed them. Throngs of people were going about their business. She was going on an adventure and couldn't care less about the smell. She was in new territory now. She was witnessing new and unimagined things. Mercy suddenly wondered if the bridge was safe under the weight of all this traffic, riding and on foot.

She giggled. There was horse dung everywhere, and everyone around her looked as though they were playing hopscotch, jumping over and swerving around all the mountains of droppings. She took her handkerchief from her dainty purse that was attached to a silk-roped chain and covered her mouth and nose, careful not to smudge her newly painted lips.

She could see the North end of the bridge. It was just ahead of her and crowded with people walking in all directions. Some hurried whilst others ambled along in the sunshine with no particular place to be.

Stepping off the bridge, she felt her stomach lurch. She was in London now and was going to make the most of it.

She loosened the silk cord and peered inside her purse. Grandma Jennings had given her a couple of coins and had told her to buy hair ribbons. Mercy had bought nothing. Instead, she had kept the money, putting it towards her savings, which she would spend today. She would spend every penny as though it was her last day on earth.

She stared in awe as she looked up at the tallest pillar she had ever seen. It was the monument, dedicated to the great fire of London. Then standing at the corner of the Monument, she wondered which direction to take. She had studied one of her grandpa's survey maps of London and was now looking for Thames Street, which according to the map would be to her left. Maybe she should take tea before reaching her final destination, she thought. Her feet were tired, and she was sure she had a blister on her left heel. Her new shoes were not made for walking, she decided.

When she found Thames Street, she decided against the tea idea. The street itself was wider than she could have ever imagined and as long as the eye could see. It was bustling with carriages, men on horseback, and women strolling, shopping, and buying fruit and vegetables from the market stalls that lined one side of the road.

There were lime-burner premises sitting just inside small alleyways, adding to the street's pungent odour. There were many new building works going on; hundreds of workmen lined the entire street. New sewage drains and what looked like half-built docks were being dug, constructed and installed. Barges were moored to the wharves, and beyond were glimpses of the river, with masts of shipping and warehouses on the far side. It was not picturesque at all, Mercy thought. This was her first taste of the city, and her lasting impressions would be of chaos, mayhem, and dirt.

She couldn't think about that now. She was far too happy to worry about turning up at the shop dirty, covered in dust, wearing dung-covered shoes, a mucky dress, and a blackened face. She would think about what to do when the time came.

An open carriage dropped off a couple of men. She approached it gingerly. This would be her very first carriage ride. She had never seen one like it and had no idea how much it would cost or exactly how far away St Paul's Cathedral was, but she was determined to get on it.

"Can you take me to St Paul's Cathedral, please?" she asked the driver.

The carriage driver tipped his hat politely, nodded his head, and jumped down from his wooden bench seat to open the carriage door.

Mercy wasn't sure how to lift the piles of material under her skirt, but she did remember that Doreen said women looked more elegant when they took hold of a petticoat hoop, which in turn lifted the front of the dress up, and avoided tripping over themselves. That was the last thing she wanted, to be lying in the muck with her legs flailing about or diving into the carriage head first.

With this in mind, she inched her hands down to her hips and eventually found a hard-boned hoop. Grabbing it from both sides, she lifted it, exposed her ankles, put her first foot onto the carriage step, and followed with the other. Before she knew it, she was sitting prim and proper on the soft leather passenger seat.

The driver closed the small waist-high door and tipped his hat again. "I'll have you there in no time, miss," he told her.

Mercy smiled to herself. He had called her *miss*. That was the first time anyone had ever been so polite to her. Where she came from, she was called the orphan or gangly Mercy Carver.

She was now completing another ambition, and she had never felt as alive. As the carriage slowly manoeuvred its way through busy Thames Street, she was amazed at just how many people she continued to see. There was a never-ending throng of new faces and costumes, of strange and colourful hats. Blimey, she almost felt as though she were in a different country altogether! People were looking up at her as she passed them. They would be wondering who she was, she thought vainly. Here she sat, dressed in a beautiful gown fitted to perfection, with fashionable hair and bonnet. She was all alone, an independent woman being driven around the streets of London in a grand carriage. Yes, she thought, they might be imagining all sorts of things about her…but they'd all be wrong.

She asked the driver what route he was planning to take, and he told her that they would not stay on Thames Street but would cross the next junction into Cannon Street, which led directly to St Paul's. It would be quicker, he added, and would get them out of the traffic jam. Mercy nodded gratefully. She was happy to be leaving the madness of Thames Street behind her. *That* was one road she would always remember, but not with fondness.

The carriage stopped at the edge of the square that surrounded the cathedral. After giving the driver some coins, far fewer than she'd expected to pay, she walked no more than a dozen feet before she came across a small but elegant restaurant and tea room. She entered and was seated at a table for two by the window. She looked out of it, mesmerised by the great domed building she had read about in one of her old schoolbooks.

She had heard some neighbours talk about excursions they had taken to St Paul's. They had all said the same thing about it on their return, that the designers, masons and builders had done an excellent job reinvigorating what had been called a dreary, dingy and un-devotional building by Queen Victoria. She had been quite distressed, apparently, at its run-down state, and had personally ordered its image to be changed and from which was instigated the design and installation of beautiful mosaics and stained glass.

When she ordered her tea, she decided on fruitcake instead of scones. To be a grown-up was a wonderful thing, she also considered. Sitting there, her spirit, her yearning to explore, to seek adventure, and to meet new and diverse societies seemed even more wondrous in her mind. Her heart told her to follow a different path than the one laid out for her. For eighteen years her grandparents had made sure she'd been fed and clothed. Neighbours pitied her orphan status and the stigma that surrounded her birth. She'd also had to endure taunts and spiteful references about her father's suicide. She knew very well what people thought about her. She was the orphan of a deranged idiot who'd plunged a dagger into his own throat, and the girl who was marrying a man almost ten years older than her father would have been if he were still alive.

Mercy looked out onto the street, cast her eyes upon the beautiful square and cathedral, and then stuck her nose in the air. She didn't care what anybody thought about her. They would probably never have tea in central London in a dress like this or see what she was seeing. She might be told how to live her life in future, but there were always dreams of escape and adventure to keep her mind busy. No one could take those dreams away from her.

Chapter Four

Sam Bigly and Eddie Gunn stood at the corner of the street a few doors away from the establishment where Mercy sat contentedly drinking her tea. They had spotted her going into the tearoom, and Eddie had decided there and then to set up shop and add her to the cargo already in the back of the carriage. She would be the final pickup on this, one of their last business trips to the capital. She would probably be one of the most highly valued, for her beauty was undeniable and probably greater than all the stock they had already accumulated.

The two men had travelled a long distance. It had taken them twenty-eight hours from the centre of Liverpool to the madam's safe house in Knightsbridge. They had done this journey many times and were well paid for their specialised job, one of danger and illegal activity that could easily see them hang at the end of a rope. It was a job that involved perfect timing, keen eyes, knowing when to strike, and knowing when to retreat. They were good at what they did, experts in the art of abduction.

They were trusted employees of a woman in Liverpool and worked exclusively for her. Both knew her well. She didn't take kindly to failure. Failure was unforgivable in her eyes. It was not in her vocabulary and not tolerated. Sam and Eddie had both seen what happened to others when she was displeased. They had, therefore, very enticing reasons to succeed every time they went to the capital. The first was the bonus they got when they returned home with a full load. The second was their continuing employment, including bed, board, and the odd fuck with one of the madam's girls.

The madam always demanded her cargo from the most exclusive areas of central London. She never travelled to London herself and maintained complete anonymity. She was the ghost at the head of dangerous but lucrative operations. In Liverpool, she was known as Madame Du Pont. The two men had always thought it a bloody stupid exercise when the madam switched accents from broad Liverpudlian to a soft French chic, depending on who she was speaking to at the time. But she was a good businesswoman, they both agreed on that. She knew how to fill her whorehouse, and they'd seen her turn men away on occasion for lack of girls or just lack of space. She could do that and do it to prominent, powerful men, who would always come back begging for more.

Sam and Eddie knew little of her past. It was clear to them that she was from Liverpool and that she had come up with a dangerous business concept that only courage and self-belief could pull off. She had made a fortune over the years and a name for herself in the most influential social circles of the industrial North. They supposed she had no family and no real friends, apart from her customers. But they did know one thing; she was one of the most, if not *the* most powerful woman in Liverpool.

All her whores came from London. She specialised in young, graceful, upper-class girls, virginal in appearance, and, whenever possible, in body. Sam and Eddie took attractive girls who still had a good chance of being untouched by a man. There were exceptions, of course, but they weren't expected to examine the girls they abducted as that was Madame Du Pont's job.

Sam and Eddie didn't particularly like the madam, but they did admire her enterprise and the profits she made. She had a mansion in Liverpool with grounds the size of a park, and she also owned a house in Knightsbridge. They often wondered why she had chosen that spot. It was a mews house with stables housing two carriages and four horses at all times. The location didn't sit well with either man as it was too close for their liking to the places where the girls were abducted from.

Eddie had asked her once why she took such risks. Why did she keep the girls so close to the abduction sites? Her answer had been quite clear, and she'd scoffed at his ignorance. "It's called hiding in plain sight, Eddie boy. It's the safest place in all London, for who would imagine that his stolen child was but a street or two away?"

Madame Du Pont had no connections on paper to the house in Knightsbridge. The man and woman who ran it held the lease. Thus, if they got caught with abducted girls in the basement, they would go down for the crime, not the madam. The team were always on hand to look after the girls' essential needs until transport day and not once had any copper knocked on the door asking about a missing girl in all the time they'd been there.

The madam, in the men's opinion, could have made a good living out of local Liverpool girls who went willingly into the Liverpool brothels. But Madame Du Pont offered an alternative experience for the type of men who frequented her house. She charged twenty times as much as any other brothel, and she had no competition whatsoever in the high end of the prostitution and gambling market.

Her gated mansion stood in the most exclusive part of Liverpool. It was far enough away from the docklands and bustling streets that surrounded it and was separated from the rundown housing areas by a large park. Only mansions and good quality restaurants sat on her side of the park, and only well-to-do people crossed it.

The mansion was exquisitely decorated. There were salons adorned with paintings on walls lined with red silk material and soft leather couches in every room. She provided private poker rooms, a bar, and servants who served champagne, French brandy and whisky in crystal glasses from silver trays.

The house had sixteen bedrooms situated on the first and second floors. Madame Du Pont's suite was on the ground floor, and the servants' quarters were in the attic.

Her whores were both beautiful and educated. They were soft-spoken, and more often than not, innocent and naive, which according to Madame Du Pont made them easy pupils to manipulate. They were all, without exception, young ladies and not common whores who opened their legs customarily for men, rich or poor.

The girls had to be well trained in the art of seduction before they were put to work servicing the madam's customers. But their training also involved brutal punishments, and on the odd occasion, death for those who wouldn't listen or accept their new situation. By the time their training was complete, the girls were either too afraid to argue or were simply defeated. That meant the madam had done her job well.

Sam and Eddie envied the madam's power and her fortune. They were the fools who took all the risks in what was a dangerous job, but she paid them good money, and as long as the money kept coming, they would do her bidding, no questions asked.

They were given a finder's fee for each girl. Forward planning and the execution of the plan itself rarely varied. It required speed, precision, and nerve. The victim was enticed to the back of the coach and its double, windowless wooden doors. Once there, the young women disappeared inside the carriage and were never seen again until they reached Liverpool.

The key to success was timing. If on the odd occasion, people or another coach came too close to their position for comfort, they would move on, and the whole operation was inevitably cocked up and cancelled.

Sam and Eddie were both young, good-looking men. Each had a nice set of teeth, wore good-quality clothing, and softened his broad Liverpudlian accent in order to fit in with Londoners who frequented the most exclusive parts of the city. Sometimes their carriage would sit in the same spot for hours or drive in circles all day just to get one girl, but there were also days when they managed to pick up two or even a third on occasion in quick succession. It was a hit-and-miss affair, a bit like waiting for the madam to give them a girl to use.

London was a vibrant city. Season after season, more girls from country estates arrived with their families to be bartered for money and power. The aristocracy and old money families attended endless balls and tea parties with the sole purpose of marrying off their daughters to wealthy and powerful families.

It was approaching late October, the final days of the season well past, but many privileged families were in town for the society wedding of the Earl of Harewood's daughter. In Eddie and Sam's opinion this was a perfect opportunity to strike for by now girls who had adjusted to London life during the past season were returning for the wedding. It stood to reason, Eddie remarked, that they'd be more adventurous and even more likely to venture out alone.

The capital's glamorous streets tempted the debutantes with independence into what they thought were safe environments. Some took tea alone, like the girl they were watching now. Some went on shopping trips, combining them with walks in Hyde Park, where young, aristocratic bucks rode their horses. Hyde Park with its romantic lake was the meeting point for many secret trysts between bucks in need of wives to run their estates and keep their family lines going, and debutantes who wanted nothing more than to become wives and mistresses of their own homes. The girls Sam and Eddie abducted had one thing in common; they were rebellious enough to go out alone without a chaperone, albeit in the most exclusive and safest areas of the city. They were confident and comfortable in familiar environments, thus allowing an easy abduction to take place.

Sam and Eddie rode around London in a Clarence cab. It was a closed transport with curtained windows. The carriage they used for the transportation to Liverpool was quite different, in that it looked more like an omnibus wagon than a private passenger carriage. It was closed in and long in length. It had tiny, high-barred windows on each side wall and heavy double, windowless doors at the back end, and written along each side was Workhouse Van. Inside, there were two long benches and enough room for eight to ten people. On the return journey to Liverpool, it was usually filled to capacity. This particular transport was always safely tucked away in the mews stables with the horses, and only ever came out on the evening of departure, for it was an ugly-looking thing that was conspicuous on these grand streets until it reached the safety and incognito of the poorer areas it travelled through.

Eddie and Sam were going home today but had found themselves in the wrong part of London due to roadworks and new drainage systems being dug on many of the roads they usually took. Mayfair, Piccadilly and Knightsbridge had been clear of roadworks, but upon leaving those areas, they'd been blindsided by diversions. Subsequent roads had led them into unknown territory. Thus, they found themselves just to the left of St Paul's Cathedral, and around the corner from the girl who would with a bit of luck, be their final, unexpected, but welcome victim.

Chapter Five

"What if she's meeting someone?" Sam said with growing uneasiness.

"Well, she's been in there for near enough a good half hour. If she were meeting someone, they'd have showed up by now. No, this little gem is alone and ripe for the picking. She's a good catch, Sam. The missus will be pleased," Eddie said in his usual overconfident manner.

"But we've already got nine. Do yer honestly think we need another one? This is risky, and we don't know the area. It might be hard getting her to walk around the corner, and I'm not bringing the carriage any closer to the square. I don't even like it sitting where it is. We should be on our way out of the city by now. Maybe we should forget it. I've had enough anyway. It's been a hard few days. I say we just pack it in and get ourselves home," Sam continued arguing.

Eddie scratched his bristled chin. Sam had a point. "You might be right, but I still think we should take her. Did you get a good look at her? Bloody hell, she's a blinder, better than the rest of them by miles. The missus will be over the moon with this one. We might even get to use her one day down the line. We'll definitely get a bonus. C'mon, Sam?"

Sam looked again at Mercy through the restaurant window and finally nodded in agreement. "You're right. Face like a bloody angel. And that body! Christ, what I wouldn't do to get her to open her legs for me." His laughter was laced with sarcasm. "We'll never get to use this one, though, only in our dreams, Eddie boy. What do you reckon...seventeen, eighteen?"

"Don't know, but who cares? She's young. I'd say about seventeen. She's definitely one of the best we've seen for a long time. So are we going to do this or not?" Eddie asked again.

Sam finally agreed. "Okay, but I'm not taking chances."

"Right then, snap to it. Get the coach."

"I will, but you just make sure you're ready for her when she comes out of there. We don't want this all sloppy-like. I'm for it, but there's a lot of hustle and bustle around here, and I'm not sure of the route out of this square we're in. You'll have to be quick with her. I'll bring the coach a bit nearer to the corner, just at the entrance to the side street behind us. It'll only be a few feet closer, but it might make all the difference. I'll get the carriage right next to the wall, and I'll have the chloroform ready." Sam turned and then added as he reached the corner, "If this goes bad, we're making a run for it, right?"

Eddie nodded absently. Sam could be like a bloody old fishwife when he wanted to be. Eddie continued to stare at the restaurant's window. The girl was still sitting there, but he'd seen her ask for the bill.

Mercy stepped into the sunlight. It was almost two o'clock, so the waiter had told her. She had ample time to look inside the cathedral, light a candle for her mother and father, and then get back on the road home. All that she had imagined in the tearoom were just that, imaginings. She would go back at the end of the day and marry Big Joe.

St Paul's sat just to the right and across the square from where Mercy stood. She pulled her bonnet down at the front, to shield her eyes from the sunlight and the dust being kicked up by horses' hooves, and started walking.

Eddie watched her and quickly looked to the corner. The carriage was now in position. He could see the horses' heads. He poured two drops of eye solution in each eye. He'd never asked what was in the stuff. Madame Du Pont had never told him. But it stung like the devil and made his eyes tear up, turn red, and swell like a bee sting. He bloody hated this part. Christ, he would end up going blind if he carried on using it. It was like bleedin' acid!

Approaching Mercy as she walked towards his position, he kept his head bowed and cried like a baby. He stepped to the right, deliberately bumping into her, and then looked up apologetically. "I'm so sorry, miss. I wasn't looking…my wife…"

Mercy looked at the man's face. His eyes were red-rimmed. Tears ran down his cheeks. He seemed to be in terrible distress. "Your wife?" she questioned.

"Yes, she's in my carriage, and she's so very sick. God help me, I don't know what to do. I got lost." He cried some more.

Mercy looked around her. Everyone was going about their business, walking and talking, carriages and horses everywhere. There were comings and goings in and out of the cathedral, and no one was taking any notice of the poor man. "Where is the nearest hospital?" she asked.

"I don't know. We were visiting relatives. Oh, God, help me. She's going to die, my Sarah. You're a woman. You'll know what to do. Please help me?"

Mercy stared at his frightened, red, tear-stained face. His expression of hopelessness melted her heart. She suddenly thought about her father. "I'll help, I will, I'll do whatever I can. Where is she?" she asked.

"Bless you, bless your kind heart. She's just around the corner. Follow me. The carriage is just a few feet away."

They were at the corner now. Mercy saw the four horses and strange-looking carriage tucked well into the shadow. "Is this it?"

"Yes, miss. She's lying in the back."

Mercy nodded. She didn't know if she'd be of any use to the poor woman inside. But she'd be contributing something, she thought, even if she just held the woman's hand whilst her husband went for help. She walked speedily beside the man.

The narrow alleyway was not big enough for two-way traffic. The man, now just to the front and side of her turned and gave her a grateful smile, and she smiled back. He led her to the rear of the carriage and opened one of the thick wooden doors. He let her pass to stand in front of him. Mercy looked into the semi-darkness. She saw the tied and gagged girls. Her eyes widened and her stomach twisted in a tight knot.

Just inside, behind the one closed door, a man appeared. She turned, terrified and confused, but instinctively knowing she was in danger.

Eddie, standing behind her, shoved her into the back of the coach with brute force whilst Sam pulled her the rest of the way in by her armpits. He proceeded to cover her nose and mouth with a smelly, wet rag. Eddie closed the door, bolting it from the outside.

Mercy's eyes began to water. She choked on the smell and taste running down her throat. Who were all these girls, she wondered through her misty, dulled mind. There were so many of them. She couldn't comprehend what was happening. She felt herself floating and then hitting the hard floor. The smell around her was horrible. She was choking on it. She tried desperately to grab the rag with her flailing arms and hands, but she had no strength to move any part of her body. She tried to shake the rag way with her head, but it was growing darker and darker around her until there was nothing. She was being consumed by the darkness...

"Right, stick some more of that chloroform on the other bitches' gags," Eddie told Sam after opening the door an inch. "We need them kept under till we get into the suburbs. C'mon, quick, tie her up and make sure her gag's on nice and tight. It's time to get home. We've done well, Sammy boy, but we've a long road ahead of us."

Chapter Six

Mercy's body rocked back and forth and bounced up and down with the coach's movements. She was falling in and out of consciousness, shivering with cold, yet unable to move her relaxed muscles. She didn't know where she was. As much as she tried, she couldn't keep her eyes open.

Time passed in a blur of dark shadows. She slept again. Then she finally managed to open her eyes and keep them open long enough to take in her surroundings. The horrible taste and smell were still deep in her throat, and she attempted to cough them out. Her body ached. Her wrists and feet were hurting, as were her shoulders and back. She tried to focus now that she no longer felt herself spinning. She was fully conscious and the terrible dream she thought she'd just had, became reality.

From her position on the floor, she could see shadowy figures, billowing skirts, and shoes of all colours. She saw the ropes tied around bare ankles first. She tilted her head back on the floor, looked left and right, and saw arms tucked behind backs. With her neck arched as far as it would go without breaking, she saw faces of terrified girls. They were all gagged with white cloths. The top of the gags sat just under their nostrils and completely covered the girls' mouths.

Mercy felt her own gag more keenly and suddenly thought she might suffocate. She couldn't breathe through her mouth. She couldn't move her lips. The gag was knotted so tightly at the back of her head it dug into her cheekbones.

Some partly covered faces stared back at her, whilst a few still slept. She tried to count how many girls were in there with her. She was on the floor with one other body, which was not moving. The girl lay directly behind her. Mercy could just see the tip of her bright pink walking boots.

There were four girls slumped on one long bench to the right and another four on the bench to her left. Some heads bounced on their neighbours' shoulders. One girl was in an awkward position with her body twisted and my head lying on another girl's lap. None could speak, but a couple of girls were persistently moaning through their gagged mouths.

Mercy looked above their faces. Her eyes scanned the walls until she saw the soft golden glow of dusk coming through a tiny window, covering the wooden ceiling in an orange hue. How long had she been lying here? Where was she? What was the carriage's destination? Questions converged on her all at once, making her pounding headache even more severe. Hours had passed, that much she did know. It would be dark soon. Was she still in London? And her final question, which should have been her first; why was this happening to her? What did they want with her and the other girls?

The pain of tightly knotted ropes became far more intense. She struggled to loosen the rope that bound her wrists, which were behind her and pressing into the hard floor that bumped every time the coach hit a stone or dip in the road. She shook her feet in an attempt to free herself, but to no avail.

Exhausted, she stared up at the ceiling and felt the first tears fall. They were a strange sensation, those tears, and she allowed them to fall freely for the first time in her life.

Chapter Seven

"How far is it now? My arse has gone to sleep. You know how much I hate those bloody pins and needles when it starts waking up again," Sam complained.

"I reckon it's about another two miles or so. Why the hell are you asking me? We've done this often enough. Christ, Sam, I can tell by just looking at the trees where we are. You sleep too much instead of paying attention. When we've finished at this rest stop, you're taking the reins. I'm knackered."

"All right, ya moaning git, stop your griping. Just get a move on and don't spare the horses. I need a drink."

The carriage had taken an hour longer than usual to reach the London outskirts. There had been work going on everywhere. They'd been turned away from side streets and main roads, and they'd ended up on the South side of the city instead of the North.

They arrived at their rest stop seven hours after starting out and three hours later than usual. The horses were labouring now, but this inn always kept spare horses for them, as did all the other inns they routinely stopped at.

The madam paid retainers, and the men with the horses never crossed her. A couple of years earlier, a man had taken her money and then hadn't shown up with the animals. He'd ended up decapitated; his head stuck on a tree branch with her anonymous compliments.

Sam and Eddie always got a free meal and ale wherever they stopped. They took their time, for after they'd had their fill, they then had the tedious task of watering the whores in the back of the coach. Food was never given to the girls. It delayed Sam and Eddie too much and was hard work. They didn't need food, the madam told them. As long as they were periodically watered, she believed there would be no harm done to their bodies, and starving them would stop shit flowing out of them every five minutes. "Just make sure you keep them watered. I want soft skins, not bloody prunes, that's the most important thing," Madame Du Pont reminded them whenever they left for London.

Sam and Eddie felt better after they'd eaten a stew with bread accompanied by a pitcher of ale. It was time to change the horses. They unhitched the four from London and led them to the stables just behind the inn. Their man was waiting, as always, with four fresh horses. He hitched them up to the carriage and then disappeared.

Eddie carried two buckets of water to the rear of the carriage and set them down.

Sam was already inside. He picked Mercy up from the floor and threw her untidily onto one of the benches. She moaned, and he slapped her across the head. He then did the same to the other girl who'd been on the floor with Mercy. She was now conscious and kicked out, hitting Sam's shin. She was punched on the side of the head for her cheek. "Try that again, and I'll choke the life out of your scrawny neck. Now shut it!"

Then he told all the girls, "Not one sound do I want to hear come out of your mouths. Next one will get more than these two got. You hear me?"

Eddie handed the water buckets to Sam, stepped up, and slid inside the crowded carriage, closing the doors behind him. He carried an oil lantern and set it down.

They shared the work. Each man untied a gag, poured water into a girl's mouth from an iron ladle, and gagged the girl again straight after.

Eddie scowled. Watering the whores got harder as the journey went on, it was so bloody time-consuming and tiring. Most, if not all the girls, usually peed themselves a couple of times before they reached the first stop, and tonight was no exception. The carriage stunk like a cesspit with vomit included. It was common for a girl to heave and sometimes regurgitate when the gag was removed. He hated the smell of it and how it looked. The sight had put him off eating porridge for life. Christ, it was like working in a zoo, tending to stinking animals by the time they got within striking distance of Liverpool.

When Eddie went back outside, Sam finished off the work. After making sure that every gag was tight enough and securely knotted, he put chloroform drops on the top part of the cloth, just under the girls' nostrils. A sleeping captive was a secure captive, as far as he was concerned. He took one last look, and sure enough, they all conked out one after the other before his very eyes.

Eddie looked at his pocket watch. It was almost ten o'clock. Nineteen hours to go, he calculated. They had about nine and a half hours of night travel in front of them. It was always as black as a bottomless pit with only a small, dimly lit lantern on the front of the carriage to guide them along the uneven and sometimes treacherous path.

They only ever came across one or two other carriages during this part of the journey. Highwaymen were not much of a threat nowadays. They had all but given up on that employment, what with night traffic on the road a rare sight, thanks to the railways.

Eddie and Sam stopped periodically to water and cool down the horses. They always had two full buckets of water attached to the rear end of the coach for this very reason. When they moved on after a half hour or so, the horses were slightly fresher and just about able to reach the next stop.

Their habit was to rest up just before dawn or thereabouts, and at the next inn they came to, they went through the same routine as the one before, eating what seemed like the same watery stew, and drinking another pitcher of ale. They were both convinced that the same cook travelled from inn to inn, and covered the length of England.

The day was coming, Eddie believed when these ventures would stop altogether. Inns were closing at night for lack of traffic, and it was harder to get someone to have the horses available, even though the men who did this job for them were well paid. The railway was going to finish off the madam's longstanding business, and that worried Eddie, for if she closed down this part of her operation, he'd be out of a job.

Chapter Eight

The carriage, exhausted horses, two men, and ten abducted girls finally reached the Liverpool suburbs. It was mid-afternoon, and the weather was fair but much cooler than the blazing London Indian-summer heat they'd left behind.

Eddie's downturned head bounced on his neck. He was unaware of the traffic build-up, the city noise, ships' horns, and putrid smell penetrating the carriage's wooden floor and walls. He'd slept for at least three hours on this last part of the journey. Sam had cursed more than once at the ease with which Eddie seemed to shut out everything going on around him. He had needed someone to talk to. Eddie talked rubbish most of the time, Sam thought, but his company would have made the last part of the journey a bit more tolerable.

Kicking Eddie's legs, which were stretched out over the footboard that partly connected the horses to the carriage. Sam shouted, "You're a right selfish bastard, Eddie Gunn. Wake up, ya lazy bugger. We're nearly home."

Eddie yawned and stretched his arms. Throwing Sam a thunderous look, he said, "Wait a minute, let me come to, will you? Christ, it's not as if you didn't sleep enough earlier."

"Well, we're in the city, just about. Keep a lookout for coppers or anyone else that might stop us for some reason," Sam insisted.

"I have to admit, du Pont's idea of having 'Workhouse Van' painted on the side was a good 'un. It tends to put most off looking in the back," Eddie commented still yawning.

"So does the bloody stink."

"Yer got that right. I don't like the look of all this traffic. The bloody Americans must be in port."

"I can see that for myself," Sam snapped, "I'm going to see if we can get down one of these side streets."

"Jesus, the whores really are smelling strong this trip," said Eddie, massaging his neck and shoulders.

"I know, it's worse than the London stink in there. I can't wait to get cleaned up and have a good kip."

"Me too. My bloody neck feels as though it's broken."

Sam glared at him. "You've got a nerve. If you had snored any louder, I was going to break your neck for you. Now, look lively, Eddie boy."

The vehicle turned off the busy port thoroughfare that ran parallel with the docks. It turned right onto a long wide road, lined with storage yards, livery stables, and an omnibus terminus. From there they headed west and continued in this direction for about a mile. They then took a sharp turn into a side street and then into another connecting to it. These streets were full of old, low-rent houses, and even Eddie and Sam hated going through this particular area. Thieves and drunks lived there, and most of them made their living stealing money and luggage from immigrants.

When they reached the final bend of the third street they'd gone through, they carefully manoeuvred the carriage onto a narrow dirt road that led to the edge of a park. The carriage steadily followed one of the many paths, branching off like veins through the grassy, tree-dotted expanse until they eventually came to another street, which bordered it on the far side.

The street they were now in was different to the ones they'd left behind. The houses were large and gated. They were in the heart of Mansions Row, where the upper class resided. Those who didn't know Liverpool well could be led to believe that they were in the countryside instead of being just a couple of miles from the docks. Most of the mansions were invisible from the street, for they sat at the end of long, winding driveways and were surrounded by high walls and trees.

Eventually, the carriage turned right and stopped in front of iron gates. Eddie jumped down, unlocked them, and opened them wide. He waited until the carriage was inside, and then he closed and locked the gates behind him.

A gatehouse stood just inside the driveway. When Madame du Pont was open for business, two men were always on hand to monitor who was coming in and going out.

Madame Du Pont's mansion and the business therein were accessible for members only. The membership document was nothing more than a fancy piece of paper embossed with a silver-leafed frame, the customer's name in the centre, the house rules, and Madame Du Pont's signature. But this document was all-important because without it there was no entry onto the premises until a thorough background check and interview had been conducted. Only the elite passed through these gates, whether it was for one night only or on a regular basis.

The driveway snaked its way around manicured lawns and trees. The carriage finally came to the rear of the mansion and turned sharply to park up inside the stable.

Both men gave a sigh of relief.

Sam jumped down and stumbled, as though he'd just reached dry land. He stretched his body, rubbed his backside, and then rolled his head from side to side. "Ah…pure luxury," he said.

Eddie joined him on the ground and did the same dance movement, swinging his hips and bending over frontwards and then backwards. "Christ, I feel as stiff as a board. I thought I'd lost all feeling in my arse forever. Thank God that's over. We did well, Sam."

"That we did. It was a hard one. I can't wait to see madam's face when she looks over the cargo. She'll be right pleased, I bet, especially with that last piece we picked up."

Two young boys smiled and waved to Eddie and Sam as they approached the carriage. One of the boys said, "It's good to see you back, sirs."

Eddie nodded and then growled harshly, "Get the horses unhitched. Wipe 'em down and feed them well, and take a look at one of the mares, it looks as though she's gone lame on her left foreleg."

Whilst the boys did as they were told, Sam closed the stable doors.

Eddie crossed to the far corner of the stable. There was an entrance situated there. He waited for Sam to join him and when he did, both men opened the door and stepped onto a landing that led to a basement, ten stairs down.

The large underground room had no windows. A fire was necessary to keep it warm, winter and summer. It was also very dark, with only small ceiling vents allowing in air and a shimmer of light.

Straw mattresses lay on the ground in two neat lines. There were five bathtubs, towels, wash bowls, soap, and rows of filled water buckets. Sam set light to the logs in the fireplace and placed the first of the water buckets on a bar that sat above them.

They were aware that Madame Du Pont didn't like her girls catching cold. She couldn't care less about them as people, but they were her bread and butter, and she cared about her income. The place had to be cosy before the girls got down there to bathe and sleep. This was rule number one.

They walked back up the stairs. Eddie spoke to one of the stable boys and ordered him to get the serving women. When he'd done this, he joined Sam, and both walked towards the carriage.

Experience had taught them not to open the carriage door until they'd covered their noses and mouths with a scarf as a mask. The stench emanating from the carriage was at its worst now that the coach was in a confined space and behind closed doors. Both men had been known to vomit.

The ten girls were in various positions inside the carriage. Some had woken up and were sitting, while others struggled to reach consciousness and were wobbling dazedly on the bench. Most were in shock and trembled, but one or two looked as though they were just about to keel over and die.

Sam was first to speak to them. "Right, wake up and listen here, all of you," he said gruffly. "I'm going to untie you one by one. My friend here," he pointed to Eddie, now holding a pistol, "will shoot you between the eyes without a minute's hesitation if you make a sound or try to run. When you're free of your ropes, you'll get down from the carriage and stand in line. I'll say again, if any one of you so much as moves or says the wrong thing, he'll shoot you for that too. Am I clear? Nod your heads and tell me you understand, for I'll not be saying it a third time."

The girls, eyes wide with fear, nodded in understanding.

They were untied one by one, grimacing but silent, and as ordered, tried to get down from the carriage. Some stumbled and fell as soon as their feet reached the ground. Legs bound for more than a day and night felt numb and had not an ounce of strength in them to hold their bodies upright.

Those on the ground crawled like babies and then attempted to stand, hanging on to another girl's skirt for support. When the last of them left the carriage, it was towed away into another, somewhat larger stall. In there, it would be cleaned and disinfected, a task the stable boys hated with a vengeance.

Chapter Nine

Mercy, dazed, bewildered, and terrified, stood in a bedraggled line with the other girls. She was afraid to move a muscle, even though her aching limbs demanded that she do so in order to free painful cramps. Terrified of being noticed or of allowing a sound to leave her mouth, all she could hear were her teeth chattering in a song of fear. She was exhausted, sick, and trying her utmost to stand on unsteady feet.

Her wrists and ankles were red raw and covered in dried blood in places because of her determined efforts to free herself from the ropes that had bound her. Pain emanated from her face. It was stinging, swollen, and bruised as though she'd been punched. Her mouth was still half-open due to the long hours she'd spent gagged, and her lips were swollen to twice their normal size with several doses of chloroform.

Horrific images floated through her mind, but she was not having a nightmare. She was not dreaming this. This was a conscious experience she could neither comprehend nor associate with anything she had ever known or imagined.

The chloroform was still lingering in her system, but she attempted to focus her thoughts on exactly what had happened to her. She had offered to help a man who was worried about his wife. The man in question was now standing alongside another man right here in this stable. She couldn't believe stupidity and trust had led her to this. It was an unimaginable horror.

Getting tied up was not an experience she had any recollection of at all. She had woken up on the floor with back-breaking pain. Only then had she discovered her tethered body. She remembered sporadic drinks of water because of the painful procedure involved. The wet, smelly rag that gagged her mouth had been pulled off her face and then replaced, stinging her skin, and the drops of liquid poured on it had sent her into an abyss of darkness without dreams each time.

She had no clue as to her whereabouts. Was she far from home or was home close by? No, she determined; home was not nearby. The capital was not that big, and they had been on the road for more than a day. She had to conclude, therefore, that they were nowhere near London or its suburbs.

Her hungry belly was rumbling, yet the thought of putting food in her mouth made her want to be sick again. Her new gown, drenched in pee and dried vomit, was a degrading and shameful sight. The dress was torn at the left-hand side from her underarm right down to her waist. She was desperate to take it off and wash her body.

Pride and vanity had been but a fleeting experience for her, she thought. That day in the dressmaker's shop and her experiences in a beautiful tearoom in front of St Paul's had been the first time she'd ever thought of herself as more than a girl from a poor London borough. It was her own vanity that had brought her to this!

This was the end of innocence and sweet dreams. How could she ever feel pure after what she'd seen and felt? She felt like an animal; no better than that. She felt like one of those black slaves she'd heard about. She was being treated like livestock at market.

What would her family be thinking right now? It was the first time the thought had occurred to her. Would they be out looking for her? She just knew they would be, but she also assumed they would look no further than the dressmaker's and Mrs McCallum's house, certainly no further than the confines of the borough of Southwark. It wouldn't enter their minds to cross the river to look for her, for that had been forbidden, and she'd always been obedient.

Had they gotten the truth out of poor Doreen and Agnes, who had displayed nothing but kindness and understanding? She was horrified at that possibility. They would be in big trouble right now with her family and especially with Big Joe. If she were able, she would take all the blame on her own shoulders. She had deliberately played on the women's pity.

Girls were sobbing. She looked to her left and then to her right. One girl was crying so loudly; Mercy thought she might get shot for it.

Just then, a girl keeled over and hit the ground with a thud. Mercy thought she might fall too; she wished she could hold on to something or someone. She thought about Grandpa Carver. She would not cry again if she could help it. He would belt her if he were here to see her crying like a sissy.

She continued to glance at the two men, who were talking in whispers and standing near the stable doors. She felt bile rise in her throat and realised that her body was beginning to sway backwards and forwards. She wasn't sure how long she could stand on her feet. She was sure she was going to faint any minute now and hoped that if she did, she would never wake up again.

Chapter Ten

A door opened. Mercy tensed and held her breath, hearing the sound of soft-footed steps coming closer from somewhere behind her. Out of the corner of her eye, she saw three women. They walked slowly, one behind the other, down the line, passing her and paying no heed to any of them. Mercy presumed by their black-and-white uniform dresses and crisp, white, frilly caps that they were house servants. All three wore aprons that began at the neck like bibs and were tied at the waist with wide bows at the back, then fell to the floor. They were well groomed, and the aprons and neat hair led Mercy to believe they had come from a grand house. She was more confused than ever. She got the impression that the three servants had seen captive girls many times before, given their total indifference and passive expressions. They approached the two men. Mercy tried to hear what they were saying, but all she saw were lips moving. A discussion was going on…about what, she didn't know.

"Right, let's get this done, Missus Parker," Eddie said. "Madame du Pont will want to inspect them, and we're already late. You get the firepit going outside, Sam, and I'll make a start on the girls,"

Sam cursed him and stood with his hands on his hips, looking ready for an altercation. "Who made you the boss? How come I always have to do the fire, and you get all the fun? I did the fire the last time."

"Aw, for God's sake, shut yer trap. Just do it, or we'll both be in the dog house. You know she won't come down here until we've got them disinfected, so stop whining like a woman and move your arse. I want a beer, and then I want my bed."

Mercy watched the man called Sam march out of a side door, banging it shut behind him. He had inflicted pain on her and the others inside that filthy, disgusting carriage. He was a pig, just like the other man, the trickster, she thought. Mercy now studied the actions of the remaining man. He was the one who had lied to her at St Paul's with false tears. *Stupid, stupid, stupid, Mercy!* Her mind was screaming.

He spoke to the servant women, pointing to the far end of the line. The women nodded. All three walked past Mercy and those next to her.

Eddie brought out a knife from a leather holster on his thigh and ran his fingers gently down the length of it from the hilt to the point.

Mercy drew in her breath. Surely he wasn't going to kill them? That wouldn't make sense. He hadn't brought them all this way just to end their lives. If she were the one holding the knife, she'd gut him. She wouldn't hesitate.

Eddie went to the first girl in the line. The girl was crying. Mercy closed her eyes. She couldn't block out the sound of moaning and tearful begging, but she didn't have to watch. She heard ripping and tearing from both ends of the line now, left and right.

Finally, she opened her eyes. She had to watch, for she would have to endure the same as the others when they got to her.

Eddie walked nonchalantly past the first girl and on to the girl right next to her. Mercy watched in horror as he took the knife to the girl's gown and sliced the entire length of it from neckline to thighs. Her hooped underskirt came off next, then bloomers, leaving the girl in a corset and unsuccessfully trying to cover her half-naked breasts and pubic region.

Eddie walked outside with the first two lots of stinking garments and reappeared a moment later.

Mercy steeled herself. She was next in line.

Eddie appeared to ignore Mercy's hatred, emanating like a blinding beacon from her eyes. She could smell his rancid breath. He was but inches away from her face. He looked her in the eye and moved in closer. Mercy tried to take a step backwards but was stopped in her tracks. The knife blade was at her throat.

"I remember you the most," Eddie told her. "You delayed our journey, but I've got a feeling you'll be well worth it. Do you like me? Tell me you like me."

Mercy swallowed painfully and stared back at him with that same shining hatred. "I like you, sir," she said.

She closed her eyes, only to open them wide a second later when she felt his wet tongue licking her face. She cringed. What was this revolting man doing? Her stomach turned over. He leant in even closer. His tongue was in her ear, out and then in again. Afterwards, it slithered back to her face, followed a path down her cheek and along her chin until it came to rest on her mouth. He parted her swollen lips. Then his tongue was inside, whipping her teeth and dancing with her own swollen tongue.

Mercy shuddered. The smell, taste, and feel of his wet tongue and saliva inside her mouth enraged her. She wanted to kick, punch, and stab him with his own knife, but instead, she stood as still as a statue with eyes staring defiantly into his own.

Mercy continued to stare at him even when the knife cut into her dress and nicked her skin at the neckline. A dribble of blood ran down her cleavage and disappeared between her full breasts. She stood like a soldier at attention, watching and hearing every rip and tear. The puff sleeves came apart. He then went back to her already torn and bloodied neckline. Pulling at the velvet with one hand, he sliced it down to her waist with his knifed hand, and the gown parted like a pair of curtains.

Mercy felt him pull the material at the waist and cut until the entire dress fell off her in two halves. When she wore nothing more than her brand-new corset, he turned from her, picked up her beautiful gown and petticoats, and marched outside again.

At this point, Mercy dared to look up and down the entire line. The three women were finishing off the remaining girls, using dressmaking scissors. They did not look up from their work nor did they utter a word. Girls were openly crying, some begging to go home. One girl fainted and was consequently slapped across the face and dragged once again to her feet.

Mercy found herself fighting tears now. This was not new to her, for she'd fought the pleasure of a good cry all her life. But she was almost naked, humiliated, and afraid of what was to come. She wanted her grandparents and her own bed. She wanted to go home, marry Big Joe, work in the grocer's shop, and let him take her night after night. She would gladly have gone back to a life she'd dreaded rather than face a future which was, with every passing moment, becoming sickeningly clearer. She suspected that she and the other girls would never see home again.

After some minutes, Sam and Eddie walked back into the stable. Mercy wondered if they had finished with the girls. She looked at the other captives, sobbing, and deduced that out of all of them, she would be the strongest. These girls were *real* ladies. They weren't common like her. Their garments; before being ripped off, had been made with quality materials and were probably very fashionable, just like hers had been. Their hair, adornments, bonnets, and jewellery also displayed classic signs of wealth and were what she expected well-bred ladies to wear.

She came from a dark place in London, a place she believed none of these well-bred girls had ever seen, heard of or imagined existed. Her home was in an area where fights broke out in the streets on a daily basis, blood was shed, and people were killed for debts owed. She had gone to school with rough girls who could bloody a nose just as quickly as any boy.

She was not a lady, not like these young women. She was more streetwise than these sheltered, high-class girls. She felt like laughing, but it would have been a scornful laugh, for she'd not been very streetwise at St Paul's Cathedral!

"Right, they're all yours," Eddie said to a serving woman. "Tell Madame du Pont we'll be here at eight tonight for her inspection and instructions. You'd better get a move on, Parker. You've got a full load to get through here, and we arrived late thanks to bloody London and its modernisation. I wouldn't dilly-dally if I were you."

Chapter Eleven

Mercy staggered tiredly with the other girls through an open doorway, down some stairs, and into a large, warm room. Once there, one of the servants spoke directly to them for the first time in a tone of voice absent of compassion. "Right, my name is Parker, Missus Parker to you lot. You do as I say, else I get it in the ear from my employer, and if I get it in the ear from her, you'll get it from me, only twice as bad."

Parker stopped talking and appeared to be looking for a reaction. Seemingly satisfied with the terrified look on the girls' faces, she continued. "You'll take your stockings off now, and then we'll be coming to get rid of those corsets. This is no time to be shy, ladies. When me and my friends 'ere, snip your corset lacings, you'll fill the bathtubs and get in. Share the tubs and scrub the filth off yourselves and then help each other. It'll be quicker. I want to see hair washed, and I don't want any moaning about the water not being warm enough. Soap and towels are over there." She pointed. "Now, are any of you on your bleeding cycle?"

Two girls nodded their heads and then hung them in shame.

Parker nodded. "Right, share a bath, you two. You'll find stitched circles of absorbent flannel and ribbons to thread through them to tie round your waists for your menses napkins over by the towels. If you lose heavy, I have some rabbit skins available too, and there had best not be any seepage once you're dressed again. That goes for all of you when it's your turn to bleed. Do you understand me?"

"Yes," all the girls whispered.

"The owner of this house is called Madame du Pont, and she doesn't like to be kept waiting, so get to it. We'll refill the buckets and heat them as best we can, but don't take our kindness as weakness, do you hear me? And another thing; don't even think about leaving this room till you're told to, understand? There are men guarding all the doors, and we don't give second chances to runaways…we provide them with nice warm graves in the garden."

After the gasps and sobs, the woman called Parker nodded to the other two women present, and the scissors came out of their apron pockets again.

Mercy watched the humiliating proceedings but refused to blink an eye. She was more terrified than ever. Bury girls in the garden? Was that a threat, or had these evil people actually killed before? When they came to her, she held her head up high, closed her eyes, and tried to retain some small measure of dignity. They stood behind her. She saw nothing but felt rough hands tug and cut her corset laces in a cruel, emotionless fashion. They pulled at her, grazing her back with the scissors, and she felt like an animal being skinned alive.

Unattached, the corset slid off her body and landed at her feet. The women then came to stand in front of her. One of them proceeded to stretch her legs apart whilst Parker got on her knees in front of her.

Mercy tried to cover her cunny with both hands, and they were slapped away. One servant pinned her arms behind her back whilst the other slapped her inner thighs. "Open wider…more," she ordered.

Mercy's body trembled with revulsion. Never had hands touched her there nor had anyone even seen that part of her body. “Please don’t do that,” she begged the women, still trying to close her legs.

“I’ll cut you if you don’t stand still,” Parker told her, “and I’ll not be taking the bloody blame if I break the skin on the most useful part of your body!”

It took great effort on her part, but after a few moments, Mercy did as she was told. Relaxing her shivering body by closing her eyes again, she thought about her family. After a few seconds, she felt another slap on the thigh and spread her legs until she thought she might lose her balance or do the splits. “What are you doing?” she shouted inadvertently.

She opened her eyes, and this time she didn’t stop the tears from rolling down her cheeks onto her chin. The scissors cut her hair from her outer pubic area right to the sides of her hole. She was nicked a couple of times but forced herself to be still as a figurine. When they’d finished with her, she was told to share a bath with a girl who was already filling it with water buckets.

Both naked and sheared girls avoided looking at each other. Mercy poured one last bucket of cold water into the bath and got in it. The bath water was tepid at best. It contained one bucketful of hot water from the fire and three of cold water that had sat just inside the door. Mercy had never seen as many iron buckets in her life, certainly not in the same room. It was better than being freezing, she thought, well used to cold baths.

She drew in her breath and sat down with her knees at her chin. The other girl followed her, gasping at the cold and weeping like a baby.

Mercy held her hand. “My name is Mercy. What’s yours?”

There was no answer.

“Please don’t cry. Don’t let them see you like this,” Mercy whispered handing the girl the bar of soap.

“Julia…my name is Julia,” the young girl whispered back. “Why are they doing this? Do you know why? Do you know where we are?”

“No. I don’t know anything. But I think we’re very far away from London. I think they’re going to sell us. I just don’t know who to,” Mercy said. “Here, let me wash your hair and then you can do mine.”

Julia stopped crying with a final throaty sob and nodded. She then pinched her nose, slid down the bath, and dipped her entire body and head under the water. When she came up for air, Mercy noticed a small cut just at her scalp. The blood had dried, and the small slit had scabbed over. It looked to be days old.

“How did you bump your head?” Mercy asked her.

“One of those men did it when they took me. I don’t know how long ago that was. I feel I haven’t slept or eaten in days. They took me to a house. I was there with three other girls, and then more came the next day.

“My mama and papa will be beside themselves with worry. We were in London earlier this year for the season. I wasn’t presented at court but my older sister was. She met the Queen four months ago. It’s her coming out year, you see. Then we returned two weeks ago for the Earl of Shannon's wedding.” Julia looked at Mercy and asked, “Were you presented this season?”

"Tell me about yourself, Julia," Mercy urged her, ignoring the question.

"My father is cousin to an Earl. I begged him to take me to London this year, even though I'm not due to come out until the year after next. I had hoped to persuade Mama and Papa to allow me to be officially presented next year instead. I'm in love you see…but I think I'm going to die here. I can just feel it." The tears spilt down her cheeks again, and this time there was no stopping them.

"You're very young to be in love," Mercy said, trying to calm her.

"I know. I'm only fourteen, but I want to marry him as soon as father allows it. His name is Charles. I should have stayed in the country with my younger brothers, but I so wanted to go to London and see the sights and attend this, the society wedding of the year. I don't want to die!"

"Julia, you're not going to die. Did you see your Charles? Did you like London?"

"Yes, London is such fun, but I so wanted to see him. That's why I was so desperate to go to the capital. He wrote to me and told me he would be at the wedding too. He's a Viscount, you know." She wept again.

Mercy looked at the servants and saw they were busy with other girls. She had to get Julia to stop crying. If she carried on the women would come over and shout, or worse, hit them both.

"Stop crying…please, you have to stop," Mercy said. "Concentrate on my questions. Tell me, how were you abducted? Were you not chaperoned?"

"I should have been, but I had secretly arranged to meet Charles in Hyde Park. I persuaded one of our family's coachmen to take me. I promised not to stray from his sight, but when we got to the park, I ordered him to stay with the carriage whilst I took a stroll around the lake. Appleby, the coachman, was very hesitant at first, but I insisted. I was to meet Charles behind a boathouse at the side of the great pond. After a short walk on my own, I found myself trapped with the two horrible men who brought us here."

Mercy had lathered and rinsed Julia's hair. Now she dipped her own head under the water. When she sat up, she wondered…had Sam and Eddie's presence been a coincidence, just terrible bad luck, or had they been stalking Julia?

Julia then told Mercy that apart from her stupidity on that day, her biggest regret was that her coachman would, without a doubt, be on the street now without a job and the lodgings that went with it. "I am so terribly ashamed. Appleby was a good man, and because of me, he will be destitute. I was a very selfish, stupid girl."

"We were all stupid, it seems." Mercy played with her own thoughts. Julia was far too young to be there. She was just coming out of childhood! Mercy looked at the other girls. She had already decided that she was different. She had heard them whisper, speak a few words, seen their graceful steps, and felt their unworldly innocence. Even in the mayhem and chaos, she'd noticed their breeding, something she lacked. Their naked bodies were unblemished, creamy-soft, and white as milk. Their smooth, silky hands had probably never washed a dish or piece of clothing.

She had also come to the conclusion that they were not all from London. She listened to whispered conversations and was quite surprised to learn that most of the girls were in fact from country estates and had never set foot in London before. They had, like her, been exploring, albeit close to where they were staying, but alone, and this had been their downfall, just as it had been her own.

Great families of dukes and earls, landowners and gentry had misplaced daughters. This information gave Mercy hope, for she was sure these families would never give up looking for them. They had the resources to scour the entire country, and when the girls were found, she would be too.

These wealthy families would also pay an impressive ransom for their daughters' safe return. She gave herself another theory. Was this why they'd been taken?

She looked at her own hands, rough with scrubbing and washing clothes with hard soap. Her skin was slightly tanned with summer sun, for she had no carriage or parasol to keep its rays at bay.

Her abductors had apparently thought her a lady because of where they'd found her and how she'd been dressed. But if this was about ransom money, she would never be returned. Would they punish her or kill her for being useless to them? Her family had not a farthing to give for her safe return.

She looked around her again and decided there and then that to stay safe, she'd have to try and fit in, both in speech and in the way she walked and behaved. Oh, God, it seemed a bleedin' impossible task after a lifetime in the Elephant and Castle!

Chapter Twelve

Once again, Mercy stood in line in the stable. This time she had clean skin and her hair, almost dry, flowed in waves down her back. She was barely clothed, wearing only a white silk shift with narrow straps. The material was almost see-through. Her nipples peeked out just above the plunging neckline, and her rounded bum cheeks were also visible.

Mercy's anger and frustration had grown even further due to exhaustion and painful muscles. She was no longer afraid. She was angry and starving.

She held Julia's hand in her own. Someone had to look after the young girl, Mercy thought. It might as well be her. In the past couple of hours, the reasons for being abducted had not become clearer. If anything her theories were bouncing around her mind like balls. She couldn't be certain, but because of their attire, she thought it a distinct possibility that they were going to be sold into slavery. Was it possible; slavery? She'd heard that practice was for black people and those convicted of crimes and later sent to Australia on prison ships. She had never seen a black man. Did slavery still exist? And what was white slavery? She'd seen something about that in a newspaper headline a while back? Did it mean white girls like these? Was she now a slave? That didn't bear thinking about!

She felt sick again and was also feeling faint, but while she had strength, she would not fall down as a couple of the other girls had. She was determined to stand tall. She was already thinking about escaping. If she got the chance, she would make a run for it, dressed just as she was. She searched her mind for possibilities. There were the stable's double doors, but they were locked. There was another side door, and one behind that, sitting atop two steps that led to God only knew where. There were no windows to slither through. But she *would* find a way out.

The clip-clopping sound of heels came from behind the line-up. Mercy had heard the door open and then slam shut again a moment earlier. She tightened her grip on Julia's hand and squeezed it, a comforting gesture without words. Julia's teeth were chattering, and heart-wrenching sobs tore from her mouth every time she exhaled. She was going to pass out if she didn't start breathing properly, Mercy thought.

Time stopped as the sound of rustling petticoats filled the expanse behind. The three servants in front of the line-up curtsied. A woman came into view and stood before them.

"Have you had any problems?" the woman asked Parker.

"None, madam. Everything is in order."

"Where are Sam and Eddie? They're late."

"They're on their way. Jimmy has just been sent to fetch them here."

Staring at the mysterious woman, who seemed quite at ease giving orders, Mercy didn't know whether to be happy or furious that the woman ignored all the captives as though they didn't exist.

She was a strange-looking female, Mercy thought. She had thick, mannish arms bulging out from the confines of her elbow-length, blue puff sleeves. Her figure was rounded, and her corset didn't do her any favours at all. In fact, if anything, it accentuated her somewhat large waist. Her huge bosom rippled like waves every time she moved an inch. They had trouble remaining within the top frill of her blue silk gown's plunging neckline. Her hair was bright red with well-defined ringlets and was adorned with various ornaments in gold and ivory. It was a wig, of course. The colour, texture, manicured hairline and perfection of every curl could not possibly be natural.

Whilst the woman spoke some way away from the line of girls; Mercy took the opportunity to study her further, this time concentrating on her face. Her double chin and layered neck sat beneath a painted, doll-like facade, and the thick layers of powder and rouge couldn't hide the fact that she was well past her prime. Yet she was not an ugly woman.

The two round pink patches on the woman's cheeks might have appeared quite comical to Mercy under any other circumstances. She looked ridiculous with her perfect bow lips painted on, to probably double their real size. But despite her painted clown appearance, the woman she was studying was intimidating. Never had she seen such a dispassionate glare from eyes that held a glint of evil, devoid of emotion and kindness.

Eventually, the object of her thoughts turned her attention to the girls.

Praying that her concentrated stares had gone unnoticed, Mercy hung her head, hoping to stand invisible amongst the group. The woman began her inspection at the far end of the line, stopping in front of each girl, lifting chins, opening mouths, checking teeth, and running her hands through newly washed hair. Venturing far across any line of decency with her physical roughness Mercy thought that the madam, as she was being repeatedly called, was behaving like a common farmer looking over horses. It was disgusting behaviour.

Mercy steeled herself. Gazing at the woman with a defiance that had been absent earlier, her nostrils took in the scent of a perfume that didn't quite manage to conceal the smell of alcohol and stale body odour. Inadvertently, she screwed up her face and then realised that the madam was staring back at her.

"What's your name, girl?"

Mercy found that she couldn't speak. She wanted to, but she was frozen in fear.

"Answer me! What's your name?"

"Mercy…Mercy Carver," she whispered.

"Well, Mercy Carver, I'll start with you for your insolence, so I will, and you best not give me any trouble. I can smell trouble a mile off…take off the shift."

"What?" Mercy said in a daze.

"I said take off the shift. Now!"

Mercy's lips quivered. "No, I won't."

The slap to her right cheek stung, but Mercy squealed from the shock of it more than any pain caused. Determined not to beg or cry, she held her head high and met the madam's cold stare. "I'm not stripping off," she said.

Madam du Pont's fingers gripped Mercy's jawline and dug into her skin, still stinging with the slap. "Take off that bloody shift now, or I swear to God, you won't see another day."

Mercy's eyes locked onto du Pont's face. Holding her breath, she was afraid to breathe or utter a sound. Her trembling fingers reached for the narrow silk straps. She pulled one down her arm and over her hand, and then the other followed. The silky material slipped off her body, down her legs, and rested on top of her bare feet. She gasped for air and for a second, stared at her nakedness.

Her arms, by her side, shot up to cover her breasts and her newly trimmed pubic area but were quickly wrenched away and pinned behind her back in a tight grip.

Parker punched her inner thighs and pulled them open like gates.

Mercy freed her feet from the shift, as she desperately tried to keep her balance. Breathless with fear and humiliation, she stared into du Pont's victorious, smirking face. She wanted to die. If only death would take her swiftly, she thought, for she could not live with the memory of this torture.

The madam was handed a black cotton glove, which she put on her right hand. She used her bare hand to push the material all the way to the tips of her fingers and then wriggled them about in front of Mercy's face. Mercy stared at it, noticing that du Pont's index finger was making a hooked finger action in front of her eyes, which then followed the gloved hand moving towards her lower body. She moaned pitifully, instinctively knowing what was to follow, "Please…please don't do this," she begged.

"Shut your trap, girl," du Pont said.

Outrage and complete despair led Mercy to lose all semblance of control. This woman was going to examine her. She was going to poke inside her hole and violate her most private parts! She couldn't allow this to happen. It would be the end of her. Her bruised body, swollen lips, and grazed wrists and ankles she could abide, but this…no, not this! She had taken as much as she would take. She wanted answers and wanted them now. She wanted to go home.

Suddenly, she heard her own voice shout, "Why are we here?"

The madam's gloved hand sat in mid-air, stopped in its tracks by Mercy's defiance.

Mercy swiped the gloved hand away with eyes that shone with hatred. "What do you want with us? Let us go. We want to go home. You can't just abduct us like this. You stay away from me with that hand, or I'll bleedin' bite it off your arm, you ugly old tart!"

Mercy was panting, breathless after her outburst, but she continued to stare into the face of her torturer. She thrust her head forward. "Don't you dare touch me down there! Don't you go to that place, or I swear I'll kill you!"

The madam nodded, looking past Mercy.

Mercy felt hands encircling her throat, from behind her. She was then kicked at the backs of her knees, which made her legs buckle instantly. Her body lay, twisted, on the ground. The madam bent down and stared into Mercy's terrified eyes. This close, du Pont's double chin and layered neck were even more evident. Her cheeks hung like flaps swinging about her face, and her ugly scowl took any semblance of womanly softness away from her altogether. Mercy looked past the madam and saw the arrival of her two abductors.

The madam's guttural, throated growl resonated around the room. "Where the bloody 'ell have you been?" she screamed at the two men. "I said eight o'clock ya couple of lazy, good for nothin' gits! Well, what have you got to say for yourselves?"

Sam gave her a shallow bow and took off his cap as a mark of respect. Eddie said, "Sorry madam, we just slept a bit longer than planned. It was a hellish journey. London's gone stark raving mad, digging holes everywhere. We tried to make up time. It won't happen again."

"It bloody better not. You know I hate being kept waiting. You should both know that by now."

"Sorry, madam. I'm sorry, honest," Sam told her meekly.

"Well, now that you've finally showed up, I need your help. I'm going to have to make an example of this one," du Pont said, pointing to Mercy lying naked on the floor. "She's a good catch, I'll grant you that, but she's a fighter, and a cheeky bitch into the bargain."

"Sam, hold her feet nice and tight. Eddie, take hold of her wrists above her head and squeeze them, so it hurts her.

"Parker, you take a leg." She gestured to the head servant. "And you," pointing to another servant, "take the other. Spread them as wide as you can…and for God's sake, make sure she doesn't move. If she so much as twitches and gets damaged down there, I'll thrash the lot of you."

Madame du Pont turned her attention back to Mercy who was crying and begging to be released. "Now you listen to me, girl. You don't speak to me unless you're spoken to. You don't even look me in the face. If you ever question me or anyone else in my employ about anything, I'll have your bloody head on a platter! You'll be told what you need to know when I say it. And as for your cheek, well, just wait and see what you'll get for that! Now, nod your head like a good girl."

Mercy complied.

"Good. I want the rest of you to watch this. When it's your turn, I don't want to hear a bloody sound coming from your spoilt, upper-class, pouting mouths, or you'll be on your backs like this one. You just remember that."

Still angry, du Pont got on her knees, with some difficulty due to an abundance of petticoats and weight. She checked the glove, wiggling her fingers yet again and making sure it was on tight. She then inserted her index finger inside Mercy's vagina and pushed it in, slowly, touching the inner sides and stretching her finger upwards as carefully as she could. She pushed it in and pulled it out a couple of times, and then smiled with satisfaction.

"Seems I've got my first virgin of the day. She's as tight as thick thread through the eye of a needle, just how I like 'em."

Mercy was pulled roughly to her feet. Her inner thigh muscles hurt. Her vagina was stinging, scratched, and hot, and her entire body felt like wobbly jelly.

Eddie and Sam held her by her underarms. The madam removed the glove and turned her attention to her breasts. "How old are you, girl?"

Mercy, her humiliation complete, sobbed like a baby.

"Aw shut it! Not so cocky now, are we?"

"I just turned eighteen, a couple of days ago."

The madam nodded, fondled Mercy's breasts, and smiled. "Good, nicely developed tits with big nipples. You're a good one, all right. Just like a perfectly ripe apple, ready to have the first bite taken out of it. You'll fit in nicely, as long as you keep your trap shut. I hope you've learned something today, Mercy Carver."

Mercy nodded.

Chapter Thirteen

After her ordeal, Mercy tried to shut out her surroundings and the terrible scenes unfolding before her eyes. She was witnessing pure evil for the first time in her life and was being crushed by the growing crescendo of anguished moans and screams coming from her fellow captives. She was glad she'd been the first. She had not been subjected to the terrible dread inflicted on the other girls' minds as they waited for their turns to be poked like a pregnant cow.

Julia, standing beside her, screamed so loud at the madam's poking, the horses whinnied and reared up in their stalls. Girls began to scatter in fright. Some went fleeing into empty stalls, cowering in corners. One girl lay on the ground, calling out in a pitiful voice for her mother. Mercy was compelled to watch the scene, yet she still felt strangely detached from it all, and for the moment, defeated.

One by one the girls were dragged back to the line, pulled by their hair. Those who deemed it better to surrender hung their heads and walked back to wait for the inevitable in silence, and eventually, order was restored.

A few minutes later, Mercy snapped out of her stupor. The madam was screaming obscenities, slapping a girl across the head, left to right and right to left, over and over. The smacking resonated around the stable. "Whore! You're nothing but a bloody whore!"

The girl shook her head, denying the claim, but the madam continued to hit her.

"You're no virgin. Don't you dare try and tell me you are with your haughty, snotty denials. Do you think I don't know the difference? I can feel your used cunt with my finger! You're as wide as the bloody River Mersey. You've had more than a few men float up and down that hole of yours. Do you know what I do with girls like you? I give them to the very worst of my customers, those that like it rough. I might even let my men here have a poke at you. That's what I do with well-used girls I pay good money for. What's your name?"

"Annabelle Fellows."

The madam turned to Sam and Eddie and smiled. "Sam, Annabelle here is yours tonight, if you're not too tired. Take her and show her how we deal with young ladies who go about pretending to the whole bloody world that they're innocent virgins."

At last, after what seemed like hours, the madam gave permission for the girls to cover up their bodies with the shifts that were still lying at their feet. She was quiet and pensive as she watched them. Then she spoke again. "Right, you lot. I am Madame du Pont. You will call me, madam. You will curtsy whenever you see me. Is this understood?"

"Yes, madam," a chorus of voices said in unison.

She continued, "I don't ever want to see a repeat of what's gone on here today, 'cos me having to bruise your pretty faces is not good for my business.

"I've invested a lot of money in you, and I need you looking good, so you'll get some rest now. You'll eat, and you'll sleep for the next couple of days, and you'll stay put until your bruises fade…oh, and just so you know, you're not in London anymore. You're in Liverpool, way up North. Your mamas and papas will never find you here, so don't go thinking for a minute they will. You won't be getting rescued, not one of you. No one in London knows you're alive. You're all dead to the world, and that makes you mine. You're my property. I paid good money to get you here, and you'll be paying me back until I've finished with you. That'll be when I believe you've passed your prime years for servicing my gentlemen callers."

She stopped talking and allowed the girls to gasp at the words she had just spoken.

"That's right; I said servicing men. You'll do my bidding or pay the price for defying me. Now a couple of you are already whores, as slack as well-fucked breeding cows. That means you've lost me some money already, and I don't like to lose money. You'll be working harder than the others to make up for the loss. You seem to like sex, so you'll get plenty of it.

"And another thing; I don't care what you call yourselves. I don't care about your family name, how wealthy your family is, or where you came from. I don't even care if you're related to the bloody queen. You're my whores now. Whores to be used by men in any way they deem fit. You'll take it up the cunny, or up the arse, for all I care, and you'll have a smile on your face, cos you *will* pretend you're enjoying it."

She stopped and grabbed Mercy by the hair, parading her up and down the line, as she continued speaking. "There'll be no telling the gents about yourselves or about where you came from. You'll be telling them that you love being poked and asking for more. There will be no trying to run away. It'll go bad for you, and you'll get much worse than Miss Mercy Carver here. You'll be battered to a pulp and left to heal until you get back to work again. Remember this; you don't fuck, you don't eat."

All the girls were crying. Madam du Pont seemed pleased with this response. She pushed Mercy back into line. "Aww, stop your bloody sniffing, the lot of you. You'll find worse out there on the city streets than inside this house. Girls like you wouldn't last five minutes without my protection."

Pausing for a moment, she looked again at the shocked, tearful faces, and smiled with satisfaction. "You've got a couple of weeks to learn what you need to know about being a proper whore and a pleasant hostess. You'll take your orders from Parker here, who'll spruce you up nicely for when the time comes for your opening night. By then you better be bloody eager for it, or else. Remember, if you try to run, speak out of turn, or tell on me to the clients, I'll cut your bloody feet off and boil them for the dogs to eat. Don't think I won't."

She stopped lecturing the shocked and terrified girls, then turned to the head servant. "Parker, get these girls fed, watered, and bedded down. Make sure you lock up properly."

With that said, du Pont turned on her heel and clip-clopped back up the couple of steps to the door, with Sam and Eddie following meekly behind.

Downstairs in the dimly lit room, the girls claimed a mattress each. Mercy gripped Julia's hand and gently guided her to the place next to her own, lay her down, and covered her with a blanket.

Food came soon after, a hot stew with plenty of meat and potatoes. The servants carried the luscious-smelling fare in steel buckets. Each girl received a bowl and spoon, along with a slice of fresh bread.

Mercy tried to coax Julia to eat. After three attempts, she realised that Julia was not conscious of the food, her surroundings, or what was going on at all.

After she'd finished eating, Mercy cast her eyes around the room.

Disbelief and shock were etched on the faces of young upper-class ladies who had heard the word *whore* over and over again. There were no more unanswered questions for any of them. Their futures had been spelt out in no uncertain terms. They would, for as long as they were useful, open their legs and be mauled, squeezed, poked, and prodded by men of any size, shape, or age. They would succumb to humiliation night after night. Their vaginas would be used, not by aristocratic or well-to-do husbands, but by any man who paid Madame du Pont money for the pleasure of it.

She looked at Julia's sleeping face for a moment and came to a decision; she wouldn't kill herself as her father had. She would escape, and when she did, she would take Julia with her.

Chapter Fourteen

Liverpool, 1860

Madame du Pont, real name Margaret Mallory, finally found the time she needed to relax before the busy evening trade began. She had been busier than usual this past couple of weeks, overseeing the inclusion of the new girls downstairs and sorting out the experienced ones upstairs. Having made arrangements for tantalising foods, fine wines, French brandies, whiskies, cigars, and champagne to be ordered for today, she felt quite exhausted. She'd packed men in every night this past week, and tonight would be even busier, for ships had arrived from America, and the American cotton men were her favourite customers.

She used to have a huge amount of energy, she thought, but the passage of time was catching up with her. There seemed to be fewer hours in a day, more responsibilities that she shouldered alone, and pains in her joints and swellings the size of apples. Thank God for opium, for without it, she just wouldn't be able to manage.

She flopped down on her chaise longue, her swollen feet slightly raised atop a silk cushion, and pondered for a moment. She barely had time to think nowadays, yet bothersome thoughts were never far from her mind. Everything was changing, and not for the better.

Her establishment ran on secrecy and trust. It always had, and she believed she'd done a bloody good job of keeping it that way, despite the never-ending possibility of betrayal.

The local coppers that knew about her and the goings-on in her house were kept quiet with regular bribes and an odd girl to use for free. But the news coming from London was not good. In the past six years, forty-eight young ladies of standing had been abducted in central London, she'd read in the newspaper. No one could possibly connect them to her here in Liverpool, of course, but nonetheless, the abduction of these girls was becoming big news.

An organised branch of coppers from The Metropolitan Police were widening their search for the girls she had just received. Their reach extended far beyond London, and they had already come to the conclusion that all the missing girls were connected in some way.

The latest newspapers from London also stated that suspicion was falling on a long-standing but as yet unknown syndicate. She had scorned this term; she was no bloody syndicate. She was a one-woman show who had pulled this off for years without the help of any other group or mastermind. She shrugged, for what she read in the papers didn't frighten her in the least. She was so very far away from London. Her safe house in Knightsbridge was secure, and its housekeepers had never been told of the girls' destination or who they were for.

Her whores would never disclose anything about themselves, for she had made examples of those who had attempted to relate their stories to customers. And as for her elite clientele, well, she had enough dirt on them to destroy their lives, families, and businesses. She made it her business to vet and find weaknesses in every single member of her exclusive club, from the poker players to the whoremongers.

Some of these so-called gents were depraved and sadistic. Most wanted virgins and youngsters, and even after those girls had been fucked for the first time, the same men came back for more, usually choosing the girls they'd deflowered.

Some men had their own sexual agendas, which she turned a blind eye to, as long as the girl wasn't strangled to death. There were also clients who simply enjoyed the atmosphere and came for the poker and the gambling. Customers arrived from far-off countries, and she saw them only for a few nights of the year, when their ships docked in from the Americas, the East, Australia, New Zealand, and Africa. After a long sea voyage, they were desperate for the feel of a woman and couldn't care less about where the girls had come from.

Cotton men from Virginia, Georgia, Louisiana, and the Carolinas were her best customers, albeit her less frequent visitors. But she made a bundle of money during their short stays. That was the reason this particular week was so important.

She had all these worries on her shoulders to contend with. She had no one to turn to apart from Parker, Sam, and Eddie.

Eddie, Eddie…he held a special place in her heart by servicing her whenever she felt the need for a man between her legs. He made her feel young and desirable.

She had always loved sex since she was a child of twelve when her uncle first introduced her to the art of being pleasured. She didn't much care about pleasuring a man, and she had the luxury of not having to; that's why she had the whores. No, she enjoyed lying back, feeling that incredible sensation of being taken up into floating clouds of blinding orgasms without having to do any of the work herself. Sex, for her, was like opium. It calmed her nerves and dulled the pain of never having been loved. She had to have it often. When it was not available, she was not a happy woman.

She opened her thighs and stroked herself until she sighed loudly with pleasure. She'd been wet with desire all morning. Eddie, with his toned young body and handsome face, never failed her. His cock knew exactly what it had to do to please her in every way, every time.

Unwillingly jolted from her thoughts, du Pont focused on the night ahead. She had nine girls downstairs. There should have been ten, but she'd been forced to get shot of one a couple of days previously, and she was still fuming about it. The stupid bitch's demise had cost her money. She was not in this game to lose hard-earned coin. She forced herself to cast the dead girl from her thoughts. Nothing was going to blemish tonight's inauguration.

They were a fine young bunch of females in the basement. The boys had done a good job in London, although it was a shame about the ones who were not as virginal as they had appeared. It wasn't Sam or Eddie's fault, of course, for it was a game of chance. But she felt cheated. "Bitches," she hissed, thinking again about the girls who had been slack. She would make sure they were used by the most brutal of her clients. They deserved to be punished. Their parents probably hadn't chastised them, so she bloody well would!

The new girls were looking good. They were completely different now to the bedraggled bunch brought in just two weeks previously. The bruising had gone from their bodies, and their feeble brains knew enough to comprehend that to speak out of turn meant death.

Madam du Pont smiled. Life was good, and it would continue to be good until she thought it prudent to close her establishment down, along with everyone in it. When that time came, and it wasn't far off, she would disappear with a new name and get herself on a ship to America. There, she would live like a queen and indulge herself in all the extravagances life had to offer. She had the means and the money. She would buy a house, hire servants, seduce men, and live the life she was supposed to live in elite American society, on an equal footing.

She rolled her tired body off the chaise longue and walked to her dressing table covered with jars, pots of rouge, kohl pencils, an assortment of powders, and red paints for her lips. She sat in the velvet chair in front of the mirror and stared at her unpainted face. Her exhausted state stared back at her. The crows' feet around her eyes with their grey, hanging bags underneath sat on each side of a slightly hooked nose. Her round, flabby face and double chin settled on a neck that resembled a plucked chicken's, slack, but with more layers. Her priceless necklace was hidden in the folds of her neck, invisible to the eye. It was her only childhood possession, a gift for her sixteenth birthday. It now choked her, but it was something she would never remove because of the small gold key that hung on the golden-linked chain.

She stood, removed her red velvet dressing gown, and studied her naked body. All trace of muscle had gone, leaving flabby arms and breasts with no rise, making them hang and swing like soft bags of flour. Her arse was also flat atop her thighs that rubbed together when she moved, giving her a permanent rash as a result. Her bloody job had done this to her, she thought, not age, not food or drink. She worked during long hours of darkness, barely saw the sun, never took a stroll in fresh air, and could not remember the last time she had been given a moment's peace.

Men had always been dazzled by her voluptuous form. She had once been sought after by the most powerful gents in Liverpool. Some of them were long-standing patrons, using her young whores, and blind to their own ageing facades.

She still possessed the power to attract men, but she had neglected her appearance of late. She would take better care of herself when she eventually shut this place down. Plenty of rest would smooth the wrinkles and ugly bags around her eyes. Her complexion would brighten, and her muscles would tighten with long, brisk walks. Parker was two years older than her, yet she looked much, much younger. She hated having to admit this, but it was the God's honest truth. Parker had never worked as hard. She'd been given an easy life, not like *her*, imprisoned by hard labour for far too long.

She carefully removed her wig and scratched her balding head, with only a few grey strands here and there remaining. She should never have started wearing these blasted hairpieces. She used to have a perfect head of hair. She stared at the red patches and scabs standing out just above the hairline and behind her ears, where residual glue remained after the wigs were removed. These scabs hurt, but she continued to scratch at them, causing some to bleed. She couldn't help herself. Her bloody itchy head was the bane of her life!

She covered up and rang the bell. Her maid would appear instantly to bathe her, paint her, dress her head with her favourite blonde wig, and squeeze her into the red corset Eddie loved so much. Then she would wait for him to pleasure her before her customers arrived and work began.

Chapter Fifteen

Jacob Stone felt the exhilaration of pride whenever he stepped aboard one of his ships. It was for him, the culmination of a year's hard work, and a pleasurable event to travel with his full load of cotton, cured tobacco, peanuts, and wheat bound for England.

Disasters had been avoided in Virginia this season. The crops had survived frost, snow, cotton worm, and heavy rainfalls, making it a golden year for Stone Plantation.

The backbreaking days of picking, drying, and storing were behind him. This year, South Virginia had produced one of the best wheat crops in living memory, although it fell short of the west's massive crop yields. He also carried the largest amount of cotton in Stone Plantation's history. The good Lord had been kind to him, and the ship was bulging at the seams with highly profitable commodities.

Jacob and his older brother Hendry owned the plantation, the ship *Christina*, and her sister ship the *Carrabelle* in equal part. Hendry was a sea captain; however, Jacob preferred to leave the running of the ship he travelled on to Jack Travis, who had served his father well for many years and who continued to serve Stone Plantation with fierce loyalty.

Spending most of this particular voyage in deep contemplation, Jacob worried not about business, but about his personal life, and especially his pending marriage. He'd spent the past weeks reading, sitting by the rails, and staring at the vast ocean, so deep in thought that the surf, the odd whale, dolphins, and biting winds went mostly unnoticed. He was not a particularly good sailor. In rough seas, he often sought refuge in his cabin with a good book or curled up in a ball in an attempt to hold seasickness at bay. On calmer nights he entertained Jack and senior crew members. They ate, talked politics, drank wine and brandies, and smoked cigars, but he had not felt the least bit sociable on this voyage.

At twenty-four years old, he was mature for his age, yet owned a playful smile, dark brown twinkling eyes, and black-as-coal curly hair that always looked unruly, no matter what he did with it. He was a tall man, well over six feet, with an athletic build and striking good looks, which had endeared him to just about every Southern Belle in the County.

He possessed a keen business mind. He had invested well, both in the purchase of slaves and of adjacent lands. He did not cheat his neighbours; he simply knew when it was the right time to strike a deal that suited all parties.

Many of Jacob's fellow Virginians still ran their plantations in the same way their grandfathers had. They resisted change, using a large force of slaves to pick their crops instead of investing money in new, technologically advanced machinery that cut down on manual labour, yielded much bigger profits, and saved money on slave purchases and upkeep.

These men had poured scorn on Jacob's investments and were now regretting their actions and seeing shrinking profits. They'd seen no need for Jacob's acquisition of strange-looking machines or the purchase of another ship, which was a rare and bold move in the eyes of many and one that left them envious. Jacob was not only a Virginian agricultural exporter, but also a major importer of commodities from Spain, France, England, and North Africa.

When the *Christina* was not crossing the Atlantic, she was moored in the Southern port of Norfolk. Jacob and Hendry's plantation was situated five miles west of the newly incorporated city of Portsmouth, Virginia, and fifteen miles from Norfolk's busy centre. It was also within striking distance of the great inland waterways and estuary of Chesapeake Bay with its bustling trading stations, large oyster fishing industry, growing towns, and hub of packet boats and steamships that ferried travellers from one island to another and all the way to the states of Delaware, Maryland, and Pennsylvania.

South Virginia's vibrant community craved European goods: silk stockings, Parisian fabrics, Spanish olive oil, copper, iron ore, and handmade silk rugs from North Africa, and Jacob and Hendry obliged them.

The two ships worked in tandem. On this occasion, the *Christina* had travelled from Norfolk direct to Liverpool, England. The voyage had taken thirty-five days on a trip whose length could vary depending on favourable or unfavourable winds.

It had been a year since Jacob had last seen Hendry. Hendry and his wife Belle were due to arrive in Liverpool on the *Carrabelle* the day after Jacob and the *Christina*. The *Christina* would be unloaded, cleaned, and tethered to the docks, ready for Hendry, who would swap ships with

Jacob, taking the *Christina* back to Europe and North Africa whilst Jacob took the *Carrabelle*, fully loaded with European goods, back to Virginia.

The two brothers had a close, loving relationship, and they worked well together. The plantation was theirs in equal part. However, Hendry had a love of the sea in his veins and cared nothing for planting. Being captain of a vessel had been his only ambition in life.

Jacob wondered and hoped at the same time that he too would find the burning passion that Hendry shared with his wife, Belle. She had given up a grand plantation life to accompany her husband on his voyages. She had gone against her parents' wishes and had been undaunted by Portsmouth society's harsh opinions of her, but not once had she regretted her decision to abide the austerity of conditions on a cargo ship.

Jacob craved some measure of passion for his own fiancée, Elizabeth Coulter, the daughter of a neighbouring plantation owner. He had grown up with her. They had attended the same balls, picnics, weddings, and afternoon teas in town with each other's families, but he had no great desire to marry her or to bed her.

He often wished he had not made an offer for Elizabeth's hand. She was comely enough, he'd often thought, with fair hair, blue eyes, and a cream coloured complexion that had rarely been exposed to the sun. She entertained well in song and piano repertoires and had a forceful character, which demanded attention, but his feelings towards her continued to be dull and lifeless, with only duty spurring him on towards marriage.

His father had wanted this union, as did her father. Stone Plantation needed a well-bred mistress to see to its everyday running. One who could organise the necessary dinner parties and play the perfect hostess without effort. Elizabeth was bred for this role. But when he thought of nights alone with her, conversing with her, sharing a bed and making love to her, his resolve weakened.

Upon his arrival in Liverpool, Jacob alleviated his body's gentle swaying, caused by the ship's movements, by taking a brisk walk around the Liverpool harbour and docks.

He stepped off the *Christina* and walked down the gangplank. His business associates were on the jetty, and he suggested that they met within the hour. This gave them time to converse with the captain, go over the inventory, and clear customs. It also gave Jacob time to clear his head, reserve two horses and a carriage for the planned evening outing, and purge his weary sea legs.

Jacob found himself in awe every time he set foot in Liverpool. It was an enormous hub for emigrants travelling to every part of the known world: Africa, Australia, New Zealand, the Indies, and his own country, America.

There were thousands of people waiting for ships that would cross oceans to new lives and new worlds. Entire families sat patiently against warehouse walls with their worldly belongings piled high beside them. Some went as far as the jetties and camped out beside the ship that would be their home for weeks on end. Other travellers strolled up and down the busy thoroughfare with impatient children who were thankfully unaware of the arduous journey that stretched ahead of them.

Dockworkers loaded and unloaded cargo, cursing the travellers who blocked doorways and passages. The emigrants were continually harassed. Some were beaten, and others lost everything. They were not allowed to board their ships until the day before or the actual day of sailing. This, in turn, meant that most emigrants spent between one and ten days in a Liverpool lodging house. Of course, there were those who could not afford such luxuries. Families who set up camp on the dockside or on a street close by with every possession they owned lying beside them.

As Jacob walked, he silently pitied the poverty and desperation that met his eyes. But he also admired the courage that shone from other eyes filled with hopes and dreams. He remembered well his own father talking about his grandfather, who had been much poorer and more desperate than many of these new pioneers.

His great-grandfather was originally from Manchester. He had also set sail from Liverpool's port, taking his family across the Atlantic in search of prosperity. They had withstood severe hardships and conditions that made the journey today luxurious in comparison.

Jacob recalled the tales of his forefathers; the journey and vessels back in the old days, his grandfather had told him, were more like slave ships. There was a fifty per cent or more mortality rate among the passengers. Jacob's great-grandfather's baby girl had been buried at sea, thrown overboard in a quick and practical ceremony that seemed to take place on an hourly basis for the families who had pinned all their hopes on a better life.

Walking through the expansive dockyard and onto jetties with his grandfather's stories still etched in his mind gave Jacob a new perspective. With every step, his admiration and pity for the travellers grew. He greeted strangers and gave farthings and pennies to children, who shrieked with delight and ran off to buy candy from one of the many small stalls in the dockyard. He asked questions about destinations and learned the reasons for such bold adventures from families who had apparently seen nothing but poverty their entire lives.

The travellers looking for a better life did not have it easy in Liverpool either, Jacob thought as he wandered through the throng of people. They were forced to pay extortionate rates in one of the many Liverpool boarding houses capitalising on a desperate clientele. They also had to contend with groups of experienced tricksters, well known for their harassment and fraud. Jacob knew all about these bands of thieves and had seen them operate many times. Their most common trick was to offer help to an emigrating family weighed down with children and life's possessions. They would then run with the family's baggage into unknown side streets that only a Liverpudlian would know. These runners, as they were called, were the scourge of human decency as far as Jacob was concerned. Yet every time he arrived in Liverpool, there seemed to be more thieves and tricksters than the time before.

He stopped to watch a ship being boarded. A family of four stood halfway down the line among hundreds of other travellers. Curious as always he asked the man, whom he presumed to be the patriarch, where they were going?

"Australia, sir," the man answered with pride. "I'm going to give my children what I never had, a full belly and a better life."

Jacob also found out that the journey to their destination, which was Adelaide, would take just under twelve weeks. He was aware that Australia was particularly popular due to the promise of gold. The Australian gold rush was being well documented, even in his own country, which was also one of the most sought-after destinations from Liverpool.

He chatted for some minutes with the mild-mannered man and then very subtly put his hand in his pocket. He shook the man's hand and gave him three gold sovereigns. The bewildered man took the coins and gasped in disbelief Jacob tipped his hat, wished the family well, and left.

Liverpool had grown as a hub since Jacob's childhood. He had first visited with his father when he was twelve years old. It was now well placed to receive emigrants from all over Europe, including from the North-western Scandinavians to the Russians and Poles, who had crossed the North Sea on steamships landing in Hull and then overland to Liverpool.

Jacob thought again about the family he'd just left. He had grown up surrounded by wealth, but most emigrants here travelled in the cheapest accommodation on board, known as steerage. This was similar to a dormitory, with bunks down the sides and tables in the centre. It was frequently overcrowded, with poor ventilation. Seasickness was a problem on the stormy North Atlantic westbound voyages. Diseases such as cholera and typhus often reached epidemic proportions as infection spread through the confined decks. As he looked at the hopeful faces eager for their new lives to begin, he wondered if they knew of the scores of emigrants who had died on board the ships without ever seeing their destinations.

After strolling back to where the *Christina* was docked, he invited his lawyer and accountant to lunch, and during three courses, conducted business. These casual discussions included financial matters, insurance issues, England's tax laws, docking rights, and the ever more expensive costs of doing business in Liverpool.

Chapter Sixteen

Lunch in the small, discreet restaurant had been going on for over two hours. Eddie was tired of Maud and Lizzie's company and their insipid conversation. He couldn't blame the women, for they had not been outside du Pont's mansion or grounds in over a decade. He supposed he'd be a boring git too if he were in their positions. In fact, if he'd been stuck there for that long, he'd be a lunatic by now, never mind stuck for something interesting to say.

Every now and then he watched the wall clock's second hand ticking slowly around the clock face. Madame du Pont had ordered Sam and him to give the girls a great time, ply them with wine, and compliment them every five minutes. Eddie now believed he'd done that in spades and that lunch had gone on long enough.

He looked across the table at Sam and gave him the nod. "Get the bill, Sam. We need to get these two lovely ladies home. They need their beauty sleep before tonight."

Eddie walked the two women out of the restaurant. Maud was slurring her words, and Lizzie's ridiculous giggling fits were giving him a headache. They'd done their duty, him and Sam, he thought. He wanted a kip and couldn't wait to get the drunken, giggling, annoying whores back to du Pont's mansion.

In the carriage, Eddie closed his ears to the women and instead occupied himself with thoughts which had nothing to do with the present company.

Sam, on the other hand, continued to play the gentleman, listening, nodding, and answering when it was required of him to do so. Maud was striking to look at, he thought, studying her beaming smile. Both women were du Pont's favourites. He supposed it was only right that she should favour them, after all, they'd been with her since they were young girls, and had grown into womanhood under her tutorage. He leant into Maud, caressed her breasts, and kissed her hard on the lips.

He looked across at Lizzie, sitting next to Eddie. She wasn't bad-looking either, but she didn't have Maud's beauty or class, he decided. Lizzie continued to giggle. The fit was interrupted at intervals by hiccups and drunken snorts coming from her nose. They were quite endearing, Sam admitted to himself.

Maud laid her hand on his arm and asked, "Sam, do you think we could do this again? I've never had such a wonderful time. It's been such a perfect day; I didn't realise Liverpool was as modern or so large. Maybe next time we could visit a museum or look at some art? Do you think we could?"

"I don't know, Maud, but I don't see why not," Sam pacified her.

Lizzie said, "I'm going to remember this afternoon until the day I die. The outside world is very exciting; I do hope the Madame will keep her word and allow us to retire soon. She did say that we were coming to the end and that we'd be rewarded for our service."

"Well, you've had a nice reward today, haven't you, girls?" Sam said.

Lizzie giggled. "It was perfectly lovely."

Maud said more seriously, "I'm going to thank Madame du Pont very much, and I'm going to work hard for her tonight. I can't bear the thought of not pleasing her."

The carriage finally arrived at the gates and came to a halt. The carriage driver jumped down to open the gates. He then led the horses and carriage inside and locked the gates behind him before taking the reins to continue up the long driveway.

Maud was singing to herself. Lizzie was looking out of the window.

Eddie and Sam closed both sets of window curtains and shared unspoken words with slight nods of their heads.

Lizzie slurred, "Why have you closed the curtains, Eddie?"

"It's time to sleep," Eddie told her.

"Don't be silly." Lizzie giggled again. "We're almost home. Open the curtains, please, Eddie?"

Eddie smiled at her and turned to Sam. "Are you ready, Sammy boy?"

"Ready when you are," Sam replied.

The two men pounced at the exact same time, grabbing the women by their throats in iron grips.

Maud and Lizzie were pushed onto their backs on the velvet seats. Eddie and Sam tightened their grips further and straddled them, as though they'd done this a hundred times before.

The women struggled, terror replacing their tipsy, happy mood. They tried to scream but could only manage to open their mouths.

Eddie pressed his thumbs deeper into Lizzie's throat. "You're not giggling now, are yer, ya' silly cow?" he panted.

Lizzie looked up at him with sorrow etched on her twisted face. Her windpipe was blocked, her throat was closed off. Her hands struggled to slacken Eddie's grip. Her legs kicked out, twisting on the velvet seat. But these were futile attempts to escape the vice-like clamp around her neck.

Eddie took hold of the back of Lizzie's head with one hand whilst the other remained at her throat. Lizzie's eyes were rolling upwards, looking at him once more with questions. Eddie smiled at her before snapping her neck with one swift movement. He took a long, deep breath and focused on Sam.

Eddie was mesmerised. Sam's face was crinkled up, eyes tightly closed, and head straight forward. After snapping Maud's neck, he opened his eyes, and pushed her dead body off the seat. Pulling the curtains open, he then stared out the window with his thoughts.

Eddie looked again at Lizzie and flicked her off the seat as though she were a bothersome cat. He punched the carriage ceiling three times to signal the driver and then looked again at Sam. "Aw c'mon, don't look so bloody miserable. It's not as if it's the first time, for Christ's sake."

"I liked Maud," Sam said, looking at her on the floor. "She was nice."

The carriage took a turn, carried on, and came to a standstill a few minutes later.

Two graves had already been dug that morning, deep inside the small woods at the back of the mansion.

Sam carried Maud in his arms. Eddie had Lizzie's body over his shoulder like a sack of flour.

Eddie tossed Lizzie into her grave, leaving her body lying twisted, with legs half way up the dirt wall. Sam followed suit, but then jumped into the hole to make sure that Maud's body lay flat and straight with arms crossed over her chest. And after saying a prayer, he scrambled out of the hole and picked up the spade.

Chapter Seventeen

Madame du Pont was dressed and ready for the busy night ahead. She looked at her reflection in the mirror and congratulated herself. She looked lovely in her new gown, she thought.

Her new whores had been cleaned up. They had been tutored so well that fear ran through them as easily as pee between their legs. Seven out of the nine were virgins, innocent and unworldly, and their aristocratic, pompous, spoilt arses had been kicked into shape.

Their upbringing made her feel sick to the stomach, for they had been given everything life had to offer without having to work, sweat, or go hungry. She, on the other hand, had fought for every crumb and farthing. She resented them, but the bitches were expensive and coveted commodities, and she couldn't let her hatred blind her. That was the truth of it.

She thought again about the incident that had occurred two days previously. She had been forced to kill one of the new whores by her own hand. The thought of it rattled her. The girl had not been a virgin, but even so, her death had meant a small loss in profits. Normally, she refused herself the luxury of losing money because of a momentary loss of control. She was much too smart to allow personal feelings to interfere with her business. But she had been compelled, for the sake of her business, to make an example out of the hysterical cow.

The girl in question had already been poked by men on numerous occasions; du Pont was quite certain of that.

There was not a man or woman on earth who knew cunts like she did. Over the years she had made it a priority to examine every single new girl that had come onto her property. A girl could lie and say she was a virgin, but *her* inspection was the only way to confirm it.

The death of the sixteen-year-old aristocrat had been necessary in order to subdue others who were displaying rebellious streaks that she would not and could not tolerate.

Screaming, the youngster had got herself out of the basement, up the stairs, and through the unlocked door. Parker, standing in the hallway, had been thrown to the ground. Then the girl started bawling her eyes out to the servants, that she'd been abducted. She somehow managed to grab a pair of scissors, and even made it into the kitchen, screeching like a banshee, and begging the cook and maids to save her. She ran to the outer door that led to the garden, and almost got into the grounds, before being subdued by the two stable boys who finally managed to silence her.

Back in the stable, the girl had cried and begged for mercy. Madame du Pont remembered now, the sheer look of terror on the girl's tear-stained face, and the way she clasped her hands in prayer. The girl had been on her knees, asking the Holy Virgin for help.

"Watch and learn!" du Pont had shouted, putting the fear of God into each and every one of them, just before she sliced the girl's throat open. The girl had gurgled for a second and then choked on her own blood.

Truth was, du Pont admitted that she couldn't have cared less what the girl had been thinking in those final seconds, but she was convinced that all those watching had learned a bloody good lesson, and after all, that had been the object of the exercise.

Recalling the girl's death, she smiled with satisfaction. Without words, she had set the rules in stone; run, speak out of turn, tell a client your dirty little secrets, and death will follow.

The other whores had the job of cleaning up the blood from the floor. They had seen the cold way in which she, the madam, could and would inflict death. Now, she had them right where she wanted them; traumatised, with broken spirits and a newfound fear that would dismiss any lingering thoughts they might have had about trying to escape.

Her belly fluttered at the thought of this evening's party and the huge amount of money she'd make off her virgins' backs. She had sent Sam and her various contacts at the dockyard to inform shipowners, lawyers, customs officers, the mayor's offices, and the head of the Liverpool coppers that a new batch of young girls were ready, willing, and available to those who wanted the first, second, or third exquisite taste.

She had nurtured the new girls. They'd been well fed and kept clean, and were ready to make their first appearances, which would propel most of them from London virgins to high-class prostitutes in a single night.

She threw a patronising sneer at the mirror. Here she sat, without being challenged, outsmarted, or threatened by any of the other Liverpool madams, and there were plenty of them. They hated her. She had no friends amongst them. Most of them were low-class sluts who had simply taken over whorehouses that they'd worked in for years.

The best they could come up with were street rats and urchins gagging to open their legs for fear of ending up in a workhouse. By the time these street whores were twenty, they were disease ridden, too slack for even the biggest and thickest of cocks. Their faces were pockmarked, and half of them were dead because of too many badly performed abortions.

She tossed her head again and ridiculed the other madams. They were stupid and uneducated in business. She was grateful to them, for her business would not be successful without their poorly run, shabby brothels.

She looked at herself in the mirror one last time before leaving her bedroom. Her new turquoise dress was complemented with hair ornaments and sparkling neck chains. She was looking exemplary. The stress of breaking in the new girls had all but gone from her. She was always a little nervous on these opening nights, as she called them. She couldn't be absolutely sure of the untested girls until the night was finally over and the last customer had left, satisfied. It was a wonderful feeling when she climbed into her bed knowing that she was so much richer than the day before.

On inauguration nights, some negative thoughts came back to haunt her. There had been, on occasion, virgins crying for mummy and daddy during their first experiences with a man. She did not enjoy complaints from the customers. They quite rightly stated that they were not there as father figures to comfort little girls, but to be pleasured.

She also hoped that no secrets left her home via customers' loose tongues. The thought of being betrayed and caught by authorities not already in debt to her or in her pocket was daunting.

She banished these thoughts and forced a well-rehearsed smile. She'd been doing this job for fourteen years, and her retirement was close at hand. She was a lucky woman with a bright, glorious future that would take her into old age. Nothing and no one would get in the way of her dreams.

Looking at the grandmother clock on the wall, she calculated that Eddie and Sam should have returned. It was a shame, for as much as she hated losing good whores who had served her well, she couldn't, under any circumstances, allow women to walk free. Her policy had always been the same and always would be. The older girls, who were no longer desired by her customers, had to be disposed of. After all, it wasn't a bloody charity she was running or a retirement home for whores.

Shame, she thought again, sipping a sherry. Maud and Lizzie had been good whores. "Cheers, girls," she said, downing the sherry.

Chapter Eighteen

Jacob Stone rode at a slow walking pace towards the main dockyard gates with his three companions in tow. He and James, the ship's first mate, were on horseback, whilst Jack, the *Christina*'s captain, and Isaac, the ship's doctor, followed behind in a closed carriage.

They had talked about this night ashore for days. It would probably end in sex, gambling, and plenty of food and drink. They had been at sea for so long that a respite of this nature was not only enjoyable but highly necessary to blow the cobwebs of monotony from their minds and release pent-up bodily urges.

Jacob had chosen to have dinner in one of the most elegant restaurants in the city, on the road called Mansion's Row. The restaurant in question provided excellent English fare of pigeon pie with potatoes and vegetables, which was always followed by a dessert tray that was second to none. The ambience was congenial, and it had the added advantage of being situated just a few streets away from Madam du Pont's mansion.

Evenings like these always held great promise and never failed to live up to expectations. As much as he enjoyed the voyage and the men he sailed with, there was nothing more alluring than a civilised night on the town and the sight of beautiful women to fill his eyes. Beautiful women were just what he needed to shrug off wearying thoughts of home and his impending marriage, he thought, riding slightly in front of the others.

Madame du Pont's premises was spectacular, and her whores were by far the best Liverpool had to offer. He was not keen on Madame du Pont herself, not since she had taken his father and his wallet full of money to bed with her when his father had been so drunk he barely knew what country he was in. She had taken advantage of his docile father that night, and Jacob would not forgive her. He had felt his father's humiliation and embarrassment afterwards as though it were his own. He grimaced now, for only a *very* drunk man would choose the vulgar Madame du Pont as a bed partner.

Jacob's father had never allowed his youngest son to bed a slave on the plantation, even when the desire was so great Jacob thought his blue balls would burst, or worse, he'd die. He'd noticed women, their bodies, and had felt the growing need to bed one just as he was coming into his fifteenth year. He'd hidden behind trees and bushes and had gone to the river, sliding between the tall rushes, just to glimpse a slave's breasts or complete nakedness when he got the chance to watch one bathe. The slightly older piccaninnies had opened his eyes and senses to sexuality. He'd spoken to his father about wanting a woman and laughed to himself now, remembering his father's answer. "Nigger women are for nigger men. It's a well-known fact, my boy, that niggers carry some goddamn awful diseases in their cocks, which then spread to the female niggers they hump."

At the time Jacob had thought that highly unlikely, as he'd seen plantation overseers and even his father's visitors bedding nigger women. He was also sure his father had bedded a few in his youth. It was a customary and hospitable gesture when receiving callers to offer all the comforts of home. Even Hendry had taken one or two behind their father's back. He, Jacob, was younger than Hendry by two years and had been naive and obedient. He'd missed out on a lot of fun, he grinned sardonically.

Nearing Madame du Pont's, he recalled the night his world had become an even greater and brighter place. His father had promised to make him a man, and he'd certainly kept that promise. Madame du Pont had found the perfect woman to bring him into manhood with ease. He remembered that first awkward moment as though it were yesterday. He, a fumbling boy so nervous he could scarce undo his trouser buttons, and the woman, an experienced and patient teacher, had enjoyed an entire night in bed together courtesy of his father, who had spent his evening playing poker with a group of men, and drinking copious amounts of whisky, which had ultimately sent him into a deep sleep on one of the salon's soft leather couches.

Jacob paid his respects to Madame du Pont's establishment on every Liverpool trip. It was a must, a need as great as cold lemonade on a sweltering summer's day in the cotton fields.

Bedding prostitutes was not one of Jacob's frequent pastimes, for he had more than enough choice among Virginia women of good breeding who were quite happy to give him their sexual favours for free. He thought again about life's hypocrisies. Many fathers had married off their Southern belle daughters as virgins when those girls had already lain with young bucks under their fathers' ignorant noses. However, the Southern code demanded that bed secrets remained just that. He wondered if Elizabeth, his betrothed, was still a virgin? Yes, she was, he determined. She had no passionate spark in her eyes. She never wore anything that didn't clasp around her neck, and even in summer, when houses and gardens were like stoked ovens, she insisted on wearing long-sleeved gowns, which gave the impression that she was a maid rather than a young Southern lady looking for a husband.

Marriage was big business in Virginia and the surrounding states. Good matches meant more power, money, and standing in the community. The games that were played amused Jacob at times. The never-ending cycle of balls and parties at plantations, sometimes a day's ride away, were frivolous and boring, but they were where introductions were made, and business was conducted, whether it be for the acquisition of slaves, land, horses, machinery, or potential brides. They were, if nothing else, Jacob thought, highly civilised in the South, with an insipid glass of punch in one hand, and a handshake deal made with the other.

The gates at the entrance of Madame du Pont's sprawling mansion were open and guarded by two men in full livery costumes. Dinner and drinks had been a grand affair as always, and now all three of Jacob's companions looked forward to tumbling some whores until the sun came up.

Jacob and James did not dismount from their horses, and Isaac and Jack remained in the carriage when they came to a halt at Madame du Pont's gates. They handed the two gate men their membership documents and waited patiently until these had been scrutinised. After a few minutes, they were cordially invited inside and wished a good evening.

Chapter Nineteen

Seating arrangements for the girls made prior to the evening entailed thoughtfulness and intelligent planning. The colour of the girl's gown and hair were important. No two girls with similar looks sat together. Each girl was complemented by her seating companion to enable her to stand out in her own individual right. Dark-haired girls sat with honey-coloured or light-haired girls. One girl was usually older than the other, and although she detested the idea of allowing them any freedoms, Madame du Pont encouraged girls who were particularly close to each other to remain seated together when standards and protocol allowed. This, she believed, made them feel more comfortable on their first night out, and if the whores were comfortable, their guests would be too.

Mercy and Julia sat with planted smiles on their softly painted faces. As instructed, their backs were straight, not hunched. Their hands lay one atop the other on ruffle-skirted laps, and their legs sat at an angle, unfolded, and with the point of toe just visible.

Mercy watched men of all ages dressed in evening attire accept champagne in crystal flutes. She knew it was champagne because Parker had told them about the guests' welcome procedure during their instructions. Mercy wondered what it tasted like. She almost wished she could drink a whole bleedin' bottle, which would in all likelihood knock her out until morning. She even wished now for the horrible, smelly drug that had been placed on the rag and then shoved in her mouth, for even that would be better than having to endure this night.

She was terrified. She did not intend to give her body to a complete stranger, but how she was going to avoid this inevitability was a different matter entirely, of course.

She looked dispassionately at her surroundings. Highly polished rosewood tables and chairs were dotted about the room. A variety of seasonal flowers in crystal vases added fragrance to the already perfumed area. An abundance of nude women posing in various positions on oil-painted canvases sat on the red velvet walls; she had seen enough nudity this past week to last a lifetime, she thought, trying to banish memories.

She found the faces of the other girls she had shared the stable with during the previous week or so. Had it been eight or nine days or weeks? Time had slipped into insignificance. Each morning she was horrified to discover that her nightmares were not dark and ugly visions from which she could awake and forget, but a reality that was ever constant.

Her dreams never altered. They had become part of her, like dark shadows accompanying her through every night. The bridge, the man, the floor of the carriage, and the murder committed threatened to drive her mad. She would not survive this hell, she believed. She was not able to abolish her need and determination to escape, as she perceived most of the other girls had. Her dreams were prophetic, she was sure of this, for she always felt the knife cut into her throat just before she awoke to Parker's morning call.

Her conscious thoughts were now a repetitious regime of fear and dread of what torture the day would bring, worry over whether she would be able to keep her temper and anger in check, and finally that tiny hope that she'd be rescued.

Her anger had grown into what could only be described as an internalised hatred of all she saw, experienced, and felt. It was further inflamed with the knowledge that she would have to succumb without complaint to another day of threatening rhetoric bestowed upon her and the other girls by the servants and the madam, whom she had come to despise with every fibre of her being.

Her only consolation was the plan she had endlessly imagined, which involved killing the madam, her two henchmen, Sam and Eddie, and Parker, a cold, calculating shell of a woman without a soul. Her mind had, in fact, killed them in so many different ways she was actually running out of ideas. These thoughts of murder had kept her sane, as had her protective arms wrapped around young Julia at all times. In protecting Julia, she unwittingly sustained a measure of self-composure.

As she continued to stare now at her opulent surroundings, she noticed that not only were the girls she shared the downstairs room with in attendance but that they had been joined by some twelve or thirteen other women whom she'd never laid eyes on before. She studied their mannerisms and body language. She questioned their seemingly satisfied expressions. Why, she wondered, did they seem to be so unaffected by this house of horrors? They appeared to be actually looking forward to being violated. She wondered if perhaps they had lost the will to fight the nightly invasions of their bodies. She also asked herself if she too would become compliant and accepting as weeks passed into months. The prospect scared the living daylights out of her.

Mercy noted that every girl was dressed in a gown which was beautiful yet daring in their cut. Although gowns varied in colour, their designs were very much the same. They were fashionable and full-skirted, revealing tiny waists below tight bodices. The necklines were low off the shoulder, with stays and corsets pushing the breasts upwards, precariously holding nipples just below the neckline. She looked down at her own breasts and blushed. The green satin gown left nothing to the imagination, and her deep cleavage made her feel every bit the whore she was to become.

Mercy was scared. She could admit this to herself but not to Julia, who discreetly held her hand under the folds of her gown. She glanced at her young friend and hid her pity and her thoughts. Julia was like a young girl dressed in grown-up clothes. She was tiny in height and so skinny that her underdeveloped breasts looked more like an extension of her ribcage. She was a child in every way, and possessed an endearing unworldliness, but that would disappear tonight, and in its place would come a hellish experience she couldn't even imagine at this moment.

Mercy sighed. She had seen cruelty and vulgarisms that had no doubt been absent from Julia's innocent and sheltered life. Even at school, she had listened to girls her age talk about being bedded by boys and men for a penny or the price of a loaf of bread. She knew just what was going to happen upstairs when she was taken, but Julia?

As the room filled with men, Mercy thought back to her first few days in captivity. They'd been filled with fear, and most of all, sadness. She'd cried for home and her family. She had wept so much that she would have sworn on a Bible that she had no tears left to shed. The humiliation, physical and mental torture and loss of freedom had taken their toll on her appearance. Her chalk-white face and wide eyes only enhanced her beauty, but Mercy was unaware of what others perceived when they looked at her. All she could see reflected in a mirror was hatred and fear, on a face she barely recognised.

Mercy watched the men walking nonchalantly around the salon, eyeing the couch areas where the women sat. They looked at her and her fellow captives from the tops of their heads to the tips of their toes, as though they were a herd of cows at market. They had all come through the salon's open double doors. She believed that just beyond those doors would be the main entrance into the house. She presumed this because she'd seen a glimpse of hallway when they'd been marched through the kitchens and into the salon. She couldn't imagine any other main entrance apart from the one off that wide-open hallway.

She wished she'd been allowed to see the house before tonight. Had she seen upstairs and where the main door was situated, she'd now have a better indication of an escape route. Maybe later on, when the place was busy, and women were moving up the stairs, she would somehow find a few seconds to slip by the crowd and flee in the direction she'd guessed the main door to be.

Julia interrupted her thoughts with a squeeze of the hand. "Mercy, I want to go home," she said with a throaty sob.

"Me too, but we can't. Everything will be all right," Mercy told her for the hundredth time, whilst still thinking about an escape plan.

"I'm so terribly scared; I just want to die. Please don't let any of these men take me. I didn't know there would be so many, and they're so old, promise me that I can stay with you."

Mercy followed Julia's tearful eyes and saw what she saw. She realised that she'd been so busy planning an escape that she hadn't noticed the arrival of even more men, now packed into the room like matchsticks. It was all beginning.

A girl captured with her was already being escorted out of the room by a man and Madame du Pont. It would be her turn soon, Mercy thought. There were so many men in attendance that it left her in no doubt that every woman there would be used more than once during the long night ahead.

Mercy turned her head and looked into Julia's eyes. This was no time to lie to the young girl. She could not protect either of them, and she would not promise Julia anything, as much as she wanted to. "Julia, you can't stay with me. You know that you *will* be going with a man. You have to be brave no matter what happens. When you're chosen, think about home, your family, your life in the country with your brothers and sisters. Hold on to your thoughts and separate them from your body. Float away with them. Let them take you to your favourite places with your favourite people. No man can take your thoughts, Julia. They're yours. And don't refuse. Don't cry. Smile and don't look afraid. You've got to do all that's asked of you, as we all must."

"But I can't," Julia insisted. "The very thought of a man old enough to be my grandfather lying on top of me, putting that thing inside me, is revolting. I would rather die. I wish Madame du Pont had killed *me* and cut my throat open instead of that other girl's. At least I would be at peace now as she is. Will it hurt…the man's thing?"

Mercy unclasped their hands and told Julia to sit up straight and smile. Parker was staring at them with those cold, unfathomable eyes.

She thought about Julia's question and decided that she would have to tell her, what she perceived to be the truth. "I imagine it will hurt a bit, more than Madame du Pont's finger, but, Julia, I know girls that like it, so maybe it won't be too bad. And just look at us. We're nicely dressed. We don't look like prostitutes, do we? Maybe these men will be kind to us. Look at those girls over there, the ones we don't know. They don't look afraid, so it can't be all that bad?"

Julia's eyes glanced at a couple of girls she had never seen before. She turned and whispered in Mercy's ear, "They look as though they're enjoying themselves. They're smiling, and giggling like silly girls. How can they be happy when I would rather end my life than sit here? Oh, Mercy, if only I had the courage to kill myself."

Mercy felt her anger growing. Julia was drawing far too much attention to herself. She was making a scene, all teary eyed and the like. They would both be punished later by Parker and the madam. She whispered sharply in Julia's ear, "Don't cry a single tear. I'll not be having it, do you hear me? You'll get us both into trouble. Stop pouting right now before someone sees you. The other girls have done this before. I bet you they all hate being violated, just as you and I hate the very thought of it. But we're prisoners. We are not bad. We shouldn't feel ashamed or disgusted with ourselves. We just have to pretend like all the others. There's nothing else for it."

Julia nodded. "I'm sorry, Mercy," she said.

At that moment, Mercy looked up to see Madame du Pont introduce one of the girls to a man who was clearly interested. He took the girl's hand and kissed it. Mercy couldn't remember her name, for the life of her, she couldn't remember. The girl stood up and curtsied to the man, and then he led her away.

"Remember, Julia, no matter what, don't fight. Just open your legs and let them touch you and do what they want with you," she said for the third time.

Mercy watched the men blend easily into the salon's highly charged atmosphere. Madame du Pont mingled, her hand kissed so often that Mercy thought she looked and behaved like a queen holding court.

Parker, Sam, Eddie, and the house servants serving champagne were circulating unobtrusively, keeping watchful eyes on girls and customers alike. Mercy came to the conclusion that Madame du Pont was very good at her job. She introduced the girl of choice with pleasantries and gushing compliments. There was no money exchanged, Mercy noted. The old hag must take the money from the men, out of sight, somewhere between the salon and the bedroom.

The planted smile on Mercy's face hid her thoughts, much darker now. She had witnessed a young girl's throat being cut open, blood spurting all over those standing too close. The girl's innocent face in death and the callous way she had been disposed of afterwards were sights that would haunt her forever. Mercy's lips continued to spread in a seemingly easy smile. She was not going to end her days an old prostitute, imprisoned and then thrown onto the streets when she was of no more use. She was not going to be killed at the hand of an old, painted woman either. She was getting out of here, come hell or high water.

Chapter Twenty

Jacob Stone and his three companions stood in the salon, champagne flutes in hands, and observed the gathering. The men had cut their usually long dinner short to accommodate Jack, who had continually urged the others to eat faster for fear of being late and missing Madame du Pont's finest.

Jacob was relaxed and felt energised. The dinner of freshly cooked pigeon pie in flaky pastry had been the type of meal he had sorely missed at sea. The good food and amiable company had lightened his mood. So much so, he now felt quite amenable towards Madame du Pont's whorehouse and looked forward to taking one of her delightful young ladies.

Jacob's father had bought Jacob's membership years ago, telling him that Stone Plantation's business had grown exponentially over the years because of Madame du Pont's establishment. "With the right foke and atmosphere, you can endear yourself to prospective clients, as long as you remember to lose a poker hand to them fokes a couple of times," his father had added with a wink of the eye.

Jacob smiled now, remembering the last time his father had been here with him. He wanted poker, he'd insisted. Instead, his father had taken three whores during the evening and had missed the poker game altogether.

Jacob continued to use this clandestine club for business purposes, for the most part. He had gained a new client or two on almost every visit so far, as this was the club *only* the wealthy and powerful frequented. Cotton factory owners, local government officials, immigration officers, judges, and even the mayor came to this mansion, all wondering how Madame du Pont came by her virginal, upper-class whores.

Having sex with the younger whores was never on Jacob's agenda. There was something distasteful about bedding a youngster, even if she was willing. He would take his time and let the others rush to claim the so-called du Pont virgins. He had no desire to break a woman in, preferring a more experienced and comfortable lover.

He grinned at Jack and said, "Well, Jack, who takes your fancy this fine evening?"

"I'm not sure yet. I'm in paradise, Young'n. I may be getting on, but I feel I could use Madame du Pont's entire stock tonight. Last time the whoaman let me in her bed was over a year ago, and I'm not one for going with slaves. It can get messy with half-breed piccaninnies running around the place. So what's a man to do? I caint spill my seeds when I'm dead, can I? And if I don't spill them soon, they'll turn into damn trees and sprout out my damn ass! What about you?" Jack asked. "Is it poker, or are you going to do the right thing and enjoy yourself for once?"

Jacob looked from woman to woman, scattered on couches like cushions, and smiled a cheesy grin. "Don't you worry about me, old'n, you just get to it. I'm still looking. See y'all later."

With that, Jacob left the others, crossing the length of the room to stand alone. He spotted Madame du Pont whispering in a man's ear. He watched her nodding her head in agreement with something the man said and studied her further. Although he disliked her, he also found her amusing in so many ways. Her clownish, over-painted face, various coloured wigs, and exaggerated French accent were all part of her facade and fascination. Why did she appear in public like that? He wondered. She was probably more attractive without all the paint, regardless of what she looked like, she was undeniably smart and resourceful. There was nowhere that resembled this place, nothing to compete with the class of prostitutes on display or the exclusive membership that included these wealthy and powerful men who could buy and sell him twice over.

As he watched her laughing now, he couldn't help but admire her business prowess, which had nothing to do with his personal distaste for her as a human being. He leant against a wall and shook his head in amusement. Madame du Pont's fair-coloured wig was bouncing and shaking atop her head as though it might fall off or fall onto her face. Jacob had the urge to laugh. He was surprised she could even manage to hold her head up. It was so laden with fancy combs and jewels. Why, he thought, does no one tell the woman just how ridiculous she looks?

A servant refilled his glass, and he continued to study her. She had strict, written rules of the house, plainly visible on his membership document. A man could approach a girl, converse with her, but couldn't touch. Madame du Pont insisted on formal introductions conducted by her or her head servant, Parker, who'd been around for as long as he could remember. After a girl had been picked, one of the two women would chaperone the man and chosen girl from the salon and discreetly collect the money once inside the bedroom.

Not all girls were the same price, for some were virgins or had very rarely been touched. Most men were happy to pay the extortionate fee for the pleasure of having one of these girls. It was an extremely civilised way of doing things, Jacob thought, in what was, after all, a whorehouse.

Madame du Pont was now gently pushing the man forward. From his position, Jacob saw a very young girl rise from a green couch. She curtsied. The man kissed her hand and then led her towards the door. Madame du Pont followed, smiling at men as she passed them. Another satisfied customer, Jacob thought. His eyes followed them until they'd left the room. Then they wandered back to the spot where the madam had stood.

He saw a woman sitting on the couch which had been vacated by the young girl. He sucked in his breath, stared at her, forgetting to breathe and dismissing every other presence in the room. He had not seen her here before tonight. She was a new addition to the house. He had not seen her earlier either, for she'd been hidden from view by the buxom madam and the over-excited old man whose bulging crotch had very publicly displayed his enthusiasm for the young girl he was about to purchase.

He steadied his breathing. His heart thumped in his chest. Butterfly wings were fluttering in the pit of his stomach, punching to get out. These were strange sensations, and none he'd ever experienced before. The beautiful creature he beheld was the most exquisite young woman he had ever seen.

He moved closer to where she sat, unintentionally bumping into people as he crossed the room. He could clearly see her emerald-green eyes now, staring unseeingly, wide, sad, and appearing deeply troubled. She held a soft, trembling, and awkward smile that was innocent and forced. Her perfect pink lips were so inviting he wanted to kiss them there and then. He wanted to caress her heaving breasts. More than anything, he wanted to hold her in his arms and soothe whatever ailed her.

She turned her head and looked around the room as though noticing her surroundings for the first time. As she moved, Jacob saw the length of her coal-black hair, kissed by candles and chandeliers. Her natural soft curls reached the centre of her back and seemed to shimmer with light, as though entwined with exquisite diamonds.

She wore a gown of emerald green, like her eyes. It covered a perfect body shape from her shoulders to her pert young breasts and down to a tiny waist where the hooped skirt then spread itself across the entire length of the couch. Never, he thought, had he seen anything as captivating, so beautiful, so fragile, and so seemingly innocent. Why would this beautiful young woman choose this life? He wondered with a mixture of dismay and curiosity. She did not belong here. She could, in his opinion, grace the greatest of houses in the land with that angelic face and body that had no doubt lain with many men. Madame du Pont certainly trained whores well in the art of innocent seduction, for this girl's demeanour was notably contrary to her job title!

He had to have her, he decided, walking briskly to the doorway to look for du Pont. He would pay her asking price; he would pay anything just to be close to the young woman who had affected him in a way that unnerved him to the core of his being. He couldn't explain the depth of his desire. Did love at first sight exist? He didn't think so. Bumping into another couple of men on his way out, he wondered if he had fallen under some unknown spell. Was he intoxicated and dull-witted, after wining and dining? Or had he simply been at sea for too long?

Reaching the lobby, he looked left, then right. His eyes travelled up the length of the curved staircase and then down towards the small connecting rooms off the hallway. He cursed. Where was du Pont? He had to find her before the young woman got snapped up by another. He turned and strode back into the salon, feeling like a lovesick fool but not giving a damn. He intended to go to the girl and stand by her side. He would wait there, pushing aside every other man who came near her, until Madame du Pont came back.

He halted in mid-step, halfway between the door and where the woman was seated. His smiling face froze, as did his body. A jumble of emotions ran through him. Parker, the whore mistress, was introducing his prize to another man, who from the back appeared to be well into middle age.

Jacob turned and made his way to the door, stood there, and watched the girl, the man, and Parker approach. His eyes followed the girl's every small step. He willed her to look at him; stupid of him, he admitted, for it would lead to nothing. But he needed her to see him.

She walked past him with eyes that stared blindly ahead, and then she was gone.

Chapter Twenty-One

Mercy climbed the stairs, sandwiched between Parker and the old man whose hands were already grabbing her buttocks. She felt physically sick. She was petrified and finally felt the taste of defeat. She had given advice to Julia, who would be going through her own hell right at this very moment, yet she too was failing in courage and finding it impossible to stop a tear from falling. She wiped it away quickly, afraid of being caught by Parker, who would later report her to Madame du Pont. She was supposed to be smiling and happy at the prospect of pleasuring the vulgar old man who was so close behind her she could hear his panting and smell his putrid breath.

They reached the bedroom, halfway down a long corridor. They entered, and Mercy sat on the bed as ordered. The man reached into his pocket and brought out a large sum of gold sovereigns. Mercy couldn't see how many he gave to Parker, but she could see from her smiling face that Parker was pleased with the transaction.

"Enjoy, sir. You have a rare beauty and innocence in Mercy. As I told you, she is untouched, but she is very willing to please you and is honoured to lose her flower to a gentleman such as you." She turned to the bed. "Is that not right, Mercy?"

"Yes, Missus Parker. I will make the gentleman very happy," Mercy answered her meekly.

"I shall leave you and return in one hour, as arranged. Enjoy her," Parker said, satisfied by Mercy's answer.

The old man was not listening to Parker and had already begun to undo his trouser buttons.

Parker walked towards the open door, and before closing it behind her, threw Mercy a threatening look to remind her of what would happen should she not perform.

Mercy looked around the room and then up at the ceiling. Sparkling, candlelit chandeliers spread across it like twinkling stars. Candles in ornate silver candlesticks were dotted around the chamber, on the walls, and on each bedside table. The entire ensemble of the place screamed passion and romance. Yet, like Julia, she wished she had the courage to kill herself.

Mercy moved further up the bed and sank her body deeper into the mattress. She could not go through with this, she suddenly knew with a clarity that had been lost to her in all the dark and horrible days since her abduction. The man was forgotten. She was now seeing flashing, moving pictures in her mind's eye. She was reminded yet again of her walk across London Bridge in her beautiful gown, the dirty rag being pressed over her mouth and nose by Eddie and Sam, the journey, putrid smells, and pain. She recalled Madame du Pont's gloved finger inside her vagina, her naked body on display in front of so many people, including Sam and Eddie, and the shame of it, as strong now as it had been then.

She shuddered, remembering Sam's and Eddie's gleeful faces and their rough hands throwing her onto the floor, holding her there, spreadeagled. She relived the endless days of watching the despair that surrounded her and then finally crying with the other girls.

She saw again the young woman's throat being cut and realised then that she couldn't even remember the poor girl's name. Images of blood, screaming, and the callous tossing of the girl's body onto a wheelbarrow as though she was cow's dung, were crushing her heart. She thought it might break altogether, yet at the same time, she was conscious of the old man's movements. His breath was quickening. He was fumbling with his trousers at his ankles now and moving as though he was racing against the clock.

She regained her senses, leaving past images behind and focused on what was going on right now. The old man was stroking his cock, licking his lips, his glazed eyes staring at her with a blank expression. She knew and accepted now that she couldn't bear it a moment longer, any of it.

She slid off the bed and stood on legs threatening to give way. This was the dreadful reality of her present situation. Stabbing pains in her head and nausea rising like a tidal wave were cursing her body, but her mind was in an even worst state. She looked longingly at the window. They were one floor up. She would gladly throw herself on the hard ground beneath and die with a cracked head than allow this old bugger to touch her. She could not allow her body to be used like this by a man who looked almost as old her Grandpa Carver. She couldn't!

Disgust crossed her face, and she swallowed the bile still rising in her throat. Her eyes were drawn to the man's old, flaccid cock, smaller than she imagined a cock to be and uglier, as it twisted in and out of his palm and tobacco-stained fingers. She realised that her facial expressions were mirroring her thoughts, something they had repeatedly been warned to hide. She remembered Parker's words; "This is the first and most important rule. Always appear amenable to and pleasured by the gentleman who is taking you."

Mercy stood in front of the loathsome man and tried to delay the inevitable. She had to think fast. She smiled but felt her lips trembling with the effort to hide her true thoughts, which she felt must be clearly written on her face. He was repugnant to her, and she was sure he saw her revulsion.

"Would you like a sip of champagne before we begin?" the words rang out at an accelerated pace from her mouth and sounded strange. She'd been trying so hard to mimic the other girls' posh speech. "It would be such a shame not to drink a toast to our union. Maybe you wouldn't mind celebrating with me. After all, you have the honour of deflowering me. It would please me very much. And it looks inviting, does it not?"

He looked at her, not really seeing her, Mercy thought. He was still stroking himself, but his cock was not growing hard, and this was obviously vexing him no end.

She tried again. "Maybe some champagne would relax you. I could give you a massage if you'd like?"

"Shut up, girl! I didn't come here for a bloody massage, and I don't give a damn what would please you or not!" he shouted impatiently. "No more small talk. Get your bloody clothes off; I haven't got all night. There's a lot more girls downstairs, and I intend to shove my cock into as many of them as I can. I don't have time for the likes of you taking your time about it. You should be ready for me by now."

"Ready?" Mercy said stupidly.

"Yes, that's right. Ready. Get your garments off. Strip. Strip fast. I'll give you the back of my hand if you make me lose my hard-on!"

Mercy stood, mesmerised by the way his eyes suddenly glazed over again. She couldn't tear her eyes away from him. His hand was moving faster, and his cock was jumping around in his palm. He was cursing. He wasn't even noticing her. He was moaning, but he was also angry because evidently something wasn't working right. He was going to take his rage out on her!

She suddenly found her sanity through the power of fear. She began to disrobe by pulling one arm out of a puffed sleeve and then reaching for the other. Her fingers trembled. She continued to tell herself that even though she was doing as he demanded, the slower she undressed, the more time she would have to think about how to get out. She looked at the door. He stood between her and the exit she so craved.

The old man approached her, cock slightly swollen and more solid now. She stared at it and involuntarily took a step backwards. The man moved towards her with angry strides, threw her onto the bed, and ripped the bodice of her dress. He pulled down the top of her corset to release her breasts and nipples, which were now completely visible from top to bottom. "Don't you dare mock me, bitch," he hissed at her. "I wasn't born yesterday. I know these teasing little games. You want me for longer to get more money out me for your whore madam."

With these words he pounced with one leg on either side of her hips, straddling her like one would a horse. His heavy weight knocked the air out of her. His hands went to her breasts. He gripped and painfully pulled them towards him. He fondled them, squeezed them, pulling at her nipples until Mercy moaned with pain and humiliation, which spurred him on even more. She looked down at her waist where his cock rested. It still wasn't hard. His upper body then leant towards her until his face was inches from her own. He didn't kiss her; instead, his head moved again until his mouth reached one of her nipples. She watched him as he sucked it like a baby would a mother's teat. Then he bit into it. Mercy finally screamed with terror, "Oh God, help me!"

"You like that, girl, don't you?"

Mercy's desperation grew, as did the man's cock. He dismounted and threw her skirts up to cover her face. He tore at the hooped underskirt, and it shimmied down to her ankles. He tossed it over his shoulder and reached for her bloomers. She lay silent and felt his awkward movements as he straddled her once again. She felt his fumbling hands on her upper thighs, attempting to spread them, whilst she tried with all her strength to keep them closed. He was going to enter her!

Twice he slapped her covered head and then said, "Bloody fucker, get up for me. Come on, don't do this to me, you bastard. Get up there!"

He let go of her thighs to stroke his cock again. Mercy pulled the crumpled skirt off her face until it lay just below her chin in a bundle of folds. She had endured the horror until now, but her mind was continually screaming, "Enough, enough!" She thought once again of death and the comforting peace it would bring. She twisted her head to the side whilst listening to his loud panting and soft moaning.

For the moment she seemed to be forgotten. She was just a body with a hole to poke and prod, that she knew, but nonetheless, she was mystified at the man's actions, his difficulties, and the ugliness of the sexual act.

She saw the lighted candle sitting in its silver, ornately decorated candlestick on the bedside table and concentrated on its light. Suddenly, she stretched out her arm and wrapped her hand around the base. It was heavy.

The old man was concentrating on holding her thighs open, staring at her vagina and trying to guide himself inside her, still without success. She was not only revolted now but was also filled with hatred and rage. She was possessed by a demon and silently thanked evil for coming to her aid. No more, she thought. No more!

She tightened her grip on the candlestick, the lighted candle shaking precariously atop it. With all her strength, she smashed the object across the side of his face. His head rolled backwards and then forwards. He swayed drunkenly, still straddling her. He seemed disoriented for a second but remained conscious enough to curse her whilst punching her full on her small face.

Mercy's nose exploded with blood and pain. He put his hand to the open wound on the side of his forehead, and she hit him again, this time catching him just at the centre of his balding hairline. His eyes rolled. He moaned. She smashed the candlestick against his head for the third time, and his body flopped to the side and fell unconscious, head first onto the pillow. He would want to kill her, Mercy thought. She couldn't stop now.

The candle lay on top of the bedcovers, which were bursting into flames, but the bloodied candlestick was still firmly in her grasp. She sat up and managed to break free of him by unravelling his legs, still straddling her in an awkward position. She clenched the candlestick even tighter and rained it down on his face, her own face receiving the blood splatter coming from his wounds. She was now straddling him, raising and lowering the candlestick, each time hitting him harder and with more rage than the time before. She stopped, out of breath, and for the first time noticing that a fire was spreading from the bedcovers and licking the bottom edges of her gown.

Jumping off the bed, she quickly peeled her clothes off until only the corset remained. Instead of trying to put the fire out, she lit the four-poster bed curtains with her gown and then threw the flaming bundle at the window curtains to spread it further. Both sets of curtains ignited, and within seconds the room was bathed in a bright orange glow.

Mercy was crying with fear, shock, and the knowledge of what she'd just done. She stood in the middle of the room in a blackened and bloodied corset, displaying her full breasts. She tucked them in with trembling hands as best she could, and for the first time carefully examined the man she'd just murdered. He no longer had a face. His head looked like a fleshy, squashed tomato. She had done that. She had bashed his skull in. She had killed this man!

Smoke was filling the room. The flames were growing higher and spreading until she could barely see. Her eyes watered, and she was blinded by smoke and stinging tears coursing down her face. She heard the window glass explode and automatically shielded her face with her arms. Glass shattered into shards. Some hit her, stabbing her bare arms and upper chest as they flew across the room.

She felt no pain. She was a dead woman, no matter what happened now. She would die in this fire or at the end of a rope…or worse, by Madame du Pont's own hands.

She sat near the door. The smoke was filling her lungs, and she coughed. She didn't care. *Let the fire take me*, she thought. She coughed again and wondered how it would feel to die. Her father had taken his life because he didn't want to go on living without her mother. She was now going kill herself too because even if she could escape this place, she could never go home and allow Big Joe to marry her, defile her, and force her to do what the old, burning man on the bed had wanted her to do.

She was not ashamed of her father anymore. She understood him now. She empathised with his decision. The fear of death was far outweighed by the pain and suffering life would surely bring. Her life was over…

Mercy's eyes were closing. Her breathing was interrupted by continuous coughing. She gulped more smoke into her lungs and then suddenly looked at the door.

"Julia!" she screamed. *My God, where is Julia?* She couldn't leave the innocent girl alone to die in this place. After crawling to the door, she turned the poker-hot door handle. Skin from her palm stuck to it and left her with an open, burning wound. The pain brought tears. She coughed again and slithered out of the room on all fours.

Opening the door brought smoke into the hallway with her. Sparks followed and flew into the air, setting ablaze the ornamental curtains that were frilled across the ceiling, pulled back, and bordered down the long hallway's walls. She had to get onto her feet. She felt herself clinging to the wall. Her breath was laboured, but she rose slowly, using one hand at a time until she was fully upright. Her face was bloodied. She wiped her eyes with the backs of her hands. Dismissing the pain in her palm, she focused on the hazy golden candlelight on the same silver candlesticks in brackets all along the hallway. She reached one and threw it at some more ornate curtains, draped across the hall's breadth like curtains found on a theatre stage. She reached another candle and did the same to curtains further down the hall. Death would have to wait, she decided. She was going to burn the whole bloody house down.

Chapter Twenty-Two

Jacob's enthusiasm for the night ahead had waned. The emerald-eyed woman had gone, but his desire for her was, if anything, growing stronger. He cursed his foolishness. Had he approached her the minute he'd seen her, he would have laid claim. Instead, he'd spent too much time staring at her and in his enthusiasm had left the salon in order to find Madame du Pont, forgetting that Parker was still there working in Madame du Pont's absence.

He was as virile as a young bull, and the little vixen had left him cursed with unreleased tension that was now paining him. Yet he wanted no one else. Should he take some other woman for the sake of sexual release it would be like partaking in a corked bottle of wine; disappointing and bitter tasting, instead of a vintage reserve for which one savoured every delicious sip. He was not *that* desperate, just cursed with a mysterious emptiness. He had not only desired her; he had wanted to hear her speak. He'd also wanted to ask the reason for her transparent misery. She was a misfit and no more belonged here than he did in England. The way she had continually pulled up the front of her bodice, albeit unconsciously, had not gone unnoticed by him either. It was troubling. Was she an innocent or a very good actress?

He casually cast his eyes around the salon, thinned out by the absence of women and men who had climbed the stairs already. His companions were nowhere in sight. He smiled. They deserved a good time. God knows they all did after the long weeks at sea. Even conversation tended to diminish towards the end of the voyage.

He brought his thoughts back to the room and the present. The women who sprawled seductively on the vacant couches were surrounded by men who had, no doubt reserved them by now, and who were currently forced to respect the house rules of, no touching or lewd language, at least in public. Under the watchful eyes of Madame du Pont and Parker, bad behaviour was known to lead to an immediate termination of membership. Many a man had been chastised by Madame du Pont's tongue, followed by a shredded membership and all future invitations rescinded. "I supply class; therefore I expect class," was clearly written on each membership document.

Jacob had often wondered at the gall of the woman. She, with her dictatorial rules, managed to manipulate every man who came here into boyish subservience. Jacob found the polite conversations, the fine manners of men, whom he suspected were chomping at the bit to tear a woman's clothes off, and the virginal pretence of some of the women, amusing.

Noticing Madame du Pont's and Parker's watchful eyes on the clock, he suspected that they were controlling the appointment times of those clients already upstairs. The whores were paid for on an hourly basis, never half hourly. The little notebooks pinned and chained to Madame du Pont's and Parker's skirts listed who was with which girl and how long he had paid for. Madame du Pont, Jacob knew, was quite capable of banging on bedroom doors if a man went over the agreed time limit. Time meant money to her. She was not the generous type when it came to that particular flexibility.

Seating himself close to the pianist, he decided to cut his losses and listen to the music. It soothed him, along with the half-filled brandy glass in his hand. Madame du Pont was going to approach him any minute, he deduced. She was staring openly at him, probably wondering why he had not picked out a woman yet when she had seen to his three companions who were already settled upstairs. He looked at his pocket watch. The night was still young, but it was too early for poker. The card games rarely began until after the first round of sexual activities had finished.

He closed his eyes and sank his body into the luxurious, soft cushions. With his eyes closed, he'd keep Madame du Pont away. He detested small talk with her, even though she was the hostess who had introduced him to a couple of good business contacts in the past. He smiled to himself. A cotton factory owner once told him that fucking Madame du Pont was like riding a bucking bull. She was, in his opinion, the most unfeminine yet exciting woman he'd ever had. He'd also added that in her younger days, she was not at all bad-looking. She had taken every customer in her stride as many times a night as she could until she realised it was more profitable being downstairs supervising than upstairs having sex.

Jacob's eyes shot open, and the pianist suddenly stopped playing as screams and shouts of "Fire, fire!" resonated from upstairs, outside in the hallway, and finally in the salon itself.

Along with Madame du Pont and everyone else in the salon, he sprang to his feet and ran out. Now, not only were there verbal warnings but an undeniable smell and taste of smoke descending the staircase.

In the hallway, mayhem met Jacob's eyes. It took him a moment to separate the chaos from what was actually happening. Girls half-dressed, some naked with only a sheet covering them, ran towards the main front doors, only to be roughly manhandled back into the salon by the doormen. The customers, on the other hand, were asked to leave the salon in an orderly fashion to seek water buckets from an outhouse behind the kitchens. It was becoming apparent that this was a fast-escalating fire that could only be contained if all men present attempted to stop the flames from spreading.

Men were buttoning up their trousers as they ran from the building. Jacob heard shouts and orders being issued outside and then the sound of whinnying, frightened horses pulling carriages, arriving outside the main entrance.

Customers who had left their trousers upstairs were comically running around in their long johns. Jacob took in the picture and pushed himself against the flow of traffic, towards the staircase, which was now a smoke-filled invisible hill. His earlier thought that the men would get water buckets and assist in putting the fire out disappeared when it became blatantly obvious that there was no such plan afoot in the minds of those men still remaining. The customers were leaving Madame du Pont's mansion to burn to the ground.

Standing by the stairs, Jacob's eyes searched for Jack, James, and Isaac. Jack appeared first, cursing because he'd left his jacket upstairs. Isaac followed, and a few minutes later James appeared, holding a woman's hand, telling her to leave.

The four men stumbled outside. Jacob looked up at the building's facade and saw that some of the first-floor windows had blown out. The flames were licking the outside walls.

Jack coughed whilst buttoning up his shirt. "I was on the second floor," he said. "The smoke had reached just about every bedroom I passed. I heard window glass smashing and ran for my life."

Isaac said, "It's a mess up there. I've never seen a fire spread this fast."

"What can we do?" James shouted to Jacob above the noise of breaking glass and crackling timbers.

"We need water!" Jacob shouted back. "Someone get some damn water. There are still fokes up there!"

"To hell with water!" a stranger shouted back at him. "I'm getting out of here. You three should do the same."

No one cared, Jacob realised. The entire household of customers were thinking about saving their own skins. Even the servants in crisp black-and-white uniforms ran outside and across the lawns until they were out of sight. There were no allegiances to the madam or her home. At some point, the firemen from the Volunteer Fire Brigade and the Liverpool coppers would arrive, but they would be far too late to halt the inferno.

Jacob suddenly thought about the woman who had captivated him earlier. Was she still in one of the bedrooms? He had not seen her run down the stairs, or outside onto the lawn. He looked at his friends and knew what he had to do. "Jack, James, go get the horses and carriage. Bring them here to the entrance and stay with them. Guard them with your lives. I wouldn't put it past these fokes to jump on the back of the first horse they see. I'm going inside. There's something I have to do. Isaac, will you come with me?"

"Well, I ain't gonna let y'all go in there alone, am I?" Isaac shouted above the noise.

Jacob ran up the stairs to the main double doors and into the corridor. Men and women were still appearing, coughing and stumbling from behind a curtain of smoke. Jacob pushed past them, going in the opposite direction, and took to the stairs, two at a time. With every step he took, the heat became more intense. Smoke was already filling his nose, mouth, and throat, and he shielded his face with his forearm.

Isaac followed closely behind Jacob. When they reached the first-floor landing, they halted. "Should we go to the top floor first?" Isaac shouted.

"No, we'll search this floor. This fire's spreading too fast. If we go up one more floor, we won't make it back down. The stairs are not going to hold much longer. You heard Jack. I reckon we have just about enough time to search a few rooms. We just have to hope that those upstairs made a run for it after they smelled the smoke." Jacob then told Isaac, "I'm looking for one gal in particular. She was wearing a green gown and had long black hair. I need to find her." Jacob coughed and wiped his watery eyes.

Isaac nodded. "I'll search as many rooms as I can."

There were three long and dark corridors. Jacob took the east wing, where the flames were highest and more intense, whilst Isaac took the west wing. They would tackle the South corridor after they had searched these particular rooms, but only if it was safe to do so.

"A quick look in every room, as far as we can go, right?" Jacob shouted.

Isaac nodded again.

Each covered his nose and mouth with a handkerchief; scant and pitiful protection but all they had, and then set off in opposite directions.

Flames licked the walls and lathe-and-plaster ceilings, which were beginning to crumble. Jacob, blinded by smoke, felt his way hesitantly, feeling for doors and doorknobs. He dodged a falling chandelier, which just missed him as it came crashing to the floor. Looking into a smoke-filled room, he shouted above the noise, "Is anyone in here?" When there was no answer, he moved on, holding and palming his way along the corridor's wall, until the heat from the wall became so intense, he had to let go.

All the bedrooms were black with smoke. Jacob believed that he had chosen the most dangerous corridor. It was becoming clear that this part of the house was where the fire had started. Flames and sparks shot upwards and outwards like a firework display. Everything in the fire's path had ignited, from flowers to decadent fabrics. The flames were rising now along the long hallways, due to soft silk materials covering the walls. All the glass chandeliers were exploding with the heat, and even the wooden floor in places was smoking, cracking, and about to burst into flames.

"Is there anyone here? Is anyone hiding in here? Come out quickly! Don't be afraid!" Jacob shouted out in every room he stepped into.

He came to a bedroom halfway down that particular corridor. Its door had crumbled. It was impossible to see anything inside at first. The flames were thicker, higher, and the heat more unbearable than in any other room he had seen so far. The fire started here, he deduced by the extent of the damage. The entire room was alight. He was just about to turn on his heel when he saw the remains of a body on top of the bed.

He got a little closer. Poor bastard, he thought. It was not even what could be described as a body. It was a black, burned-out shell. There was absolutely no way to tell if the remains were male or female. His heart suddenly felt heavy. What if it was her? What if she'd been left here to die?

Just then, Isaac ran down the length of the hallway. He was shouting Jacob's name, yet under the noise of the flames his voice sounded as quiet as a whisper. "Dear God, it's completely unrecognisable," Isaac said, entering the room. "I don't even know what gender that corpse is. Come with me. I've found something…I think it's what you're looking for."

Jacob ran behind Isaac, asking no questions. Time was of the essence.

Isaac suddenly stopped, making Jacob stumble backwards. "There are two women in here. I caint get them out. Quickly, we ain't got much time."

Panicking, Jacob agreed with Isaac. Smoke was making him feel drowsy and strangely relaxed. He would be unconscious soon.

The room was filled with smoke, just like all the others, but flames had not yet taken hold.

"Under the bed," Isaac said.

Jacob heard a voice whimpering incoherently. The men got on their knees, lifted the silk bedspread, and stuck their heads underneath the bed frame. The two women clung to each other, huddled on their sides. One was unconscious, the other bloodied and moaning, in shock, and unaware of their presence.

"Julia, please, we have to get out," the woman mumbled over and over again, still unaware of Jacob and Isaac.

Jacob and Isaac pushed the bed towards the wall until the two women were in a position to hold onto. Jacob couldn't see the women's features through the smoke under the bed, but as the bed slowly moved towards the wall, their faces and bodies became more visible.

Isaac pulled the first woman out by locking his hands behind her back and just below her shoulders, whilst Jacob pulled her towards him by her ankles. She was the youngster Jacob remembered from earlier. She was unconscious and completely naked. "Get her downstairs and outside," Jacob said. "I'll be right behind you with the other one."

Jacob helped put the girl into Isaac's arms and covered her with the bedcover. He then concentrated on the other woman. He grabbed her by her closest arm and pulled. She too had just lost consciousness.

Struggling, he felt his lungs filling with smoke. He coughed, and then pulled the woman towards him. Once she was free of the bed, he managed to swing her body up and over his shoulder.

Chapter Twenty-Three

After Madame du Pont had given calm and precise orders to Eddie and Sam, she dismissed the doormen and then ordered Parker to accompany her. She also sent orders to the coachman to bring her best carriage around to the rear entrance of the mansion and to wait there behind the trees, unseen, until she came out.

The whores must not, under any circumstances, leave the building alive, she told Eddie. There had always been the possibility of a scenario whereby she would have to make a run for it for one reason or another; an enemy's loose tongue, betrayal, a dissatisfied customer or servant bent on spiteful revenge. Any one of those scenarios involved disposing of all evidence that might be prejudicial towards her. The garden was filled with bodies of missing women, and now her current stock of whores would have to die in order to keep their mouths forever shut.

Her most loyal entourage knew exactly what they had to do. She had drummed it into them over the years. They would not let her down, for if she were arrested, they would accompany her to the gallows. This she had also made very clear.

The women had been rounded up. Three or four were missing, and this worried her. Time was no longer on her side, but as she was always optimistic in the face of adversity, she could only hope that they had been trapped and burned to death upstairs. Either way, she had no more time to think about the missing girls. The others who had tried to flee on the shirt tails of clients had been grabbed off them, kicking and screaming, and were already in the salon. They would be kept there until every client had cleared the premises.

She was finished here. The fire inside the house had spread too far. There could be no redemption, no business as usual tomorrow or the day after or ever again. The bloody house was falling down about her ears!

As soon as the firemen and coppers arrived, she'd be questioned, and a can of worms would be opened. Not all officials were on her payroll. Some honest coppers and magistrates would not treat her well. She could not afford to have girls roaming free and accusing her of abduction and forced prostitution.

Before she tied up her loose ends, she had to be sure that the clients had already left. She was told they had, apart from four. She knew this because two horses and a carriage outside the main entrance were being protected by two of the four Americans, she had seen earlier. The other two men, she assumed, were missing, dead, or dying. She couldn't wait any longer to ask questions.

Marching into the salon, she looked keenly at the frightened, screaming faces staring back at her. They were begging her to release them. She could see the terror in their eyes and hear it in their tearful voices. She turned from them and nodded to Eddie and Sam.

"The moment Parker tells you I am in my carriage, light this room up and make sure you bolt the bloody door behind you. Do what you have to do…Parker, you're with me."

For all her outward calm, Madame du Pont was in shock and devastated. Her entire life was falling apart. Her empire had collapsed, and she had just given the order to murder twenty or so girls. Their deaths would be quick and painless, she told Parker, soothing herself. They would be overcome by smoke and would not feel the flames burn their bodies.

Parker nodded in agreement, without emotion, as was her way.

Decision made, du Pont's first destination was her suite of rooms. As she hurried across the hallway to a door, which would have easily been mistaken for just another wall panel by those who had no idea of its existence, she grabbed at her chain with the small key attached and yanked it from within the folds of her neck. The chain broke, but she didn't stop to pick it up. It was the key she wanted.

She opened the panelled door with another key and walked into a small hallway, where three doors stood closed. "Parker, get me three gowns and one for travelling in, some stockings, shoes, and corsets. My three favourite wigs, face powder, rouge, kohl, and lip paints. That's all I'm taking. Do it quickly."

The smoke had reached downstairs and was now inside her suite. She had no more time to think or to plan. She would travel light. Money was the key to everything, and she had that in abundance. All other possessions could be replaced once she reached her final destination.

Inside the room starting to fill with smoke, she guided herself to her locked private closet. The small key from her neck chain opened this door. Behind a loose panel, obscured by piles of garments, was a wall safe. She turned the dial to four, two, eight, and six, twisted the handle and opened the door. She found just what she'd come for, and sighed with relief.

Piles of bank drafts sat in neat bundles. On top of the money were identity papers. She would have to wear the black wig, as she was described as black-haired in the papers. She had been dark haired back in her youth but hated that colour now since it made her look older.

She looked at her real name, Margaret Mallory, and a false date of birth, making her five years younger than her fifty-five years, plus the fake city of birth, Manchester.

Running an illegal business had taught her many things, the most important being that one should always be ready to make a quick exit should the occasion require it.

Rolls of pound notes, dollar bills, and gold sovereigns filled the rest of the safe. She shouted for Parker, who came running with two leather valises. One was filled with the clothes requested earlier, and the other was to be filled with the gold coins that Eddie had always sworn to guard with his life. He would go with her. She could not do without Eddie to protect her, or his young body, which she would continue to enjoy until her last breath.

Parker helped du Pont to change out of her evening gown and then used cotton strips to bind the paper money to strategic places around her body, underclothes, stockings, and corset. Parker then dressed du Pont into a slate grey, plain crinoline dress with a high collar. When she ripped off the madam's fair wig, she was slapped for being too rough. She stumbled backwards and then carried on with her labours, gingerly attaching the long, black curly hairpiece to a balding, bleeding head. Sticking a pile of paper money under the black-and-grey-trimmed bonnet was du Pont's idea. The head accessory partially covered the wig and was tied securely with a silk bow around her neck.

Madam du Pont studied her new, matronly appearance in the mirror. Wiping the layers of paint off her face, she applied a more subtle lip colour. "If I ever find out who did this to me, I'll bloody boil them in vinegar and then rip off their skin," she said. "Right, Parker, go give the order to Eddie and Sam. Tell Eddie to get rid of Sam when they've finished with the whores. He's to use the pistol. Noise doesn't matter anymore. He knows where to follow us. Be quick about it."

Chapter Twenty-Four

Mercy drifted in and out of consciousness. She thought she might be dreaming, for as always, she saw terrible things and misty silhouettes floating and dancing before her. She grappled with them, as one would when trying to catch a patch of mist in the hand. But these nightmares were different somehow, for she felt physical pain. She was being bounced around, and her body was thumping up and down on a hard surface. If she could only open her eyes, maybe she could understand why?

Thick smoke…fire…fire, she remembered now. She saw the candlestick, the man, and blood spraying out of his head like a fountain. Her heart beat faster. She was putting the puzzle together, remembering certain events, but not all that had led her to this actual point in time.

She wasn't dreaming. She was awake, yet couldn't keep her eyes open long enough to get her bearings. She was continuously losing herself to a void that contained no memory of time or events. She felt hammers striking her head. Her hand hurt, burning like a thousand bee stings. As she bounced along, images in her mind's eye intensified. After leaving the bedroom and the disgusting old man, she'd crawled into the hallway, searching for Julia, shouting her name. No; screaming out her name above an angry eruption of crackling wood, smashing glass, and shouts from people running down the smoky hallway. Then there had been noise everywhere.

At some point, she'd fallen over something, and her head had smashed into a sharp corner; a table or the arm of a chair, perhaps? She remembered her fingers touching the rapidly swelling egg-sized bump on her forehead, the blood seeping into her half-closed eyelids and then dribbling down her cheek. She lost time and events. Then…Julia's face, she saw Julia, she remembered now…Julia bending over her and screaming at her to get up.

Somehow she had risen to her feet with Julia's help. She was dragged by the hand and was then pushed to the ground and told to roll under a bed. She didn't want to be there at first, but Julia, naked, with skin blackened by smoke, had continually screamed that they'd be murdered if they went downstairs.

All her instincts had told her that they would die under that bed, but she also believed Julia. She was so very tired, and her head was spinning. She felt a sticky substance all over her body. She was too tired to worry about what that was.

Julia had fallen asleep. Mercy had tried to shake her awake, but then her own conscious mind disintegrated, and darkness took over completely.

Where was Julia now, she wondered. She tried to shout out for her, but her voice was lost. She'd been struck dumb. Managing to crack open an eye, she realised that she was being carried like a sack of flour. Her head was bouncing against the small of a man's back. Who was carrying her? Her head was pounding. She was choking and felt incapable of swallowing any more smoke-filled air. She was dangling and swaying. Her ribcage felt the hard shoulder muscles beneath her. Sam or Eddie had found her.

She was beaten, and her death would be ugly. She felt the man's panting breath and his body's vibrations when he coughed. She struggled to be set down. Her tiny fists pummelled the man's back. Wiggling her upper body, she attempted to fall off his shoulder. Her bare feet kicked some part of him. But they were all feeble attempts. She was tired and captured like a small bird in a large fist. She felt hands and arms grabbing and holding her buttocks and thighs even tighter than before. She had no strength left to fight. Someone probably had Julia too. Their throats were going to be cut open, just like that other poor girl. Maybe Madame Du Pont would do it herself. Death was going to take her one way or another. That was her last thought before she spiralled into darkness again.

Jacob reached the hallway downstairs and staggered out of the main doors. Jack and James stood at the bottom of the small flight of exterior stairs holding on to the frightened horses.

James ran forward and took Mercy from Jacob's arms. He laid her on the grassy verge next to the young girl whom Isaac had brought out moments earlier.
"Goddammit, Jacob, what were you thinking?" he shouted.

Jacob waved him away and sank to his knees, trying to catch his breath and clear his head. "Don't worry about me. I'm all right. See to the women."

Isaac was attempting to revive Julia, who had stopped breathing.

James placed his jacket behind Mercy's head and gently examined her bloodied face and body. "She's lost a lot of blood, but I can only see one injury to her forehead. Where is all this blood coming from?" James asked Isaac.

"I'll see to her in a minute," Isaac shouted back. "I'm losing this one. James, help me.   When I tell you, pinch her nose and breathe into her mouth with one steady blow. Do you understand me?"

James nodded and obeyed Isaac's instructions.

"Can you save her?" Jacob asked, still dazed but staggering onto his own two feet.

No answer.

After a minute or so, Isaac and James stopped what they were doing. Isaac put his ear to Julia's mouth and waited. Julia shook violently, retched, and coughed. The four men sighed with relief.

Jacob's eyes followed Isaac as he moved onto the other woman, lying unconscious. Looking closely at her, he felt his heart soar. It was her, Jacob kept thinking. The beautiful, unconscious face belonged to the young woman who had captured his heart earlier. He'd been convinced of it upstairs, but her face had been hidden by hair. Whilst he was carrying her, he'd felt tingling vibrations run through his body. He had connected to her closeness. It was inexplicable, but goddamn, that's what he'd felt.

There was such a lot of blood, he thought, looking down the length of her body. It was not only on her face, which was entirely covered with it, but her body, legs and the scant corset she wore were also caked in it. "Isaac?" he asked, searching for answers.

"I don't know, Jacob. It can't all be her blood. She has a large bump on her head, but the cut's not deep enough to cause this." He looked up at the others. "Most of this blood belongs to somebody else."

At that moment, screams from inside the house redirected their attention. All four men had been under the impression that they were the last to leave. No one else was in sight. The madam hadn't been seen by any of them since the first sign of smoke, and they had presumed that she'd left with her whores from another exit. The entire house was in flames now, and the roof was beginning to creak and cave in. She was probably long gone, yet they all heard screaming coming from the ground floor inside.

"The salon…I saw some women being taken in there," Jacob said to the others, slightly mystified. "There are no windows in that room. There's only the small glass banner that runs along the edge of the ceiling and double glass doors. If they are locked, the women won't be able to get out. We need to get back in." Jacob turned to Isaac. "Look after the two girls. I'm counting on you not to let anything else happen to them. Leave now. Get yourselves and the girls back to the *Christina*. Put them in my stateroom. And Isaac, don't leave them until you're certain they're all right and comfortable."

No one argued.

James followed Jacob. They went to their horses. Both men got their Colt revolvers and holsters from the saddlebags. "Use it if you have to," Jacob said.

James nodded in agreement.

The salon door was shut but not locked. Screaming was clearly coming from within, sounding loud and desperate. Jacob turned the doorknobs and pushed both the heavy doors inwards. He stepped into the room with his gun cocked and ready. James followed, holding his Colt, arm outstretched.

Jacob's eyes took in the scene before him. His stunned expression also displayed a rage he rarely felt.

A man was lighting up the curtains and fabrics, setting another fire. The women had been corralled in the corner of the room furthest away from the doors. Another man was holding the women hostage at gunpoint. Jacob's instincts took over.

Jacob shouted above the noise coming from the screaming women, "You two! Lower your weapons and step away from the women!"

Eddie turned; torch in one hand, gun in the other, with a mixture of surprise and anger crossing his face.

"I said put the gun down, or I swear to God, we'll kill you where you stand. Now drop the gun!" Jacob shouted again with his weapon pointing.

Eddie looked at Sam. Sam with a terrified look on his face, bent down and laid the cleaver he was holding down on the floor.

Jacob and James concentrated on Eddie. James shouted, "Don't be stupid. You don't want to die tonight. Put the gun down!"

Eddie shot one more look at Sam, and then at the two guns pointed in his direction. Bending over, he gently laid the gun on the floor. "I'm not dying for that old cow!" he shouted, raising his arms in the air.

Sam looked into the barrel of James's gun and also raised his hands above his head. "Don't shoot," he pleaded in a high squeal.

Jacob and James took their eyes from Eddie for just a second and looked at Sam, who was now crying like a baby.

Eddie took advantage of the situation, for after managing to side step behind Jacob's half-turned body, he reached the door and ran without looking back.

"Goddamit!" James shouted. "I'll go after him."

"Don't bother. Let the coward go. We need to get these women to safety. You take this sniffling son of a bitch outside and hold him."

James grabbed Sam by his jacket collar and pushed him towards the salon doors. As he left the room, he shouted over his shoulder, "Jacob hurry up, you ain't got much time."

Jacob grunted to himself. He would have liked to have pistol-whipped the bastard that ran away to within an inch of his life, but the priority now was to coax the frightened women to go with him. "Come on, ladies. Follow me. I'm not going to hurt you. We have to leave right now!"

The women clung to each other. Jacob couldn't understand their reluctance to move. They were afraid of him. He holstered his gun and walked to the doors, opening them wide. "Run as fast as you can and get yourselves home. No one else is going to hurt you," he told them. "Go on, get out of here!"

His words brought them to their senses, and they scattered like rabbits. Jacob checked once more that no one had been left behind in the salon. Satisfied, he joined James outside.

Sam continued to stare at James's gun, now inches from his face. "I was just following orders," he sobbed. "She told me to do it. Don't shoot me, please. Don't kill me. I'll give you no trouble."

"Shut up," Jacob told him. "James, what shall we do with him? Personally, I'd like to take him to the po-leece, but I'm in no mood for questions I can't answer or for staying up half the night."

"Let's leave the goddamn coward here."

Jacob nodded. "Good idea." Pushing Sam with the barrel of his gun, Jacob reached the closest tree to the house. James got the horse's tether rope from the saddlebags and then with Jacob's help, tied Sam to the trunk.

"You can explain to the authorities what happened here, and with a bit of luck, they'll take y'all in for further questioning. I do believe y'all have a lot of explaining to do," Jacob said.

Sam's face was a picture of panic. "Please sir, if those girls get to the coppers I'll be done for. Have mercy, sir," he sobbed. "I didn't want to work for that old witch. She made me do terrible things. Don't leave me here…please let me go, I promise I'll lead a good life."

"Shut your mouth," Jacob said. "Tell your sordid story to the po-leece."

When Jacob and James were satisfied that Sam was securely tied to the tree, they mounted their horses and rode away from the burning mansion at a canter.

As they rode in the darkness, Jacob said, "I guess we can consider our memberships here, terminated."

Chapter Twenty-Five

Madame du Pont's carriage raced through her property's grounds. The curtains were closed, and du Pont and Parker, sitting inside, held on for dear life as the carriage swayed precariously around the tight bends on the road.

Madame du Pont was cursing the world, yet she was also displaying a rare vulnerability. Sobbing, she could barely get the curse words out of her mouth. Her face was as white as chalk, her body trembled, and she absently wrung her hands together.

The carriage driver and co-driver headed straight to the docks at gallop's pace, as per du Pont's instructions. When they approached the entrance, they slowed, entered the dockyard's main gates, and parked in a dark, secluded spot near to the ticket offices, which remained open all night.

After sniffing loudly, du Pont fell silent, unwilling to engage in any conversation with Parker. Her mind was racing, and every time Parker spoke, she raised her hand, palm outward, to silence her.

Her best option was America, she thought. She had always fancied that country. It had been her choice ever since the day she first thought about her retirement. The New World seemed to be a more civilised place than the others she'd considered. She could not contemplate the likes of Australia, which would be filled with penal colonies and hordes of crooks and criminals.

No, for her, America was the place to be. The gentlemen from the Southern states had always impressed her with their manners and ardent displays of respect for her whores. She deserved to have respect now, not as a madam but as a lady, and she had enough money to buy it.

She hoped Eddie would remember exactly what she'd told him about booking the tickets for a big Southern port. He could be a bit scatty at times, and knowing him, she would end up in bloody Boston with all the undesirables.

As she sat inside the carriage waiting for him, she wondered if her orders had been carried out to the letter. The mansion would be in cinders by now. Coppers, firemen and officials would be crawling all over it. The burned corpses of her whores would be found, of course; there was no getting around that. She could only hope that the women had caught fire quickly and that their bodies would be unrecognisable. The idea of even one surviving scared her to death. She tried to look for a positive outcome and found one. Once she got on that ship for America, she'd never have to put her feet on English soil again.

For a moment she thought about her house in London, as she also had plans for that. The house in its fine location was worth far too much money to ignore or leave unsold, and its future would now have to be addressed.

It had been quite the day…a day that had begun with promise and ended in disaster. Glancing at Parker, she thought. The woman was loyal, but that loyalty was going to be tested to its limits as soon as passage on a ship had been secured.

As time passed, du Pont's disposition became one of nervous anticipation tinged with concern and annoyance.

Eddie had still not arrived at their designated meeting point. She had no idea what could be taking him so long. She had given him strict instructions, and he knew that she would be worried. It was bloody inconsiderate of him to dally like this, she thought angrily.

More time passed. She wanted to stretch her legs. The docks were quiet, but there were hundreds of people sleeping in the docks' narrow streets and in front of warehouses. She was safe inside her carriage. It would be folly to even step outside it. The drivers had a rifle and pistol and would shoot anyone who threatened her, but even with their protection, she was carrying a great deal of money on her person, not to mention the fabric carpet bag, filled with gold, sitting next to her. If that went, she'd be finished.

She heard the sound of running footsteps getting closer to the carriage, and then Eddie's voice identifying himself to the drivers. Her body relaxed, and she sighed with relief. Eddie had not disappointed her after all.

"Get in here, Eddie," she hissed softly through the closed window curtain.

Eddie opened the door, stepped into the carriage, and closed the door behind him. He had a flushed face and was perspiring, panting like a hunting dog, and smoothing down his damp hair.

Madame du Pont's keen eyes captured his expression. People were like open books, and she never missed a trick. She looked at his nervous posture for a moment and then spoke. "Eddie, tell me it went well. Tell me you didn't cock it up."

Eddie shifted his body in the seat.

"Tell me they're all dead; out with it!"

"I'm sorry, madam. The whores got away. I was interrupted by a couple of those American buggers who were intent on freeing them," Eddie told her with downcast eyes.

"How many got away, exactly?" she asked him with an icy stare.

"All of them…and Sam, they got him. They had guns. They were going to kill me, so I ran. I didn't even have time to get my horse. Look at the state of me! We need to get on the ship as fast as we can…"

"I know that, you bloody fool! What do you think I'm doing, sitting here for my own bloody pleasure?"

"I know you're desperate to get on, and I've sorted it…it's done. America. We're going to Norfolk, Virginia. I got one first-class cabin like you asked and one in steerage. There, that's what you wanted, isn't it?"

"Good, that's good, but I want on right now. I don't want to wait until morning, not with whores running around, thanks to your incompetence. You're a dozy git sometimes, Eddie Gunn! You tell that ticket master that I don't care how much it costs. Bribe him till he can't say no if you have to. Go! And bring the ticket master back with you. I want his personal escort to the ship. Christ almighty, Eddie, thanks to you, all those bitches are running around Liverpool like headless chickens, spilling their guts and telling tales on me."

Eddie nodded whilst opening the door and stepping down. "I'm sorry. I'll make this right, I promise. I'll be back in a jiffy. Just stay put and don't get out of the carriage. I'll be five minutes."

Up until now, Parker had remained silent, but anger was clearly evident on her face. "Have we got to share a cabin then?" she asked. "I was supposed to get my own first-class ticket. What's going on here?"

Staring at Parker with eyes no wider than slits, du Pont spat out, "Watch it, you. Who do you think you're talking to, ya cheeky mare? What made you think you could get the same comforts as me like you're my bloody equal?"

Parker stopped panting with rage, took a deep breath, and leant over, bringing her face inches from du Pont's angry glare. Her expression was, as always, cold, and now impassive. "Have you forgotten after all these years of playing queen bee to all and sundry that I'm your bloody sister?"

Madame du Pont opened her mouth.

"No, you don't get to speak," Parker warned her. "Shut your mouth and keep it shut. You're going to listen to me for a change. You've been so consumed by your own self-importance all these years you've forgotten that I'm your elder by two years. You should be showing *me* some bloody respect…Margaret, I've kept your secret for long enough, and there'll be no more *Madam* coming from my lips. Our new identity papers say, Margaret and Myrtle Mallory. It's our father's name. Our real names, at last. Parker is dead, and so is your Madame du bloody Pont!

"You're not my mistress, you never were, and I finally deserve the pickings of my labour just as much as you. There's no more brothel and no more French accent. It's over!" She moved in even closer. "We *are* equals, and this equality starts right now."

For once, du Pont squirmed in her seat. “I know that, Myrtle. Everything is different now. I agree we’re equal, with equal money and status, but there is something you still have to do.” “No, there’s bloody not!” Myrtle hissed back. “I have my own money to do with what I please. We agreed right from the start that when our venture ended, you would stop bloody well bossing me around. So I don’t need to do anything else for you.”

Myrtle looked at the valise. “And another thing, I want a cut of that gold in the bag that I had to carry onto the carriage. I deserve it, and I’m going to have it just as soon as we land in America. It’s only right, and you know it. I worked hard in that mansion. Your bed was bigger than the blasted room I slept in. I slaved for you and never told anyone who I really was because I promised you I wouldn’t. But no more, do you hear?”

Myrtle sat back and stared long and hard at her younger sister, whose face had turned a cherry red. Margaret’s lips moved, but no sound came from her mouth.

“Are we clear?” Myrtle asked again.

“Yes, we’re clear, but Christ, I’ve just watched my whole life go up in bloody flames. Can you not give me some time to grieve?”

“It was my life too, what little life I had.”

“Why didn’t you speak up sooner if you were so unhappy? You could have left whenever you wanted to.”

“Leave? Why? Half the business is…was mine. I put up with you because you have the better business head and you seemed to enjoy killing young women. But you need to forget who you were and think now about who you’re going to be. That’s what I’m going to do the minute we get on that bleedin' ship, and I take off this uniform for the last time."

Madame du Pont lowered her eyes to hide her rage. She felt like strangling her own sister to shut her up. No one had dared speak to her like that for nearly two decades. Myrtle was her elder sister, but she had no brains to speak of. She'd always been as thick as the pig shit on the farm they used to live on. She'd still be living on that farm, milking cows, if it weren't for her. Myrtle was an ugly bitch into the bargain and would never have found a husband to keep her. Christ, even their father had agreed with her on that point before he died.

There was silence. Myrtle was right, though. She did deserve a retirement, but she would still have to work for it, du Pont decided.

"Myrtle, I need to say something. I agree that there is no more Madame du Pont. The name will never be mentioned again because she went up in flames with Parker. Does that suit you?"

Myrtle nodded her head victoriously.

"It's going to take time for me to adjust, but you're right, we have to look to the future now and put Liverpool and the whorehouse behind us."

"Exactly right," Myrtle said.

"You know, we've been lucky. We played with the devil for more than fourteen years, and we both came out unscathed, without losing our souls."

Myrtle laughed.

"What's that laugh for?" du Pont asked.

"When have you ever had a soul? You were a soulless bitch from the day you were born. You loved killing and beating those girls."

"So what? You loved watching me do it to them! Anyway, that's all over with. We've got other, more important matters to discuss right now."

"And what might they be?" Myrtle asked, forever suspicious of her sister.

"We're going to a port called Norfolk, Virginia…that is, me and Eddie, are going."

"What the bloody hell do you mean by you and Eddie?"

"We'll find a nice, small country house with a big garden, and we'll get ourselves some of those nigger slaves they've got over there," Margaret said, ignoring Myrtle's question.

"Answer me, Margaret. What do you mean, you and Eddie? What about me? You're not thinking about leaving me here, are you? You wouldn't dare!"

Margaret's eyes widened and displayed just the right amount of hurt. "No, of course not. I'd never leave you here, ya' daft bat! You're going to London, to Knightsbridge."

"What?"

"Myrtle, listen to me. We have a house there that's worth a lot of money. We're going to have to sell it because we're never coming back to this bloody island. You can have more than me out of the proceeds. Sixty-forty in your favour. You've got two men here to take you when they drop me off at the ship."

"Get lost, Margaret. I'm getting on that ship, even if I have to fight you for your bloody cabin!" Myrtle raged.

"The house will sell in a week, a month at the most," Margaret insisted. "Then you can join us. I'll have a lovely place all set up for us by the time you get to America."

"No, I'm not doing it," Myrtle protested again.

"But you've always wanted to see London, haven't you? You'll be a couple of months behind me, that's all. Think about it. You've got all the power. You'll be the one to give orders to folk, and I'm going to trust you with the money."

Myrtle began to whimper. Tears were streaming down her cheeks. "No, no, bloody well, no, ya' selfish bitch," she said. "You planned this all along, didn't you?"

"No..."

"Don't lie to me, ya bleedin' cow. I'll not go to London for you. I'm going to America, and you had better make all these years I've put in worth it for me."

Margaret sniggered. "Myrtle, Myrtle, you don't understand, you don't have a choice. How are you going to get to America when you've no ticket, and I've got all the money? Who do you think Eddie and the two drivers take their orders from? You'll go to London because I'm telling you to go, or you'll stay in Liverpool and walk the streets. And if you put your hands near that carpet bag, I'll cut it off…oh, come on, don't look so bloody glum. You know I love you, and I'll miss you…"

"You make me bloody sick, you conniving old whore," Myrtle said.

Chapter Twenty-Six

Mercy was awake, but she remained as still as a statue, with her eyes tightly shut. Eventually, she found the courage and cautiously opened her eyes halfway. She heard soft breathing beside her and turned her head on the pillow. She moaned softly with the pain that came with the movement. Opening her eyes fully, she saw Julia lying next to her, sound asleep and with a peaceful expression on her young, innocent face.

Mercy poked her head under the sheet and blanket in order to examine her body. It was aching all over as though she'd been punched. Oh, dear, God! She was naked. Her cheeks blushed and stung with heat, and she pulled the covers up to her chin. Where were they? Her body was clean. The sticky mess had gone, and she smelled of lavender soap. Some unknown person had bathed her.

She touched her head. The bump was still there and was giving her a headache, but it had been covered by a bandage that was wrapped around her head several times. Who had cared for her? She looked at her right hand. It was burnt, the way her hands had burnt many times before whilst cooking at home, in London, but it too was bandaged and smelt of herbs.

She tried to gather her thoughts and put them into order: The flames, the smoke, the fire engulfing Madame du Pont's mansion. The memories converged in her mind, overcrowding it and making her head ache even more.

She covered her face with trembling hands. She had set the fire. She had killed a man. *My God, I did, I killed him!* Other people might have died too, because of what she did. She hadn't thought about all the innocent people in the mansion. She'd just wanted to destroy it. She was going to burn in hell, if not today, then someday.

Where was she? She looked around the cabin and listened for a familiar sound. There were scrapings and thuds and men shouting orders coming from the other side of the wooden ceiling. How could she have slept through such a racket?

There were soft swaying movements beneath her, rocking her gently in the bed. It felt soothing, and she was somewhat calmed by it. She was on a ship. She was alive on a ship…but why? How had she come to arrive here?

It was a man's cabin. She could smell the remnants of tobacco and cologne. She could see maps, a spyglass, and masculine adornments. On the floor sat a pair of boots, and a crumpled up shirt. Trousers were strewn over the back of a chair. This was not Madame du Pont's ship? Did the madam have a ship? Were she and Julia still her captives? If not, to whom did this ship belong?

She struggled to clear her mind but found it difficult to think about her present situation. She was suddenly hit again by images of an old man, his nakedness, his murder by her hands, her setting a fire and spreading it everywhere with candles and her own gown.

Visions of blood now came to mind, gushing from the man's head and blinding her as it spewed everywhere like a fountain. The blood had been sticking to her body. She shuddered. Her mind heard the shouts from men and women, screams filled with fear and panic. There was a memory of a man's voice. It was a soothing, soft drawl in an accent she'd never heard spoken before last night. It told her she was going to be all right. "You're safe now." To whom did that voice belong?

Julia stirred but slept on.

Mercy realised that she had slept better than she had in weeks. She was in a real bed with soft white sheets and feather pillows. She snuggled deeper into the bed, revelling in its luxury. She'd never laid her head on a pillow like this one. She was used to a sack filled with newspaper that scratched her face and made a noise every time she moved her head. There was also a blanket and soft sheeting on this bed. She was warm and cosy. She somehow felt safe. Even the memories of the previous night couldn't stop her from enjoying this one lavish moment.

Her eyes closed. She was so tired, but she had to get out of bed, find clothes, and, more importantly, see where she was. Fear descended on her again like an unwanted companion, taking away her short-lived moment of peace. No, she couldn't go anywhere. She would be safer in here.

Were they prisoners? She panicked. What if they had been carted off to be sold on to someone else, someone even worse than Madame du Pont?

She turned, lifted her aching body to a kneeling position, and stuck her head out of the open porthole just above the bed. There was an array of ships at anchor; so many ships she couldn't count them all. Twisting her head as far as it could go, she could just see the outline of jetties and buildings behind them. Finally, she looked down and saw the water lapping against the hull of the ship. They were somewhere near docks, on a ship and in a grand cabin.

She continued to stare out of the porthole. An accumulation of different noises were coming from the docks and from the ship itself. It sounded as though cargo was being loaded or unloaded. She could feel tremors as large objects, or maybe crates were being moved. She understood nothing. She looked again at Julia, serene, and wondered how the girl could possibly sleep through the disturbance.

Mercy thanked God for Julia's survival. Her small, childlike body had probably been violated, yet she slept soundly and appeared to be at peace, without nightmares of rape and fire. Mercy hoped with all her heart that this was the case and that Julia would sleep on and on with the horrors of the last few weeks absent from her dreams. She would have to wait until Julia awoke to find out all that had happened to her after she'd been taken away by the man and Madame du Pont.

It was ironic, she thought. She had gladly taken on the task of protecting the youngster, yet Julia had saved her. Julia had found her, helped her up from the floor, and had taken her to the room where they'd been rescued…but by whom and for what purpose?

Mercy lay her head back down, and it sank into the pillow. She was too tired to think anymore. She could hardly keep her eyes open. She should sleep, she decided. She had to sleep for just a while longer. She'd be no good to either of them if she felt like a dead cat.

She yawned and turned to face the wall, snuggling comfortably into the mattress. They would have to try and escape, but her head ached. She'd sleep just a little while longer…

Chapter Twenty-Seven

"What the hell were you thinking, Jacob? This ain't a damn passenger ship. Goddammit, what's the crew going to think?" Jack growled.

Jacob smiled, just as he always did when Jack put on his fatherly hat. He found it refreshing because most of his subordinates, both on the ship and at home on the plantation, bowed and scraped when speaking to him. They used the word *master* at the end of every sentence. Jack was overfamiliar, overprotective, and in general overbearing, but Jacob liked this side of Jack's character. He took the edge off the loneliness that had engulfed Jacob since his own father's passing.

He took another sip of coffee, tore some bread off the long loaf, and then placed a chunk of cheese on top of it. After taking a bite, he chewed it but continued to face Jack's blazing stare. "What should I have done, Jack?" he finally said. "One girl was near to death, and the other needed stitches on a head wound and was unconscious. Should I have left them lying in front of a burning building? Taken them to a hospital, where they would probably have been thrown out on the streets of Liverpool? Or done what I did and tended to their injuries and made them safe for the night? What would you have done?"

Jack grumbled and mumbled something, then shook his head. "I know. I know you're right. I would have done the same as you. But they can't stay here. We're in the middle of unloading, and your brother's arriving any minute with the *Carrabelle*. I'm just saying you'd better decide where to drop 'em off afore the end of the day. Or have you forgot that we gone set sail tomorrow night?"

"No sir, I've not forgotten that," Jacob said with humour. "But until Isaac has a look at them, makes sure they're all right, and most importantly finds out where they came from in the first place, they stay, and they rest."

"And then what? You think those whores have nice comfortable houses to go back to?"

"I think they might, and that's what I intend to find out. Don't worry old man. We're not going to take them across the Pond with us."

Jack scoffed at Jacob again. "And if they ain't gotten no families? They're prostitutes, dang it. Don't think for a minute you're saving Southern belles here. Both of them will prob'ly leave this ship and search out the nearest whorehouse outside the docks. It's all they know."

Jacob grew serious now and shot an angry look Jack's way. He was not convinced that the two young women, one no more than a girl, had been at Madame du Pont's of their own volition. There was something in that sad green-eyed woman's expression that had made him want to save her from the minute he'd laid eyes on her.

"Jack, don't judge them just yet. You know as well as I do that Madame du Pont's whores are different from any others we've seen on our travels. You know about the rumours. I'll admit that I've never actually heard talk, personally, but you read the secrecy clause on your membership just as I did. If du Pont was running a legal business with legitimate whores, why was there the need for this dang secrecy? You didn't see what I saw last night. All the women, without exception, were fighting to get out of that house, and when I found them in the salon, they had a gun, and a damn machete pointed at them. I have a gut feeling that we've been paying blood money. If we have, we better pray to God that we've not been harming innocent women all these years."

"Well, I assure you, I aint never took no virgin to bed in that there house," Jack retorted. "I admit what you're a saying might hold some truth. But if, and I say if, they were held captive or whatever else you're imagining, why did none of 'em ever speak up? The one I bedded last night smiled all the way through me a fucking her, and she knew exactly what she was doing. Now if she did'n wanna be there, why daint she tell me or just leave? That's all what I'm a saying, son."

Jacob was picturing the enigmatic green-eyed woman again. He couldn't get her out of his head. Maybe he just didn't want to believe she was a whore and had lain with God knew how many men. "You might be right. I might be imagining something that ain't there. But that woman…Jack, I caint think about anything else. The look on her face last night… Nope, I caint be wrong. She was scared like she was looking for a way out. When I carried her downstairs, she was fighting all the way, screaming at me to let her go. Does that sound like a prostitute to you?"

Jack softened. "Look, there's differences between what you want to be true and what is true. So she got to you. Got under your skin…she's not the first, and dang it, she prob'ly ain't gonna be the last."

"No, it was more than that, goddammit! I felt her fear. I saw it in her eyes!"

"Well, I guess we'll know more when the doc speaks to 'em?"

Jacob nodded. "Yeah, but until then, old man, we've got work to do. I want to be finished in time to meet Hendry and Belle when the *Carrabelle* comes alongside."

Jacob walked with stooped shoulders along the narrow passageway towards Isaac's cabin. His smile had gone, as was the need to display the good-humoured banter he'd set in place to pacify Jack and to hide his annoyance at being told what to do on board his own ship. Jack was very dear to him. He would never disrespect him. But he was going to have to give him some bad news, and it would probably break the old man's heart.

Jacob's decision to give Jack a comfortable retirement was purely business, but it hadn't been an easy decision to make. He'd noticed Jack's mistakes and bad judgment on this voyage. He wasn't as agile or mentally efficient as a sea captain should be. The thought of having to tell him that James was going to take over after they got home was like being surrounded by a dark, looming cloud of guilt. It would inevitably force him to give Jack the news before they docked in Norfolk.

With every step, Jacob's worried frown grew. It was the same expression often planted on his face at home when something or someone was bothering him, only this time he was being bothered by his own thoughts. Jack was right. He could do without women on board his ship, yet he couldn't help but look forward to meeting the stunning green-eyed beauty again. He wanted to know her name, where she'd come from originally. He didn't want to find a gutter-mouthed whore. He wanted to hear a soft, innocent voice, watch her perfect lips move as she spoke. He wanted to be near her, even though she would disappear from his sight after today. He had thought about her all night as he tossed and turned in an empty guest cabin. He was still perplexed as to why she had such an effect on him and why, when he'd seen her covered in blood, his heart had been shattered into shards. He didn't know what the hell was going on with his feelings, as they were usually steady and very often indifferent to female charms. He wanted her gone, off his ship, but not as much as he wanted to see her, and he'd be damned if he didn't give himself that luxury.

Isaac opened his cabin door. Jacob watched him yawn and then grumble like an old man. "Did I wake you?" he asked.

Isaac raised an eyebrow and scowled. "What do you think? I was up half the night with those two women you invited on board. I gave them some laudanum and went back a while later, and they were sleeping like babies. I washed them and patched them up. They didn't stir, thank God. I figured they wouldn't be too pleased about being undressed and messed with by yet another man."

"How were they when you left them?" Jacob asked.

"The older one has a concussion. I put in a couple of stitches on her forehead, cleaned a particularly nasty burn on her hand and treated it. As for the younger one, she was breathing easier by the time I left the cabin. They should have had a good night's sleep and will be fit enough to answer our questions. I'll tell you, Jacob, you were right about the elder of the two. She's a rare beauty…sure never seen a woman to match her. Once I cleaned her face, she took on a whole different appearance...anyway, enough of that. Come in. Tell me what you want me to do?" he said, already knowing the answer.

Jacob felt relief run through him as he listened to Isaac's good news. "I want you to find out how they are. Examine them, then ask them where they come from and if they want to go home. Ask them why they were in that goddamn house, especially the younger one. Find out everything you can about them. It just don't add up. There's something not right about all this."

Isaac looked pensive and then anger spread across his face. "I have to agree. I wanted to be sure before I said anything, but…I think the younger girl was raped. I believe she might have been a virgin before last night. When I bathed her, she was bruised, badly, and there were bloodstains between her legs. I've got no facts but speaking as a doctor; I have to conclude that she was taken by force."

"Damn, Damn it!" Jacob said under his breath.

"I'll go see them and report back to you and then we'll take it from there. Oh, I sent someone out to buy what a woman needs to dress herself," Isaac added as an afterthought. "It's probably one of the strangest orders I've ever had to give, but he's back, so I'll get them to dress. I reckon' they wouldn't wanna be seen without clothes on."

Jacob nodded, but his mind was racing, and his heart was heavy. "Dear God, I hope we're wrong, Isaac. Taking a whore to bed is one thing, but raping a terrified girl is a different matter altogether."

Chapter Twenty-Eight

From the highest vantage point on the top deck, Jacob watched the last of the ship's cargo get loaded off. He signed the many customs documents and finally concluded his business on the *Christina*. All hands were on deck, cleaning, scrubbing, and making sure that every part of the ship from bow to the hull was in pristine condition for the *Carrabelle* crew's embarkation.

Jacob watched the last of the cotton crop from Stone Plantation disappear around a street corner on a cart. He sighed with relief but also with a sense of pride. He was watching his year's work reaching its final destination, and that in turn brought thoughts of home and what he'd have to face when he got there.

The overseers would be busy right now, getting the fields ready for new seeds. His slaves, under the watchful eyes of his foremen, would be ploughing and digging, but by the time he got home, work in the cotton and tobacco fields would have stopped completely. Cotton seeds would not go into the ground until the end of March. The tobacco plants would be scattered into the soil shortly after that when spring rainfalls began. The accumulation of perfectly timed agricultural procedures was why he was able to leave the plantation at this, the quietest time of the year.

Jacob's eyes casually scanned the dockyard and vessels alongside. Its latest arrival was making final docking manoeuvres. He recognised the iron sailing steam ship instantly, and his heart filled with pleasure. There was no mistaking the *Carrabelle,* with her four funnels, and tall masts. Her beautiful lines, speed, and size made her one of the finest ships afloat. She had cost them dear, but she was worth every cent. Jacob had never set foot on her decks. Hendry had taken her on her maiden voyage, just thirteen months ago, and according to his letters, she had surpassed his wildest dreams. She was five hundred and fifty feet in length, dwarfing the *Christina.* The ship had a speed of up to thirteen knots, four steam engines for the paddles, and an extra one for the propeller. Her total power was estimated at seven thousand horsepower, and she had almost double the number of crew members as the *Christina.*

The rapid growth of their business had taken Jacob and Hendry by surprise. The *Carrabelle* was trading throughout Europe. It was doing so well, Hendry had informed Jacob by letter, that plans were underway to expand routes into Asia. Yet in the midst of their optimism was a nagging voice, reminding them that the outcome of the upcoming elections on the sixth of November, might halt not only their growth but also devastate their entire business operation.

There were four candidates for the American presidency. Abraham Lincoln, the Republican for the North, posed a clear danger to the Southern slave states. His campaign for anti-expansion of slavery and slave owners' rights issues, threatened the South's economy, and way of life. Lincoln's Northern rival, Illinois Democrat, Steven A. Douglas, was a moderate on the slavery issue. Douglas hoped popular sovereignty would enable democracy to triumph, so he would not have to take a side on the issue of slavery. Jacob did not approve of Douglas.

He was a candidate sitting on the fence, shying away from making a defined campaign manifesto.

As he pondered over his country's politics, he wondered whether it might not have been prudent to remain at home to vote. He had dallied with the idea for weeks. Constitutional Union Party candidate, John Bell, from Tennessee had Virginia's backing. He had the ear of most of the Southern slave states, but Abraham Lincoln had a greater following in the industrial North. The fourth major candidate, the incumbent Vice President, John Breckinridge, had broad support in the South, but it seemed none in the North.

In just a few short days, Jacob believed America's fate would be decided. Her growing standing with the rest of the world would now be tested; such was the looming threat of dissolution of a United States. An old saying of his father's came back to haunt him; those who stand idle in elections cannot declare protestations at an unfavourable outcome.

Jacob dismissed America's political wrangle, and instead, turned his thoughts to matters even more pressing. He looked at his watch. He still had time to speak to the two women, make arrangements for them, and get to Hendry and Belle in time for luncheon.

Isaac marched towards Jacob with a thunderous scowl on his face. Jacob had never seen the mild-mannered man look as angry. He put his thoughts aside, walked towards him, and whispered in his ear, "Not here. I'll hear whatever you've got to say in private. No need for the men to listen in."

In the wardroom, Jacob poured them each a shot of rum. Isaac's face was red with rage; he looked as though he needed the rum.

"Isaac, out with it. What did the women tell you? Jesus, you look like you want to beat the shit out of someone."

Isaac drank his shot in one and slammed it on the table. "We were right. Goddammit, but if I could find that whoring madam, I'd kill her with my bare hands. These girls were abducted from London…London! The young girl is family to an Earl.

"They were both lifted off the street in different places but by the same two men. My bet is they were those two bastards we caught last night trying to burn the women in the salon."

"Dear God," Jacob said, shocked. "How were they abducted?"

"They were tricked, snatched into an enclosed vehicle, drugged, chloroform probably, and then tied up, gagged, and carted off to Liverpool along with eight other women. They were kept in a room underneath the stable. They don't know how long for…it could have been days, weeks…but that's not the worst of it. It seems that all the women in that place were taken captive at some time or another. Jacob, those two women in your stateroom witnessed murder. They were subjected to torture. Jesus Christ Almighty…it beggars belief!"

Jacob swore. He poured another rum shot for each of them and pushed his fingers through his hair. His hands were shaking, and he was filled with guilt. He'd think about Madame du Pont later. His priority now was the well-being of the two girls. "How are they doing…physically and mentally?"

Isaac shrugged. "Physically, they'll both recover…mentally…? What do you think? The older one is bruised black and blue down one side of her face, and I'm bettin' someone hit her. She won't talk, but those green eyes, Jacob, I felt as though I was being pulled into them. She never said a word the whole time I was with them."

"Nothing? But you asked her where she wanted to go?" Jacob asked.

"I did, but like I said, she didn't open her mouth. I never heard one word from her. The youngster's called Julia, and she did the talking for both of them."

"And the woman…do you think her head injury is serious?"

"I reckon the stitches I put in last night will have to stay in place for best part of a week. She's not fit enough to walk around the streets of Liverpool on her own, put it that way. She's got a bad concussion and needs to be monitored. I think she's still pretty much dazed, but we have to get her to talk so we can find out where to send her back to."

Jacob watched Isaac pour another shot and noted that he seemed deeply affected by this turn of events, and by the mystifying green-eyed woman. Jacob asked, "What happened to Julia when she was taken upstairs? Did she tell you anything about that?"

"Not much. She told me that she had not fought the man off, but he hurt her. She said du Pont threatened to kill them if they spoke about themselves or didn't comply with the customers' wishes. I swear I will kill that woman if I ever see her again."

"Yes, you already said that. Why the hell did none of them speak up? Ask for refuge? Ask to be taken out of that place?"

"I don't know. But you, me, and every other blind fool who went there were duped."

Jacob's anger was growing, and most of it was directed at himself. "Well, now we know they didn't say anything 'cause they were being threatened by du Pont. Goddammit, Isaac. I knew something was up with the older one. I should have gotten to her sooner. I had a feeling in my gut that she was scared."

"You're attracted to her, ain't you?"

"That doesn't matter right now," Jacob said curtly. "What's concerning is that those women were held at gunpoint last night, and those bastards were going to kill them to keep their mouths shut. I should have hanged the one we caught instead of tying him to a damn tree. Dear Lord, it'll take some getting over this, unless I c'n find the man that escaped, rip his balls off and shove 'em up du Pont's ass!"

"Jacob, we have to make sure that whore mistress doesn't get away with this."

"I'm with you there, but first we have to make it right and get the women back to their families. I'll go now and try to get the other one to talk. We can get them both on a train to London…and we'll make sure they're safely escorted."

Jacob's mind was spinning. He was desperate to find out the woman's name, but he had to concentrate on practical matters first. He said, "Did Julia give you an address?"

"She did."

"Okay. Get a telegram to her family, and order one of the men to look into train times. And send Jansen to get the local po-leece here too. They need to know everything we know about du Pont's criminal activities, and they damn well better catch her before she makes a run for it. Her man too, that bastard that got away last night."

Chapter Twenty-Nine

Mercy was deep in her own thoughts. She was free. Madame du Pont could not hurt her anymore. Julia had been promised safe passage home this very day. She had given the doctor her family name and where they lived in London and was repeatedly told that arrangements would be in hand before the end of the morning. Julia was going home to the loving arms of her family. *She*, on the other hand, was going to rot in hell.

When the doctor came, Mercy had held her tongue, preferring to listen to Julia's long story, instead of telling her own. The doctor had been shocked, Mercy believed. She'd seen disgust and anger in his eyes and now began to wonder if the man she'd killed had also been ignorant of the truth. Would he have pitied her had she told him that she was a prisoner? Would he have left her alone, maybe even helped her escape? Had she taken a life when all that life had wanted was what he'd paid for? She was racked with guilt. At this moment she could not speak or listen to anything other than her own recriminations.

She stared out of the porthole, hiding her shame from Julia. Julia had done herself proud, Mercy thought now. She'd imparted every piece of information, every memory, and every detail of the torture and murder they had both witnessed in Madame du Pont's house of horrors. She had left some details to the imagination, regarding her rape. She had thanked God and his angels, telling the doctor quite simply that the man had hurt her, but he had not damaged her soul. God had turned off her mind to his actions, and she had therefore not involved herself in the ordeal.

Julia's bravery and maturity were still new to Mercy. She had not seen this side of the girl's character before. Julia had shed a few tears, which she wiped away with annoyance, but Mercy took that as a good sign. The poor girl might still be in shock and unable to comprehend what had happened to her. She could wake up tomorrow or the day after, fully realising the extent of the horrors she had lived through. But today, she was revealing a serenity and dignity, well beyond her years.

She watched Julia eat a hearty breakfast, but she couldn't think about eating. Her stomach was knotted, and waves of nausea threatened to spill over. She could barely talk. She was afraid to talk. She was filth, a murderess and arsonist.

No one back home would believe what she'd done. There, she couldn't even bring herself to kill the rats that scurried across the floor in her grandma's house. She wouldn't have hurt a fly. Yet here she sat in a grand cabin with blood on her hands and with the guilt of knowing she had snubbed out a life, or lives, like candles.

She could not speak as Julia had, for she was not a victim. She could not talk about the fire, for she had set it. She could not bring herself to utter the name Carver, for she was terrified that by giving it, she too would be sent home.

Home? No, not home. She fought the very idea of it. She could never go back to her grandparents' house…ever. She would rather wander the streets of Liverpool until she died or was killed.

She thought about her impending marriage. She hated Big Joe more than ever, yet he was not the guilty party. Her grandparents had sold her to him with no regard for her feelings, and that made *them* guilty in her eyes. They had done it to survive, to feed the family, to buy her new garments, and to make their lives easier, but they were just as bad as the slave traders she had heard about, living in distant lands. They were almost as bad as Madame du Pont!

This terrible ordeal had taught her more about life than she could have ever imagined. The world was a cruel place, where money had the power to buy people, enslave them, and kill them on a whim. She had seen this with her own eyes. She'd been bought and paid for like the whores at the du Pont manor, but Big Joe would not receive his merchandise. She would rather slit her own throat in a Liverpool back street than give herself to him. Best her family and Southwark thought her dead.

The stateroom's door rattled with a loud knock. Julia stopped eating. Mercy stared unswervingly at the door, wondering who would enter. Fear once again crept up on her. Coppers could be lurking outside. They'd take her away in chains. Someone might have witnessed her appalling deeds.

Fear was going to live with her for the rest of her days. Fear of the unknown, the constant worry that death would result from a wrong word or action. Fear of ever walking out alone. Fear of the madam finding her, taking her to some dark place and slitting her throat. Peace, Mercy knew at that moment, would only come after she was sure that, Eddie, Sam, and that bitch were dead.

Mercy heard a second knock. It was a gentle, unthreatening tap. She looked down the length of the table. There were breads and cold cuts. The maps had been removed. Flowers had been brought and sat in a crystal vase right in the centre. Whoever had ordered these kind offerings delivered by the doctor might be on the other side of the door.

Mercy whispered in Julia's ear, "It may be the nice doctor, Julia. And he was kind, wasn't he?"

Julia nodded without taking her eyes from the door.

"Come in," Mercy said with a soft tremble in her voice. Her heartbeat quickened, and she prayed.

Jacob took a hesitant step inside the room. He stood just inside of the door, hat in hand and with no intention of moving closer. He looked at the young woman and the girl, and his heart melted. His eyes met the woman's, and he couldn't tear them away. He tried to focus on Julia, but his eyes automatically slid back to those green eyes.

She was just as beautiful as he remembered, even more so bathed in the mid-morning light pouring through the open porthole. She was dressed in a dark blue gown, which would have looked ordinary on anyone else. She, on the other hand, with those vibrant green eyes and flowing hair, was like a rare, exquisite doll. Her bandage had been removed, and the sutures, sitting at the centre of the swollen area, were visible just beneath her hairline. Jacob's heartbeat quickened, and he attempted to calm it. He had questions and needed answers.

Mercy looked at the stranger, and grainy images surfaced in her mind. There were dark, blurred outlines and flames dancing, but his face was also there. She was back in the bedroom, being pulled from underneath the bed. She was thrown over a shoulder. In the misty images that followed, she remembered his face again, outside on the grassy verge. He'd saved her. She remembered now. She'd seen him for just a split second before he hauled her out of the room.

She studied him more carefully and waited for him to speak. He seemed as tongue-tied as she. Her fear drained away, for as she watched him, all she could see and sense were kind eyes and concern. He stood tall and was broad shouldered. She caught herself thinking he was handsome. She was mesmerised by his deep brown eyes that were locked onto her own. How could a man be so perfectly formed?

"Good morning, ladies. I'm sure glad to see y'all looking better. My name is Jacob…Jacob Stone. Welcome onboard the *Christina…*"

"What are you going to do with us? Why are we on this ship?" Mercy interrupted him, afraid he'd read her mind. Jacob smiled, and Mercy noticed his perfect white teeth. Her words had come out the wrong way. They had sounded abrupt and ungrateful. "I'm…I'm sorry for interrupting you, Mr Stone," she stuttered.

Jacob waved her apology away. "I'll tell you everything you want to know, but first I wish to know *your* name and where you're from?"

"Why?" Mercy asked, feeling heat flush on her skin.

"I need to know who you are, in order to get you safely home to your family. I know that you are Miss Julia Cavendish," he said to Julia, who stood and curtsied. He turned to Mercy. "But you I know nothing about. You need to give me some information, like Miss Julia here has. Believe me; I just want to set this right. You've both been through a terrible ordeal."

"You'll never set this right," Mercy said in a voice laced with anger. "But you can help Julia. She is cousin to the Earl of Sussex. Her family is staying in Knightsbridge, London. If you want money, I know for a fact they'll pay whatever you ask."

"I assure you, I want no money from anyone," Jacob's voice sounded hurt.

Mercy saw the hurt in his eyes. She'd insulted him. Oh, God, she was making a mess of things.

Jacob said, "Isaac, my ship's doctor, is already seeing to Miss Julia's travel plans, but you, Miss, I need to know what we can do for *you?* I'm asking you your name so that I can inform your loved ones that you're safe. There is no ulterior motive here."

Mercy couldn't take her eyes from him, yet she was now unable to speak. She was like the dumb halfwit that lived in her street back home, robbed of speech and brain. What if this man only wanted her name to turn her in? What if Madame du Pont was already telling lies about her? Oh, God, what if this man saw her do the things she did last night? She jumped at the sudden sound of his voice.

"I come from Virginia in America, and that's where I'm headed tomorrow. I'm going home, and that's all I want for you.

Mercy waited for him to tell her she was wanted by the coppers, but he seemed to be done speaking. She took a deep breath. She might be condemning herself to death, but she had to give him answers. She looked at Julia. The girl was going to be shocked and mortified to hear that she'd bathed with a commoner in the same bathtub.

Then she watched the dark-eyed man with hair as black as her own. He was hypnotising her with those kind eyes that were boring holes into her soul. She had to speak. "Did all the other girls get out? Did they escape too? Did anyone die in the fire?" She needed to know these things first.

"Your fellow captives are all right. I saw to their release, myself."

Mercy heard herself choke on a sob. She threw her hand to her throat. "I'm sorry. Forgive me. I was so worried about them. We both were."

Julia nodded.

"When we were looking for you, we found a charred body," Jacob said.

"You were looking for us?" Mercy heard the words tumble from her mouth.

"We were looking for anyone who might have been trapped upstairs."

"Oh, I see."

Jacob continued, "Please don't think about last night. Just know that I believe all the women in that place were saved from the fire and from Madame du Pont, who will, I assure you, be hunted down and punished. The local po-leecemen would like to ask you a few questions about her, if you can surely manage it, Miss, and about your experiences. They want to help. Will you speak with them?"

"Speak to the coppers? No!" Mercy shouted without thinking. "No, I don't want to talk about it. Julia has told you everything. It's all true. Julia, do you want to speak to them?"

"No. I just want to go home, please," Julia said.

Jacob nodded. "Okay. No one will compel you to answer any questions, but I still need your name," he told Mercy.

"Mercy…my name is Mercy Carver. I come from the poorer side of London, on the wrong side of London Bridge. I have no family and no one to go back to. I'm an orphan. I don't…didn't have employment, and I don't want to go back to those streets."

Julia's mouth was open. She stared at Mercy as though seeing her for the first time. Mercy threw her an apologetic look and refused to look at Jacob. "I'm sorry I'm not from a rich family, Julia. I thought you would have guessed that by now. You all spoke so nicely, and I tried to copy you to fit in. I thought Madame du Pont might kill me if she knew I had no value."

Mercy then looked at Jacob. His eyes were dark and unfathomable. She thought she saw anger in them. Was he disappointed too?

Julia said, "Mercy, I don't understand. You're very beautiful, and you had on such a lovely gown, and your hair…I thought you came from a family like my own. You don't speak as I do, but you looked like a lady. So you mean you're poor, a commoner?"

"Yes, on both counts. Looks can be deceiving, but I assure you, I'm poorer than a church mouse and as common as the muck on my street," Mercy told her, hurt by Julia's snobbery. "I'm just a girl from the wrong side of the river who wanted to have tea and look inside St Paul's Cathedral. There, now you know. I was in the wrong place at the wrong time, and that's why I was taken."

Mercy lowered her eyes in shame. She felt as though she'd just committed a crime. She looked up at Julia's eyes again and noted that they were looking at her in a different light. Her shocked expression had not abated. Mercy's disappointment in Julia was now turning to anger. "And the dress you talked about…I borrowed it from the local dressmaker. I saved up for a year to have my day in London."

For a moment there was silence. Mercy fiddled with the bandage on her hand. Why was she surprised? Julia was a spoilt young girl who had probably never cavorted with a low-class woman in her life. Mercy had no doubts now that her friendship with the young girl was over. She was well aware of her station in life. She was the kind of woman Julia's family would employ to work in their mansion's kitchen, not one who would ever be allowed to sit upstairs to drink cups of tea and eat dainty pastries. She had hoped, for just a short time this morning, that maybe, just maybe, Julia would ask her to go home with her. But the Julia she'd known, protected, and soothed had gone.

Mercy finally looked at Jacob and saw pity. She had to get off this ship now. She didn't want pity from either of them. "Please, sir, I want to go now. I can look after myself. I'm sure I'll find employment here in Liverpool. I don't need your help or anyone else's, for that matter. Please, just get Julia home. That's all I ask."

Jacob looked at Mercy's tired face and saw fear written across it. She had tried to hide it from him and Julia, but as she sat there like an innocent, lost child, wide-eyed and apprehensive, he instinctively knew that with nowhere to go, no one to help her, and no funds, she would be doomed to an early death, or worse, forced to become the very thing he had just rescued her from.

"Mercy…may I call you Mercy?" he asked her.

Mercy nodded.

Jacob said tentatively, "My doctor tells me that you have a concussion and that your head is still swollen. You have sutures, which, if not treated properly, may become infected. I implore you to stay a while longer, at least until tomorrow morning. I can find you some respectable lodgings for a few months and give you funds until you find employment. Allow me to do this for you."

Mercy's eyes filled with tears that slid down her cheeks. She'd never heard such kind words or experienced this much concern. His kindly character and handsome face were chiselling away at her hard, impenetrable facade. Her strength had always been her greatest ally, but this man's smile and patient, sensitive character took her breath away. She was left panting in short, sharp bursts.

He was undoing her family's sacred teachings. They had told her never to feel sorry for herself and never to cry in public during moments of weakness. She had been taught that it was dangerous and unwise to allow another person to see her with her heart on sleeve. But this man,

Jacob Stone, was dragging her heart and soul right out into the open, making her vulnerable and turning her into the same pitiful creature her grandpa had despised for as long as she could remember.

Her mind wandered to the one person her grandpa still hated; her father, Thomas. He was continuously blamed for Grandpa Carver's all too frequent angry outbursts. In his eyes, Thomas was a man without strength of character, courage, or will. He'd never forgiven his son. He would go to his grave cursing him for the act of suicide that had gone against everything the Carvers stood for, their stoic acceptance of misery, hardship, and poverty. A Carver accepted a life without vision or ambition to raise himself above and beyond the trials that God had set him.

Mercy gulped for air, but she could no more control her tears than she could her own self-pity. What would it be like and how would it feel, she wondered, to have such a man as, Jacob Stone, by her side to protect her, displaying kindness towards her every day in deed and word? How lucky she would feel to have those piercing eyes and that handsome face look at her lovingly in the morning and at the end of the day.

She wiped her tears and realised that she'd been crying for quite some time. She was a pitiful creature. Her head was pounding again. She sat up straight and tried to recuperate the small amount of pride that she still possessed but couldn't find. She was resolute in her decision never to go back. Forward, she told herself, forward was the only direction she would take from now on.

"Thank you, Mr Stone, for everything, but I really don't need your charity. I would just like to rest a while longer. My head hurts."

Chapter Thirty

Jacob walked onto the jetty, still thinking about Mercy and wondering how he could help her when she had repeatedly turned down his offers of assistance. She was stubborn and afraid, and she intrigued him even more now. She had fire, ice, and spirit in her veins, yet she was as soft and vulnerable as a kitten.

She was determined not to return to London. It was not his business to ask why she had come to such a steadfast decision. Her young companion, Julia, had not offered Mercy safety or refuge with her aristocratic family. This had disappointed him, but he had not been surprised. The two appeared to be close in friendship. Mercy had obviously looked after the young girl in the past couple of weeks, judging by the way Julia had clung to Mercy's side, yet he understood Julia's reluctance to take Mercy with her. Mercy would be considered undesirable in Julia's world. She had no family, no title, and no money. Though her voice was as smooth as honey, her accent was markedly different from Julia's. Mercy would not be considered a good companion, and she would never be accepted as Julia's equal.

As he walked towards the *Carrabelle*, late for his reunion with Hendry and Belle, he realised that he was finding it difficult to think about anything other than Mercy Carver. He didn't want to say goodbye to her at the end of this day. He was neither rash nor impulsive, and he was not a naive, inexperienced man. He was master of a hundred or so slaves and owner of a plantation and two ships, yet he wasn't capable of dismissing a woman he barely knew from his mind. Mercy, why even her name was intriguing, beautiful, and sensual. She had begged for kindness through her eyes. He doubted she'd ever known real affection in her entire life. She had cried openly, unaware that her tears had crushed him. He'd wanted to take her in his arms and promise her his protection. He wanted to take away her darkest and most abysmal memories.

He shook his head in wonder. Maybe he would never see her again, but he was enamoured by a London commoner called Mercy Carver.

Chapter Thirty-One

Jacob stood on the *Carrabelle*'s deck and stared open-mouthed at Belle.

She stood beside Hendry, radiant and amused at Jacob's shocked expression. Gone were her usual britches, shirt, and braces. In their place was a gown, which cleverly but not entirely hid her pregnant state.

"Belle, how did this happen?" Jacob asked stupidly.

"Ask your brother; he caused it," Belle smiled and responded happily. "You should have seen his face when I told him, Jacob. We were in the Bay of Biscay at the time in twenty-foot waves and a darn wind that threatened to topple us. I was sick right in front of him, and y'all know what he said?"

"No, ma'am." Jacob smiled.

"He said, 'Don't tell me after all this time you've suddenly become a bad sailor. We've been through much worse than this. Go an' lie down, and don't let the men see you!' Ornery fool. I was sick for days, but not because of the dayum weather. He never cottoned on 'til the buttons on my britches finally popped. Why, it took another month or so afore I plucked up the courage to tell him."

Hendry spoke at last. "Now hush, honey. You'll be making my brother think I'm an idiot. If you had told me sooner, I would have gotten you on a ship back home. Be honest. That's why you didn't tell me 'til we were in North Africa."

Jacob kissed Belle's hand and then hugged her so gently she laughed out loud. "I'm with child. I'm not a china doll, so if y'all gonna to hug me, Jacob Stone, hug me!"

"I missed you, my sweet Belle." Jacob laughed. "I swear I never imagined this day would come. This is going to change everything. It has to." He grabbed Hendry by the shoulders and slapped him on the back three times. "I'm happy for the both of you. Hell, I'm going to be an uncle! But you do realise you caint stay on board a ship now, don't you, Belle? How far along are you?"

"Oh, I guess about five months. Maybe a little more."

"Five months…Hendry?" Jacob looked to his brother.

Hendry nodded and smiled. "Don't worry, Jacob. It's been decided. Belle and I are going home with you on the *Carrabelle*. You're going to have visitors at Stone Plantation for a while. Hope you don't mind. We figure we'll be landlubbers until the baby's at least a year old. I don't want to miss his or her first steps and first words. This wasn't planned, but we're mighty happy about it."

"And I'm over that horrible sickness now, so don't worry about me. I'll be fine getting across the Atlantic. I can't wait to tell everyone," Belle jumped in.

Hendry beamed again. "Yep, she's never felt better nor looked more beautiful. We spoke to a doctor in Marseille, and he doesn't see a problem with Belle taking this one last voyage. All we need to do now is find a new captain and navigator for the *Christina*, although I doubt we'll find a navigator as good as my Belle."

Jacob looked at the bump on Belle's stomach, still trying to take in this momentous news. "You love the sea, both of you. Are you sure you can deal with living on land? And Belle, should you really be taking this long trip? It's going to be pretty rough going across the Atlantic."

Belle laughed. "Don't worry about me, Jacob. Worry about yourself. Why, y'all get sick just sailing in a milk pond let alone any squall!"

Jacob opened his mouth to protest, but Hendry stopped him. "Look, we know this is a shock. Y'all have to let it sink in. We've got a lot to talk about, and lunch is waiting in the stateroom. Why don't the three of us discuss it down there?"

Jacob followed them, pensive about Belle's condition. Yet even with Belle's health in mind, his heart soared. He was going to be an uncle. Even better, he was going to have his family back at Stone Plantation.

Over lunch, Jacob realised that his face or voice must have given something away when he revealed of his night out. He stumbled over his words as he relayed the entire story, and was well aware that he mentioned Mercy's name in just about every sentence.

Belle first posed the question. "I can see y'all fond of this Mercy woman. You only met her last night and you didn't even speak to her, yet you caint stop talking about her. I don't understand?"

"Belle, how can you of all people say you don't understand? You and Hendry were like a couple of victims under a voodoo love spell ten minutes after you met at that picnic."

Belle and Hendry laughed together. Hendry said, still smiling, "You've got us there. Love is a wonderful, mysterious happening. I've never seen you like this, so I can only believe that *you* may think you've been spellbound too. Belle, who are we to question my little brother's feelings?"

A serious expression crossed Belle's face. She believed in love at first sight. Jacob was right; it had happened to her and Hendry. But Jacob was engaged to Elizabeth Coulter, a friend. She was spoilt, and she cared more about being mistress of Stone Plantation than she did about Jacob. Unfortunately, a woman's ambition for position in the South was all too familiar. Many of her friends married for money and comforts, not for love. If Jacob broke his word, he would never be forgiven. South Virginia would make him a social outcast.

She tactfully said, "Darling Jacob, have you thought about Elizabeth in all this madness? You're getting married afore Christmas. That's just a couple of weeks after we get back. Hendry and I were so happy when we decided to go home because it meant we could be at your wedding. Do you truly think, you, a Southern gentleman in every way, can break your word to the Coulters? Why, it's unheard of. They'll make bad enemies. You know that, don't you?"

Jacob hung his head. Belle was right, but he damn well knew what he wanted, and it wasn't Elizabeth. He suddenly knew that with or without Mercy in his life, Elizabeth would never be able to fill his heart. Mercy had opened his eyes to his real feelings. He had felt alive this morning, just sitting with her. It was as though the universe had finally shown him what had been missing in his life.

He answered with the truth as he saw it. "I ain't never been in love, Belle, y'all know that. This woman has captivated my heart, and I feel like a goddamn prisoner. I have done so since the very first moment I laid eyes on her. All I want to do is sit with her, talk to her, 'n be with her. I've nothing else to say. This dang woman has turned my brain into swamp mush overnight, and that's all there is to it."

Belle rose and hugged Jacob. Tears were in her eyes. "Big, strong, Jacob is in love. You know, something crossed my mind only this morning. I just hate the thought of being cooped up in the cabin for more than a day, but Hendry insists I take things easy. Why, he won't even allow me to do my job unless I'm sitting down. I believe I may need a companion, Jacob. Old bossy boots here will never allow me to work on deck, not in the squalls we're expecting in the Atlantic." She looked up at Hendry, and he nodded. "Why don't you ask your Mercy Carver if she would do me the honour of keeping company with me on the voyage?"

Hendry said, "Belle, this is the woman in you talking, not the sensible, ship's navigator. That, my love, is one of the worst ideas you ever did have." Looking at Jacob, he continued, "Jacob, be sure about this. You could be setting yourself up for a fall. The Coulters will rub your nose in the mud if you let Elizabeth down."

"I can take care of the Coulters," Jacob said.

"Then you better go get this Carver woman, but I don't know how the hell y'all going to survive the shit-storm that will be waiting for you back in Virginia."

Chapter Thirty-Two

Isaac stood sombrely and at a distance to witness Julia saying goodbye to Mercy. He couldn't begin to imagine what terror they had experienced together and what memories would haunt them to their graves. He saw no panic or fear now, just an outpouring of sadness coming from Mercy, the sweetest, most beautiful woman he had ever beheld; a woman he could easily fall in love with.

He thought, watching the women, that just as their two worlds had collided, those same two worlds would now separate. Julia, with her aristocratic family, would erect an impenetrable barrier against the common, poor, and desolate young Mercy Carver, who had, by all accounts, protected her friend like a bear with her cub. It was a sad situation, and it was also unfair. But in caste, Mercy was almost as low on society's ladder as a slave on the streets of Portsmouth, Virginia.

Mercy finally turned with head held high and the dignified poise of the finest of ladies. She looked at Julia once more and smiled before disappearing below decks.

Isaac went to Julia. "Everything is in order, Miss Julia. Don't you worry about a thing. Those two men beside that carriage on the jetty are from the Liverpool police station. They're policemen. They will escort you all the way to London and right to your family's door. A telegram has been dispatched to your father, so you needn't fret. They'll be expecting you."

"These two men…are they good men? Will I be safe with them?" Julia asked.

"Yes, miss. They are highly respected law men. They have letters of credentials to prove who they are. I interviewed them myself. They're going to protect you. No one else will ever harm you again, Miss Julia. The entire Liverpool police force is out looking for Madame du Pont. She'll be caught, don't you worry about that. I swear you're in safe hands now."

Julia looked at the hatch that led to the stateroom. "I so wish I could take Mercy with me, but my father and mother would never allow me to associate with her class of person. I'm ready to leave, thank you," she told Isaac.

Mercy sobbed silently on top of the bedcovers and tried to imagine all that was to come. She had stupidly turned down money and lodgings, which could have been the one saving grace that might have led her to employment of some sort. After learning to talk more like a lady and how to walk with grace at Madame du Pont's, she believed she could possibly get a position in a large, well-to-do house, but she had no references or notes of recommendation. She could try the lodging houses and work in one of them, cleaning or cooking. The owners might even give her a free bed to sleep in. She was sure there would be many such lodging houses in Liverpool, especially with a port bigger than the Elephant and Castle. She vehemently shook her head. Only as a last resort would she go into a workhouse, only if all else failed.

She looked around the cabin thinking if only she could remain here forever. She felt safe, warm, and unafraid for the first time in weeks. She had nothing but the dress on her back, bought for her early this morning. She still had a bit of a headache, but that would go eventually. As for the stitching on the wound, well, she would just have to cut them out herself at some point, when it had healed.

Her biggest problem, she imagined, would be to procure a safe place to sleep on streets filled with strangers, some from foreign lands. There would be thieves and men who would violate her in a second if they saw her alone and vulnerable. She could be sold into servitude or whisked off to Australia. Her journey would be fraught with dangers, and she dreaded the very thought of this new life of hers. This led her to once again think of home and her choice never to go back there. Big Joe came to mind, and all thoughts of home were banished as quickly as they had come. Anything would be better than a life with him, even death.

She rose reluctantly from the bed and wrapped a black woollen shawl around her shoulders. There was no point in sitting here alone any longer.

Chapter Thirty-Three

Jacob walked as fast as he could along the jetty from the *Carrabelle* to the *Christina*, trying not to appear like a man in a hurry or a thief on the run.

As he stepped on board the *Christina*, he ignored the movements of the men and the comings and goings of their belongings. Some of the ship's crew were changing over. Many had been on the European route for too long and were eager to return home to Virginia, whilst others in Hendry's crew were European and did not wish to cross the Atlantic. As he walked across the crowded deck, he noticed that, as always, some crew members were there because it was a social occasion.

Jacob had introduced a custom whereby every member of both crews received a tot of rum, which was dispensed by the quartermaster. Usually, he used this time to speak to the men, hear any complaints, and listen to new operational suggestions from the more experienced crew members. But he didn't have time for niceties today. Ignoring their greetings, he waved away their questions and made his way straight to the stateroom to find Mercy.

He knocked on the door and waited. There was still no answer after his second attempt. Opening the door cautiously, he called out Mercy's name.

The stateroom was empty, and all signs of the previous occupation had gone. The bed had been neatly made up, the cabin was clean, and the only evidence of Mercy Carver and her young companion was the lingering smell of feminine, flowery lavender.

"Goddammit," he voiced out loud. He'd missed her. She'd left earlier than he'd anticipated and without a goodbye. She might have gone with Julia, but he doubted that. She might have simply slipped off the ship without anyone noticing, but he couldn't believe that either.

He took to the ladder attached to the passageway's bulkhead, climbed it two steps at a time, and reached the deck. Once there, he called loudly for silence in an unusually sharp tone. "Did any of you see the women leave the ship?" he asked all present.

"Yes, sir, Mr Stone," a voice from the crowded deck shouted back. "The young 'un left first with the doc, and the other left not ten minutes ago."

"Come closer, man," Jacob ordered. "Did the young lady leave alone?"

"Yes, sir. She just upped and went and never looked back or at anyone on her way off. She stood on the jetty, kinda thoughtful like, but I didn't see which way she went," the crew member told him.

"Come with me, Carson. I've got a job for you."

"Yes, sir, at your service, as always, sir."

Jacob walked down the gangplank with Carson at his heels. His heart was thumping. He was unwilling to lose Mercy now. "We're going to look for her. You take the jetty's right and walk it as far as it goes. I'll take the left end and head to the port gates. Do you understand me?"

"Yes, sir. If she's still in the area, we'll find her. Doubt she'll have gotten as far as the gates yet. She didn't look to be in no hurry to me."

"Do you recall how she looks and what she was wearing? It's important that you do and can spot her in the crowds down there."

"Oh, I remember her, all right. I could never forget a face like that, begging your pardon, sir."

Jacob nodded, giving the man a cold stare, and then gave one more order. "If you find her, Carson, for God's sake don't scare her off. Her name is Miss Mercy Carver. Tell her Jacob Stone would like permission to speak with her on an urgent matter. Speak gently and make sure you get her back onto the *Christina.* You make dang sure she doesn't get away from you. Am I clear?"

After the man had nodded, Jacob turned and began his search. The main thoroughfare led to the port gates and was a long, straight road if one didn't take a fancy to the many shortcuts along the way. Not knowing the port, he doubted Mercy would head for unknown territory like small, often dangerous lanes and narrow streets filled with runners and cargo holds. No, Mercy would be smart enough to realise that she'd be safer if she walked to the gates by the most public route, and that's what his gut told him to do.

He passed a multitude of people boarding ships. Mid-afternoon was the busiest time of the day, for this was when most ships began their boarding procedures. He knew the system well. Very few ships left in the morning, preferring to set sail at nightfall, just as he did. There was no plausible explanation for this where he was concerned because the *Carrabelle* and *Christina* only held cargo. But when passenger ships left in the late evening, it allowed the crew to concentrate on their jobs instead of spending the first few hours at sea working hard with the added weight of bothersome travellers and screaming children running around their ankles.

Night sailing ensured that most passengers; by now exhausted with long days of waiting to board, went straight to their allotted bunks and slept the night through, waking up next morning to the sight of an endless ocean of water. Passengers were discouraged from roaming around the decks, day or night, and were given just an hour or so a day to inhale fresh air into their lungs before being urged to go back down below.

Jacob was tall, and that gave him an advantage, for he could look over the heads of most men, thus had a better chance of spotting Mercy, even from a distance. He walked on, head moving and eyes focusing left to right. He even turned around to look backwards and double-checked that he'd not missed her slight form in the crowds. Eventually, he saw her, and his heart and stomach lurched, leaving him breathless.

She was, as he'd thought, heading for the port gates, and ultimately the city. He wondered if she knew what a snake-infested pit it was. It could swallow a lone woman whole, and no one would care or notice. Bodies were found stabbed, shot, or beaten to a pulp every day. There were many good people around, but there were also those of the same ilk as the two men who had tried to kill a bunch of women in the du Pont mansion.
Jacob quickened his pace. He'd met her for a reason. He'd saved her for a reason. Now she was in his life. No matter what was in his future, she was supposed to be in his present.

Chapter Thirty-Four

Mercy walked on and then turned around in a full circle just to make sure she wasn't being followed. She saw no one she recognised and walked on again, this time manoeuvring in a zigzagging pattern to the left, where the ugly grey buildings stood, blackened by steam, coal, and smoke from remnants of small fires lit by travellers. In her mind, being close to walls would give her more security.

She looked up at the very top of the buildings and saw that most were flat-roofed. She brought her eyes down to focus on the wide doors, some shut, some open. From where she stood, she could easily make out what was inside these great shell-like sheds. They had three walls, but the doors were so wide at the front they took up almost the entire frontage without brick or mortar being required. Inside the huge, open-spaced buildings were crates and equipment coming and going to foreign lands. She suddenly wished she could find refuge inside a crate, fall asleep, and wake up on the other side of the world.

Tucked between two of these buildings was a small bakery. She stopped to look through the glass window, seeing bread, sweetmeats, and pastries on shelves, three high. Her fear of being found by Madame du Pont or her henchmen, Eddie and Sam, was not her only concern. Having no money to buy food and no safe place to sleep were more fearsome and much bigger problems. She had no purse with shillings or farthings. She had the clothes on her back, which would begin to smell and darken with mud and dirt within days. She could bear the cold and probably find a discarded crate on the roadside to sleep in for a night or two, but she would have to beg for water and food, and that was the most terrifying thought of all. She had always been poor and had gone without food for a day or two, but she had never had to beg for anything in her life.

She cursed her foolish pride. Had she accepted some funds from Jacob Stone, that kind, wonderful man, she would have avoided these added worries. She should have taken enough to get her safely on a train, which would have taken her out of harm's way and allowed her to start afresh somewhere else.

Her name rang out loud and clear. She recognised the voice. She turned from the window and saw Jacob Stone, the American, now standing inches from her.

They were forcibly pushed together by the crowd. The noise in the port was deafening. Bags, babies, sacks of clothes, heavy boxes, and even pots and pans rattling made it impossible to hear what Jacob was saying.

Mercy stared open-mouthed and felt a rush of pure joy coursing through her body. She was practically in his arms, unable to take a step backwards or sideways, and could hardly contain her happiness.

Jacob held her elbow, and she allowed him to guide her inside the small bakery. A queue of people stretched from the counter and snaked all the way outside into the street. Jacob walked past the counter, still holding on to her elbow, and took her to a curtained-off area. Behind the curtain were tables and chairs filled with those who could afford an afternoon tea in luxury. Jacob found them a small table for two sitting against a far wall.

Mercy looked into his sparkling, kind eyes and felt her insides flutter as they had this morning when she first met him. He was smiling. He was happy to see her too.

Jacob allowed Mercy to order tea and cake before he spoke. This also gave him time to rehearse the words he wanted to use lest he come out with a load of incoherent drivel. He looked into her nervous and enquiring eyes and waited until she was comfortable before he spoke. "I'm sure glad I found you in time, Miss Mercy. I thought I was too late."

"I don't understand. Too late for what? Have I done something wrong?" Had he come to hand her over to the coppers? Had he found out what she'd done? Were the authorities behind him or lurking close by? She shot glances in all directions and then brought her eyes back to him. She relaxed her body as soon as he opened his mouth to speak.

"No, ma'am, you've done nothing wrong," he told her. "You may be an answer to a prayer…not mine, that would be my sister-in-law's prayer. You see…"

Tea arrived. Jacob was grateful for the distraction. He was making a complete ass of things when usually he had no problem articulating his words. Mercy had a strange effect on him. He was grappling with words and looking into her beautiful emerald eyes at the same time. They were disconcerting and left him fumbling.

"I was disappointed when I got back to the *Christina* and found you'd already left. I thought I'd never see you again, and that would have been a tragedy. You see, I specifically went back to search you out and to speak to you. I want to offer you employment."

Mercy opened her mouth to speak, but Jacob silenced her. "No, wait, please, afore you say anything, let me finish. I don't want you to be afraid or think ill of my intentions. I just need you to listen to my proposal afore you give me your answer. I promise you I'll answer any questions you might have and put your mind at ease if you'll just hear me out. Will you allow me to do that?"

Mercy nodded but nervously bit her lip.

Jacob cleared his throat. He unintentionally forced his fingers through his hair before taking in and then exhaling a long, deep breath.

"I've just met up with my brother, Hendry, and his wife, Belle. They're presently on our other ship. The ship is called the *Carrabelle*, and it will leave for Virginia with us onboard tomorrow night."

"Yes?" Mercy had to say, now impatient with curiosity and hope.

"Belle is with child and has only four months left until she comes to term. She and Hendry have lived on the sea, but of course, this changes everything. They now find themselves having to give up their lives onboard ship to go home with me. She asked me just an hour ago to find a young lady who could keep company with her on the voyage. She's going to be spending a lot of time in her cabin. If you knew Belle, you'd agree that she's a woman who doesn't take kindly to being cooped up like a chicken. Miss Mercy, it would mean the world to her if she had a female companion…not a servant, you shouldn't think that at all. She needs someone to talk to, play rummy with, or just to stroll on deck with every once in a while. My brother's afraid for her health."

"She's a woman working on a ship?" Mercy questioned, still unable to comprehend anything else he was saying.

"Yes, it's rare, I know, and her family are not best pleased. But Belle and Hendry love each other and won't be parted. Forgive me, but I told her about your situation, that you might be happy to have this opportunity. I know I'm asking you to leave your country and go to an unknown land, but you would be doing my family a great honour if you agreed, and you will be well taken care of. So what do you say?"

Mercy realised that her mouth was open. She snapped it shut and repeated his words in her mind. She could scarcely believe Jacob's offer, yet he had made it abundantly clear. This astonishing and kind man was asking her to go to America and leave England behind. He was offering her the chance to get rid of every rotten memory and more…the pain suffered in her short life. She would have employment, funds, and dignity, which were things even her grandparents had withheld from her. A new life, she thought, and a new world.

Again tears threatened to spill over her eyelashes. The thought of remaining in Liverpool had been a necessary but rotten proposition. Now the very idea of it was abhorrent to her. Five minutes ago, she had walked the road with a heavy heart, dreading the moment she would pass through the gates and onto the strange and dangerous Liverpool streets. Jacob Stone had come and cast aside her despair. He had replaced it with hope and a future that sounded better than anything she could ever imagine here in England.

Mercy was just about to say yes, but then a troubling thought struck her. "Mr Stone …erm, Jacob. I like the sound of your proposal very much, for I certainly don't want to remain in this city. I'm scared if the truth be told. I have nothing and no one. I'll be very honest with you; I see no hope for my situation. But what will happen to me when I'm no longer needed by your sister-in-law? Surely she has family, sisters, a mother, and friends who will keep her company. What will I do? Will I be cast out onto the streets in a foreign land?"

Jacob shook his head in horror. "That will never be the case. We look after our own. You'll have funds and freedom. You'll never be left to wander any street alone, not while I draw breath."

Jacob said nothing more. Instead, he watched her mind at work and waited for her to speak again. Mercy needed to ask her questions; more questions, he deduced by her transparent expression. She had to be sure and content with her decision. He would hate himself if he were responsible for any future unhappiness or doubts that might plague her already tattered life.

Mercy finally looked up at him. He gazed at her with a candid expression as though he could read her mind. It unnerved her. He was the only person she'd ever known who had the ability to *see* her through the facade she'd been building around herself for years. She said, "You say you own a plantation. Is it like a farm? I've never been on a farm. I've never seen the countryside or smelled fresh, clean air or seen a sky without a smoggy haze. But I'm a quick learner. I could work on your farm when your sister-in-law no longer needs me, couldn't I?"

Jacob smiled. "You needn't worry about that. I have *a farm*, as you call it. In Virginia, my farm is called a plantation. I'm a planter. It's full to the brim with workers. I have so many I hardly know what to do with them all at times."

He grew serious when he next spoke. "This must be scaring you. I'm asking you to step into the unknown, but you will have a bright future, I promise you. My family will be in your debt, and we'll always look after you. I give you my word as a Southern gentleman. You will *never* have to worry about being without funds or dread seeing Madame du Pont or whatever that despicable creature's name was ever again. Say yes…if not for me, for Belle."

Mercy's heart was pounding, yet it felt as light as a feather, she had never felt such happiness or so blessed. She smiled, and her face lit up. "Yes. Yes, Jacob, I accept your offer. It would be an honour to keep your sister-in-law company. I won't let you down, not one little bit."

Chapter Thirty-Five

Mercy slipped the nightgown over her head, pushed her arms into the wrist-length, frilly sleeves, and pulled the soft garment down to her ankles. She looked at the wall clock. She had two hours before she would have to dress for dinner. She would spoil herself with a brief nap. She lay on top of the bunk, rested her head on the soft pillow, and watched the last of the day's grey light peek through the porthole. She sighed, happy and contented after another fulfilling day with her new friend, Belle.

After two weeks at sea, Mercy had found her sea legs and was surprisingly healthy, even during the strongest of winds and roughest of squalls. Belle had given her an entire wardrobe of gowns, coats, shawls, and hats, but Mercy had found herself more at home in the 'britches', shirt, and long woollen coat. She remembered Belle's words; "There's no need to traipse around this ship in cumbersome gowns." Belle had laughed when Mercy brought *corsets* into the conversation. "I declare Mercy, I caint remember the last time I had to wear one of those detestable undergarments on a ship. My gowns are much simpler. They allow me to breathe freely."

Before leaving Liverpool, Belle had been forced to purchase new gowns, nightgowns, and undergarments that would be comfortable right up until the bump on her belly grew to the size of a giant pumpkin.

Mercy smiled fondly. That's what Hendry called Belle nowadays…his pumpkin.

Mercy had grown up with a sewing needle and thread in her fingers and had managed to widen Belle's britches, albeit with other materials. Belle in return had given Mercy more garments than she'd ever owned in her entire life.

As days and nights passed, Mercy found herself more and more at ease with the affluent family, and their crew. This comfortable integration was due in part to Belle's efforts, as she'd made it clear from the first moment they met that Mercy was on board as her companion, not as a servant. Luckily the women had discovered common ground in character.

Mercy thought about the last two weeks. Belle was the best of companions. She was kind and light-hearted, and her stories about growing up in Virginia and on her parents' sprawling plantation entertained both of them for hours.

Belle also spoke about Stone Plantation and its beauty. She was adamant that it was probably *the* best and most prosperous plantation in South Virginia. Mercy had wanted to know more about her new home but was told that she should just wait to be overwhelmed when she saw it with her own eyes.

During her first few days aboard, Mercy had listened but had spoken only when urged to do so. Belle seemed to sense her need for silence and never questioned or forced her to talk about her life. This thoughtfulness was what had drawn Mercy closer to Belle. As days and nights passed, reservations, fear, and self-loathing faded with the island Mercy had left behind.

She smiled again, snuggling now under the sheets and blankets. She was supposed to be the companion. It was her job to make sure Belle was not alone, bored, or tired of being confined. But Belle had turned the tables and had taken it upon herself to entertain Mercy, thus giving her time to come to terms with her recent past quietly. Belle began almost immediately to invite her into a world she'd always dreamed about. She showed her maps and explained routes from country to country. She spoke about her home, saying that Virginia had once been an English settlement in the year, 1607, at a place called, Jamestown. Mercy couldn't imagine how ships managed to sail across this ocean, almost 260 years ago. Mercy also found out that red-skinned people lived there. They were called Indians. Black slaves, called Negros, *did* exist after all and were very important to the white fokes who lived in Virginia.

Belle described Morocco's and Tunisia's great souks and the Atlas mountain range, the Portuguese coastline and the Strait of Gibraltar, as well as Spain's eastern coast. Mercy hadn't even heard of some of the countries and was in awe of the sheer size of the world.

Belle's parents were alive and well, as far as Belle knew. They adored her and she them, but she was sure that they would never fully forgive her for making a decision that was both selfish and incomprehensible in their eyes. "I thought my parents were going to have a seizure when I told them of my plans. They threatened to lock me up in chains and have my marriage annulled. It was unheard of. Everyone frowned upon my decision, even my brothers, who always knew I was a not quite the Southern lady I should have been. They sure didn't mind when I climbed trees with them and threw apples from the highest branches when we were children. Oh no; that was all great fun until I became a woman. Then it was, 'Talk like a lady, don't show your ankles, don't walk too fast, and don't run.' Men don't take kindly to women who talk too much and know too much. Why, you would have thought I'd turned into an entirely different creature the moment I grew breasts!"

Mercy pictured Belle in her mind. She was of small build and had fair hair. Her skin had darkened with the wind, rain, and sunny days at sea. She had a naturally friendly face, which was more interesting than beautiful, but Mercy thought she had beauty in spades. It was in her smile, her animated expressions, and her eyes that lit up and shone like beacons whenever she spoke about Hendry.

She recalled Belle's words, so profound and filled with emotion. "I'm the luckiest woman alive. When I was home, my days were filled with picnics, balls, and parties, but none of those grand occasions meant anything to me if Hendry was not present. Now, should he not be with me, my life's blood would stop pumping, a summer's day would chill me, and I would be as the dead, without reason or means to breathe. I love him so much, Mercy. I hope you're as lucky as me one day because there's no greater joy than loving and being loved. Hendry is a wonderful man. He's the reason I spend my life on a ship and why I'll always be by his side, wherever he goes. There's no money and no amount of comforts to equal a full heart."

Belle was the epitome of what Mercy had always imagined an older sister to be: caring, affectionate, and protective.

Mercy thought about Julia often, but instead of picturing the closeness they had shared, all she remembered now was the coldness and disgust. Yes; disgust had been reflected in Julia's eyes. Julia had saved her life, and Mercy would always be grateful to her for that, but Julia had also taught her that friendship could be fickle.

Mercy's peaceful thoughts of Belle and her new life to come had been interrupted by memories she would rather forget. She rose from the bed and poured herself a glass of water, drinking every drop without pause and panting afterwards.

She sat on top of the bunk this time with her legs crossed, elbows atop them, and fists holding up her chin. Belle was not Julia. Belle was honest, and Mercy was drawn to that honesty. She remembered the moment she too had lowered her guard and had let the details of her life spring forth like gushing water. They had been sitting in Belle's cabin, talking about England. Belle told her that she was not too fond of Liverpool but yearned to visit London, and then she had asked Mercy to describe the capital.

Belle now knew every tiny detail about her life, and Mercy wasn't sorry, not one little bit. She had stumbled at first when describing the day of her birth, as told to her by Grandpa Carver. But because of Belle's understanding, she no longer felt the shame that had followed her throughout her life. Mercy realised now that she could think about her parents without feeling she had to banish them into some dark corner of her mind.

Belle was the only person she'd ever met who had urged her to think kindly and fondly of Thomas Carver. There was no shame, Belle told her, in loving someone so much that you wanted to die with them. She had added that she could not envisage living without Hendry and that she understood Mercy's father's anguish. Belle added, that in her opinion, the act of suicide was a selfish and cowardly act, but the shameful act would be to marry a man or woman one didn't love.

Mercy had then decided to tell her everything, from her secretly arranged marriage to Big Joe to the awful day at St Paul's when her life changed forever. Belle's tears were comforting, as was her rage, and at times, disbelief. Mercy omitted the murder and fire from her story, for she believed that even Belle, the most understanding of people, would not want a murderess as a friend.

A tap on the door jolted Mercy from her thoughts, and she climbed off the bunk. Dinner was not for another hour or so. She prayed that nothing was wrong with Belle or the baby. She cracked the door open, hiding her body behind it, and showed just one eye to the person on the other side of it.

A crewman stood there and bowed slightly. "Good evening, miss. This note is from Mr Stone…Mr Jacob Stone. He asked me to wait for your reply."

"I'll just be a minute," Mercy told him.

She closed the door and leant her back against it. Her heart was thumping at the mention of Jacob's name. She tried all day, every day, not to think about Jacob, yet he was always in her thoughts. She wanted to be near him, to gaze into his perfect face, to feel the strange vibrations that connected her to him somehow when he was near, and to hear his comforting soft, Southern drawl.

She understood Belle's need for Hendry, for she felt the same way about Jacob. He had been distant since she'd been on board. She knew by his frequent absences from the dinner table that he had absolutely no interest in her. He was, as far as she could tell, going out of his way to avoid her.

She stared at the envelope and wanted to tear it open, yet she hesitated. She had no idea why Jacob would be writing to her. Being captivated by him was not a satisfying or pleasant feeling. She felt like a prisoner yearning for a guard to bring food to sustain her, though when he did, it was never enough. She was left wanting more. She found these new and intense feelings unnerving, for they were exactly the feelings Belle had described when talking about Hendry.

When Jacob was present, Mercy's world lit up. Time flew so fast she barely had time to live and enjoy the moment. There had been nights when he'd declined to have dinner with his family. She'd sat at the table, wishing for the conversation to cease, the meal to be over, and a quick exit so to sleep and awaken the next morning with hopes of seeing Jacob on deck. She didn't know if she loved him, but she did recognise that her insatiable need to be near him had led her on an unhealthy path that left her both mystified and frustrated.

She pulled herself up straight and mumbled angrily. She had once again let her mind wander and had left the poor man waiting outside. She pulled the note out of the envelope and took a deep breath.

My dear Miss Mercy,

Dinner has been cancelled. Belle and Hendry have decided to eat alone and retire early. I wonder if you would do me the honour of dining with me in my cabin. Dinner will be served at seven o'clock. I would very much like to talk to you.

I am at your service,
Jacob

Mercy's hand shook as she once again cracked open the door. The crewman was standing patiently and bowed again at the appearance of her one eye.

"Please tell Mr Jacob I will be there on time," she gave her verbal reply.

"Yes, miss. I'll go inform him, and then I'll come back and fetch you. A body can get lost here if it don't know where it's going," he drawled in the now-familiar Southern accent.

Mercy thanked him, and he left. He was right. She didn't know where Jacob's cabin was. She had only been inside three cabins and had seen many more doors and stairwells to the lower decks. It could be anywhere.

She took some deep breaths and ran to the small hand mirror. She picked it up and looked at her flushed face and dishevelled hair. There was no time to pin her hair up or paint her face, but there was time to pick out a gown and at least brush her hair into some order. She was going to eat with Jacob and might even be alone with him. She didn't know what he wanted to talk about. Whatever his reasons, he had left her innards in a twisted knot and her whole body shaking like a blob of jelly.

Chapter Thirty-Six

Jacob shuffled the plates and wine glasses around the small table for the umpteenth time, uncommonly nervous and unsure of what tonight's outcome would be. Mercy would either make him a very happy man or she would spurn his advances, in which case, she would also destroy his dreams. He had thought about this moment the entire day. Would she accept his invitation? Would he have the courage to tell her that he loved her? The last thing he wanted to do was scare her or put her in a situation where she felt trapped. He was well aware that the last time she'd been alone with a man in a room was the night she'd been taken upstairs in the du Pont mansion. She'd never spoken about it. He had questioned Belle as to Mercy's well-being, but Belle knew nothing, or if she did, she was not talking to him about it.

He'd fought Mercy every dang day, trying to avoid being too close to her, not wanting to look into those eyes or feel the blood inside him boil up when she was near him. No woman had ever gotten under his skin like this. Sure, women had brought out his primal urges. But Mercy? She had captured him, body, heart, and soul. He'd found the strength to do the right thing and stay away from her. He watched her from a respectful distance. But the time had come to lay his cards on the table and declare what was in his heart. He was man enough to admit that his initial feelings for her had not wavered, if anything, they had intensified.

She was more precious to him with each day that passed. The black rings around her eyes had gone, and the light in her eyes was, if possible, brighter. Her cheeks had a healthy glow, and she had filled out, leaving the gaunt, haunted look behind in Liverpool.

He had also come to see her true character. She was lively and talkative. Even her voice seduced him with accent and words, which at times made no sense to him or anyone else on board. She was desperate for knowledge. Every time he saw her, she was holding a book in her hands like a prized possession. Belle urged Mercy to read and write; she'd had a very limited education and wanted to better herself, she'd informed Belle. She was, as he'd always known, full of spirit and pride.

Jacob smiled. Mercy's efforts to speak like Belle were amusing, but he suspected that her speech exercises were important to her. She'd admitted to all of them one night at dinner that she was happy to be leaving her country behind and didn't care if she ever saw it again. Jacob wondered if Mercy's desire to sound like a Southern woman was about her desire to fit in or if, in fact, it was an attempt to wipe out her past; one he knew nothing about.

Belle already loved Mercy, and for this reason, so did Hendry. Jack and Isaac were becoming fond of her natural good humour, her desire to be helpful to Belle in any way possible, and her genuine interest in America's history. Mercy endeared herself to everyone because of her ability to laugh at herself, and her tinkling laughter was infectious.

Pouring rich red wine into a small goblet, he once again tried to make sense of his feelings. At first, he'd been intrigued by her silence. He'd felt a fatherly…no, he couldn't say fatherly, more a brotherly need to protect her. Even brotherly was a stretch now.

He got up and paced to the door and back, and to the door again. He then sat at the table and moved the condiments a couple of inches to the right. The stakes were high. He had fallen in love with her, but she had given him no reason to believe she returned his feelings.

Tonight he would know for sure. He had to know one way or another before the ship docked in Virginia. He would go through hell for her. He would take the inevitable shitstorm, as Hendry called it. She would ruin his reputation, and he'd be cussed by all who knew him. He didn't care. He finally admitted this too. He loved her, everything about her. He wanted her, not for a day, a week, or a year. He needed her in his life, for he sure as hell couldn't imagine her not being in it.

Mercy Carver had stolen his heart. If she felt as he did, their union would destroy his relationships with some of the most affluent people in South Virginia. Elizabeth's Southern pride would be crushed. Her heart? He didn't know what was in her heart. All he knew for certain was she was delighted at the thought of becoming mistress of Stone Plantation.

He knew Elizabeth well. She had the same lifelong ambition as all the other Southern ladies he knew. Their need for power and status was inbred. Her gaggle of brothers and bullish father would try to destroy him socially. But Stone Plantation was a force to be reckoned with, and the Stone family name was powerful in its own right.

Elizabeth and her family would not take kindly to being left at the altar, but he would accept their insults and attempts to excommunicate him from society. He would accept everything that life threw at him if Mercy was by his side and if she returned his love.

Mercy arrived at exactly seven o'clock, dressed in a red silk gown that had tiny buttons from the square neckline to the waist. Her hair glistened with health and flowed to her waist in waves. Just a hint of red covered her lips.

Jacob opened the door and dismissed the crewman. He kissed Mercy's hand. She gave a small curtsy, as she had been taught by Parker. "Good evening, Jacob," she said.

"Hello, Miss Mercy. You look lovely," Jacob said, ushering her inside. "I'm happy you decided to join me. It's not much, just some cold meats and cheese. But the bread is fresh, and we can have a drop of wine. Does that sound good?"

Mercy smiled, trying to hide her nervousness. "It sounds lovely. I'm hungry," she told him. As always, the sight of him sent her into a state of girlish stupidity. She hovered by the door and watched him pull the chair out for her to sit.

Once seated, she clasped her hands on her lap and followed him with her eyes until he sat down beside her. She suddenly wondered if she was up to the task of being alone with him. She hoped that he would do all the talking, at least to begin with, because at this present moment she found herself without a single thing to say.

Jacob served the meat and poured red wine into her goblet. She looked at it for few seconds and then gulped it down in an attempt to settle her nerves. Her eyes watered. She spluttered and coughed as its warmth hit the back of her throat. When it had cleared, she apologised.

Jacob laughed softly and poured water into a glass. He handed it to her, still smiling. "Maybe you should wash that down with a little water. Wine can bite you when you least expect it. It can kick you like a mule. I don't want to have to carry you back to your cabin."

"It tastes so nice, blimey, it's as smooth as milk!"

He laughed again. "How are you? You do look better. The ocean and salty air seem to suit you. Belle sure is happy to have you with her. Do you like my family?" The words tumbled out.

Mercy wondered which question she should answer first. "I do love this sea air. It's so fresh and not at all like the smelly water in London. And I like your family very much. Everyone on board has been so kind to me. You look so like your brother, yet he's very different." She pushed that thought through her mouth and blushed.

"Oh?" Jacob said, raising an eyebrow and giving her a quizzical look.

"What I mean is…he's quiet, and he's gentle…not that you're not gentle. He just seems..."

"He doesn't talk as much as me? He's not as loud? He's a little more reserved? You're probably right. But he wasn't always the quiet one."

"Tell me about him," Mercy said, wanting to shut up.

"Tell you about my brother? Hmm, let me see…well, we're close in age, and I consider him a good brother and friend. He loves the sea. He's good at what he does, and he'll make a great father. When I look at him now, I see a contented man who doesn't want for anything as long as Belle's by his side. He reminds me of my mother. Hendry and I were youngsters when she passed, but I remember that she was loyal. She loved my father to distraction.

"Hendry is a lot like her in many ways. But don't be fooled. I don't believe you are seeing the same Hendry I saw a year ago. Even I am seeing him in a different light on this voyage."

"Why?" Mercy asked.

"Well, for starters, he has Jack to share the load of captaincy. He's tired, although he won't admit it. Two years at sea is a long time, and he's desperate to get Belle home. I believe this baby will be good for both of them. Rest and some time on land is just what they need. I'm happy to have them at Stone Plantation; it'll be like old times."

"They're very much in love, aren't they?" Mercy said.

"Yes, they are. Hendry would never admit this to anyone, but I saw them both on the day they met, and I think my brother was smitten by Belle after one conversation."

"Do you think love can happen that fast?" Mercy asked.

"Yes, I believe it can. You only have to look at them to know that they're meant to be together. Maybe God has a divine plan for all of us."

"What do you mean?" Mercy bit her lip.

"I'm not an overly religious man, but I believe that a higher power has a hand in mapping our lives to a certain extent. I don't think we're meant to journey through life alone," Jacob said honestly. "I think Hendry and Belle are two halves of a dollar bill…together they're rich, but apart their lives are worth nothing. Have you ever been in love, Mercy?"

Mercy laughed, but it was a sardonic, bitter sound. "No, I was not allowed to meet boys or go out with them for walks or picnics like the other girls in my neighbourhood. My grandparents kept me at home most of the time. I would have got a right slapping if I'd mixed with boys my age."

Jacob's face was filled with confusion. Mercy could almost hear his thoughts. She'd told him that she had no family.

Mercy stared at her food and wondered what Jacob would think about her if he knew the truth about Big Joe, her grandparents, her mother and father. She took a bite of cheese, aware of Jacob's eyes on her. She would have to tell him. Belle already knew; he might already have been told. "Jacob, I lied to you. I do have a family, of sorts."

"Tell me," Jacob urged with soft encouragement.

When she finished speaking, Jacob was holding her hand, and she was wiping a stray tear from the corner of her eye.

She looked at his fingers entwined with her own and realised she had been so consumed by her story that she'd missed the moment he'd reached out and touched her. She pulled her hand away and picked up her fork as an excuse to free it. His touch was overpowering, and his pity was unbearable. She failed to see the hurt in his eyes and said, "Jacob, please don't pity me. Everything has a place, and my story belongs to the past. I won't forget where I came from; I'm not ashamed of being poor. I don't hate my father for abandoning me. But I am sorry I lied to you about not having any family. Please forgive me. I couldn't let you send me back to London; I just couldn't."

Jacob nodded. For a moment there was a comfortable silence between them.

Mercy felt lighter, as though a weight had been lifted. Some lies and secrets had been brought out into the open. She'd been compelled to tell him the truth, even if he now despised her. She looked at him then, and to her surprise saw that he was smiling gently. He wasn't disappointed, and she could tell that he wasn't angry either. She smiled and dismissed the previous conversation by saying, "Please tell me about the cargo you're carrying. I want to know everything."

Jacob talked animatedly for an hour or so. Mercy drank in the sound of his voice and gazed unwaveringly into his dark eyes sparkling in the candlelight. They appeared to be sitting a little closer together, and she might have imagined it, but she was sure he'd pulled his chair a little closer to her.

She heard about all the spices and commodities that filled the holds and listened to him talk of their destinations. Now and then she asked a question and hoped that she didn't sound like a silly girl without a smart thought in her head.

She was happy, but time was speeding by, and she didn't want the night to end. Life was coursing through her. Her heartbeat and breathing were normal, but she felt as though tonight were the first day of her life when breath poured forth outside a mother's womb. She had never felt this alive.

She wondered if she should offer to leave, but then remembered that he'd asked her here because he wanted to speak to her about something. She watched him play with his thoughts and without thinking laid her hand on top of his. "Jacob, you wanted to talk to me. Is there bad news?"

"No, there's no bad news." He smiled. "To tell you the truth, I just needed to see you. I think about you, Mercy, and I wanted to be alone with you."

Mercy's eyes widened. This was not what she'd expected him to say.

"Am I scaring you?" he asked.

"No…I didn't know…I thought you were hiding from me. I'm not sure I understand what you're saying?"

He stroked her fingers, squeezing them gently with his strong hands. Mercy's heart began to race, and she felt her cheeks burn. She looked into his face, and her eyes were drawn to his mouth. She lifted them and looked into his eyes. She sucked in her breath and found it suspended and difficult to exhale. Jacob continued to stare at her without changing his expression. Her mind grappled with what she now knew to be true: Jacob desired her. He wanted her, maybe, as much as she wanted him. His eyes were watering, and he was unable to speak, just as she was unable to tear her eyes from his face. The only difference between them, she realised now, was that in the last two weeks he'd hidden his feelings, whereas she'd been a fumbling wreck every time she'd been near him.

Jacob sighed and took a deep breath. "Miss Mercy, you've upset my neat and organised world. Dammit, woman, you've turned it upside down and inside out, and it's time you knew this."

He moved closer until she could feel his breath and the tip of his nose tickling her face like a feather. "May I kiss you?" he whispered.

Time stood still. Mercy's heart was racing, and she swallowed a lump stuck in her throat. She was about to be kissed for the very first time, and she desperately wanted his lips on her mouth. It was almost as though she already knew how wonderful it would feel. A strange sensation was covering her body like a shroud of light. Her skin tingled, and she felt a small ache between her thighs. It was a strange and annoying sensation. She didn't know what it was, but her heartbeat was quickening even more. She stared into his eyes and nodded. "Yes, Jacob. I would like that."

His lips touched hers, and she closed her eyes. She felt the softness, the teasing magic that caused her to ache for something more profound. His tongue slid across the outline of her mouth. Then it slithered inside and connected with her wet tongue. The burning sensation on her cheeks heightened as his kisses grew more ardent and intrusive. Her mouth was open, and she let out soft moans of pleasure as he got to know every inch of it, inside and out. Waves of pleasure crawled up and down her body. The ache between her thighs was becoming uncomfortable. She needed more than his kisses. How she knew what she wanted was a mystery, but her body was uncovering secrets she had never known existed. Her mind had no part to play in what was happening. It was as though a primal sense had been awakened inside her, and all she had to do was follow it. If he stopped now, she thought, she would quite possibly die with unspent desire.

He laid his hand on her gown's bodice, and she allowed him to slip his fingers inside it. He cupped her breast and softly squeezed her nipple. She felt it grow hard and moaned again. Then she pulled away from him and stood up.

Jacob's eyes were filled with hurt and guilt. She saw his disappointment and bent down to kiss him. She stood up straight again, unafraid, eyes shining seductively. She undid the tiny buttons on the front of her gown. One sleeve slipped off her shoulder, and the other followed.

Jacob came to stand in front of her. Her dress was sitting at her waist. Her breasts were partially hidden by a cotton bodice, which Jacob removed tentatively from her shoulders and arms. His eyes never left her face, as he took off his evening coat. She grabbed the bottom of his shirt with her two hands. He raised his arms, and she pulled it over his head. Her gown fell to the floor. Her undergarment followed, leaving only bloomers to hide her nakedness. His hands caressed her shoulders and then slid down her body to her hips. He tugged gently at her bloomers and drew them to her knees. They fell to her ankles, and she was left standing naked before him.

No words were spoken between them. No words were needed. For a second, she thought that maybe this would be a mistake that she would never be able to fix, but she didn't care about mistakes or what he might or might not think about her behaviour. She had never wanted anything so much in her life.

Jacob kissed her neck, gently pushing her hair away. He undid his waist buttons, and his trousers fell to his ankles. He stepped out of them and led her by the hand to the bunk.

She lay down and realised that she had no clue what to do next. But when Jacob explored her body with his hands, mouth, and tongue, there was no need for lessons of any kind.

He came to lie on top of her, one elbow on the bed holding his stomach just inches from her own. Then he arrived at the place where Madame du Pont's cotton finger had been. The image was dismissed. She spread her legs wider. He stroked her, and she thought she might scream with pleasure.

He guided his manhood inside her, and as it pushed its way up, her body suddenly jerked backwards, and she screamed.

Jacob stopped moving. He stopped breathing, devouring her with his eyes. They were questioning and surprised. "Mercy, you're…"

"Yes. I'm a virgin," she whispered. "But please, Jacob, please don't stop. I'll die if you leave me now."

"My God, I didn't know…"

"Sshh, please love me, Jacob," Mercy begged again.

Jacob's rhythm started gently, slow, and tender, but he kissed her with an even deeper passion than before. She rose and fell with him in perfect harmony, as though she'd been born with the knowledge.

He thrust deep inside her, and now there was no pain. She was floating on air. She felt faint with pleasure, yet still, she hungered for more. She lifted her hips off the bed to meet him and heard herself panting as they moved together faster, and with an urgency she couldn't quite fathom. And then a new and previously undiscovered sensation flashed through her, forcing a loud moan from deep within her throat to echo around the room. She buried her mouth in his shoulder. Her body rose up, suspended in air, and shook with pleasure. Then it slowly descended to lie flat again on the mattress.

She heard him say, "I love you, Mercy," just before his body tensed, he shuddered, and his seed exploded inside her. He moaned loudly too before she felt his body relax, and then he lay spent, partially on top of her, as they both tried to regain control of their breathing.

This is love, Mercy thought at that moment. It was not what she had expected at all. There was no discomfort or pain throughout; that had lasted but a few seconds. There was no shame or disgust in the act. There was only pleasure; so much pleasure, there were no words to describe it. Their souls had joined, loving and worshipping each other's bodies. She was no longer a virgin, and her heart was no longer her own. She belonged to Jacob Stone now in both body and soul, and she was changed forever.

Jacob caressed her face, and she kissed him again. She faced him, feeling drowsy and limp. She wanted to say so much to him. She wanted to tell him that she'd been the one responsible for murder and fire, for then there would be no more secrets between them. Instead, she lay contented in his arms, feeling his hands stroke her hair. Her secrets would remain hidden for a while longer. She would not and could not break the beautiful spell he'd cast…not tonight.

Chapter Thirty-Seven

Jacob opened his eyes just as the sun was peeking its head above the eastern horizon. He held Mercy in his arms, listened to her soft breathing for a moment or two, and then slid slowly and quietly to the edge of the bed. He pulled back the sheet and saw bloodstains. He lay on his back, stared up at the ceiling, and captured the previous night in his mind.

Mercy had given him the greatest of gifts. She had come to him willingly and without reservations. For him, she was the perfect lover. He was now in unknown territory, filled with love and passion.

His mind was in turmoil. He wondered if he should despise himself even a little for taking her innocence when he held a secret that would most likely crush her. Would she have given herself to him had she known about Elizabeth? No, she was proud, too damn proud for her own good, he believed. She'd been willing to walk the streets of Liverpool without a cent rather than accept the money he'd offered her. That was the measure of the woman.

He fought now against what he knew to be true. He could try all damn day to tell himself no harm had been done. No matter how many times he said those words, he *had* betrayed her trust. That was a fact.

Mercy, the most honest woman he'd ever met, would not have gone near him knowing he belonged to another woman. In fact, he felt sure that had she been informed of his situation, her rejection of him would have been accompanied with a slap to his face.

He was feeling conflicted. Should he tell her about Elizabeth and about his plans to call off the wedding? He could use all his powers of persuasion to convince her that all would be well and that patience was required on both their parts until he sorted this mess out. Or should he take the coward's way out and say nothing? He could tell the others to keep quiet and make sure Mercy didn't find out about Elizabeth until after he broke off the engagement. Belle, Hendry, Isaac, and Jack were not stupid; they knew how he felt about Mercy, and they would not betray him. But would they respect him or admonish him for his deceit?

He thought about their lovemaking and felt himself harden again. Had he been wrong to presume she'd been with a man, willingly or by force, at least once? Christ Almighty, she'd been imprisoned in a whorehouse for weeks! It was only natural to think she'd been used, broken in, or raped by a customer, or by one or both of those bastards he'd found trying to set fire to the other women.

He got up, dressed, and found his usual tray with coffee pot and cup on the floor outside in the passageway. He poured himself a cup and sat at the small table, watching Mercy sleep on, despite the aroma of fresh coffee filling the cabin.

Her face held a peaceful expression. He could almost see an aura of light surrounding her. Being in love was not an everyday experience for him. He felt like he'd been put under a spell.

He laughed at himself. He was seeing lights! Next, she'd be floating on air like an angel. Her face was angelic, and he marvelled at her resolve in overcoming her terrifying experience.

His thoughts raced back to the du Pont mansion, and he felt the familiar, burning rage grow inside him. Mercy had been upstairs for at least a good half hour before the first screams and the first sign of smoke. What had happened in that bedroom? Why had the old man not taken her?

He tried to remember the smallest of details from that night. Mercy had been semi-naked when he'd found her. She wore nothing but a torn corset. It was covered in blood…but whose blood? How had she escaped the man? What had happened between them? Where did the man go when fire struck the building? Had he run like all the other cowards?

An image jumped into his mind like a flash of light, and he tried to resist it; the burned body on the bed. Was it possible that the blood on Mercy's body belonged to that corpse? Had she refused him, fought him off? Mercy was sweet and gentle. Violence was not in her nature. But against all the odds, she'd left the mansion a virgin, and for the life of him, he didn't know how *that* was possible.

Mercy opened her eyes and saw Jacob sitting at the table, head down, writing something in a log book.

"Good morning," she said sleepily.

"Mercy, you're awake." Jacob smiled warmly. "I have some coffee. It's still warm. Can I pour you a cup?"

"Yes, please. I'm beginning to like coffee."

"As much as wine?" Jacob teased.

Marcy laughed, sat up, and pulled the sheet up to her chin, holding it in place with one hand.

Jacob smiled again and raised an eyebrow in amusement. "Put this on. You'll be more comfortable." He handed a shirt to her, and she slipped it over her head. The sleeves were far too long, and he rolled them up for her. She then took a full cup of coffee from him and savoured every warm sip. She was still smiling. She was unable to stop smiling.

Jacob sat on the edge of the bed and hated the thought of what he was about to do to her. The questions invading his mind had to be answered. An incredible future together awaited but Mercy's secrets would grow like weeds and eventually destroy her and everything that was beautiful and pure about her. Those secrets would sit between them, like a giant chasm.

He began, hesitantly at first, "Mercy, are you happy?"

"What does my face tell you?" she asked him, grinning.

"It tells me that you feel the same way about me as I do about you. I love you, Mercy. I've never said those words before to any woman, but I want to say them every single day to you from now on."

"I love you too. I think I've loved you since the moment we met, although I didn't truly know what love was until you kissed me. I'm very happy. I've never known such joy."

"You know I'll never let you go. You're stuck with me now. But I believe we need to get something out in the open, just between us. No one else needs to know anything about it."

"Of course," Mercy said, feeling uneasy. "What is it?"

"It's about Liverpool and Madame du Pont," Jacob said.

Mercy panicked. She was reading his mind, for she knew what was about to come. She dropped her eyes, unable to look at him. "Jacob, you're scaring me."

"Look at me," Jacob urged. "I love you, and that will never change now. You have my whole heart. I will never allow anyone to hurt you. But I have to know what happened to you in that bedroom before the fire. I saw you go up the stairs with a man, and that's why I thought…"

"You thought he'd taken me?"

"Yes, that's what I presumed. I guess I was wrong. But you were with him for quite a while, and men didn't go to that mansion to have polite conversations."

Mercy's face turned a deep red. She opened her mouth a few times but was unable to articulate her words. He was watching her, and she wanted the bed to swallow her. She couldn't tell him. "Jacob, please don't make me. I don't want to talk about it or even think about it, ever. Don't make me say something that will cause you to hate me. Please, Jacob. I beg you. Ask me anything else about my life, and I'll tell you, but not about that night."

Jacob was torn. She was in pain, and he was the cause. "Mercy, please trust me. I could never hate you, and I don't want to force you to relive that terror. But if secrets stand between us, they will eventually lead to our downfall. They will eat away at you. They'll reside inside your beautiful soul. They will turn it dark and will corrupt all the happiness I aim to give you. If you don't share this with me, I will always wonder, and you will always be hiding."

Mercy felt the first tear fall. She was going to lose him. He wouldn't want a murderess by his side. He would be disgusted by her cruelty. She had knowingly put everyone in that house at risk to fulfil her own purpose, and she already accepted that she was going to hell when she died.

He took the cup from her trembling hands and then held her to his chest. "My darling, just say it. Tell me what happened and then we'll both let it go."

Mercy heard herself cry. The tears had come so suddenly she couldn't stop them, no matter how much she tried. She was sobbing so hard she couldn't speak, even if she wanted to. He rocked her in his arms. Finally, the tears subsided just enough for her to breathe and find her voice.

"I went into the bedroom with him. He was mean. He shouted at me to undress. He was disgusting to me, and I felt sick. I was angry and knew I couldn't go through with it.

"I thought about jumping out of the window. Death would have been welcome." She took another deep breath.

"Go on." Jacob kissed her forehead.

"The man slapped me, and he tried to get his thing inside me. I couldn't let him do it. God help me, but I couldn't! I hit him with a candlestick. I wanted to get him off me. The candle set fire to the bed, and he was still on top of me, so I smashed his head with it again and again and again! I was so terribly scared…I didn't mean to kill him, and then the fire grew so quickly. My gown was on fire, so I ripped it off and threw it at the curtains. At first, I wanted to die in the fire, because I knew if I were found *she* would cut my throat. Then I remembered Julia. I left that man on the bed. I set fire to the hallway. Julia found me and dragged me to another room, and you found us. So now you know. I killed a man."

Her tears exploded once again. This time they were even more heart-wrenching. She had determined to keep this to herself until the day she died. She had thought she could bury it, along with everything else that had happened. But the floodgates had opened, and she was drowning in pent-up sorrow and regret.

Mercy expected Jacob to push her away. She thought she would see hatred. Instead, she lifted her tear-stained eyes and saw love; the same love that had been present before she'd admitted to murder.

"Jacob...say something," she sobbed after a long silence.

He wiped then kissed both her eyes. "Hush, Mercy. Please don't cry anymore. It's all right; everything is going to be all right. You were a prisoner. You were being forced and threatened. You had every right to defend yourself. The man with you probably didn't know he was forcing you, or maybe he did. Either way, he had no right to hit you or to enforce you to do what he wanted in the face of your objections. He should have left and taken his anger out on that wicked du Pont woman."

"But I took his life...I took a life," Mercy still sobbed.

"Yes, you did, and you will have to live the rest of your life knowing that. But I need you to promise me that you'll forgive yourself. You're not a murderess. You were a victim. You were protecting your body. I doubt you were even in your right mind after all you'd been through." He kissed her again.

"And as for the fire…it was an accident, to begin with. You made it spread, and though you might not believe this now, by doing that, you saved your life and the lives of other innocent girls held with you. They're all free now. No one died, apart from the man who would have raped you and beat you. Julia went home because of you. And all those other women did too."

"But I could have killed everyone…"

"But you didn't," he reminded her.

Mercy was still sobbing, and every now and again she gulped for air. Her mind was digesting his words. He didn't blame her or hate her, and he was still holding her. She felt as though a pressing weight had been alleviated. Guilt would remain with her. She would never shed it, but she could now learn to live with it and pray for the man she'd killed. She would say sorry to him every day for the rest of her life. And it was true that she had set the other women free. She hoped and believed Madame du Pont would never be able to kill or hurt another girl. The madam was ruined.

"Jacob, why did you go to such a place?" Mercy found herself asking without prior thought.

Jacob played with her hair. Every now and then he wiped one of her errant teardrops. He said candidly, "Whorehouses have been around since the beginning of time. Prostitution is probably the oldest employment that exists. Women have always followed armies into battle and were available to soldiers for money at the end of a day's fighting. The greatest civilisations, the Egyptians, Greeks, and Romans paid for sex, and women were not ashamed of what they were. But I swear to you, had I known the truth about Madame du Pont, I would have reported her to the highest authority. I would never, never take a woman without her consent. Mercy, in all the years I've been going there, not once did I see sadness in any woman's eyes…until you! Why did you not speak out?"

"I watched her slice a young girl's throat open!" Mercy shouted now. "We were all terrified…I was so very very scared."

Jacob crushed her to him. "I feel your pain, my darling," he said. "I'll help you forget. We will never speak of this again, but I swear to you, if I ever cross paths with du Pont, I'll kill her."

Chapter Thirty-Eight

South Virginia, December 1860

Mercy and Belle had been on the road for a little under three hours, travelling in a leather-seated carriage with copious amounts of blankets flung over them to keep the bulk of the bitterly cold, still air from penetrating their skin and bones. They were accompanied by four outriders: two crewmen from the ship and two of Jacob's overseers from Stone Plantation.

After leaving the Norfolk Port area, they drove down Main Street, to a small harbour and dock. There, the party boarded a packet boat, which ferried them across the Elizabeth River, docking in Portsmouth's North Landing.

Afterwards, they had encountered a few shallow rivers, fords, and streams, but to the west of Portsmouth, lay a drier landscape. The endless fields were mostly brown, layered with frost, yet every now and again large patches of green coloured the magnificent view that met Mercy's eyes.

She asked Belle about the dense forests, the likes of which she'd never seen. She tried to remember the strange names of the trees: dogwood, beech, and yellowwood. The trees were bare of leaves, for the most part, but even so, to Mercy's London eyes, they were magnificent and breathtakingly beautiful.

Mercy's mouth had been open almost the entire way. Belle had joked that had it been summer, she'd have caught and swallowed a hundred flies by now. But Mercy didn't care how she looked. She was mesmerised with the naturally rugged land and endless sky.

She listened to the menagerie of sounds around her, enhanced by the stillness. The calls of invisible wildlife and birds came from within the dense thickets and swamps. The small rises in the dirt track yielded yet more surprises when the carriage mounted their small peaks.

At times the landscape changed completely and was flat, organised and bordered by white picket fences, which looked dull against the white sky. Open fields were behind the picket fences and were manned by black men and women, who were already beginning to furrow the land under the watchful eyes of white overseers.

Mercy's deep inhalations also amused Belle, but Mercy didn't care about that either. For the first time in her life, she told Belle, she was breathing in sweet, country air, filling her nostrils and lungs with an array of delicate, flowery perfumes she had never before experienced. Belle laughed and told her there were no flowers in mid-December, but Mercy wasn't convinced. She smelled the sweetest of aromas. These perfumes brought to mind her grandmother's story about her father, Thomas, and his dream to live in rural England's pure air. She was fulfilling that dream for him, and she didn't care how stupid she looked.

Mercy looked across at Belle now and saw that she was fast asleep. She took another blanket and covered her friend right up to the chin. Then Mercy continued to take in the breath-taking scenery.

She shivered now, alone with her thoughts. She wasn't particularly cold. The tremors spreading up and down her spine were mainly due to the shock and horror she'd tried to hide from Belle earlier. She'd seen unimaginable poverty on her own streets in South-East London. Young children and adults dying from hunger and disease were everyday occurrences, and she'd learned to harden her heart and dim her sorrow. But she would never forget the cruelty that had met her eyes not five minutes after landing in this beautiful new world.

Belle had seemingly chosen to completely ignore the ebony men and women who were paraded in lines down the Norfolk jetties and into the town. But Mercy had been traumatised and so deeply saddened at the sight of them; she wondered now if she would ever be able to accept this new culture where white people found it entirely reasonable to treat black-skinned folk like animals.

She first noticed the shackles that imprisoned this race. They were bound at the ankles, wrists, waists, and necks. The irons on their half-dressed bodies dug into their skin, leaving bloodied streams. The shackles looked heavy and cumbersome, like thick bracelets, attached to inch-wide chains that jangled loudly with each step taken. Some of the wretched creatures with iron necklaces suffered deep dents around the neck, which were crusted and infected, making the dried blood pale pink in colour.

The men and women were hunched over, weighted down, and more miserable-looking than any stray cat or dog she'd ever seen on Southwark's streets.

She pitied the women who were without most of their clothing, leaving some of them bare-breasted and devoid of any dignity. Despite assurances from Belle that they would be given more suitable clothing, at some point, they still reminded her of her own humiliation on that first day in Liverpool, when Madame du Pont had displayed her insatiable need to humiliate and abuse young, naked bodies. It had been days since Mercy had thought about that mad, evil woman. She refused to allow her into her thoughts now, so she imagined her dead.

Mercy had kept her tongue still for the most part, knowing that this was Virginia's culture and tradition. She hated the very idea of enslaving a man, woman, or child, but Jacob had forewarned her that she would have to accept it. Here in the New World, things were very, very different.

Her obsession with slavery had begun one night when she'd listened to a conversation between Jacob and Hendry. They had decided that on arrival, Mercy and Belle would head straight to Stone Plantation, whilst the men would remain in Norfolk for four days, first to unload the ship, and then to purchase four new house slaves.

Later that night, she lay in bed, wrapped in Jacob's arms, and asked him why he needed to buy Negros. She remembered the conversation well, every single word, and was still appalled and sadly disappointed at Jacob's reasoning and politics.

"Slaves are an integral part of life in the South," he told her. "Without them there would be no cotton, peanuts, or tobacco grown. These are the wheels that turn the great Southern economy and are highly profitable export businesses."

Mercy had argued that it still didn't give him or anyone else the right to buy and sell a person, just like her and just like him apart from skin colour, no matter what race or circumstances. She was met with a fierce and heated defence.

"Mercy, niggers, are not like us," Jacob began, patiently as always. "Their brains don't function in the same way as white fokes, and they have very little intelligence. They wouldn't understand or appreciate what freedom is all about. Their minds wouldn't be able to function without their master's direction. And to be fair, all we've done in the last two hundred years is take them from the African jungles, where, no doubt, they spent all day dangling from trees and eating each other over open fires. We freed them from that life. It's as simple as that."

Mercy parried, "But maybe they are clever. Maybe they could read and write better than me if given a chance. How do you know what's inside their brains if you don't ask or test them?"

"They know how to sing and dance. They can cook too, and very well, but it took our great-great-grandmothers to teach them. They make babies the same way we do, but that's about it," he said.

Mercy grew angry at his attitude and refused to check herself. "Jacob, you look down your nose at them the way our vulgar rich aristocrats look down their snotty, bleedin' noses at us commoners in England. I don't like hearing you talk like this. You're kind and gentle, not cruel and…and all snotty like a dandy."

Jacob laughed and then kissed her. "Look, I know this is all going to be new to you, but we're not monsters. I don't whip my slaves unless they run away, and then I have to make an example of them. I even allow them to marry, and that's rare where I live. That's very rare, Mercy. I've come to recognise that they do have feelings, just like us. But if they decide to marry, they have to be damn sure there's not a whole bunch of piccaninnies running around their feet."

"Piccaninnies?"

"Children, young 'uns. We can't take care of large nigger families, so it's up to them to control their urges."

"Well, that's not fair, is it? No one tells you to control your urges! And what happens if they do have children?"

"Why, I look after them. Some get sold on when they're older. It's evolution mostly. The old die and younger generations take over. We don't drown them at birth." He laughed at her horrified expression. "Mercy, I own my slaves. I paid good money for them. But it doesn't mean I'm a cruel monster. They are my labour force. They eat for free and sleep under a roof for free. Aren't your workhouses just as bad?"

Workhouses had been Mercy's worst nightmare growing up. She'd been threatened time and time again that she'd end up in one if she didn't obey her grandfathers' strict house rules. She frowned. What would her grandparents be thinking right now? She wondered.

Jacob pulled her closer to him. She kissed his bare chest and listened to his breathing. Then he spoke again. "I'm worried about all the talk that's going on, and you need to know why, seeing as how you're going to be a Southern lady. Slavery may seem cruel in your eyes, but without slaves, the South would be destroyed. I didn't like what I heard before I left for England. The great industrial

North believes in its wisdom that slavery should and will be killed off in the very near future, but that's wrong.

"We need to expand slavery into neighbouring states to keep our agricultural industries alive. If we don't, we'll lay waste to land that's been overused. Lincoln and his Republicans in Washington believe we should be freezing out the slave trade entirely. We caint allow that to happen.

"We'll fight to keep our ways if we have to. The Northern politicians with their fine factories and machinery plants think they have the God-given right to tell us what to do. They insult our States' rights and over tax us. They're throwing mud in our faces 'cos without our niggers our lands would be nothing but dirt."

Mercy wanted to argue but unfortunately didn't have a clue about what her argument should be, apart from her objection to the whole barbaric idea of slavery. She decided, therefore, to listen and keep her mouth shut.

Jacob had got out of bed and had poured her some wine. Sadness had crossed his face, followed by anger. She had opened a wound. She'd offered an apology for bringing up a subject she knew nothing about. He'd kissed her and had then told her a story, which would live with her forever.

"Mercy, thirty years ago, there were about twenty thousand nigger slaves in Virginia. Now you're calling them people, but back then a few of them terrified and massacred around sixty of our Virginian neighbours. They were like wild African animals, not people at all.

"Nat Turner was the name of the slave who started the revolt. He came from a plantation near Jerusalem in

Southampton County, not too far from Stone Plantation. According to my father, there were around sixteen thousand people living in the county at that time, and only six thousand were white folks. We had to keep the niggers on a tight leash 'cos they heavily outnumbered us…you understand that, right?"

Mercy nodded. "What happened?"

"Nat Turner was the scourge of the earth, a murdering bastard. He was a carpenter. He learned to read and write, which was illegal to begin with. He wasn't whipped and didn't work in the fields. In fact, he had an easy life, yet his animalistic traits told him that he was supposed to be killing white folks, as many as he could, regardless of age and sex.

"Through reading the Bible, Turner got it into his head that he'd received a calling from God, and that it was his duty to free the slaves. My father was always convinced that Turner had planned his attacks months afore they took place. That was just conjecture at the time and has turned into nothing but myth now. What I do know is that he started his killing spree on a small farm near Cabin Pond. It belonged to the Travis family, who were hard-working and never did harm to a living soul."

"Why did he begin there? What made this Nat Turner want to kill *these* people?" Mercy asked.

"I don't know. I don't think he cared who he killed, as long as they were white. The only orders he gave to his followers were to wipe out as many white folk in the county as possible. I suppose Travis Farm was as good a place as any to start. Turner got there with his nigger friends, and he was the one to climb in the window on the second floor. It was in the dead of night, and the house was asleep. He and his men killed Mr and Mrs Travis with axes and bashed their newborn son's tiny body against the fireplace."

Mercy covered her mouth and mumbled, "Oh my God, that's terrible."

"It was. Then they moved on to killing another twenty or so whites on six other farms. Turner murdered his nine-year-old owner who'd inherited him and who'd treated him decently. Mercy, treating them decent is what I try to do, but you have to know that the more you give them, the more they take advantage of your kindness."

"What happened to Turner? Did he get caught?" Mercy asked, imagining the horror.

"He did, but not before he killed some more people and forced other slaves to join him. Those that didn't want to kill their masters ran into the woods to hide from the violence.

"After Travis Farm and a few others had been ransacked of horses and guns, Turner reached the home of Thomas Barrow. He was a good friend to my granddaddy, Hendry. My father remembered seeing Barrow's dead body and my granddaddy crying like a baby. Barrow was hacked to death, but he was a good soldier right to the end and managed to hold the niggers at bay until his wife escaped to safety.

"During that same day, Turner marched his men on to Jerusalem, the county seat. They turned off onto Barrow's road…Captain Barrow built that road with his bare hands for his neighbours' benefit. Anyway, Turner's men got to Levi Waller's house. He ran a small school and

Turner, that bastard nigger, killed eleven whites there, most of them children.

"By the time the niggers had reached the intersection of Barrow Road, most of the white fokes had gathered to stop him, my grandfather and father included. There were a few shots fired, but not many were injured.

"Turner's men started marching up a long lane that led to a plantation, but when they got there, they came under attack from fokes inside the house. The slaves on that plantation were loyal to their master, and they also attacked Turner's band. He was then on the run, heading Southwards.

"You know, Mercy, the sad thing is that he was responsible later for hundreds of slaves being executed, whether they'd been involved or not. I guess everyone was just so damn angry, and revenge dulled the pain and grief. It wasn't right, and my granddaddy wasn't right for whipping every male nigger on our land, but that's what he did. That's the cold truth.

"Turner was finally caught after months of searching by militias who'd come from as far as Richmond. He'd been hiding in a hole that he'd dug afore the revolt, not far from where he came from. Maybe he knew it would end badly?"

"How did he die?"

"He was hanged by the neck. He confessed to everything he'd done afore they killed him. My granddaddy and father watched his execution. They told Hendry and me the story as soon as we were old enough to understand the difference between whites and niggers.

"I'm not saying that everything we believe in is right, but there have been slaves in Virginia for more than a hundred and fifty years. Like I said, mine live in wooden houses, not holes. They have three meals a day. They sing, dance, and laugh. You'll see that they have their own structured community on my land. There's a few of them who raised me, and I love them like family. Tell me, what do you think would happen to them if they were free?"

"I think they would learn to read and write and become doctors or teachers just as easily as a white person. What do *you* think would happen?" She threw back at him.

"There would be chaos and killings. Half of them would starve or wander until they fell down and died in some backwater swamp. They'd be like tamed animals going back into the wild, unable to adapt..."

"Mercy…Mercy, open your eyes."

Mercy snapped her eyes open, and Jacob's face and voice faded. She would see him in four days, and then he would ask her the most important question of her life. She was going to be his wife. She was sure of it.

"Stone Plantation is just around this next bend in the road," Belle said. "Are you ready to see your new home?"

Chapter Thirty-Nine

Margaret Mallory sat in the lobby belonging to one of the many small Norfolk boarding houses. She already hated the dirty streets of what, to her, was a small town, compared to her Liverpool. Neither could she abide the dust, the noise, the filthy sailors who got drunk every day and night then their falling over and losing consciousness in the street, plus the sounds of sporadic gunfire. She detested the strange slatted half-door entrances into saloons, where men were so loud, and the women had no class. Christ, she missed her opulent surroundings with maids and cooks, and good shops to buy the new wardrobe of clothes and hats that she so desperately wanted and needed.

Her intention to live in a quiet house on the outskirts of Norfolk had been discarded. The desire she had for a small but elegant country house had grown to fever pitch, so much so that she'd employed a Mr Coutts to take her this very morning to look at some properties that were on the plantation belt, not too far from the affluent city of Portsmouth.

Her impatience to leave the boarding house matched her bad temper, and Eddie bore the brunt of it. He sat at another table, and as she watched him devour some bread and cheese, she almost wished she'd left him behind in England. The anger she harboured towards him had grown in the last month, ever since his refusal to come to her bed on the ship. He had a bloody cheek. Sex was the main reason she had bought him his passage, for God's sake!

She continued to stare at him, hating his newfound insolence. “I’m not having sex with you again,” he’d told her. “I’ll have sex with women my own age from now on, and if you don’t like it, you can bugger off. And another thing, if you want me to be at your beck and call like a dog, you’ll have to pay me well for the privilege. I can get a job anywhere in America. I don’t need to put up with you or your high and mighty ways. This is a land of opportunity we’re going to, and there will be lots of possibilities for the likes of me.”

She had never particularly liked Myrtle’s company. Myrtle’s deadpan eyes held the same expression regardless of gentle conversation or heated discussion. But Margaret was beginning to miss her almost as much as Eddie’s body. If only she didn’t need the jumped-up git, she kept thinking, looking at his gob full of food.

Eddie’s official title, Margaret told him, would be that of overseer, but he would also be expected to fetch and carry whatever she needed. She needed him this morning. Mr Coutts would be here any minute, and she didn’t want Eddie to know how much she was spending on a house. No, she decided, he wouldn’t be privy to any more intimate details of any kind. She’d pay him what he wanted, but he *would* be her dog from now on, nothing more.

“Eddie, come over here!” she shouted across the empty dining room.

“Yes, ma’am,” he said. Getting up, he strode cockily towards her.

Margaret liked the new title to fit in with the Americans; *ma’am* had a nice ring to it. It was much better than Mrs Mallory or madam. And it made her sound more like a lady.

"I want you to go to the slave auction today. There's one on this morning. I want four of them niggers by this afternoon."

"But what if you don't find a house? Where are you going to keep four niggers?" Eddie asked.

"I'll get a house; don't you worry about that. And I'll make sure it's mine to move into by the end of the day. I have it on good authority that this is what will happen if I want it to happen, so you just leave that to me. The houses I'm going to see are all empty, and that's all you need to know.

"Bring them niggers here, but not before five o'clock and, Eddie, if you have to tie them to trees outside town until then, do it. I'll be all sorted by five. Do you hear me?"

"I hear you, but it all seems a bit quick to me," Eddie said, scratching his head.

"Shut it. I know what I'm doing. I've been assured the paperwork is done quickly here. I'll worry about furnishings tomorrow. I'm not staying another night in this filthy place," she told him haughtily.

"Well, if you're sure. And what type of niggers are you looking for?"

"How the bloody hell do I know? I've never had one before. Just get a selection. Two women and two men, and make sure none of the men come with a woman they're fond of. I don't want them having sex together; I want them working. Now have you got it all in your head?"

"I haven't got any money," Eddie told her.

Margaret went into her bag and brought out a large pile of dollar notes that she'd bought the day before. She would use the gold to buy the house, which was quite acceptable, Mr Coutts had told her.

"Here. Get the cheapest ones you can, but make sure one of the men is to my liking. I want plenty of muscle.

Eddie took the carriage, also purchased the previous day, and rode towards the market after being given directions by the owner of the guest house. He'd thought long and hard about his future life in America. He could turn his hand to almost anything and was young enough to make a good life for himself. He'd had his fill of du Pont. He couldn't stop thinking of her as du Pont. She'd always be du Pont to him…big, fat, ugly du Pont!

He was glad he'd finally told her that there would be no more sex with her. His stomach had held enough bile and vomit hidden behind forced erections and false, sweet words. She'd made him want to puke for years, ever since she'd taken him to her room when he was fifteen. He hated the smell of her body, the feel of her crinkly skin, and floppy tits and cunt. He hated kissing her hard, thin-lipped mouth, but he'd been desperate, and desperation could make a young boy do just about anything.

He'd stick it out with her until he'd had his fill. He had thought about throwing her overboard when they were on the ship, but she was an asset, for she could open doors, get him introductions, and pay for his lifestyle. As much as he wished it were so, money wasn't the most useful commodity here, it seemed. You had to be in with the right crowd, and that's where the old bitch would come in handy.

He'd pilfer a bit here and there and get his own bank account. Madam du Pont thought he was stupid, a body without a brain, she'd often told him, but he wasn't just a body. He was clever and cunning. He laughed. He'd already gotten one over on her. Parker would never be seen again. He'd paid the two carriage drivers to bury her on the road to London after they'd killed her. The couple who lived in the Knightsbridge house would stay there in comfort until they passed away. Madam du Pont never had found out that they were his parents. No one knew about that little gem of a secret, not even Sam.

Chapter Forty

Jacob, Hendry, and Isaac rode with the wind at their backs towards Elizabeth's family plantation, situated far to the west of Portsmouth. The journey was long, but Jacob's mind was not on the scenery, his satisfaction at being home, or the highly successful trip that was now behind him. Instead, he thought only about the following hours when dreams would be shattered for some, and he would be forever branded as a rogue without a decent, gentlemanly bone in his body.

He was well aware that in voicing his decision to call off his wedding to one of Virginia's finest daughters, along with truthful declarations of love for an unknown Englishwoman, Miss Mercy Carver, fate would shape a sharp, twisted turn in a path that had been mapped out for years. He also believed that his new path would be filled with widespread condemnation from a genteel society in which being a gentleman was even more important than the amount of wealth one possessed.

Jacob had thought about telling Mercy that he was engaged. He would have put her mind at ease with the promise to break all ties with his betrothed, but that would not have been the gentlemanly thing to do. Elizabeth deserved better, for she was the victim of this cruel act. Therefore he'd decided that she should be told that it was over before he promised himself to another woman.

He felt a tiredness sweep over him; a deflated morale, an ache for Mercy, and a dread for what was to come. He wanted to go home, as did Hendry and Isaac.

Isaac had been distant and pensive of late. Their once forthright and honest conversations had been forced ever since the last days on the ship. He suspected that he would lose Isaac's friendship altogether in the next few weeks, for he was making it quite clear that he was no longer happy in the South.

Snow was just beginning to fall. Jacob lifted his face to the white, freezing flakes that were starting to settle on his hat. He loved winter and its gentle pace. Warm nights around the fire, reading, when there was very little activity in the fields was always welcome during this season. They were the complete opposite to his gruelling summers when there was no respite from work or time to enjoy the beautiful, hazy summer days of his youth.

He remembered those days with fondness, he and Hendry swimming in a lake, followed by picnics, tree climbing, and apple picking that often turned into an apple fight and a few black eyes. Now, especially now, he yearned for those days again.

His homecoming had been a bittersweet affair. The ship had been unloaded and was undergoing repairs. Everything had gone smoothly and without any of the usual delays caused by the Norfolk port authority, whose unorganised bureaucratic systems were not up to par with their English counterparts. Jacob had been chomping at the bit to leave Norfolk but had been delayed an extra day because of events that were both troubling and dangerous to his beloved South.

It was the custom for him to meet up with other plantation owners at this time of the year when ships came back from their Atlantic trading voyages, and Christmas was just around the corner. This social gathering was going to be even more enjoyable, Jacob had believed, for Hendry would be with him, welcomed home by many who had not seen him in years.

When Jacob, Hendry, and Isaac walked into this particular meeting, however, there was an atmosphere of quiet contemplation, even anger from some, and grave concern on the faces that greeted them.

The meeting had taken place in the new Stewart's Hotel, recently refurbished and packed with leading politicians and slave owners. Mayor William. W. Lamb, first elected in 1858 and just newly re-elected this year, was also in attendance.

Jacob liked William Lamb. He was a fair man and possessed innovative ideas on how to expand and better the road and rail routes into Norfolk to facilitate agricultural movement to and from the dockyard. Politically, he espoused extreme points of view, but Jacob had voted for him twice now, as had everyone who had any say in Norfolk's expanding financial vision.

Immediately noticing the dreariness in the hotel dining room, Jacob guessed this was because of unspoken words that lay waiting to be released from tongues that had held aggressive and hateful rhetoric for far too long. Greetings were without the usual regaling of Christmas festivities just beginning. Instead, quick greetings were followed by talk of war, secession, and defiance towards the newly elected Republican government in Washington.

Isaac, being a Northerner and Bostonian, had remained tight-lipped and on his best behaviour when talk of the national election reached a frenzied tirade of outbursts and expletives bordering on treason. Jacob had been grateful for Isaac's self-control, for he knew that Isaac was and always would be loyal to the North, Lincoln, and the North's point of view regarding slavery and States' rights.

All the Northern candidates had presented a danger to the South, everyone present had agreed, but no one had been more feared by the Southern states than the winner, Abraham Lincoln. The news of Lincoln's victory on November 6 had not come as a shock to the new arrivals. Hendry, Jacob, and Isaac had often spoken on this subject whilst at sea, and all three fully expected him to achieve a landslide victory. But Lincoln threatened to destroy the South with his outlandish policies on slavery. He would demolish an entire economy and kill morale. He was the South's worst nightmare, and now that nightmare had become a reality.

Mayor Lamb had made it quite clear that he would do everything in his power to obstruct and form a resistance against the North from passing any more laws that threatened the South's way of life, and more importantly, livelihood.

As Jacob listened, he'd shuddered with foreboding. Lincoln's popularity in the slave-free Northern states would make men take up arms and invade the South, should Lincoln demand it. In addition to that dismal assessment, the talk of dissension and a new confederacy in the making by some of the Southern states unwilling to engage in any talk of reducing, or God forbid, rejecting slavery, was growing.

Jacob had pondered the future. He realised that in his ten-week absence across the Atlantic, the political landscape and mellow Virginian political opinions had changed at an alarming rate. The South had lost its voice. It had very little support in Congress, with no powerful advocate. His assessment was, therefore, that without dialogue and diplomacy, violence and war would become a necessity in order to keep what legally belonged to the Southern states.
Jacob's horse stumbled on a small rock and jolted his thoughts back to the Coulter Plantation, just coming into sight on the horizon. Elizabeth would be expecting him to show up at some point. She kept abreast of his journeys and seemed to have a very reliable spy who somehow always knew of his exact movements. It wouldn't surprise him to see her wearing her battle dress; an extravagant gown with jewellery befitting a princess, just in case he was to arrive unannounced, which was exactly what he was going to do.

Isaac rode slightly behind Jacob and Hendry and was consumed with his own thoughts. At the meeting yesterday he had come to realise that he'd spent enough time in the South. He was fond of the Stone family. He loved the open Virginia countryside and his voyages to Europe, but trouble between the North and South was coming. The chasm between the two cultures could not be crossed through political dialogue, not this time. He could sense anger and disdain spewing out of some of the men he'd met in Norfolk. God forbid this hatred from spreading to violence, he pondered, but after what he'd seen and heard in Norfolk, his initial reaction was one of fear. War would tear the country apart, and it was on the horizon, waiting to rise up and burn the country he loved.

His loyalty was unquestionable. He was a Northerner. He hated slavery and all it stood for. He was intelligent enough to know that life was a whole lot easier to navigate when he remained silent on the slave issue. But every time he sat with these grand plantation owners overseeing the niggers' backbreaking work, shackled bodies, and whiplash scarring, as though slaves were born and bred for the sole purpose of serving white masters, he cringed with shame.

He was going to make his way North to follow Lincoln, a man with great vision. Imagine if he'd voiced that opinion yesterday, he thought.

It was during the two-day meeting in Norfolk that he'd decided to head North straight after his last visit to Stone Plantation. He'd kept this news to himself, but he was now set on returning to his family and his own people. As much as he loved Jacob and Hendry, they were not his people.

Time to get married, his mother had stated in her last letter to him.

It's time you came home, darling, she'd written. *It's about time you thought about settling down with a loving girl from Boston. I have a hankering for grandchildren before I get too old to enjoy them.*

It's time to be a real doctor in the hospital with your father and with real patients. And it's time you took your loyalty to our nation seriously.

That last statement had scared him. His mother was not the kind of woman to talk about political goings-on, no lady did.

As he rode, Isaac suddenly became mildly anxious. The very thought of leaving Virginia brought on a heavy, dull ache. It didn't stem from any geographical love for the South. No; it was his love for Mercy Carver that was leaving him despondent and miserable, more miserable than he'd ever felt. Loving Mercy was futile, yet she filled his every thought. She and Jacob were inseparable, and so much in love with each other that it seemed to him only God had the power to separate them. But he loved her nonetheless, and only God could wipe clean the passion that resided in silence within his heart.

He felt an inexplicable exhilaration of life in its purest form course through his veins when in her presence. He would never have her, hold her, or make love to her. He would never tell her how he felt, no matter how much he wanted to. She confided in him, laughed with him, and teased him on occasion. She vented her numerous questions at him about America and his city, Boston. She told him all about the poverty she'd witnessed and lived through on some of the poorest streets of London, and about the rats that were her playmates, crawling over her rough bed-blanket at night on the kitchen floor.

He missed her now, just as much as Jacob did, he guessed. But Jacob would see her in two days, and they would marry. Isaac could only hope that by removing himself back home to the North, his heartache would subside. Life would dictate another path that might or might not include love, and his dreams would be redirected into a more realistic realm.

Mercy; his Mercy, a secret never to be shared, yet always in his mind's imaginings. He hoped she would fade from his memory and he would be released from the pain that haunted him.

Chapter Forty-One

The three men rode their horses through the stone entrance to the Coulter Plantation. They passed slaves mending fences and overseers watching them on the way. The toilers were then forced to up tools for the day because of a sudden blizzard that blinded them. Jacob, Hendry, and Isaac held their hats on whilst attempting to guide the horses at a decent pace down the long road that led to the Coulter house, built in the same colonial style as the Stone Plantation house, although slightly smaller in size.

When the house finally came into view, Jacob noticed how grey and jaded it looked. His house would look the same. Plantation houses were never painted in the winter. To do so would be a futile exercise. The winter of rain, snow, and mud would leave its imprint on the facade until spring when cleaning would begin. No one bothered with appearances at this time of the year, and all properties were as dull and bleak as the weather.

Jacob's belly was turning, twisting and knotting so much now that he thought he would be sick. This would be the hardest and the worst thing he'd ever done or would ever have to do, but whenever he thought about Mercy, he was filled with unfaltering determination and courage.

They reached the front of the house. The small roundabout in the centre of the driveway and just a few feet from the stairs leading to the main doors still housed some hardy plants, and sturdy cacti that didn't mind winter cold or summer heat.

The horses halted at the main entrance and were immediately taken away by two slaves to the stables. Jacob told the men to wipe them down and feed them.

"Are you ready for this?" Hendry whispered to Jacob.

"He's as ready as a chicken with its neck laid out for chopping," Isaac replied, laughing.

At that moment, Mrs Coulter, Elizabeth's mother, scuttled outside in her enormous crinoline gown. It was as wide as the doorway. She was forced to pull in the enormous underskirt hoops to get through even that generous space.

Mrs Coulter had a very small head and would have resembled a knitted teapot-cosy had it not been for her floor-length shawl. Staring at Jacob, her eyes were welcoming but at the same time frozen with confusion and questions. After her initial surprise, she flicked her eyes to Hendry and then Isaac, welcoming them with a generous Southern smile.

"Why, Jacob and Hendry Stone, to what do I owe the pleasure? I declare, you two boys are the last people I expected to see here today. And Isaac, it's always a pleasure to greet one of our Northern neighbours. But I surely am all of a fluster, 'cos I wasn't anticipating you, Jacob, especially today!"

"I hope this is not an inconvenience?" Jacob said, beginning to feel uneasy in the absence of the rest of the family, who at this time of the day would usually be taking tea together by the fire.

"Of course it's not an inconvenience, Why, I'm just flushed with joy at the sight of you boys. You must come in, and of course, you'll stay the night? I believe we're set for a mighty storm; it may last for days! Jacob, you must tell me all about your grand adventure. And Hendry, I do declare you get more handsome every time I see you. Why, it must be three years since your last visit, and Belle, you must tell me all about her. She's such an interesting character. I declare I don't know how she manages to live at sea when she could be perfectly comfortable right here in Virginia, waiting for your return. But that's Belle, always the tomboy."

Mrs Coulter went on and on and didn't stop talking until they were inside her hallway. Jacob had opened and closed his mouth various times, but couldn't get a word in edgewise. Where the hell was everyone, he wondered? Where were Elizabeth, her father, and her brother?

"Now you boys know the rules…boots off. I can't have my lovely rugs muddied, now can I?"

"No, ma'am," said Jacob.

"I wouldn't dream of it," Hendry said.

Isaac simply did as he was told.

House servants were lining the hallway. Mrs Coulter wasted no time in organising them with various tasks. "Matilda, fetch some hot chocolate and cookies for these gentlemen, and tell cook I'll be having guests for dinner. Steven, get Mona and Susan to ready three rooms and make sure there's a fire lit in each." She turned to the men, who were now displaying wet socks. "Come into the drawing-room, boys, just as soon as you take those wet jackets off. I have a bright fire going. I'll get you warmed up in no time."

"I've come to see Elizabeth, ma'am. Is she home?" Jacob finally got the chance to ask. He had a sinking feeling that Mrs Coulter was alone in the house.

"Why, Jacob, I was so happy to see y'all, I didn't get around to telling you that my husband, Elizabeth, and my George have gone to Stone Plantation to see *you*. They left early this morning. I'm sure they're there right now, as we speak. Elizabeth insisted on seeing you as soon as she heard you were back, and you know how my daughter is when she has a bee in her bonnet, why, there's no stopping her. She was so excited, and what with the wedding less than two weeks away, she just couldn't contain herself.

"My husband told her to wait until we were sure you were at home, but she insisted that, as you'd arrived in Norfolk three days ago, it was more than likely you'd be at Stone Plantation by now. You know Elizabeth, she can be as stubborn as a mule."

Jacob's face was as white as the snow outside. This was a disaster. Elizabeth, her father, and her brother would be sitting in his house talking about the wedding. Mercy would have learned he was getting married by now. She would be devastated. He had landed himself in hot water. He had completely miscalculated the timing and his fiancée's quick thinking. Elizabeth and her family had left nothing to chance and had outsmarted him. His heart was thumping as the dire consequences of his actions hit home.

He looked at Hendry and Isaac for support. Both of them were probably thinking the same as he. Hendry looked as though he wanted to tell him he was a jackass, which he'd been saying out loud for two weeks. Isaac eyed him with a pitying smile.

They would have to stay the night, of course, but then, what if the blizzard worsened? Would they be stuck here for days? Jesus, this was going to be a long night or maybe even days. The more time Elizabeth spent with Mercy, the more she'd revel in wedding conversations. Mercy was proud. She'd be angry, and she'd also be feeling hurt, let down, deceived, and worse, untrusting of him and his words.

He gained some composure and said, "Thank you, Mrs Coulter, ma'am, it's very kind of you to put us up. We just need to eat something. I can't speak for Isaac and Hendry, but I'm dead on my feet. It'll be an early bed for me, and we'll leave at sun up, weather permitting. I'd hate to keep Elizabeth and her father and brother waiting."

"Now, Jacob Stone, you know I won't allow you to ride out until the weather permits, not even if you begged me. Why, you're practically family already, and I'm sure my boys and Elizabeth will be well taken care of in your home, just as you will be here. Who is at Stone Plantation, might I ask?"

Jacob stared blankly at her and was relieved when Hendry spoke for him.

"Belle's there. She went home as soon as we docked. She'll be mighty happy to see Elizabeth and keep company with her. We have some great news, Mrs Coulter. Belle's with child. I'm going to be a father. That's why we've come home to stay a while."

Hot drinks and cookies arrived. Jacob smiled gratefully at Hendry. He could talk about Belle and the baby all night without being urged to do so, and Mrs Coulter would be happy to listen. They would eat dinner and hold polite conversation. Isaac would be interrogated as usual about the North, his family, and his view of the South's slave expansion plans, which were all over the newspapers. As Mrs Coulter rarely paused for breath, all he would have to do was nod in agreement until it was time for bed. He drank the hot chocolate, thawing out his cold bones and dreading the night ahead, not only here but for those at Stone Plantation.

Chapter Forty-Two

Mercy yawned and then stretched like a contented cat. She'd slept the night and half the day away in a luxurious four-poster bed and was now feeling refreshed and eager to once again explore her new home. She got out of bed and realised that the fire was still lit. She'd slept through the sound of logs being piled onto it throughout the night. The heat inside the room made everything outside look even more picturesque. As she sat on the window seat, watching sheets of snow falling, she believed she'd never be as happy as she was at this present moment.

She'd seen very little of her new home in these first two days. The weather had made it impossible to walk any distance at all, and so she had contented herself by exploring the house and keeping company with Belle.

Their arrival had generated great excitement within the household. Servants had scurried out of every door and had lined the hallway. Belle's pregnancy and her own fresh face raised a few eyebrows and more than a few whispered questions. The house slaves had been dressed beautifully. The slaves were not afraid, had a lot to say, and didn't wear shackles. They were not raggedly dressed, and most importantly of all, they seemed happy. In fact, the entire house had an air of warmth and love, and she had felt at home almost immediately.

Mercy had been given a slave the moment she arrived. The girl, Abby, was roughly her own age, and she talked non-stop in a high, accelerated voice about how excited she was to meet someone from another part of the world. Mercy could barely understand her. She found Abby's incessant chatter irksome after an hour of unpacking but put this down to being overly tired and wanting nothing more than a hot bath, a tray of food, and bed.

Abby called her "Miss Mercy" after or before every sentence, depending on where she took a breath. Mercy found this amusing, but Belle had warned her that although slaves were allowed to express themselves, a strict owner-slave relationship still had to be maintained.

Mercy dressed quickly in a dove-grey gown piped with black and carried a black woollen coat, hat, gloves, and scarf. Belle had promised to have her escorted around the entire plantation, but she'd be happy to see just a fraction. It was not a day to be outdoors for any length of time, no matter how much she wanted to explore Jacob and Hendry's vast lands.

As she reached the top of the curved stairway, she heard the sounds of a woman's laughter, men's voices, and Belle issuing orders for tea. She raced down the stairs. These would be the first visitors to Stone Plantation since her arrival. Had Jacob arrived with guests? She stopped and smoothed down her hair. She would have liked to have taken the time to look her very best, but if Jacob were home, she would throw herself into his arms, regardless of how she looked or how wet he was from the blizzard outside.

She entered the drawing room. A woman, much taller and fairer than she, stood beside two men, one older and the other roughly the woman's age. The woman was removing a hooded fox fur cloak. She was beautiful, Mercy thought. Her hair was the colour of gold and sat perfectly in ringlet lines to her shoulders.

Mercy turned her gaze to the two men. The older man, a father figure maybe, helped the woman with her coat, and the younger, fair-haired man was laughing with Belle.

All three turned to settle their eyes on her. She felt unsure of herself in the presence of these people and looked keenly at Belle, waiting to be introduced. None was forthcoming. Planting a smile on her face, she took matters into her own hands. "Hello. I hope I'm not interrupting."

"Mercy, you're awake!" Belle finally exclaimed. "I'd like to introduce you to our closest friends. You should have seen my face when they arrived. I was so surprised to see them, especially with the weather being as it is."

Belle walked towards Mercy and pulled her to the centre of the room. She introduced her first to the woman. "Mercy, this is Miss Elizabeth Coulter, of the Pinetrees Plantation."

Mercy curtsied, as did Elizabeth. Each woman looked the other over with polite curiosity. Mercy liked the woman instantly but couldn't help but see a certain resentment flashing in Elizabeth's eyes. She took a step backwards and was then introduced to Elizabeth's father, who greeted her with a broad smile and open admiration.

"Miss Mercy, it's a great pleasure to meet you. I hear an English accent?"

"Yes, you do, sir. I'm from London…South-east London, to be exact."

"And what do you think of Virginia? I believe it must be a complete change in culture and scenery for you. I'm sorry you've been greeted by this weather, but the dang winters here can go from sunshine to a blizzard in a single day. Y'all will get used to it."

"It snows in London too," Mercy told him. "In fact, it's probably snowing there right now. The snow's much nicer to look at here, though. It's pure and white. In London, it turns very quickly to brown slush, and it's not nice to walk on or to look at."

Belle interrupted, "Mercy, this is Elizabeth's brother, George, and Mr Coulter's son, of course. He's one of Hendry's dearest childhood friends."

"It's very nice to meet you, Miss Mercy. You're very lovely; I have to say."

"George! Don't be so forward." Elizabeth scowled.

"Well, it's true, she is lovely. What, are you afraid you won't be the belle of the ball anymore? Don't like competition, do you, my dear sister?"

Elizabeth tossed her head and laughed disdainfully. "Why, what do I care about being belle of the ball, George? I'm getting married in eleven days, and I won't need to compete with any single girl in the county ever again. I have my beau, and I couldn't be happier about it. Isn't that right, Pa?"

"Yes, it sure is, my darlin' girl. George, stop teasing your sister. You know how disappointed she's feeling right now."

Mercy listened to the chatter, which carried on until they were all seated and tea had been served. She had been forgotten for the moment and was glad, for it gave her time to study the Coulter family. She took a quick look at Belle, who was strangely quiet and distant. Belle's manner towards her had changed. There was an underlying look of trepidation in her eyes. Mercy had spent enough time with Belle to gauge her moods and was beginning to feel the first tinge of anger. She hoped Belle wasn't ashamed of her or embarrassed to call her friend in front of her fancy visitors. That would make her just like Julia; unwilling to understand and accept Mercy's background.

Jacob's name had been mentioned several times. Elizabeth seemed to be very fond of him, and Mercy felt resentment building. She was jealous! She, Mercy Carver, was jealous of another woman. Elizabeth obviously knew Jacob very well. She was calling him 'my darling Jacob'!

"So, Miss Mercy, how long do you plan to stay at Stone Plantation? I do hope it's a long visit. You sure brighten the place up," George said.

Mercy smiled. His jovial banter was not rude, as his sister thought. He was being playful. He reminded her of Isaac, always teasing her and she him in an easy-going friendship.

"I honestly don't know how long I'll be staying," answered Mercy. "But I hope that it'll be for a long time. I love Belle, Hendry, and Jacob, of course. Belle's just like the sister I always imagined having."

"So you have no other plans, Mercy?" Elizabeth asked.

"Well, no, actually, I don't."

"In that case, I will have to make sure to put you on the wedding guest list, although the invitations have gone out now, and it would be better if you had a partner. Why, I don't think we have any single ladies attending unescorted. I'll speak to Jacob about it when he gets here."

Mercy's eyes widened, and she stared at Belle, who refused to look at her. She willed Belle to look her in the eye. Her breathing was becoming uneasy. Her heart was pounding fast, her head was spinning, and she was sure that the Coulter family were staring at her. She had to say something. She had to know the answer to the question that was tearing her heart apart. "Thank you for your invitation, Elizabeth. You must be very excited about your wedding. Are you marrying a local man?"

Elizabeth laughed; her father and brother too. Belle looked down at her lap, hiding her eyes. Mercy looked at the laughing faces; laughing at her, or laughing at the question? She wasn't sure.

Elizabeth stopped laughing and looked at Mercy impassively. "Why, Mercy, surely you must know who I'm marrying after being on that long voyage. They must have told you that I was marrying Jacob on his return. How could you not know this? Did my Jacob not tell you?" Elizabeth turned sharply towards Belle. "Belle, did that fiancé of mine not talk about me at all?"

"Of course he did, Elizabeth, but you know Jacob better than anyone. He doesn't talk much about his personal thoughts, although I do know he's looking forward to the wedding. Mercy probably wasn't around when he spoke of you. You know Jacob is a terrible sailor. Why, we hardly saw him. And I was spending all my time in my cabin with Mercy for company…"

Belle's voice trailed off, and an uncomfortable silence ensued.

Mercy had heard enough. She was struck dumb, felt as though her breathing had stopped, was seeing double, and couldn't look at anyone. She hated Jacob and wanted to kill him and herself. She felt disappointed and hurt by Belle, who had hidden this from her…they had all hidden it, Jack, Hendry, and Isaac, who had always been very understanding. She had told Jacob all the secrets about her London life. They had all betrayed her. Jacob had used her as the prostitute he thought he had saved. He had taken her virginity, and now he'd broken her heart. She wished she'd died in the fire.

Mercy felt all eyes on her. She stood up, as ladylike as possible, and made a point of pouring more tea into all their cups. She couldn't allow herself to be seen like this: weak, pathetic, a crushed woman who had just had her heart cut out and served up on a plate to a woman called Elizabeth.

Mercy tried to steer the conversation away from the wedding, but Elizabeth hadn't finished. "Well, I just hope this horrid weather has gone in time for Christmas and the wedding. Pa, what will happen if no one can get to Pinetrees? I'll just die! I want the whole county to see my gown."

"This blizzard will pass in a day or two. Don't you worry your pretty little head about it," her father said.

Elizabeth dabbed tearless eyes with her delicate lace handkerchief. "I just think Jacob has been too selfish and mean. Why couldn't we have gotten married in the fall like I asked? Why did he have to go on that stupid voyage to England this time? It's just not fair! Pa, you must tell him how badly he's treated me."

Belle stood on shaky legs. She'd heard enough and wanted to comfort Mercy, who was behaving more like a lady than Elizabeth. She looked across the room at Elizabeth, who was pathetically sobbing. Her father was holding her hand, and her brother looked bored. Belle had to get out of the room. She was getting a headache.

"You know, I feel a little faint," she said. "Now y'all must make yourselves at home. Your rooms should be ready by now. Why don't we meet for dinner at seven? I'm awful sorry, but being pregnant seems to make me tired all the time. Mercy, would you be a dear and help me up the stairs? I'm going to lie down for just a little while."

"Of course I will," Mercy said, grateful to have an excuse to leave. "When I get you all tucked in, I think I'll take a short walk…just around the gardens. I've got my coat and hat all ready."

"But you'll freeze to death! You can't go out there, not in this weather," Mr Coulter said, shocked.

George jumped in quickly, saying, "I'll be happy to escort you if you like, Miss Mercy?"

"No, thank you, George. I like walking alone," Mercy said.

"Pa, don't fuss so. I'm sure a walk will do her good. She has such a grey pallor about her. And George, you know it wouldn't be seemly for you to escort Mercy alone. Think of her reputation," Elizabeth said as though Mercy had already left the room.

Mercy laughed. "I'll be fine. Thanks, all of you, but I'm actually very used to the cold. We Londoners are hardy souls. I've got my hat and coat, and I don't think five minutes of fresh air will do me any harm. It was interesting to meet you all. I'll see you at dinner," she said, following Belle from the room.

They walked up the stairs in silence. Upon entering Belle's room, however, Belle broke down and held Mercy to her. Tears streamed down her face. Mercy felt their wetness on her own cheeks.

Mercy looked into Belle's face. Her sorrow and guilt were heartbreaking. Mercy wanted to shout, scream, and call her a traitor, but she saw that Belle was suffering as much as she.

"Sshh…Belle, don't upset yourself. Think of the baby. It's all right," Mercy told her.

"No, no, it's not all right! I should have told you about Elizabeth and Jacob…we all should have told you. We fought with Jacob about it for weeks, but he was determined to sort this out in his own way. Mercy, Jacob is at Pinetrees right now if I'm guessing right. That's the Coulter's Plantation. He was going there to tell Elizabeth that the wedding has to be called off. He was going to do and say the unforgivable because he loves you. He loves you so much. Dang it, Mercy, Jacob should have told you. You would have understood, wouldn't you?"

"Of course I would have," Mercy told her truthfully. "I came into Jacob's life after his engagement. He should have told me, though, on that very first night, when he said he loved me…oh Belle, I hurt so much."

Belle nodded and held Mercy to her again. "I know, I know, darling. But you have to forgive him. He'll just die if you leave him."

Mercy had heard the words, "Jacob loves you so much." She knew them to be true, but the closeness between them had now ended. He was getting married to another woman.

"That woman downstairs believes she's getting married in eleven days' time. She will have her wedding dress hanging up, ready to wear. The cake will have been made. The ceremony, the invitations…oh God, Belle, Jacob can't break it off now. It would ruin him. I can't allow him to destroy his way of life for me. I'll never fit in here…not with my accent, my common upbringing, or the reputation of being a marriage breaker."

"What are you going to do? You can't leave. You'll break him!"

"He has broken me!" Mercy said miserably. "Rest now. I'll be back in a little while. I need a brisk walk. I always feel better after a fast walk. It will clear my head."

"Please, Mercy, don't leave Jacob…"

Mercy walked back down the stairs and picked up her coat, gloves, hat, and scarf that were lying over a chair. As she put them on, she heard raised voices coming from the drawing room. She stopped to listen, hidden from view behind the door.

"Did you see the look on her face, Pa? She wants Jacob; I know she does. What if he wants her too? I'll be ruined forever. I'll never be able to go out in public again. Oh, Pa, please don't let Jacob throw me over like I'm common white trash…like she is!"

"Don't you worry, darling, Jacob will marry you, even if I have to shove a rifle in his back. He won't defile your reputation or our family's fine name. I'll make dayum sure of that."

Mercy covered her mouth to stop the sound of wretched sobs escaping. Tears fell onto her hands, rivers of tears that couldn't be stopped. She stumbled quietly to the door and opened it, slipped through it, and went out into the freezing cold.

Chapter Forty-Three

Jacob, Hendry, and Isaac arrived at Stone Plantation tired, hungry, and eternally grateful to have made it out of Pinetrees. They had left the Coulter household just after midday, as soon as the wind had dropped and the snow was but a soft flurry.

The snow had been deep, too deep for any sensible person to even think about riding out in it. But they had all agreed that they couldn't spend another night with Mrs Coulter and her incessant talk of her wonderful daughter and her wedding plans.

Belle saw the three men ride up the drive and her heart lurched. At last Hendry had come home. These past days had been a living nightmare, and she'd missed him terribly. They'd never been apart for so long. In the five days since she'd seen him, everything that could go wrong had. Pulling a shawl across her shoulders, she rushed down the long staircase to greet them.

The Coulters were gone. She had been furious to learn that they'd left before she awoke. Their suspicions had grown regarding Jacob and Mercy. She had barely been able to keep the truth from them after they'd goaded her with question after question about Mercy. Mercy had not attended dinner. Instead, she had complained of a headache and had eaten alone in her room.

Belle was no fool. She suspected the Coulters' departure without a goodbye, or a thank-you, was because they didn't want to be present when Jacob arrived home.

They were not going to give him the chance to explain himself. Elizabeth had manipulated this, Belle reflected angrily. Unless Jacob met her on the road, it would be far too late to call off the wedding. She wouldn't put it past the Coulters to take an alternative route, just to make sure they didn't meet Jacob halfway. If she were in Elizabeth's position, she might do exactly the same thing to hold on to her man.

Belle reached the bottom of the stairs and called out for Handel. He was in his sixties and was bossy and authoritarian. He knew he was loved like a father by the two Stone brothers. He used this knowledge to his advantage, giving Hendry and Jacob a telling-off every now and again when he thought they needed to be put in their places, and both brothers allowed the slave this leverage.

Having given the order to ready the house, Belle left Handel to issue his orders to the other house slaves.

The three men walked wearily into the hallway. Hendry and Belle hugged and kissed.

Jacob interrupted them in a shaky and nervous voice. "Are the Coulters still here?"

"No, they left before the house stirred. Jacob, I think Elizabeth is suspicious."

"Of course she is. She doesn't miss a trick. Goddammit, what the hell do I do now? Where is Mercy?" he asked, realising she was nowhere to be seen.

Belle's eyes filled with tears and then she broke into heavy sobs. She'd been brave and controlled, but now that Hendry was back, she didn't need to be strong anymore.

"She's sick, Jacob. She's very sick. She went out in that blizzard yesterday. She was upset when Elizabeth talked about your wedding. She wouldn't listen to me and went for a walk and got lost. She eventually found her way back in the dark, but then she got a fever early this morning, and no one will let me in to see her."

Belle sobbed to Isaac, "I'm so glad you're here, Isaac. Please go to her. I'm very concerned. I wanted to be by her bedside, but everyone was worried about me coming down with something…and the baby."

"Oh, God, this is my fault. Where is she?" Jacob stumbled up the stairs.

Belle shouted after him, "She's in your father's room. Abby is with her."

Isaac paled. He thought quickly. He ordered one of the house slaves to fetch his bags and raced up the stairs after Jacob. If Mercy was down with a fever, she could be in real danger. He would have to improvise as far as medicines were concerned. His heart was as heavy as a rock, and his mouth was dry. Mercy had suffered so much already. He wanted to punch Jacob in the mouth, friend or no friend. His stupid ideas on how to handle this whole nasty business had been noble but futile. She deserved better.

Jacob sat at Mercy's bedside and was openly crying. Isaac stood at the door for a second and felt tears sting his own eyes. He wondered if he was crying for his tormented friend or for Mercy, who lay unconscious. Her face was tinged greyish white, and in complete contrast to her damp coal-black hair spread across the pillow.

"Jacob, get out of the way. I need to get closer. You don't have to leave, but you have to stand aside." Isaac took his two medical bags from the slave. He took out the stethoscope first and loosened Mercy's damp gown. Her head was still, but every now and then she whispered jumbled words. She was perspiring badly and burning like a hot poker. He placed the stethoscope on her chest and listened to her lungs. They were rattling as she breathed, and he was in no doubt that infection had set in.

"What's your name, girl?" Isaac asked Abby.

"Abby, sir. I don't know what to do," she said, also crying.

"Abby, I want you to do exactly as I say. Bring me some water with ice and some rags. Put this medicine, two full teaspoons of it in a glass of boiling water, and hurry."

Isaac looked at Jacob's frightened face, and at last, his heart melted. Jacob was very much in love; as if Isaac hadn't known that already. Now was not the time to think about *his* feelings for Mercy. "Jacob, this is serious. It could be influenza."

"What can I do?"

"We need to bring her temperature down. Keep piling on cool, wet rags. They need to be placed on her forehead, her neck and across her chest, even under her arms and changed when they get warm. She needs to drink sips of cold water. The medicine I sent Abby to fetch might help. I picked it up in Liverpool. It has some herbs, eucalyptus, and roots they say can clear the lungs. I don't want to bleed her, but I might have to."

Jacob's eyes widened in fear. Bleeding was only done in extreme cases nowadays, and the treatment had very little success. “Dear God, what have I done? I’ll never forgive myself if…”

“That’s enough of that talk,” Isaac told him sharply. “Help me sit her up against a stack of pillows. It may help her breathing.”

Mercy heard the sound of their voices from some distant place. She tried to open her eyes, but there was a fire. The flames were all over her body, and she couldn’t get away from them. She screamed Jacob’s name. She was at a wedding, but no one wanted to sit next to her. She was ashamed…everyone was staring at her. Elizabeth was laughing, and Jacob was her groom.

“Jacob, no…no, Jacob!” Mercy shouted in her dream.

Jacob listened to her calling his name. He had no right to feel sorry for himself. Mercy and Elizabeth had every right to hate him, as did Belle, who had endured Elizabeth’s company. He’d behaved like a son of a bitch!

Abby and another house slave arrived with a basin of water mixed with a little snow. Abby carried a tall glass with Isaac’s medicine in one hand and soft cloths in another. Her eyes were tired and puffy. Jacob took the glass and told Abby to wait outside the room for further instructions.

He and Isaac dampened down Mercy’s burning body with the cool, wet cloths. Isaac ordered the slave who remained to fetch a bowl of boiling water.

Jacob watched helplessly, while Isaac poured the foul-smelling medicine into Mercy’s mouth.

Later, they suffered the stench of eucalyptus steam rising from the boiling water in the bowl Isaac had ordered. It was placed and held just under Mercy's nose.

Mercy could smell the strong aroma flowing into her nose and then taste the bitter liquid running into her throat. Maybe it was that horrible drug again…were Eddie and Sam here? Had they finally found her? She moved her head from side to side, attempting to escape the drug, but had no strength to do anything further. She tried to open her eyes, but they were stuck together. She couldn't watch herself burn; that would be too horrid. Every now and again she felt someone lift her head and pour another type of liquid into her mouth. This one tasted even worse than the drug. She tried to call out for Jacob, for he would save her again, she just knew he would…

Jacob held the bowl whilst Isaac dabbed her continuously with the wet, cooled cloths. When the snow and tepid water in the basin melted, he ordered more of both to be brought, and the bowl refreshed.

They repeated cooling her, medicating her, and placing steaming eucalyptus inhalations carefully under her nose. Neither man left Mercy's side until the next morning.

In the grey light of dawn, Mercy was no better. Her breathing was still laboured, and the burning heat in her body had not noticeably subsided. Jacob slept now with his head on the edge of the bed and his body on a chair.

Isaac hadn't slept at all. He had tended to Mercy, and along with Abby, had continuously dampened her down with the cool water. He had decided to open a vein in her arm, and her blood trickled into a bowl. The medicine that Isaac had bought in England was still being poured into her mouth, tiny drops at a time from a spoon. The steaming bowl of water and eucalyptus had been changed constantly throughout the night. There was nothing else they could do now but wait and pray.

Hendry and Belle held each other in bed. Belle told Hendry all about the Coulters' visit. They talked about the wedding, and both agreed that it was too late for Jacob to call it off. In four days' time, they would all have to leave for Pinetrees for the wedding and Christmas festivities that would follow.

"How are we going to convince Jacob to go when Mercy's lying here so ill?" Hendry asked.

Belle said, "He won't leave her like this, and he's still determined to call it all off."

"Well, he can't. It would be the end of him…and of us. Some of our cargo comes from Pinetrees and the other plantations around Portsmouth. We would all be ruined, not just Jacob."

"But he loves Mercy. How can you worry about business when his happiness is at stake?" Belle said angrily.

"I know he loves her. I've never seen him like this with any woman. He wants to marry Mercy, but sometimes duty and honour have to come first!" Hendry said sharply. "Belle, things are not good here. There might be big changes next year in how we deal with the politics of this country. Jacob's problems are small in comparison to what might happen in the South."

"What are you saying?" Belle looked into his face.

"I'm saying that if the North continues with their anti-slavery policies, some of the Southern states may secede from the Union."

Chapter Forty-Four

On the fourth day, Mercy's fever broke, and she finally opened her eyes. She looked around the room. She couldn't remember where she was at first. She wasn't afraid, yet she remembered feeling flames engulf her, a dead man, her bloodied hands, and Jacob's face. She opened her eyes wider. The room was bright, and the light hurt them.

First, she saw Jacob. He was holding her hand. At the other side of the bed was Isaac, dampening her brow. Both men were smiling. Why were they smiling? She wondered. Her mouth felt terribly dry, and her body was damp and ached all over.

Her memory began to return. Jacob and Elizabeth were getting married. She'd gone for a walk. She'd fallen in the snow too many times to count. There had been dips in the fields, and small hills all hidden by the thick layer of snow that had been so high in places it had reached her knees. She hadn't meant to walk so far, but the blizzard had been dark and wild, like her mood. She felt as weak as a newborn baby now and couldn't move her head or raise a smile to the two men in return.

She stared into Jacob's eyes and saw his love. It was still there, but then she remembered the Coulters. Tears dribbled down her cheeks, and Jacob dabbed them away.

"It's all right, my darling. You've been very sick, but Isaac is making you better."

Mercy tried to speak, but her mouth couldn't release the words. She turned her head away from Jacob and looked at Isaac. He looked so tired and afraid. Finally, she smiled gently at him and then fell into a deep, peaceful sleep.

Leaving Abby with Mercy, Jacob and Isaac headed to the dining room.

Belle was sitting with Hendry. Breakfast was being served, and for the first time in days, Jacob and Isaac ate a proper meal.

It was going to be the most difficult, heartbreaking day of Jacob's life, but he knew what he had to do. Looking at the others, he said in an unsteady voice, "We'll have to leave at noon."

"I'm sorry, Jacob, but I'm not going with you. Hendry will stand by your side. I'm not leaving Mercy," Belle said.

"I figured, and I agree with you. I think it would be better for you to remain here. It's too cold for you to travel in your condition, and I would feel happier knowing you were with Mercy. She's still so very weak, and she'll need someone to talk to."

"And to clean up your mess," Belle said, and then regretted her words. "I'm sorry. I didn't mean that."

"You're right. This is my mess, and I am leaving you here to deal with it. Jesus, what have I done?" Jacob said in a voice laced with guilt.

"You've been a dang fool," Belle, spat.

"It's a miracle she pulled through at all," Isaac said. "I thought we were going to lose her. She's a fighter, a real fighter, our Mercy."

"Yes, she is. And she's also badly hurt. Jacob, she won't be here when you get back. You do know that, don't you?" Belle said miserably.

"She will. She has to stay. I don't know how to fix this, but I'll figure it out," Jacob told her.

"So you think you're just going to walk back in here with your new wife, and Mercy's going to be at the door to welcome you both? There are times I want to slap you!" Belle's eyes were sparkling with anger.

"Belle, please. I'm at my wit's end. I don't want to marry Elizabeth Coulter. I want to marry the woman I love upstairs. But you know I have to do this, for you and Hendry too!"

"Don't you dare blame Hendry and I. You should have been honest."

"Don't make this harder for me."

Belle shook her head. Tears stung her eyes. "Say no. You don't have to go through with it. I agreed with Hendry last night, but I've changed my mind. Don't do it, Jacob…I implore you!"

"Hush, sweetheart. Don't you go upsetting yourself. Jacob has no choice, and y'all getting all riled up won't change that. He has to marry her. There ain't nothing else for it."

Jacob's conflicted emotions were mixed with complete exhaustion. He shook his head and shared his thoughts with the others. "Y'all know Elizabeth wants to be mistress of this plantation more than she wants me. I reckon she might not want it so bad now that you two are home," he said to Hendry and Belle. "She might…"

"No, she won't call it off," Belle interrupted. "She's got her mind set on this house, and in her mind, only God Almighty is going to stop her from having it. But I don't think that woman has any love for you either, Jacob, and that gives me hope."

Jacob murmured, "Hope, what hope do you see?"

"Hope that Mercy will remain calm enough to see that running away from you isn't the answer. We've been talking about this, Hendry and me, and we're going to ask her to stay in our townhouse in Portsmouth. When you've settled in, you can go see her whenever you want. We'll all make sure she's financially secure, and she can recuperate there. I know it might not work, but at least it will give you time to convince her that all is not lost."

"Goddammit! Am I the only sane person here?" Isaac said angrily, looking at Jacob. "Do you really think that Mercy will agree to become your mistress? Listen to yourselves! Do you think you can own her like you own your slaves? Jacob, are you figuring on using her when you tire of being with your wife. She's got her pride! Jesus, she's still alive because she's strong and resilient…for the love of God, let her go. Give her enough money to start over and don't be so fucking selfish!"

"Isaac! My wife!" Hendry warned him.

Isaac ran his fingers through his tousled hair and put his hand up. "I apologise, Belle, but I've heard enough. Jacob, you're exhausted, you're not thinking straight. Belle, you seem to be on some quest for a happy ending. And Hendry, you sit there silently defending your brother when you should be telling him not to marry a woman he has no affections for. I ain't goin' to your wedding neither, Jacob.

I won't sit there and listen to speeches and vows and choke on your wedding cake! I'm staying here to make sure Mercy is on the road to recovery before she storms out of this house. Then I'll take her wherever she wants to go. No one here should put silly ideas into her head about becoming Jacob's concubine. You Southerners with your backward traditions make me feel sick to my stomach! Mercy's only eighteen years old. She deserves a life, a good one. You brought her to Virginia, Jacob, so you have to think hard now about what you're doing and how you're going to let her go. Because let her go you must, and if you don't…!"

"What, you'll look after her? Is that what you wanted to say?" Jacob shouted back.

Isaac stood up to leave and then faced the others, who were still shocked by his outburst. "If you throw Mercy aside for Elizabeth Coulter, I will make it my duty to take care of her."

"Yeah, I reckon you'd like that, wouldn't you, Isaac? Do you think I haven't noticed how you look at her? You're in love with her. Any dang fool can see it. But why? How can you be in love with a woman who loves another man and has never given you any cause to hope?" Jacob mocked. He was now also on his feet and had moved towards Isaac. "You're happy about this situation! Why, I believe there's nothing you'd like better than to take Mercy for your own when I'm out of the way."

"Yes, damn you, I do love her, and God knows she'd be much better off with me than remaining here, waiting for you to call on her!"

Belle stood up and banged her fist on the table. "Enough! Both of you sit down, right now." She was sobbing. "Isaac's right; if you marry Elizabeth, Jacob, you have to let Mercy go, she deserves better...oh God, this is awful. How could we have even thought about her being a mistress? We're being selfish, Jacob...we are," Belle sniffed. Belle's tears calmed the situation. She slumped forward and covered her face.

"If either of you two upset my wife again, I'll throw both of you out of here," Hendry threatened. "Jacob, I'm your brother, and I hope you know that all I want is your happiness, but not marrying Elizabeth will ruin you, and you know it. Virginia's looking at some tough times up ahead, and you, me and every other planter round these parts will need all the friends we can get."

"I know, Hendry…God help me, I do."

Defeat resonated around the table. No one spoke; no one ate. In two hours, Hendry and Jacob would leave, and Jacob would marry Elizabeth.

Jacob got up and walked from the room. He wouldn't, couldn't say goodbye to Mercy. He would write her a letter and beg her to wait for him in Portsmouth, where he'd go to her and promise her a solution.

Chapter Forty-Five

Mercy lay awake and stared at the ceiling. Candles were lit, the fire was blazing, and her headache was receding. Abby had just bathed her, and she wore a clean cotton nightgown. Abby sat in an armchair, watching her as always. The poor girl had not left her side in days. Mercy had seen her face every time she'd opened her eyes, even when it was for just a moment.

The door opened, and Belle walked in. Mercy held out her hand, and Belle came to sit on the bed. She held Mercy's hand and kissed it. "I love you very much, Mercy, you must know that. You gave us all quite a scare," she said, stroking Mercy's forehead.

"Jacob has gone, hasn't he?" Mercy whispered.

Belle nodded, unable to say the word, yes.

Mercy cried softly, without strength, to vent her sorrow. She lay listless, staring again at the ceiling, and then looked once more at Belle. "There was nothing else he could do. I understand him, but Belle, I feel dead inside. All my hopes and dreams…gone."

"No, darling. You mustn't think like that," Belle told her, but without conviction. "Love finds a way. It always does."

Mercy gave her a weak smile and then squeezed Belle's hand. "Jacob gave me life. He saved me more than once. I will always love him…always. Without him, I would never have known the meaning of happiness. My heart was full of it. I suppose my memories of him will have to be enough for me now."

"No, you're wrong. Many paths will be open for you, and along the way, you will find love again. Even I believe we can love more than once. I also believe that great things can happen. Opportunities are endless on our journey through life. As God is my witness, I'll pray every day for you, and I'll ask for love to find you."

Mercy closed her eyes, yet tears managed to squeeze between her eyelids. "As soon as I feel well enough to get up, I'll leave. How long do I have before Jacob returns?"

"A week; eight days, maybe. Mercy, please don't think badly of Jacob. He couldn't say goodbye to you. You were still too ill. He didn't want to upset y'all when you were finally sleeping peacefully. You slept for two whole days, and your fever has gone. He left a letter for you." She watched Mercy's face as Mercy digested her words. "Do you want to read it when you are alone?"

"No. Read it to me. Please."

Belle's hands shook. She dismissed Abby. "Bring tea for Miss Mercy and me," she ordered before Abby left. "And something light to eat for Miss Mercy too.

"Are you sure you don't want to read this alone?" Belle asked, hoping Mercy would not make her say Jacob's words out loud.

"Read it. My eyes hurt."

Belle nodded and took the letter out of her dress pocket.

My dearest Mercy,

I know that you must hate me, and I caint blame you. I want you to hate me, for I have been dishonest and unspeakably cruel to you.

I want you to know that my love for you is sincere in every way. You are the love of my life. You will always be in my heart, filling it with joy but also with immeasurable regret because of what I must do. There will not be a day that goes by when I don't think of you and when I don't hate myself and wish that I had done things differently. I have ordered Isaac to open an account for you in the Portsmouth bank. I refuse to allow you to say no to the money that will be placed there for you.

Belle and Hendry have a house in Portsmouth, and it is yours to live in. We are only a few miles apart, and I pray that you will wait for me and grant me the opportunity to convince you that this marriage to Elizabeth will not deter me from having a future with you. I will find a way to resolve this.

I realise I am asking much from you, but I promise you that love can and will overcome all. You and I are meant to be together, Mercy. Please, please wait for me, and let me prove to you that even if I have to leave my home and disappear with you to wherever the wind takes us, I will do it. I have the money and the means to begin a new life. Belle and Hendry are with me on this decision. I just need time.

My love, always

Chapter Forty-Six

Isaac settled Mercy and Belle into the carriage and took one last look at the house, which held fond memories. He knew as he joined the ladies, that he would never see it again.

The carriage was quite luxurious, with thick curtains at the windows and velvet seats; one for Belle and himself, and the other long enough for Mercy to curl up on. There were bearskin rugs, pillows, and flasks of hot drinks, including even more of the chicken broth that Mercy had sworn never to drink again after being forced to taste it for nine consecutive days.

Handel and Abby followed in another carriage, which also carried the ladies' belongings. It would be their task to look after and care for Mercy.

Belle was going to visit with her parents, whose grand townhouse in the city of Portsmouth was situated in a highly populated residential area just off the long, tree-lined avenue at the heart of the city.

Belle thought about Jacob and the look of misery on his face when he left for his wedding. He'd looked at her, made her promise to look after Mercy, and said, "The next time I set foot in this house, I'll be married to the wrong woman. How ironic God is."

Belle had the strength not to display pity or sorrow at Jacob's plight. She had urged him to part on good terms with Isaac, but they had parted with a handshake and a single word of goodbye. She watched Isaac look back at the house, sensing that he would never return and that this would be another regret that Jacob would have to live with.

Mercy snuggled down under her blanket and smiled at Belle and Isaac. As the carriage left Stone Plantation's fine arched entrance, she wondered if she would ever again set foot in it. Once more her path had been diverted in an instant, her destiny changed, and her dreams shattered.

With her eyes closed, she concentrated on the smooth rocking movement of the carriage over ground that had shed the snow so deeply on that fateful day. It lay only on higher ground now and in small, sparse patches, thanks to the week of mild weather over Christmas. Mercy heard Isaac speaking to Belle. He had saved her life. She would always admire and love Isaac. "So kind," was her last thought before a deep, dreamless sleep took hold.

Watching Mercy sleep, Isaac wondered what it would be like to hold her in his arms, to see her look at him in the same way she looked at Jacob. During his heated argument with Jacob, he hadn't denied his feelings for her. He wished he could take back some of the spiteful words he'd spoken. He also wished he didn't have the intense feelings he had nor the bitterness that grew in his heart every day. Convinced he could make Mercy a happy woman and give her a grand future if she were his and if she would only let Jacob go.

He would remain in Portsmouth for a week or so, and try to convince Mercy to leave with him. If she refused, he would begin the long journey home to Boston alone.

Chapter Forty-Seven

Mercy was feeling better, so much so that she decided to take a walk to the haberdashery store to purchase ribbons for the belated Christmas party to be held that very evening at Belle's parents' house. Abby had asked to join her, but Mercy had ordered the slave to stay home. Mercy had not been left alone since her arrival and wanted nothing more than time to herself and a brisk walk. Abby insisted that she take her medicine. Mercy was not keen on this idea. It made her light-headed and sleepy. But she relented after being threatened with, "Miss Mercy, I'se be telling Mr Isaac you be disobeying his orders."

As she left the house, she laughed. She was taking orders from a slave and obeying them!

Out on the street, she breathed in the crisp, fresh air under a blue sky and thought again about just how lucky she was to be alive. Hendry was home, and Jacob would be at Stone Plantation with his new wife, yet she was happy. He was close by, and any day now he would find an excuse to come to her. Life was short; she kept reminding herself. Happiness was fleeting. She had tasted it, wanted more, and would fight tooth and nail to hold on to it.

She felt no jealousy towards Elizabeth; rather she pitied her. Jacob loved *her*. Soon Elizabeth would come to realise this and give him up, for what woman would want to be with a man who loved another? She saw no happiness in her life without Jacob. No moon would look bright, no sun would warm her, and no other man would take his place in her heart. She was a mistress now, and it was an ugly word, but she was sure that one day she would be his wife. She would hold onto that dream.

She was immediately taken by Portsmouth's beauty and character. Its long main road was an avenue lined with tall trees, giving it a country air. Shops were colourful with wooden slats painted in white, cream, and terracotta. There was an array of small tearooms with covered terraces looking onto the street, which Mercy could envisage being comfortable and cool in the summertime.

There was a beautiful old church that sat on the corner of a row of shops. She stopped and noticed a small gate and entered. She followed a path which took her to the rear of the building, and there she found a graveyard. Some of the headstones were so old that the names written there had all but faded into the stone itself. She did see a few that clearly belonged to the long-dead soldiers who had fought in 1776 to free America from Britain. People had left plants and flowers. The graves were extremely well cared for. She left the church and decided to go straight to the haberdashery before having a more in-depth look at the city centre. Belle had given her directions. Having only one road to manoeuvre, Mercy had to walk just a few hundred feet before the shop came into view.

Eddie Gunn stood just outside a saloon in Portsmouth and spotted the woman walking gracefully down the street towards him. He recognised her immediately, and his mouth gaped open with surprise and shock. Mercy Carver! He'd never forget that name, that face, or that body naked in the stable. Mercy Carver, the troublemaker; the girl who would have got her throat cut on that very first day had she not been a high-value virgin.

He slid around the nearest corner, wondering what to do. Mrs Mallory, as he'd been repeatedly reminded to call her, was at a party. She'd been quite the popular guest of Norfolk and Portsmouth's finest families lately, with her tales of widowhood and cotton factories gaining her the respect and admiration she'd been determined to find in this backwards country.

Her new farm, sitting to the west of Portsmouth and was on prime land, had also endeared her to the plantation belt. She'd be gone till tomorrow, Eddie thought. She would curse the world if she knew Mercy Carver was here, able to point the finger at her, reveal her for what she was and what she'd done. If truth be told, he was just as worried. He didn't know the law here or what the law would do if the Carver woman accused him of abduction. How the bloody hell had she ended up here? That's what he wanted to know. How did she get on a ship? Why was she dressed in finery? Who was her benefactor? She'd have him in jail before the bloody cock crowed. She probably had some old git looking after her for sexual favours, or worse…who knew the bloody sheriff!

He was sweating now. What would Mallory want him to do? He laughed. It was obvious what Mallory would want to do…he would have to kill Carver, and it would have to be done quickly.

Eddie thanked God Mallory had all that land now. She could start another graveyard like the one she'd had back in Liverpool if she had a mind to. He had a gun; a Colt in a holster. It was easy to get guns here. He had a brand-new rifle and two more guns back at the farm too. Never met a savage Indian yet, though, he reflected, getting distracted easily after a few whiskies.

He cautiously peeked out from a porch and saw Mercy go into a shop. A plan was beginning to form in his mind. He still had his skills. Abduction was what he was good at; he just hadn't done it in this country yet.

His horse and trap, he concentrated now, were tethered with Moses, his slave, just a short distance from where he stood and not far from the shop she'd gone into. No more than a hundred yards away. Mercy Carver was feisty; he knew that. She wouldn't go with him without a fight. But she was up against the best; he reminded himself. He'd abducted her before, and he'd do it again.

Mercy left the haberdashery, telling the woman who owned it that she would be back to pick up her packages. She had decided to buy some wool. She would knit a shawl for the baby. It would be a nice surprise for Belle. She turned left and walked towards the restaurant she had seen earlier. She was beginning to feel light-headed after having spent so much time recently indoors and was surprised at how tired she felt after just a short walk. As she walked, a feeling of peace swept over her. She was a stranger here, yet she felt at home.

A hard, pointed instrument poked her back, and a strong hand grabbed her shoulder. The sound she heard sent her mind into turmoil. So shocked was she to hear Eddie's threatening voice in her ear, that she froze, paralysed, stricken with fear, and unable to scream, run, or answer.

His words echoed loudly in her mind, though in reality they were whispered softly.

"Move forward. Don't speak, don't struggle, and I won't shoot you where you stand. Smile and nod your head."

Mercy nodded, and he punched the gun into the small of her back again. She wanted to say something. Why couldn't she speak? Dizziness washed over her again.

She walked in a daze, pinned between Eddie and the row of shops. Eddie ran the gun teasingly up and down the side of her body. He stopped abruptly and spoke to a slave standing by a two-horse trap. "Be as quick and as discreet as you can, Moses, in getting me and my friend here home." He dug the gun in even deeper until Mercy thought her ribcage might crack.

Eddie pressed her body against the open entrance to the trap. He moved the hair covering her ear and whispered again, "Get up into the seat and smile at anyone who passes by. I swear to almighty God, if you make a spectacle of yourself, this gun will make a hole in your back, and the bullet will fly out your stomach." He held her arm so she could enter the trap and bowed in a gentlemanly fashion for effect.

As Mercy put her foot on the step, her leg gave way. Eddie held her up with the hand that was under her arm, pushed her onto the seat, and then jumped up quickly, all with the agility of a cat, to sit beside her. She looked down at her side just above her waist and saw the glint of his gun peeking out of his jacket, resting over his arm. He punched the gun into her again, smiling sweetly at the same time.

"Just a short drive for you and me, Mercy Carver. Then we'll have a nice little chat. What do you think of that, eh? Happy to see your old pal, Eddie, again?"

She still felt light-headed. She wished she hadn't taken that medicine before she left home. It was clouding her mind and slowing her down. She felt as though her brain had been pickled. Eddie was speaking, but his words were coming out of his mouth in slow motion and made no sense whatsoever. Her movements were lethargic. Her arms felt heavy. Even her head felt too heavy for her body to support.

She wanted to live. She wanted to see Jacob again and feel safe in his arms. But for the life of her, she couldn't snap out of the drowsiness that had taken hold.

She looked at the back of the driver's shiny, bald, black head and wondered why he was not helping her to escape from Eddie. As the trap sped down the road, she knew her life was in danger. At the very least, she should scream, gun or no gun. But Eddie was evil, and he *would* kill her, even if it meant he had to make a run for it afterwards.

She finally found her voice, but it was slurred. She sounded like a drunken man. She ignored Eddie and talked directly to the slave as he pushed the horses into a soft canter through a quiet, hedge-lined lane. "I don't know your name, but they'll hang you for this. Is that what you want? This is a bad man…his name is Eddie, and he kills women. If you stop now and help me, I'll make sure you're rewarded. I'll get them to set you free. I know people." There was no response.

Mercy cursed Abby again for making her drink the bloody medicine that she normally took before a nap. Then she cursed herself, for ultimately she was the one who'd drunk the bleedin' stuff. God's grace, if only she didn't feel so dizzy or relaxed. If only her mouth weren't so dry. If only she could think straight!

Eddie laughed. Mercy's body was swaying next to him. "What's up with you? You sound like a halfwit. Where's that Mercy Carver spirit we all hated, eh? Gone soft, have you?" He laughed again and pushed her body into the corner of the seat, where the half canopy hid most of her from sight. He moved along the seat with her until there was not an inch of space between their bodies.

Putting his arm around her shoulder, he continued to smile and make small talk about how nice the weather was. They were taking back streets where there were very few houses.

Mercy panicked. Her heart was thumping, yet she was not displaying her terror. She tried, with great effort, to free herself from Eddie's grasp, but she was as weak as a day-old babe. She looked around her while trees, houses, and the road began to jump and sway before her eyes. Eddie was saying something about getting a warm welcome from Mrs Mallory. She looked at him through her blurred vision and said, "Who is Mrs Mallory?"

"Oh, that would be Madame du Pont to you, Carver."

Her head fell forward, and white spots bolted in and out of her vision. She repeated the name…du Pont, oh, God, she was going to die today.

Eddie watched her head loll to the side. Her eyes were closed. He was thrilled but not exactly sure what was up with the girl; the same girl who'd put the missus's patience to the test, it had all been too easy. She was too easy? He'd taken risks, as always, but this was not London, and the street had been almost empty where he'd found her. It was probably too cold for these Southern gentry. He quietly despised the lot of them. He'd come to what he could only describe as a small kingdom with exaggerated politeness and protocols, weak, tasteless beer, and bitter whisky, and where every white man was king of his black subjects. Christ, this had been the best day he'd had here so far, he thought. He was actually beginning to enjoy himself.

He looked at the woman next to him…Mercy bloody Carver, all weak and submissive like. Not what he'd expected from *her*.

He thought about what to do when they got home. He'd fuck her; that was as sure as his next beer being served to him by one of them black slaves in the house. He'd keep Carver alive until the missus got back tomorrow morning. He'd demand a nice bonus and the pleasure of watching du Pont kill her in any way she saw fit.

Chapter Forty-Eight

As Mercy was dragged down from the trap, she took a quick look at her surroundings. She stood and inadvertently yawned. Eddie laughed again.

"Bored, are we?" he asked her.

Mercy ignored him and looked around her. An attractive wooden house with a wrap-around porch greeted her. There were two barns close to the house, where she believed she would be taken to be killed. White, waist-high picket fences surrounded open fields, and beyond were dense woods. This was du Pont's lair, she thought with hatred and disgust. She'd see her any time now, gloating, laughing, and no doubt delighted at the prospect of killing again.

She was pushed forward, not to one of the barns, but to some stairs at the side of the house. At the bottom of these stairs was a passageway with an old wooden door at the end. The wall of the house was on her left, and an earthen bank was to her right.

Eddie opened the door with a large, rusty key. It was dark inside, but Mercy could just make out a small landing and then some wooden stairs. She shuddered. It was like a black hole down those stairs.

Eddie stopped in front of her and lit a fat candle. He moved down the stairs. A poke in the back from the black man encouraged her to follow Eddie, carefully all the way to the bottom.

Eddie placed the candle on a table sitting against the back wall of the airless room and lifted keys off the hook above it.

Mercy was watched by the black giant, who had not given any indication of what was going to happen. Then, surprising her, he pushed her hard against a side wall, knocking the air out of her lungs. He forced her to the ground with a strength that made her squeal with fright and then calmly attached iron bracelets to her wrists.

Eddie moved closer, guiding the slave with the candle. She was being shackled, like the black people she'd seen in Norfolk.

Eddie tossed the slave the keys, and he locked the shackles in place. He then lifted her arms high above her head, and she moaned in pain. One long chain was attached to the central bar between the wrist shackles. She craned her neck in the semi-darkness and could make out an iron shaft sticking out of the wall, with a ring at the end of it.

The slave took a padlock from Eddie and hooked it to her chain. He then attached it to the ring at the end of the wall shaft and clicked the lock closed, until both shaft ring and her chain connected like a necklace. He tugged at the chain and then at her metal wrist cuffs. He nodded to Eddie and threw the heavy keys back to him, and Eddie hung them again on the wall.

Eddie slapped the slave on the back and got down to Mercy's level. He lifted the candle to her face, blinding her.

Mercy's arms felt as though they would break at the shoulders. Looking into the light, she saw nothing. Eddie's bad breath assaulted her nostrils, the candle's flame burned her cheeks, and to make things worse, her arms were becoming unbearably painful.

Eddie's fingers whipped her head around to face front. His head suddenly swooped in, and his mouth connected with hers in a deep, penetrating kiss. He said, "If I had my way, I'd kill you right now and be done with you. But, as it stands, keeping you alive will bring me some more of those dollar bills. So I'll be back later, depending on how I feel after I've eaten a delicious cooked chicken and drunk a few beers, and then we'll have some fun to pass the time. You'd like some fun before you die, wouldn't you, Mercy? I can give you that, something nice to take to your grave."

Mercy jerked her face away from him. She couldn't bear to look in his direction.

"Hmmm, we've got all night, you and me," she heard him say. "Mrs Mallory won't be back till morning, so you can enjoy a night with the rats and your last day on earth thinking about what a bad, bad girl you've been. She'll finish you for good this time."

Mercy spat in his face. "You're a bloody rat, Eddie. No; you're du Pont's dog, wagging your tail when she gives her orders. Well, I've never been scared of dogs nor rats," Mercy threw at him. "Let her come. And when she gets here, be sure to tell her that it was me who burned down her bloody house in Liverpool. See how she likes that!"

She still refused to look at him, but she heard his intake of breath and felt his fist connect with her cheek. Her head banged against the uneven wall. She cried out in pain. Then she finally saw his face as it came within inches of her own. She spat at him again, aiming for his eyes. Her mouth was dry, but a smattering of saliva dribbled down his forehead.

He wiped the droplets away with his sleeve and surprised her by smiling. Then he laughed. "You clever bloomin' whore. So it was you who destroyed du Pont's empire? I have to give it to you, you've got spunk." He laughed again. "And as for me being her dog? She doesn't even know you're here, so she didn't order me to take you. That was me, all me…woof, woof! You'll be a nice surprise for her when she gets home."

"I'll look forward to seeing her, so I will," Mercy told him defiantly. "And I'm not a whore. I left that bloody house a virgin."

Eddie ignored her words. "Oh, she's going to have a great time finishing you off. It won't be a quick slice of the throat, though, I'll tell you that for nothing. She's going to make you suffer slowly, and I'm going to enjoy watching."

"I'm not scared of you or her. Do you hear me? I'm not scared!" Mercy shouted as Eddie moved away into the dark shadows.

She watched both men climb the stairs. The door opened, and then the candle was snuffed out. She was left in the darkness, terrified and alone.

Chapter Forty-Nine

Mercy sat in the black, freezing-cold room, defeated, afraid, yet strangely calm. Her cursing bothered her, and she silently said sorry to God. Her arms were so very painful that she decided to try and stand up. Twisting her legs, she brought her knees up to her chest and turned to face the wall. She then palmed her way up the rough stones until she stood at shoulder level with the iron shaft that held the rings, padlock, and chain. She turned around again and leant against the wall with her arms mercifully lying at a more or less correct angle.

She sighed with a half sob. Madame du Pont was going to inflict excruciating pain on her body. She'd seen what the woman was capable of. Her bravado in front of Eddie had only stoked the fire, for when du Pont found out that Mercy had burned down the mansion, she'd make her suffer all the more. *You're stupid, Mercy Carver, stupid and prideful.* She could kick herself for those words to Eddie.

God had swooped down to effect vengeance on her for murdering an innocent man. He had brought du Pont to carry out the sentence for him. Only God could have made this situation come about. This was her punishment, her comeuppance, as her grandfather used to say. "You'll get your comeuppance, girl, if you do this or do that."

She sobbed now. Grandpa's judgements had been lenient in comparison, a caning or a few slaps on the backside with a shoe, a couple of days without food…but this? She should be screaming at the thought of dying. Why wasn't she screaming? She felt numb and witless; that was why. She found it impossible to imagine not being alive. She pictured her throat being sliced open and felt nothing. She saw herself being punched and stabbed, again nothing. Death, she decided, was just unimaginable.

Mercy's breath caught in her throat. She stared into the darkness, swearing she had heard a voice coming from somewhere in the basement.

"Miss…miss, can you see me? Over here…I'se over here."

Mercy clearly heard the soft, deep voice, but she couldn't see an inch in front of her face. She focused her eyes, looking to her left, right, and front. The sunny morning had gone, and the grey light outside was almost redundant. Even the small shaft of light shining through a hole in the stone wall had diminished.

She heard a rattling of chains, and again, and a third time. She was not alone in this dungeon? Who was here with her? Whoever was there, he'd remained silent while she was being shackled, and had been completely ignored by Eddie and the giant slave.

"Who are you? Where are you? I can't see you. Are you chained up too?"

"I'se here, miss, against the other wall…near the table. My feet is shackled, real tight. I'se sittin' on the floor. I can't move."

"I'm sorry. I can't see you," Mercy said again, trying desperately to locate him. "Can you see me?"

"I sees you, miss. I sees you when you come down here." He rattled the irons again to give her direction.

This time, Mercy looked to where she remembered seeing the table, and then to the right. The chains were still rattling. The noise was as heavy as the irons. She looked again. The small shaft of light from the broken wall stone settled on specks of dust falling softly down the wall diagonally in front of her. The ray of daylight cast itself upon them. She followed the dust until it settled, and then saw the outline of a head. The man's body was impossible to make out; however, the sand-coloured dust was like tiny, shining crystals raining in the air. She focused her eyes on the head and said, "Rattle the chains again, but harder this time."

He did so. She noticed that every time he rattled his chain, the anchored wall shaft moved slightly, which in turn made the dust fall.

A thought entered her head. She turned to the wall behind her and felt its texture with her palms. She scraped her fingernails along the grouting between the stones. It was soft, yes…just like sand. Every time she shook the iron shaft, sand dust fell.

If she could wiggle the shaft enough, it might just come loose from the wall.

"What's your name?"

"Nelson…Nelson Stuart from Stuart Plantation. They gone now, the massa and mistress; gone to live in the city. Sold me at auction to Mr Eddie and the devil woman," he said even more miserably.

"Nelson, I'm Mercy, Mercy Carver. I'm going to try and loosen the shaft like the one high above you. Can you try too?"

"I gone did try, Miss Mercy, but I ain't been able to reach it. I'se as strong as the ox, but I caint stand on my feet to get at it, on account of being in irons."

Mercy nodded in the darkness. "Nelson, how often does Eddie come down here?" she wanted to know.

"I'se ain't got no way a knowin'. I ain't got no way a telling how long I'se been here, but he ain't come with no food or water, and I knows it's been day and night twice now. I'se mighty thirsty. I'se don't reckon I'se sees morning'."

"I'm going to try and free myself, and then I'll unlock your shackles. Do you know how to pray?"

"I sure does. I'se prays to the good Lord every day," he told her proudly.

"All right, then. Start praying."

There was hope; Mercy kept repeating in her head. If she could just get the shaft out of the wall before Eddie came back, she would be free.

"Please God, please God, save me. I can do this. That bleedin' woman is not going to get me again. Please help me. Come on, you bloody stupid wall, fall down," she whispered in the darkness.

After some time, and now with bleeding palms and fingers, she admitted that the shaft wasn't going to move enough to come all the way out. It was hammered in far too deeply.

She leant against the wall, not quite ready to give up, but panting for breath; she was exhausted. She would kill for a drop of water. "I'm sorry, Nelson. I don't think I can do it."

"You can do it, Miss Mercy. You got to do it, or you be dead in the morning. You can do it. I'se knows you can."

Mercy's silent tears were broken by soft sobs. She had cried more this past year than she had in her entire life. But this was no time to cry. She had to keep trying to loosen the shaft. Did she want to die a horrible death? No! Did she want to see the face of that vile creature, du Pont, again? No! She would rather rip her hands to shreds than die here at *her* hand.

"I'll try," she told her faceless companion.

She grunted and panted, twisting and turning the shaft. She pushed it up, pulled it down. It moved slightly from side to side, around and around, until finally, in one circular movement she felt it loosen. It became easier to move in all directions after that. She giggled. "Come on; you bleedin' stupid thing. Get out. I can do this. I can do it!"

She pulled at it. The shaft moved out an inch, bringing with it dust that stung her eyes. She pulled again, leaning back and using the weight of her body for leverage. The dust was thicker this time, and sand was breaking off in lumps. She pulled again, as hard as she could, and suddenly found herself on the other side of the room, sitting on a sore backside.

"Nelson," she groaned. "Nelson, I did it. I did it. I'm going to find the keys."

She heard his sigh of relief. "Lord above, you'se gone and did it. Hurry, Miss Mercy," he urged her.

Mercy moved on all fours with difficulty. Her shackles, chain and padlocked shaft made it hard for her to do much more than shuffle her body in small awkward movements. She did not want to stand. She was blind in the darkness and would probably bump into something and knock herself out. The floor was safer. Finally, her knuckles hit a wall, scraping them. She grimaced. Her hands were bloodied and torn already, but she didn't care. Again she palmed her way up the wall, using her hands to feel for the hook that held the keys. She pictured Eddie holding the candle and knew that the keys were halfway up the wall and halfway along it. The heavy shackles restricted her movements. She tried to hold her arms up, but the irons fought to bring them down. Her fingertips tapped along, and then she felt the keys. They jingled at her touch.

"Don't you bloody well drop them, Mercy," she whispered. Grasping the keys in her right hand, she cried with relief. "Nelson, say something," she said quite loudly.

"I'se here. Follow my voice. I'se here. That's it. I hears you chains. Them be gettin' louder."

Mercy touched a leg and took a sharp breath. "Oh, I'm sorry," she said nervously. She followed his leg with her hands to his ankles and found his shackled feet. Tracing the centre bar, she found the keyhole. Her hands were shaking, cumbersome, and difficult to manoeuvre, but she managed to get the first of the three keys in her fingers and tried pushing it in the hole.

"No, not that one," she told Nelson. She tried the second. It slipped in and turned to the right, and the shackles sprang open.

Mercy then used Nelson's body as a guide. She pulled herself up by his torso until she stood upright. Lifting her arms high above his head, she got to her feet, felt the wrist chain, and followed it to his hands. She found the shackles and smiled.

This time she found the right key on her first attempt. The shackles once again jumped open, crashing to the ground. The noise was loud, and she began to panic. "Nelson, unlock me…quickly," she begged him.

Nelson found her fingers and took the keys from her. On his third attempt and with the last key, she was freed from her chains.

Chapter Fifty

Mercy and Nelson found the rickety wooden stairs and stumbled up them. At times they missed a step or stubbed their toes on the next step's underbelly, but eventually they reached the top platform. Nelson felt the door panel and then found the knob. He turned it. It was unlocked.

"Ha! That's what you get for being a cocky git!" Mercy whispered, thinking of Eddie.

The door creaked open a couple of inches; just enough to allow Nelson to see what there was outside. He looked, creasing up his face in the daylight, and then turned to Mercy, who was trembling with fear and excitement.

"Sssh, Miss Mercy. We's gotta run for it. I don't see nobody, but that don't mean they ain't there."

Mercy nodded, staring into Nelson's ebony face. It was swollen to double its size down one side. One eye was shut and looked like a fat black bubble. His nose and mouth were caked in dried blood. She put her hand up slowly and touched his cheek. He jerked his head back at the intimacy.

"I'm sorry they did that to you, Nelson," she murmured sympathetically.

He said nothing and opened the door. Mercy followed him out into the short, open passageway with three more steps leading upwards at the end of it. She then saw his back, his ripped shirt and lash welts, broken skin with flesh hanging. She covered her mouth with her hands to stop from venting her shock, anger, and sadness. She was surprised he'd made it up the stairs.

They peered over the grassy bank that bordered the passageway. They were at the side of the house, which meant that they had only a very short run to the thick treeline that sat to the left of them.

"Are you ready to run, Miss Mercy?" Nelson asked.

She nodded in silence.

Crouched down again, Nelson was ready to take the first steps forward, but Mercy grabbed his arm. He swung his head around.

Mercy stared at him again. Another plan had come to her in the last few seconds, and it didn't involve running. Her wits were with her, she was determined, and now all she had to do was convince Nelson to stay with her.

"Nelson, I'm not running away on foot. You need to get your back seen to. You won't last a day and night if we don't try and stop it from getting infected. And you will be a fugitive. If you get caught, that bloody big cow of a woman and her faithful dog will hang you or whip you to death. I know the buggers!" Mercy's eyes were flashing with rage. "There are things we need. I want a gun and your ownership papers. I want a horse because I'm too tired to walk…Nelson we have to do this properly. Madame du Pont and Eddie are not going to kill anyone else. I swear they're not."

"But Miss Mercy…"

"No, Miss Mercy nothing. How many slaves are here?"

"She got three more; Moses and two girls."

"Will Moses stop us?"

He nodded angrily. "He real happy here. He ain't never been beaten. She like him, and he ain't no friend to me."

"Well, I don't care. I'm not leaving without the things I need. Will you help me?"

"It's too dangerous," Nelson said sadly.

"Will you help me, though?" Mercy asked him again.

Nelson winced in an attempt to smile. "I reckon I'se will. Be my pleasure. But I'se don't hold out much hope of us be gettin' away."

They climbed the steps and then skirted the side wall to the corner until they reached the back wall of the house. Mercy looked over to a barn and saw horses outside, tethered by reins to a bar. There were no saddles, and she had never been on a horse's back, but they were hers to take nonetheless. She was filled with thoughts of vengeance. She clung to the hatred now overwhelming her. It would give her strength and courage.

They came to a window, and she looked through it from the ground up. She saw the room was unoccupied, and they moved on. She looked through the next window they came to, crawling behind Nelson in a gown she now cursed. It was a damned nuisance.

The room was a kitchen. Two girls were present. She grabbed Nelson's leg and put two fingers up, pointing to the kitchen window. He nodded, and they moved on.

They came to a door, which Mercy believed to be an outside pantry door. She looked back at Nelson, who confirmed her suspicions with a whisper. "It be leading to the kitchen, Missy. The girls ain't gonna stop us if we tell them be plenty quiet. Mr Eddie, I'se guessin' he be in the drawing room drinkin' or eatin'. Moses be always with him; when he not upstairs with the mistress."

Mercy thought for just a moment. This was becoming a stupid idea. She still felt weak; she doubted she could overpower a chicken, never mind two men, unless…

"We need to find a gun first."

Nelson nodded. "Mr Eddie hangs his gun and belt in the hallway closet. Mrs Mallory don't allow no guns in the drawing room."

Mercy had questions but decided that now was not the time to ask. They had to act quickly. "We'll get the gun. We'll hold them up and get Eddie to give me your papers. We could tie them down with something…no, wait, we could shackle them in that basement…"

"We's need to get dat gun," Nelson reminded her. He opened the door, and they sneaked into the kitchen through the inner pantry door.

He silenced the girls with his finger. They nodded submissively, shocked by the sight of his tortured face and even more shocked at Mercy's appearance.

Outside the kitchen was the dining room. The two slave girls confirmed in whispers that both men were in the drawing room.

A kitchen door led straight to the hallway. Mercy prayed. Her actions were those of a madwoman, but her mind screamed that she had to see this through to the end.

She nodded to Nelson and took the lead, slipping into the hallway. The closet with the gun that Nelson had told her about was not within the drawing room's line of sight. Mercy slowly and silently turned the doorknob, opened the door, and saw the gun and holster hanging on a hook. There was a rifle there too, and she handed that to Nelson. She reached up and pulled the gun out of the holster. She hadn't a clue how it worked. She turned it over in her hands. It was heavier than she thought a gun would be.

She had seen her grandfather Carver once cleaning a pistol. It had not been the same as this gun. His had been much bigger, with a longer barrel, but it had a similar lever on the top. How hard could it be to hold a bleedin' gun and make it look menacing? She pulled the little lever back, cocking it, but not knowing what her action meant.

Nelson nodded, whispering, "You gone made the gun ready to fire."

She saw the trigger and a small catch. She didn't know what the catch was for but slid it back anyhow. The thick, round barrel dropped out of position and hung loose. She looked into it. There were six conical shaped balls inside, in separate compartments. She pushed it back into place with a small click and looked at the trigger and the cocking lever again. "I think it will definitely fire now, she whispered. "There are balls and grease in these compartments." Picking up boxes of bullets, she added, "I'll take these bullets, too. You check that rifle, seeing as you've probably seen one before."

Snoring could be heard coming from the drawing room before they even got to the open door. Mercy knew that this was the moment to conjure up all her hatred to hate with all her might. She closed her eyes for a second, remembering everything Eddie had done to her.

"Make sure that rifle doesn't go off," she whispered to Nelson.

She poked her head into the drawing room. Eddie and Moses were asleep in armchairs. She gestured to Nelson to follow her.

"Wake up, Eddie, ya lazy git. You too, ya big, ugly giant!" Mercy was scared, but she let the anger rise, bringing flashes of the past towards her.

Eddie's shocked expression and the black giant's wide, frightened eyes left her feeling cold and confident.

"How the hell did you get out?" Eddie asked.

"That doesn't matter. I want Nelson's ownership papers. I want your partner to sit on that chair over there while you get them," Mercy told him.

"Fuck off, Carver. I don't take orders from a woman, especially a whore."

"Then I'll shoot you. I'll shoot you where you sit because that's what I fancy doing. I mean it, Eddie, I will kill you."

"And you'll bloody hang for it."

"Why? No one knows I'm here. Anyway, what if I do? It'll be worth it just to know you'll never hurt anyone again. Get the papers. Look in that desk over there. They had better be there, or I'll follow you all over the house till you find them and give them to me. Nelson, find some rope."

"I ain't goin' for no rope, Miss Mercy," Nelson told her.

"I've counted the balls in this gun. There are six. I'll be fine. Go find some rope."

"Get them papers first, Miss," Nelson told Eddie. He looked at Mercy. "I'll go get dat rope when he done give you the papers."

Mercy nodded. "You're right. I wasn't thinking. You stick that rifle in *his* face." She pointed to Moses, now sitting on a chair in front of Nelson.

Eddie laughed. "You're going to die, Mercy Carver. You're not getting out of here alive. You dare to hold me at gunpoint; I don't think so." Eddie spat out the words without drawing breath. "You're a stupid girl thinking you can best a man."

Mercy raised the gun higher, pointing it at his head. "I will best you, ya big lout. Do as I say and then we'll see who's stupid here."

"All right, all right. Calm down. I'll give you the bloody papers. Nelson Stuart, belonging to Mrs Margaret Mallory, right? Is that what you're after?"

Mercy nodded.

"So what's the problem? No need to tie me or Moses up, is there? We'll let you go. You've got the guns, remember."

Mercy nodded, becoming strangely hypnotised by Eddie's power. It was as though she were back in the whorehouse, terrified of him. "Shut up, Eddie. Just get them," she said, hardening her voice.

"All right, but don't do anything daft. I'm going for the papers," Eddie said. "You were right; they're here, in the desk drawer."

Eddie turned his back on her, bent over, and stretched his arm across the breadth of the bureau. He opened a drawer, rummaged through it, and then slowly lifted something. Nelson had a better view of the drawer than Mercy, and could now see a gun in Eddie's hand. He screamed, panicking at the sight of it.

"Gun…he got a gun!"

Mercy heard Nelson's shout and reacted like lightning. She aimed the Colt at Eddie's back. The gun was cocked, and she squeezed the trigger. The bullet hit him, nicking the back of his left ear.

For a second or two Eddie looked stunned. Mercy stared at the back of his head, but then she too saw the glint of a gun in his hand. Adrenaline pumping through her, she squeezed the trigger again, and again, and again.

The snap and whistling sounds were deafening. With each shot, Mercy saw Eddie's blood explode and spray outwards from the centre of his back. Her finger wouldn't stop squeezing the trigger until she heard Nelson scream her name again. "Stop shooting! Help me, Miss Mercy!"

Turning, she saw him wrestling for the rifle with the giant slave. The noise of gunfire still rang in her ears. Moses was overpowering Nelson. The gun was being turned towards Nelson's neck. Mercy aimed the gun at the giant's head, squeezed the trigger twice in quick succession and screamed, "No!" She continued to squeeze the Colt's trigger, which now made nothing more than a clicking noise.

The slave's head disintegrated. Blood splattered on Mercy's gown and face. He hit the ground with a sickening thud.

Nelson's voice once again brought her mind back from the brink of complete madness. Her entire body shook. She looked down. His big hands covered hers. Nelson's fingers were on the gun barrel, and hers, still clicking the trigger.

"Hush now, Miss Mercy. It's over," he said.

Mercy realised that she was still screaming the word *no*.

"Miss Mercy, put the gun down. That's right, now. Put the gun down. There ain't nothin' more to fire at. They be dead now, ain't no doubting that."

Mercy stopped screaming and stared blankly at Nelson. She watched her arm being lowered and saw the gun being taken from her grasp. She looked at the gun in his hand as though it were some wondrous, magical creature that had just saved her. She forgot to breathe for a few seconds. Then she exhaled with piercing sobs of fear and disbelief. As she wept, she fell to her knees.

Nelson watched her torment unfold. The two girls tiptoed in and stood at the door, in silence. Only Mercy's cries to God were heard. Only her prayers for forgiveness broke the stillness in the room.

After a few minutes, calmness descended upon Mercy. She stood up and walked to the far side of the desk. Bending down, she looked into Eddie's face and lifeless eyes. She pushed his dead body off the desk and watched it hit the floor, feeling nothing but remnants of hatred. Papers; she needed to find the papers. Rummaging through the top drawer, she found what she was looking for, and smiled. Eddie had not lied. The papers were there for each of du Pont's slaves.

She took the one with Nelson's name and tucked it into her bodice and then she picked up a map of Virginia and also decided to take that.

Approaching the two girls, who shied away from her in fear, she told them, "I'm sorry to have put you in the middle of this. I'm going to have to tie you up. If I don't, you'll both get into bother with your mistress, or, you can run away," she added as an afterthought.

The girls shook their heads, looking shocked at the very idea of it.

"All right, but you understand that you are staying here with a cruel woman? And you understand why I have to tie you up?"

They looked at each other and nodded.

Nelson said, "I'll go find dat rope now. You gotta take off that there dress, Miss Mercy."

Mercy looked at her wet, bloodstained gown. "I'll go look for something to put on and see if there's anything else we can take with us, like money and food."

Mercy suddenly grabbed Nelson's hand. She said, "Nelson, you do want to come with me, don't you?"

"You saved me, Miss Mercy. I'se yours now. I'se gonna look after you. Ain't no more harm gonna come to you, not while you got ole Nelson. But where we gonna go?"

"Don't worry about that just yet. Tie the girls up, and then come look for me."

Nelson nodded.

When Nelson left the room, Mercy turned her attention to the girls. She was calm and poised and couldn't understand why she wasn't still screaming with the shock of it all.

"I know you're scared, but those were bad men. This one," she said, pointing to Eddie, "was going to have me killed tomorrow. Your mistress was going to cut my throat."

"He *was* bad." One of the girls spoke for the first time. "He done took me every day, and was real rough. I'se real glad he dead," she added, spitting on Eddie's dead body.

"Please, don't tell on me when your mistress gets home. If the sheriff comes, tell them that a bandit or a thief killed these men. Will you do that for me?"

The girls looked at each other.

Mercy could only guess what they were thinking. She hated the thought of leaving them here with du Pont. But she was about to embark on a perilous journey with one slave and couldn't, wouldn't take responsibility for three. If the girls agreed and stuck to a story, they wouldn't be harmed. But if du Pont threatened them and they told her the truth, du Pont would beat them and send all hell after Mercy. She wouldn't give up until she'd crushed Mercy once and for all.

"I'm asking you to lie and to never tell the truth about what happened here. And you mustn't blame Nelson because he didn't do anything. I killed the men," Mercy said, pleading with her eyes.

The two girls nodded in unison. "We ain't gonna say nothin' 'bout no woman been here, we promise. And may the sweet Lord bless you for killing that evil on the floor," one said.

Mercy sighed with relief. She couldn't be sure if they would stick to their word, but if they could, even just for a day or two, it would give her and Nelson a good head start.

"Thank you. Now, do either of you know where your mistress keeps money?"

"I do," one said. "I'se see'd her one day with a money box in her bedroom. I knows she puts money in her boots too."

"Could you go get all the money for me?" Mercy asked her.

The girl beamed. "I can surely do that."

"I can get you's both some food for sure, Miss," the other girl said.

Chapter Fifty-One

A dense cloud covering hid the stars and moon. In the barn, Mercy held a lantern up whilst Nelson saddled a horse for her. She had never felt as alive or so grateful to still *be* alive. The shock of what she'd done had now worn off, yet she could scarce believe she had killed two more men. She was still shaking, hanging on to an outward calm for dear life, but she was traumatised. Had she been alone, she would still be sitting on the floor, weeping.

She felt no guilt or sadness at the murders just done. She felt no pity for Eddie, nor the giant slave, or for herself and her present situation. But she needed Jacob. There was nothing she wanted more than to be in his arms right now, for he would make everything right.

She stared into Nelson's beaten face. Nelson would hang for these murders if he stayed. Madame du Pont would accuse him, wondering at the same time how he broke loose from his chains. The idea of taking Nelson somewhere safe was ridiculous. She didn't know the country. She hadn't even had a chance to see the bulk of Portsmouth. Yet her instincts told her to help him, for she could never live with herself if he were blamed for the murders *she* had just committed.

The two slave girls had tended to Nelson's back. He hadn't cried or uttered a sound when they cleaned and disinfected his wounds. The only indication of his suffering had come from his tightly clenched fists, his trembling lips, and his face, which had perspired. Had Madame du Pont arrived home, Mercy would have shot her without hesitation. This thought also scared her.

She had saddlebags filled with food and water. She was taking blankets and spare clothes, and now both she and Nelson wore thick winter jackets. She had dollar bills stuffed inside the bodice she still wore. There was money, and plenty of it stuck to her right and left breasts, and even stealing the money couldn't conjure up guilt.

She also took shackles and the key that fit them. They lay solidly inside a bag that would be right next to her at all times. She had a feeling they would come in handy at some point, for what woman travelling alone would allow a slave to walk beside her on the road, unshackled?

She had gone through the cupboard in the hallway and had found ammunition for the guns. There were two different types. She compared the balls inside the rifle's barrel with the balls in a box and found them to be the same. Nelson showed her how to load the Colt. He used to do this for old Massa' Stewart, he told her. She watched him fill the barrel's compartments with powder. Then he pushed in the conical balls, and finally, greased each compartment, telling her that this would stop one compartment from igniting another. She had the packhorse laden with everything she could think of, including a small pan for cooking, but there was no room for Nelson to sit on its back. "I still don't see why we can't have a horse each," Mercy told him. "It's not as though there's not enough of them here."

"Miss Mercy, if those white fokes see me, a nigger slave, on a horse, they be shoot I'se dead for real. An' I ain't never sat on no horse."

"Me neither. But we've got to do it, or else we'll never get far enough away from here. I'm not going to get up there on that horse and watch it go at a snail's pace with you walking beside me. We'll just have to share a horse for now and hope we don't fall off."

"Ain't no problem riding together be night, I'se do reckon. Ain't no one in them woods for miles," Nelson said.

"Good. We'll get as far away as possible, and then we'll rest when the sun comes up."

"But I'se got to be takin' you home to you's fokes," Nelson said.

"We're not going home. I thought you knew that. I know your mistress better than you do. She'll have us both hanged. Just finish getting the saddle on, and then we'll see about where we're going."

Mercy, aware of Nelson's questioning stare, thought again about what she was going to do.

Home and family? No. She couldn't go back to Portsmouth. Madam du Pont would go to the sheriff, crying about her murdered men, especially Eddie. She would report her missing money, and Nelson would be hunted like a fox. And what if du Pont spotted her like Eddie had? The old hag would find a way to get to her and might even accuse her of the killings out of spite, with or without proof. And the two slave girls, whose names she hadn't even bothered to ask for, might be tortured into telling du Pont or the sheriff the truth. She couldn't bear to think about that.

Jacob had understood why she murdered the man in Liverpool, but these killings were becoming a habit! She was a multiple murderess now and wouldn't be safe in Portsmouth, not from the law, or from du Pont. And those she now loved; what would they think of her if she appeared in Portsmouth with this story? No, she thought sadly again. She had destroyed any hope of getting back to Jacob because she'd pulled that trigger.

What if they waited there until morning to kill du Pont? That would finish off the sordid tale completely, and she would never have to think of the vile woman again. But she remembered Jacob's story about Nat Turner, the slave. Nelson would not only be blamed for killing the two men, but also a white woman. He'd be hunted from here to the North, east, and west. They would use dogs and trappers. He'd be caught, eventually, and sliced up like a dog's fleshy meal. Blimey, the situation was bad enough without adding du Pont to the list of killings. Sweet Jesus, Mercy thought, what was she becoming?

Mercy thought hard. She'd heard that slaves were free in the North and lived among the white people there. They had houses, ate in restaurants, mixed at parties, and had jobs. She believed it because Isaac had told her so, and he was from a place called Boston, which lay far North of here.

Why shouldn't she take Nelson to the very first Northern state she could reach? It wasn't a bad idea. Afterwards, she'd return to Portsmouth and tell everyone she had been abducted by bandits, Indians, or thieves. She had plenty of time to weave a story. She would cry like a Southern lady.

Mercy was inspired to be more optimistic about her future. Pessimism was being overturned by hope. Some of her fears were probably unfounded. With the powerful Stone family by her side, du Pont couldn't and wouldn't dare to show her true colours. She was not strong enough now or in any position of power to threaten anyone. Mercy smiled for the first time. She was going to see Jacob again after all, but only after she had completed her mission.

Mercy told Nelson to get on the horse. She was wearing one of Eddie's shirts, and a pair of britches held up with braces. She had crumpled her own soiled clothes, and they were inside one of the saddlebags. She would bury or burn everything she'd worn today. After pulling her hair high into a knot, she covered it completely with Eddie's hat, and then tied the leather hat strings tightly around her neck to keep it from falling off.

She snuffed out the candle inside the lantern. Nelson pulled her up onto the horse's back to sit in front of him. Her body seemed high off the ground, she realised with some trepidation. Turning towards Nelson, as much as was possible, she said, "You know, I learned a lot of things on the ship I was on. We're going North, and I know a bit about the stars." She looked up. There were no stars. "The North Star is up there somewhere, and I know how to follow it. We need to get into the woods and ride as far and as fast as we can, and pray we don't fall off this animal."

"Where we be goin' Miss Mercy? You wanna be goin' right side or left?" he asked, confused.

"Go to the right and hope we don't end up in the middle of Portsmouth. Pray that we'll have a clearer sky tomorrow night. We've got a long way to go, and I intend to set you free, Nelson Stuart!"

Chapter Fifty-Two

Jacob, Hendry, and Isaac sat nervously waiting for the sheriff to update them on the investigation. Mercy had been missing for three days. Isaac had gone to pick her up for the party and had been deeply worried when he was told by a distraught Handel, that she had not returned from her outing that morning.

Isaac and Hendry had gone straight to Sheriff John Manning, who had immediately asked for a posse be put together and dispatched to all areas of Portsmouth, its outskirts, and east as far as Norfolk. A missing white woman was a serious event. As the hours passed, it became apparent that Mercy was either lost or had been abducted. No one dared to mention murder just yet.

Jacob had returned to Stone Plantation with Elizabeth, filled with emptiness and regret. He'd begun to notice his bride's numerous and infuriating habits. He knew that he possessed many flaws in his character, but it seemed to him that Elizabeth, for all her Southern breeding, failed to see any of hers.

Elizabeth was discourteous in her opinion of others. She didn't seem to give a damn about the well-being of anyone but herself and constantly spoke about her own desires, from her wardrobe to her ideas on how to completely remodel everything in Jacob's house in order to leave her indelible mark upon it. She had pounded him with questions about Mercy, even on their wedding day, and had insisted that the English woman was just too common and would, therefore, never be invited to any picnics or balls at Stone Plantation, forthwith.

Elizabeth wasn't that different from any other Southern woman he knew. She was a product of a traditional upbringing, as part of which, girls were overindulged, and bred purely for marriage, without thought to intellect or sense being part of their tutorage. Elizabeth followed the old Southern idea that all wives had a duty to conceive but were not necessarily expected to enjoy lovemaking with their husbands. They had made love only once.

Mercy had spoiled him for life. He now knew the joy of being with a selfless, lovable woman who displayed an open and honest character, a disarming smile, a curious mind, and a natural passion. She was invisible now, yet always present.

On their fourth day at Stone Plantation, Jacob entered the dining room and found Elizabeth at the breakfast table. Grasping a bundle of papers in his hands, he hoped he looked sufficiently worried for her to ask what was wrong with him. When she carried on eating, saying nothing but a good morning, he took matters into his own hands.

"I have to go into Portsmouth this morning. I'm taking my fastest horse and won't be away long. Hendry forgot to take some vital papers with him, and he'll need them for the port authorities."

"Oh, but you caint go, Jacob!" Elizabeth moaned and stamped her foot under the table. "What will foke around here think? This is our honeymoon. I want to be alone with you here. And you did promise to talk to me about the new colours for our bedroom today. It's not fair!"

"I know, my sweet, but I'll be gone just a few hours. I'll bring you a nice surprise back," he said.

"You will? What will you bring me? No, wait. Why don't I come with you, and then I can choose? You'll have to wait until I change, though. I should look my best. I don't want those silly girls in Portsmouth thinking I've let myself go just because I'm a married woman, now do I?"

"No, of course not," he said, sounding appropriately shocked at the idea. "But that's why it's better if I go alone so that I can get back to you as quickly as possible with a nice new gown that will make you the envy of every woman in Portsmouth." Jacob was growing agitated at the sound of her voice. He added for good measure, "And I'll bring you a new bonnet to go with it. No girl in Portsmouth will ever laugh at you, my dear."

"That's so sweet of you," she gushed.

Elizabeth was forgotten now as Jacob continued to wait with Hendry and Isaac.

Sheriff John Manning, a long-time friend of the Stone family, had taken over the new sheriff's building whilst Jacob had been in England. He had his own small but private office and deputies under his command. The entire building had been refurbished since Portsmouth had been incorporated as a city.

Sheriff Manning was ensconced in his office with a woman, and the three men were growing impatient and aggravated with him and with each other.

Jacob's face was ashen. He tried to digest the terrible news that had been delivered to him within minutes of his arrival at Hendry's Portsmouth house. There, he'd found Belle and Hendry, who had done their best to explain what had happened. Jacob had raged at both of them for not getting a message to him the moment he'd returned to Stone Plantation.

"There are at least fifty men out of Portsmouth involved in the search, and about a hundred covering Norfolk. It is New Year's Eve today, but they'll keep looking regardless. I'm sorry, Jacob," Hendry said. "You must feel like hell, but understand, you have a new wife who already suspects you're in love with Mercy. The last thing we wanted was for you to up and leave Elizabeth your first day home to look for another woman, particularly when that woman is Mercy!"

"I am living in hell," Jacob told him honestly. "And I am sorry for bringing my hell to your door. I'll apologise to Belle, of course. She didn't deserve my outburst, especially with her being in a fragile condition."

"She understands, and she's tougher than she looks. But, goddammit, Jacob, I've never seen my Belle cry as much as she has these last few days. She knows all about Mercy's ordeal in Liverpool and is beside herself with worry. She loves Mercy. We all do."

Jacob turned then to Isaac. He had been surprised to see him still in Portsmouth. He'd thought he'd never see him again. "Isaac, I'm so sorry 'bout the things I said to you afore I left. Thank you for being here. When you were out with the posse, were there no signs, nothing to give us hope?"

Isaac shook his head. He'd barely slept in three days. He was dead on his feet, but he'd go out again today, this time overnight. They were widening the search. "Three days have passed, and I believe Mercy has gone…really gone."

"I don't believe that! You know how tough she is," Jacob barked.

Hendry put his hand on Jacob's shoulder and forced him to look at him. "Jacob you're not thinking straight or being realistic. Mercy left our house, a stone's throw from all the stores she needed. There were no corners to turn, no dark or dangerous alleyways to get lost in, and just one street to manoeuvre. It was mid-morning. There is no way Mercy could have lost her bearings. She's got a good head on her shoulders. She would have asked directions."

"What are you saying?" Jacob asked him with a thunderous look.

"I'm saying that I…we, believe, she could have been taken by someone or numerous people, but that's just one theory."

Flashes of anger and then anguish alternated in Jacob's eyes. If this was what had happened, he'd kill the bastard responsible. That was his only thought and the only words he could hear in his mind.

"Have you considered that Mercy might just have decided to leave of her own accord because of your marriage?" Hendry asked. "We caint overlook that possibility."

"No!" Isaac butted in, surprising Jacob and Hendry. "No, Hendry, you're wrong. I saw Mercy the day before your party. I took some medicine to her. Though she was still weakened by the virus, she was also excited and happy. She didn't run away. My gut tells me she didn't."

Jacob rose to his feet. He'd had enough of sitting and waiting. He didn't like what he was hearing. He would lash out at someone very soon if he wasn't careful. "Who is he in there with?" he demanded of the deputy on duty.

"Some woman called Margaret Mallory," Jacob was told. "She's been coming in here for two straight days. Her overseer and a slave were murdered out at her farm…used to belong to the Gibsons."

Jacob nodded. "Yeah, I remember old man Gibson. That's a tough break for a woman to handle."

"Well, I reckon she's a tough old bird if you ask me. She's English, been here bout three or four weeks. The dead overseer came with her on the ship, name of Eddie Gunn. Been with her for years, she said."

Jacob's head spun. Eddie Gunn? Mercy's abductor in London had been called Eddie. He was du Pont's henchman and one of the men who tried to burn the women to death. Was it possible?

"So she's all alone now?" Jacob asked him, trying to sound calm, attempting but failing to steady his fast-thumping heartbeat.

"Yep. Says she's all alone and scared. One of her slaves has run away too. Guess he did the murders. We're out looking for him."

"And where was she when the men were murdered?"

"Away at the time, visiting with the Harpers at some party or other. Lucky for her, cos the damn nigger would have had her too, I reckon."

"Yeah, she's a lucky woman," Jacob agreed.

"Yep. There were just the two men and two nigger girls in the house. Them nigger girls were tied up in the kitchen...alive but didn't see a dang thing, so they told me."

The name Eddie and the fact that he and this mysterious Mrs Mallory were both English must be a coincidence, surely. Could du Pont be in there? He needed more answers.

"So the two girls, how come they saw nothing?"

"I dunno, Mr Stone. All they said was that it was a big fella, wearing a jacket, gloves, and some sort of mask covering his face. All they saw was a pair of eyes."

"A mask, huh?" Jacob said. He wondered why a slave from the farm, known by the two girls, would be wearing a mask. That didn't make any sense...

"I saw the bodies, Mr Stone. There was blood everywhere. That poor Englishman never stood a chance. The fella had three holes in his back, and half his ear shot off...in the goddamn back! Can you believe that?" the deputy said. "That nigger's gonna get strung up as soon as he's found. You just wait and see. Ain't gonna be no trial. Trouble is we already got two posses out on account of that missing Englishwoman. What is it about the goddamn English? It was a nice quiet Christmas, and then the English came and blew the goddamn city down with their shenanigans."

Jacob had a hundred more questions, when finally the office door opened and he spun round ready to face the woman who would confirm or deny his suspicions.

Sheriff Manning escorted the woman out. Jacob recognised her immediately. His mouth went dry, and his heartbeat quickened again. She had less paint on, and a more conservative wig, light brown in colour. She was dressed in mourning black, but it was her. The woman was a damn chameleon. By now, Hendry and Isaac were also on their feet. They saw the woman and looked to Jacob, who warned them with his eyes to say nothing.

Jacob casually turned to the window. Hendry and Isaac also turned from her and began a soft-voiced conversation.

Jacob's mind raced, but his conclusions were quick to come. Madame du Pont and Eddie had something to do with Mercy's disappearance. His gut told him that. He knew Mercy and her past better than anyone, even better than Isaac, who only knew the half of what happened that night in Liverpool.

This was no coincidence, du Pont, Eddie, and Mercy were inextricably connected.

Jacob's heart soared. If Eddie was dead and if a slave was dead, then maybe, just maybe, Mercy had been the one to kill them? He knew this theory was bordering on the ridiculous; a young, defenceless woman being abducted and then getting away by shooting two grown men. But he also knew that if Mercy *were* dead, du Pont wouldn't be here.

The missing slave was puzzling. Had he taken or killed Mercy?

Goddammit, it was time to get out of here. There was no going home for him, not yet.

He felt sure Mercy was out there, on the run, either afraid of being caught for murder, and, or, eaten up with guilt. He smiled to himself. *That's my girl, Mercy,* he thought with pride. *You're alive. I know you are.*

Jacob looked out onto the street with thoughts of murder on his own mind. He would take revenge on du Pont regardless; that was a given. But now he needed to concentrate on du Pont's parting words with Sheriff Manning. He blocked out everything but the sound of her voice.

Margaret Mallory dabbed at her tear-stained eyes after glimpsing Jacob, Hendry, and Isaac. She recognised them instantly. Christ, she'd known she might bump into some of her American customers at some point. She'd come here to this part of the world because of them and their gentlemanly ways. But if they recognised her, she'd be finished in this city. City? Bloody stupid…Portsmouth was as small as her neighbourhood in Liverpool!

With her back to the men, she spoke quietly to the sheriff, who was patiently waiting for her to stop crying. "As I said, you can find me at the Langton Boarding House. I'm not living in that house of death on the Hampton Roads another minute, not until that slave has been caught and hanged. I think I'd die from lack of sleep. I'm so alone and vulnerable, you see. If only I had a husband to protect me," she sobbed a little more.

"Don't you worry about nothin'," Sheriff Manning told her. "We'll swing by your place and make sure it's all locked up tightly for you."

"No…well, that's very kind of you, but like I said before, I've taken my valuables. I'd just like the house to be left as it is for when I return. It's all cleaned up, and I made sure it's locked. I can't stand the thought of anyone else going near it just now. You understand, don't you, Sheriff?" She dabbed her eyes a little more.

"Of course, if you're sure…?"

"Quite sure. Please, just remember I must be informed as soon as you find that murdering black man. I would hate to think of others being put in danger because of him. He's a horrible, horrible creature, Sheriff."

"You have my word, Mrs Mallory. The nigger won't get far," Manning assured her. "We've got dogs out and some of my best trackers with them. We almost always get our niggers back, though some do happen to die of their own accord. He won't last long in this cold weather, I reckon. He'll freeze to death. It's more than likely we'll bring his corpse back. You sleep easy, Mrs Mallory, and don't you hesitate to come back here anytime."

"Thank you, Sheriff." Madame du Pont stretched out her arm, let her hand grow limp, and waited for the sheriff to kiss it. Once he did, she walked to the door and left.

Jacob, Hendry, and Isaac walked back to Hendry's house. There had been no new updates from John Manning. The posse would set out again within the hour, he'd told them.

Jacob had another idea, which he wanted to run by Hendry and Isaac. His plan was simple.

Seated in Hendry's drawing room, Hendry and Jacob explained to Belle what they'd seen and heard. All, without exception, were feeling more hopeful because of du Pont's presence in the sheriff's office. They agreed that had Mercy's body been found by du Pont, she would not have come forward with such keenness and drama. Instead, she would have tried to draw attention away from herself, not towards herself. They'd just heard about a damned expensive funeral for Eddie Gunn, with four plumed horses, a black carriage, and *her* in black garb following behind with the new acquaintances she'd ingratiated herself with!

Isaac and Hendry listened to Jacob's plan. They thought it sound, and after a light lunch saddled the horses, ready for a ride out to the Hampton Roads.

Before leaving Belle's house, Jacob sent a messenger with a letter to Stone Plantation, informing Elizabeth that he was not returning this day or the next. It was his civic duty to join the posse searching for Mercy Carver and the missing slave. Mercy was Belle's dear friend, and he was doing this for Belle. He finished by saying that he would be home before she knew it but then decided to add, out of a sense of duty, that Elizabeth was welcome to join him in Portsmouth.

Chapter Fifty-Three

Jacob smashed a window on the ground floor, knocking out the remaining shards of glass with his rifle butt. He climbed in, followed by Isaac and then Hendry. They spread out, going from room to room. The downstairs rooms smelt of disinfectant. They had been cleaned thoroughly, yet blood splatter still remained visible on part of the drawing-room wall. Jacob rummaged through the desk drawers, but each one contained little more than bills and writing materials.

The men met in the hallway and concluded that, as far as the house was concerned, there was nothing to suggest Mercy had been there.

They searched the barns next; nothing. The horse stalls and paddock had been cleared out. Jacob suggested that the horses must have been taken by Sheriff Manning and his men.

They came to the side of the house. Jacob stopped, noticing the small passageway that led to a door. "We'll take a look in here. Then we'll have a look around her land." He kicked a stone. "Goddammit, I thought we'd find *something*," he said, frustrated.

The basement door was locked. The men tried to kick it in, but it was stubbornly strong. Jacob told the others to stand back and pointed his rifle at the keyhole. He fired a couple of shots, and the door flew open inwards. They left the door open for light but saw that it wouldn't be enough once they got down the stairs. Jacob asked Isaac to bring candles from the house.

Jacob and Hendry waited at the entrance. Hendry was first to hear the muffled sounds coming from below. "Jacob, I think there's someone down there."

Jacob's heart raced. "Mercy!" he shouted. He moved quickly and stumbled down the stairs, but when he reached the bottom, he saw nothing but a black hole. A woman's muffled sounds were growing louder. He shouted to Hendry, "Where the hell is Isaac?"

Isaac appeared. "I'm here, Jacob. We're coming down."

Each man held a lit candle. They turned to see a room about fourteen feet long and ten feet wide. They saw the black slave girls tied and gagged in one of the far corners. One girl was mumbling through the rag gagging her mouth. The cotton was bloodied.

Jacob gasped, sympathy for their plight reflected in his eyes. "Oh, my God," Was all he could mutter.

Isaac undid the gags.

The girl moaned softly and stared unseeingly. Her entire face was damaged. Teeth had been knocked out, and her jaw bone was broken. Both eyes were swollen shut, and her black skin had been torn by what looked like fingernails. Even in the soft candlelight, they could see the red and blue bruising on her ebony face, which had lost all structure.

Isaac took a closer look at the other girl. He looked up in the orange glow and shook his head. Her beating had been more severe, coupled with an open wound on her throat. A dried blood trail completely covered her shabby dress.

Hendry took the live girl outside and laid her on the grass, putting his jacket on top of her freezing-cold body. She cried in silence, unable to voice her suffering properly because of the wounds to her mouth and jaw.

In the basement, Jacob asked, "How long Isaac?" "A day, no more," Isaac told him, after examining the body's lividity.

Jacob carried the dead girl's body up the stairs and into the softening light of late afternoon. The sky was grey with not a patch of blue. His mood was as dark as the sky while his hatred for du Pont as bright as the hidden sun.

He knelt on the ground and was reminded of the last time he and Isaac had lain girls onto grass and tended to their injuries.

"Déjà vu," Isaac said, reading Jacob's mind. "Is there no end to du Pont's cruelty?"

Isaac was with the other girl, who was still breathing laboriously. Her eyes were rolling upwards. She tried to speak but couldn't utter a sound. He asked her if he could lift her dress. There was no response. He lifted it gently to just above her belly and saw the bruising and distension. Isaac looked at Jacob and Hendry and said, "She's bleeding internally." He held the girl's hand and whispered softly, "Who did this to you?"

She stared at him once more, trying to open her mouth, and then she stopped breathing.

"We know who did this," Jacob said, standing over the bodies.

"I've seen some beatings in my time but never like this."

"There ain't no animal that kills for pleasure the way du Pont does," Jacob said, angrily.

"No sir, I reckon she enjoyed tearing these women apart." Isaac looked up to see Jacob rubbing his eyes. "We can't take them back with us to Portsmouth. If du Pont did do this, it means she might have found out Mercy was here."

"That's exactly what I'm thinking," Jacob agreed. "She more than likely tortured them to get to the truth about who killed Eddie. Their story to the deputy didn't make sense to me. So who were they covering for?"

"The slave?" Hendry suggested with a shrug.

Jacob shook his head. "I don't think so. If the missing slave murdered the two men, why would the girls lie about it? No; they were covering for someone else, someone more vulnerable. I'm guessing du Pont got that someone's name or description from them, and then she had to shut them up. It has to be Mercy. It has to be."

Isaac stood and took Jacob by the shoulders. "Are you telling us that you believe Mercy killed the men and then ran away with a slave of her own accord?"

"That's precisely what I'm saying." Jacob smiled.

The three men decided that they should not accuse du Pont of these murders, for if they did, she would take Mercy down with her and accuse her of the double murder. Mercy would be called a whore, Jacob reminded them. She would become a fugitive, a wanted woman, a woman who had run away with a nigger slave.

Jacob had no proof of anything, yet he *knew* Mercy was alive. She was out there, somewhere, and his only mission now was to track her down and bring her home.

He stared at the two dead girls for a moment and said, "We need to bury these girls in the woods. For the moment, du Pont will just have to torture herself wondering where the slaves are and who has them."

Isaac creased his brow with worry. "Jacob, she saw all three of us in the sheriff's office. She looked right at us. I know it was just for a split second, but she's sure to make some kind of move on us at some point…even if it's just to make sure we won't tell anyone who she *really* is."

"Or she'll keep her mouth shut and stay in the shadows," Hendry gave as another opinion.

Jacob agreed with Isaac. Madame du Pont lived to be centre stage. She wouldn't remain in the shadows. She needed friends, and she'd be wondering right now if they'd given her away to Sheriff Manning. Let her wonder, Jacob decided. This was becoming more like a game of chess, and he intended to win. He said to the others, "I've got no idea what that woman will do next, but we'll let her make her moves. The best way to fight her is to keep our mouths shut. If we don't give her any reason to suspect us of knowing what she's done, she'll be blind. She'll want to know why we're ignoring who she really is. When that time comes, she'll seek us out."

Chapter Fifty-Four

Mercy shivered. She had never felt cold like this, not even in the coldest London winter when her grandfather very often spent the coal money on drink and it was colder inside the house than outside.

The air bit into her face, leaving it red and raw with chilblains, which she could only imagine must appear horrific to anyone who looked at her. Her eyes continuously streamed and were hurting her, so much so that it was becoming difficult to keep them open. Every breath she exhaled was like a grey fog that lingered in the stillness of the night. Now, in the early morning, her breath left her mouth like a white cloud. She wrapped a dirty shirt around her face, leaving only her eyes visible. Better to look stupid, she thought than to freeze to death or have frostbite on her skin.

She and Nelson had been on the run for eight days and nine nights. She knew this because she had marked a small cross on the linen map with each sunrise. The skies had been kind. They were clear, and the moon was growing. The North Star and great Venus were bright. Their presence had guided Mercy's path through the Virginia countryside in the long hours of darkness. Having left Portsmouth far behind them, she decided to rest at night and travel during daylight hours within deserted, dense woods.

They slept in thickets, always surrounded by trees and never anywhere in the vicinity of dwellings, even when those would be barely visible in the distance. They had been lucky, for on two occasions they had found shelter in abandoned cabins, and even the horses had been given respite from the cold by being under the same roof as them.

They ate sparingly now but had all the water they needed from small streams that were like veins running through the land. When Mercy was sure they were in isolated positions, she got the gun and rifle out and practised shooting, using targets placed in the soil of banks or hillsides. She began from close range, and every day put more and more distance between her and the target.

Shooting guns had become an obsession with her. She wanted to be a good marksman, an excellent shot. Guns would kill animals that they could then eat. A gun or rifle would keep her and Nelson safe from any bandits they might come across. Her gun had killed Eddie, and she was alive now because of it. She slept with her Colt under her blanket. She had to be ready for anything or anyone. She was confident, for she had, through practice and determination, become a talented shot.

This morning they came across a small river running through a clearing of tall grass. The water was crystal clear, with a pebbled floor where fish were darting back and forth. She'd catch a few. She'd done it before, and though she wasn't particularly fond of their taste, they were a good source of nourishment, and that's what mattered.

Small sheets of ice floated casually along with the soft current, bumping into logs and branches and breaking up like shattered glass. She turned to Nelson, standing slightly behind her, and said, "Nelson, I have to do this. I'm filthy. I have to wash off the grime. I still feel as though I've got the stench of blood on me. I'm going in."

"You gonna freeze to death, Miss Mercy," he said, shaking his head. "Ain't no way you gonna come out of there without gittin' the influenza."

"I've just had influenza. I won't get it again. I'm going in and so are you," Mercy said defiantly.

"No, ma'am. I'se sure ain't, Miss Mercy. No, sir, I ain't going in there with no ice or fish a bitin' d'es legs."

Mercy rested her hands on her hips and looked at him with determination and authority. "You will so go in. You're as dirty as me…dirtier even! You need to clean your wounds and wash all that dirt out of your hair. We've got soap, and we're going to bathe, and smell like flowers. Then we'll eat and continue on. You'll feel much better afterwards, I promise."

"No way, Miss Mercy, no way," Nelson said again.

"No arguments. I own you, remember," Mercy said with a mischievous giggle. Nelson looked miserable. He had apparently lived an easier life than she had in the Elephant and Castle!

"I'll make a deal with you. You make a fire and start heating up those beans. I'll bathe, and then when you come out of the river, you'll have a nice warm fire and something hot to eat. Doesn't that sound good?"

"All right den, but I ain't likin' it. I reckon we's can die in dat dere water," he moaned again.

Mercy stepped on the pebbles on her way back to the shoreline, hurting her feet on the odd jagged stone. The embankment was rocky, but just behind the rocks stood rushes and bushes as tall as she was. Behind them were fir trees that stretched for as far as the eye could see. Their camp was set just a stone's throw from this river but was well sheltered from the forceful wind.

Her hair was dripping wet and clean and covered the entire top half of her body like a black blanket. Stepping onto the rocky bank, she grabbed her bodice, tucked the dollar bills into the bodice cups after she'd fought to get it back on, pulled on a clean shirt, and buttoned it up to her neck. She pulled up the trousers, tightening the braces, and then finally sighed with relief after donning the thick woollen jacket.

When she reappeared, the fire was just beginning to rise and give out some much-needed heat. She walked to the pack horse, retrieved her hat, and after pulling her hair back into a topknot, stuck the hat on. She smiled at Nelson, whose face was filled with undisguised disapproval. Mercy stared right back at him, undaunted.

"Before you say anything, Grandma Sylvie always told me that a person's soul left through the top of the head and cold air filled a body by entering through the top of the head. So that's why my hat is covering my soaking wet hair."

"I ain't sayin' nuttin'," Nelson told her moodily.

"You don't have to. You're like my grandma; she was an open book. I could tell exactly what she was thinking just by looking at her face, and I know what *you're* thinking right now. Now take the soap, off you go, and don't come back till you're clean. I mean it."

Mercy stirred the beans. She was agitated and hated not knowing exactly where they were. She was well aware that they were slightly off course. She couldn't detect the big river's pungent smell at all now, and the terrain had changed from flat to rocky. She believed they were now far enough away from Portsmouth and any search party that might still be looking for them, but she couldn't be certain. How far would Virginia go to find a runaway slave? Especially one who'd probably already been found guilty of murder. Would they be hunted whilst still inside the state of Virginia, even the most Northern part? The Metropolitan Police in London had wanted posters printed and placed all over England when hunting criminals. Was it the same way here?

She looked at the map she had found along with the other papers in du Pont's house, and had to squint, focus, and refocus until she found her starting point. The map was old, probably more than twenty years old as the material had turned yellow. The writing and all the important names of the towns had faded, and it had been folded so many times there were open slits on every crease, which made many names and words disappear completely.

She drew her finger along it on the right-hand side, pushed it upwards, and found her starting point; Portsmouth. Her finger glided across to Norfolk and then upwards to the great inland waterways and islands of the Chesapeake Bay Estuary. She had hated that part of the journey. Had she been there under any other circumstances, she would have thought it beautiful. Being a fugitive, she had instead found the highly populated waterways both dangerous and worrying.

Mercy shuddered. She had found it necessary to shackle Nelson and lead him like a dog. They had gone through turnpikes and over toll bridges. They had boarded a small packet boat in one of the bays that took them across a narrow stretch of water to another island. Once there, Mercy had flicked her eyes over the other passengers waiting to board an even bigger packet boat, which would take them over a wide stretch of water in the bay area. There had been no sign of a sheriff or anyone else displaying interest in her or Nelson, but there *had* been too many people around for Mercy's liking.

They had managed to find a quiet spot, devoid of hordes of travellers, and had boarded the last boat of the day, which held no more than a few stragglers.

The boat crossed the Hampton Roads, also noted on the map as being called Tidewater, a part of the Elizabeth, James, and Hampton rivers. Mercy had closed her eyes, breathing in the fresh air, and was immediately reminded of Jacob and her night-time conversations with him on the *Carrabelle*'s deck. *Dear God, I miss you, Jacob*, she thought.

Her eyes watered with the pain of losing him. She wiped the tears away with an angry scowl. This was no time to be feeling sorry for herself. She concentrated once more on the map, remembering the fear she had felt on those crossings. It had crept into her veins, making the blood race to her heart that in turn thumped so hard she was left breathless. There had been so many people milling about, going here, there, and God knew where.

They had gotten close to the town of Hampton, where there would have been hot food, but she had refused to go near its centre.

Mercy had believed that taking the coastal route, with intermittent water travel, was the best and quickest way to arrive at the next state, which was Delaware. But she had not taken into account that it was probably the most dangerous route. There was, she had eventually come to believe, only so many crossings and harbour towns, and they would have been caught at one of them, she was sure of that now.

They had rested on the outskirts of Hampton that night, although sleep had been as elusive as a hot meal. At first light, they rode the eight miles to Newport News, and that was where she'd seen the wanted posters in full view of everyone coming off and going on the packet boats.

Her eyes had scanned the board plastered with posters. She saw Nelson's first. It read:

Wanted dead or alive,

Dangerous slave who goes under the name of Nelson Stuart, wanted for the murder of two men. One of the murdered men was negro, and slave, the other a white overseer. He is of thin build, over 6' in height, and is owned by Mrs Margaret Mallory, from Portsmouth, Virginia. He is to be approached with caution and brought to the nearest sheriff or marshal, dead or alive. 1,000 dollars reward.

Mercy had stared at it, noting the pathetic and inaccurate drawing of Nelson's kind face. The image looked like any other black man in Virginia, or in the world. It was a caricature, an ink drawing of a round head with a wide nose and full lips. It was not the kind, thoughtful, and gentle soul she had come to know. She had been insulted by that poster.

She had then found her own likeness on another poster, which was much more detailed and sympathetic.

> *Missing*
>
> *Miss Mercy Carver. Beloved friend and resident of Stone Plantation, Portsmouth, Virginia. Missing since December 28, 1860. Mr Jacob Stone will pay a handsome sum of 5,000 dollars reward for anyone who brings her in alive to any sheriff or marshal.*

Mercy had felt her body tremble at the sight of her name. She had believed that they'd already travelled far, yet she and Nelson were still being hunted…unconnected, but both hunted all the same. They had taken the first boat westward from a harbour in Newport News. The last town they had skirted was Smithfield, where she'd bought some supplies. From there, they had headed Northwards, always avoiding populated areas, and stopping to rest only when necessary. Mercy was annoyed with herself for not taking the time to study the map carefully. She had made many mistakes in such a short period of time. If she weren't so cold or miserable, she'd find it funny, for so far they had travelled east, North, west, and were now slightly North again, yet still within striking distance of Portsmouth! Blimey, she thought, she wasn't a good navigator. She wasn't even that good at following stars. Thank God she had steered them in the right direction, for had she taken one more wrong decision, she and Nelson might have ended up going South, and straight back to Portsmouth itself.

She stared without seeing and unconsciously stirred the pot of beans dangling from a wooden spit above the fire. That fire had promised much, but had, after many attempts to revive it, dwindled into not much more than a pile of ash blowing in the wind, with only a hint of flame left. It was a pitiful fire, she thought. It was not warm and welcoming and hardly produced enough heat to steam the bean sauce.

She looked up and lifted an eyebrow in amusement. Nelson had returned and was desperately trying to dry his tight, wiry, curly hair that was as wide as it was long. She laughed. "You may as well stick your hair in the fire if you want to dry it," she told him. "It's the worst fire I've ever seen."

"I'se got lots of I hair," he pointed to Mercy's hat, "But all dat wet hair stuck under Mr Eddie's hat ain't never gonna dry," he told her.

Mercy smiled at his earnestness, but she had no time to discuss her hair further. "I say we bypass towns from now on. We'll eat like the pioneers did. We'll trap rabbits or catch fish. And I've decided to go a bit more to the west. What do you think?"

"I'se don' know, Miss Mercy. I ain't never seen no rabbits, an' I aint never been North of Portsmouth 'fore now," Nelson told her.

He didn't like the sound of going west, he thought to himself, but he would go where she went and would never let harm come to her. He'd promised her and the good Lord. "Ain't no freedom in the west, Miss Mercy, but I'se sure didn' like d' way dese men look at you on dat boat."

"Yes, I noticed. I was scared they were going to ask me where I was going when I wasn't even sure myself. I don't think we should chance all those places along the river again. Going west will mean that our journey will take longer, but it'll be safer. I bet there will be more wild animals to eat."

Nelson nodded. He liked the sound of that.

Mercy unfolded the map again and looked North. They would not be able to get to Delaware if they did go towards the west. She drew her finger across the map again and said cheerily, "Right. I think I've got it. If we go slightly more to the west, and then we follow the North Star again, we should come to Pennsylvania eventually. I believe that's a free state for black people. My…my friend, Jacob Stone, told me where the free slaves live."

She folded the map and put it back in the saddlebag and smiled again at Nelson. "Let's not worry about anything right now. I'm starving, and these cold beans look good."

Chapter Fifty-Five

Jacob had ridden as far as he could and for as long as possible before finally giving up because of bad weather. No one he had questioned on his journey through the Chesapeake Bay and the Hampton Roads had recognised Mercy's likeness or remembered a woman with her distinct accent.

Mercy had now been missing for over two weeks. Virginia was looking at a harsh winter, with more blizzards and snow than the state had seen in years. Even at the coast, the snow was piled high, and conditions had been treacherous with cruel horizontal winds blowing without respite during short days and long nights.

It was mid-January and his Northern advance all the way up to the Delaware River, stopping in every small, large, or port town, had yielded nothing. He was weary and broken-hearted but had not given up hope of seeing Mercy again.

He had thought about many things on that journey. He wondered how it was possible to feel so much joy one day, only to lose that extraordinary feeling of complete fulfilment the next. Mercy had given him the great love he'd always imagined existed. It had surpassed all his expectations. He didn't only love her; he craved her, felt her with him even now, and saw her every night in his dreams. They were still connected by some inexplicable power. That was why he *knew* she was still alive. He physically ached for her. It was both comforting and tormenting to believe in his heart that she was well.

He was a few miles outside of Portsmouth, but instead of turning his horse left, which would have taken him into the city, he turned right and headed towards du Pont's house. His torment had grown with each mile. He believed du Pont could lift some of the heavy burden from his shoulders by giving him answers. He would use force, if necessary. He would kick her door down, and he would remain there until he got information that might give him a better understanding of what had happened to Mercy. He was convinced that du Pont would have returned to her farm by now, in fact, he was counting on it.

His horse whinnied at her front door. He dismounted and tethered the reins to a wooden post. Through lace window curtains, he saw candles flickering. He stood for a moment, trying to hide and contain the hatred he felt towards du Pont, and then stepped onto the porch.

A slave woman opened the door. Madame du Pont stood behind her, dressed in a cream-coloured gown which displayed the shape of her hanging, saggy bosom. Gone were all the necessary tools she usually used to enhance her looks. She had no corset to hold up and shape her bosom and pull her in at the waist. There was no jewellery to hide the folds in her neck or earrings to cover long, dangly lobes. Her wig was old, showing bare netting on bald patches. Yet her face was caked with powder and rouge, black kohl pencil on top and bottom eyelids and eyebrows, and bright red paint smeared above and below her lip line in an attempt to hide the wrinkles that surrounded them.

She stared at Jacob, blinking with surprise and then folded her arms across her chest, displaying her annoyance.

Jacob removed his hat, shook the snow off it, and barely managed to hide his inner desire to kill her. "Good evening, Madame du Pont," he said.

"It's Mrs Mallory now, Mr Stone. What do you want?"

"Are you going to invite me in?" Jacob asked.

At that, du Pont pushed the slave girl aside and came to stand in the doorway. She poked her head out and looked around to find out if he was alone. He was the last person she wanted to see. She didn't like the way he was looking at her, not one little bit. "No. It's late. I was just going to bed, and I'm not accepting visitors."

Jacob pushed her and the slave aside he strode into the drawing room and waited for du Pont to join him. He warmed his hands by the fire and glanced at his tired bearded face in the mirror above the fireplace. "I see you have another slave," he said when she entered the room.

"I have, and I plan to get more. What's it to you?"

"Just an observation," Jacob said.

"John Manning, my dear friend, got her for me. John and I have been stepping out together, you know. So, Mr Stone, why are you here?"

John Manning was a damn fool, he thought. Jacob continued to stand in front of the fire but turned to face her. "Oh, I think you know why I'm here."

"No, I don't know, so you best be telling me before I throw you out."

Jacob laughed at her. "I'll leave when I get what I've come for. Don't threaten me."

"Well, go on, out with it then."

"I want information about Mercy Carver," he told her.

"Mercy Carver? Why do you want to know about her? I do know her, of course, but I can't help you. I don't know where the girl is…England, I suppose. She was just a well-used whore who came to me for a job, just like all the other whores did. You must know this, Mr Stone, you visited my mansion many times to fuck my girls."

Jacob felt his rage rise to the surface. He returned her contemptuous look. "Yep, I guess I did, so you can drop the 'Mrs Mallory' act with me. I know who and what you are. I know the truth about how you acquired your whores. I know that you beat them, tortured them, and killed God knows how many. I despise you. If I weren't a law-abiding citizen, I'd take you to that basement of yours, shackle you to the wall, and beat you to death. But I'm not like you. I'm a decent human being, hoping that justice will catch up with you, one day."

As she sat down in an armchair, du Pont stared with loathing at Jacob. She'd been waiting for something like this to happen, although she had suspected it would be much worse. Ever since she went to the sheriff and saw Stone and his friends there, she had known one of them would try to make trouble for her, eventually.

"If you think your insults bother me, you're mistaken. I've known tougher men than you who tried to best me and couldn't. Let's just get down to business. You want to know about Mercy Carver, and I want to know why you haven't told anyone who I am and how we met in Liverpool. Am I correct?"

"That's about right, so let's not waste any more time. What do you know about Mercy Carver's whereabouts?" Jacob asked.

"All I know is that she was in Portsmouth and then disappeared. I was shocked to learn she was here. How the hell *she* managed to get herself on a ship to America, I'll never know. What's your interest in her?"

"It doesn't matter what my interest is. I'm here for answers, and you're going to give them to me. I know she was in this house. Your man, Eddie abducted her. I know this because the two slave girls you murdered informed me that she'd been imprisoned here and had escaped. They told me everything afore they died at your hands." Jacob saw and heard her intake of breath. "Don't waste my time denying it. We both know it's the truth, so don't insult me with lies. You tortured those innocent girls, and I suspect you got information from them. I'll stand here all night 'til you tell me exactly what they disclosed to you about the night your two men were killed."

"Eddie and Moses were murdered in cold blood!"

"I don't think so. They probably deserved to die, same as you."

"I'll report you to the sheriff, so I will. You've no right to be here, badgering me like this. You're trespassing, and I can get you charged for that!"

"I told you once, and I'll tell you again, don't threaten me."

"It's not a threat. I'll do it. I'll drag your bloody name through the mud. What would your wife think of this, eh? You barging in here without so much as a by your leave. I've been seeing a lot of your Elizabeth."

"What?"

"Oh yes, me and her have been keeping company ever since you went off gallivanting, looking for your whore. I'm having lunch with her tomorrow. She's become quite dependent on me. I'm such a good listener, and she has so much to say about you."

"You'll stay away from my wife!" Jacob blazed.

"Oh, hit a nerve, have I? Well, it's too late for that. She's told me all about you being a rotten husband, and she'll be telling a lot more people soon, you mark my words. She likes my company, and I've got a lot of tasty titbits to tell her, none of them nice where you and Mercy Carver are concerned. So don't you bloody tell me what to do. I'll swat you like a fly! That's right, Mr Stone, you just try telling tales on me to your wife or keep me away from her, and we'll see who's sorry then. If you make any accusations against me, I'll make sure there's a warrant out for Mercy Carver on a charge of murder.

"I'll tell everyone you killed my two slave girls and buried them in my garden. Oh, I know where you put them, all right, and I know it was you and probably your brother and that Isaac. I'll take you and your whore to the depths of hell with me if you don't leave me alone to get on with my life in peace." She shot him a look filled with hatred.

"You'll never have peace, not while I'm alive," Jacob told her.

"Don't you dare bully me, ya big bugger! I'll not be having it. Mercy Carver *was* here, though I doubt she was abducted. Do you want to know what those black bitches said? They said Carver killed my Eddie and Moses. They told me she took off with that black git, Nelson, and they said she wasn't sorry for killing poor Eddie. There, what do you think of that?" She glared at him.

Jacob digested her every word. She had just confirmed that Mercy had been alive and well when she had left the farm. He remained outwardly calm, but his heart was thumping. He'd never wanted to kill before, but he did now. It would be a pleasure to wring du Pont's neck.

"Did the slaves tell you where she was headed?"

"No! I'm telling you nothing else."

"Jacob believed that du Pont didn't know anymore. "Listen carefully. You *will* stay away from my wife," he warned. "You won't go near my brother and sister-in-law either, or there will be hell to pay. And if you call Mercy a whore once more, I'll break your goddamn neck. I'm warning you, don't take my reticence to dispose of you for weakness. I will destroy you when I'm ready."

"You can't destroy me! Didn't you hear what I just said? Mercy Carver murdered my Eddie and Moses. I've got the sheriff in the palm of my hand and his cock in my mouth to keep him happy. I've got your wife running after me like a puppy dog because you're neglectful of her. I have Virginia's finest inviting me to their parties, and enough dirt on you and Mercy Carver to bury you both. So tell me, what are you going to do for me? Are you going to keep your mouth shut, or are you going to force me to cry like your mealy-mouthed wife and tell everyone what you and Mercy Carver have done?"

Jacob was losing patience. She had ingratiated herself into his family. He dreaded to think about what Hendry and Belle must be going through. They had obviously not given her real identity away or acknowledged it. She had also gotten Sheriff Manning into her bed. She was toying with him, and he now knew that talking was not going to get him the information he needed.

She sat back with a look of smug satisfaction on her face.

Jacob's anger was mounting. His breathing quickened, he was being consumed by hatred. Storming across the room, he ripped the wig from her head. She squealed, and a fearful expression crossed her face. He pulled her out of the chair, marching her to the mirror with his hand gripping the back of her neck. The kohl along her bottom eyelids ran in straight lines down her cheeks, along with her face powder and tears. His heavy hand drew across her eyes and mouth, swiping the red paint off her lips until it was all over her cheeks, chin, and jawbone. Her face was pushed towards the mirror until her nose touched it. He forced her to look at her reflection, fingers digging into her skin.

"Look at yourself. Take a good, long look at your balding, scabby head. See your wrinkly skin and ugly face. Look at all the ugliness inside you, out in the open, sitting on your face. I'll drag you down the Portsmouth Road like this. I am one of the most powerful men in South Virginia. There is not a politician, judge, or jury that won't do my bidding. So don't test my patience, you damn murdering whore!"

Her fear was visible as she stared at her reflection, mesmerised. "You're a bastard. I'll scream, and my slave will come running," she hissed at him.

Jacob drew his gun, turned du Pont around to face him and pressed the tip of his Colt into her forehead. He pushed it hard against her skin, giving it a circular dent. Cocking the gun, he stared into her face with eyes blazing.

"Make a sound, and I'll blow your head into this damn mirror. Now tell me about the night Mercy Carver was here…and I surely do mean, everything?"

"I need your word that you'll keep your mouth shut about me?" she sobbed now.

"You're in no position to bargain, so stop your tears. You're not human enough to cry. Start talking," he ordered.

"The slaves…they told me that she looked at a map. She had this stupid notion of getting to the North with the slave, Nelson. The girls wouldn't tell me at first, but then they spilt their guts. They gave her food, and she stole guns and all the ammunition. The bitch took the same gun she killed Eddie with. That's all I know. I don't know anything else!"

Jacob believed her. He holstered his gun and then pulled her back from the mirror and threw her into the chair. Picking up her wig, he tossed it into the fire and then turned to face her.

"You've tested my patience, du Pont. I have never afore and will never hurt a woman, but you I would kill without a moment's hesitation. Way I see it, you've got two choices. You can leave now and never come back, and you might live a long and miserable life 'cos that's what you deserve. Or you can remain here. But if you decide to stay, know that I will make your life hell, and it will be short. I may not do what I'm aiming to do today or tomorrow, but your past *will* catch up with you. You have my word that I am going to kill you for what you did to Mercy and those innocent girls, both here and in Liverpool. You won't walk down a street in South Virginia without looking over your shoulder because I'll always be watching, deciding whether it's the day to abduct you, take you to a backwater swamp, and cut your throat wide open."

"You can't talk to me like this! You can't tell a woman you're going to kill her and get away with it. You hurt my head, ya bugger!" she screamed at him.

"I will get away with it. As God is my witness, I will. I've never met pure evil afore, yet here you sit right in front of me. Send a note to my wife. Lunch is cancelled. Don't so much as try to see her again or go near my brother and sister-in-law. Remember one thing. I can protect myself and Mercy from you, but who is going to protect you from me?"

Jacob put on his hat and then he turned to her the door. "This conversation never happened. Are we understood?"

"Yes, we're clear on that, and it suits me just fine. But I'm not going anywhere. You don't scare me, and you'll not be stopping me from seeing who I bloody well please! If you say anything about me, I'll make up so many stories about you; your bleedin' head will spin. Now get out of my house…ya backstabbing lout!"

Chapter Fifty-Six

Jacob finally arrived at Hendry's townhouse. Elizabeth was in their bedroom, Handel told him. Mr Hendry and Miss Belle had retired.

He ordered a tray with cold meats, bread, and hot chocolate, and told Handel to get a hot bath ready for him.

He forced his aching body up the stairs to the guest bedroom and found Elizabeth brushing out her long, straight hair. "You're still up," he said.

"As you can see, yes, I am. So you're back, or are you going to leave again in the morning?" Elizabeth greeted him sarcastically.

"Yes, I'm back, my dear," he said. "Are you well?"

"I'm well enough as if you care. I'm spitting mad. You abandoned me, and I am still a new bride. I just don't know what our friends must be thinking. Your behaviour is unforgivable, Jacob. It's despicable."

He answered a knock at the door. Two servants carried buckets of hot water and filled the tub in an adjoining room, warm by a raging fire going in the hearth. Jacob closed the door between Elizabeth and himself, undressed and got into the tub's inviting warmth, which, he thought, should just be enough to thaw him out and calm the anger that still lingered.

After dinner, Jacob joined Elizabeth in bed. She was asleep, or so he thought. He was exhausted, yet he was hungry for the feel of a woman…any woman, for in his mind she would be Mercy, and he had never needed Mercy more. He caressed Elizabeth's body, dreaming of Mercy, eyes closed and a small, pleasant smile planted on his mouth. He was jolted out of his dream when he suddenly felt Elizabeth tossing his hand aside.

He snapped his eyes open in shock. He looked up at her, sitting with her back now resting on fluffed-up pillows, arms crossed over her breasts, hidden under her baggy cotton, floor-length nightdress. She wore a scowl that had managed to wipe out any trace of sweetness on her face. She had a right to be angry, Jacob thought. He would allow her barrage of insults and would accept her punishment, whatever that might be. He waited patiently whilst she continued to rage at him with a stare alone. Finally, he said, "All right, Elizabeth. Say your piece."

"I don't want you to touch me. I've not long bathed, and I don't want to be sullied. It's too cold to have to get out of bed to clean myself."

"Oh, I see," was all he managed to say. He was surprised to be having *this* conversation.

Elizabeth pouted like a sullen child and began again. "It's obvious to me and everyone else in this house that you are in love with that Englishwoman. Belle isn't even taking my side. Why, she barely speaks to me anymore, and Hendry is just like a puppy dog doing her bidding."

"That's called love, my dear."

"Well, I don't care what you call it. You will never see that Mercy Carver woman again, so it makes no difference one way or the other. She'll be dead somewhere by now."

"She might well be dead in this cold, lying under a tree, rotting as we speak. Does that please you?"

"Don't you dare be sarcastic, Jacob Stone. You know fine well that you've humiliated me in front of everyone from here to Norfolk!"

"I think that may be an exaggeration. I'm sure folks are too busy hibernating from the cold at the moment to be bothered about us."

"You are not a gentleman. To think I could have had any man I wanted...but somehow I chose you," she told him. "Why, I don't know what I was thinking. But since we are married in the eyes of the Lord, you had better treat me right, or my family will hurt you and your brother. It's just as well my poor mother doesn't know what I've been a going through. Her heart wouldn't take the shame of it all."

"Then let's be thankful that it's too cold for your mother to entertain and hear all about your shame. Now answer me this...why are you so damn mad about another woman when you've just thrown my arm away? Don't you want me to caress you?"

"I don't want you to make love to me. I don't need *those* affections. I just need you to be a good husband, especially in front of our friends and anywhere in public," she stated, surprising him again.

"But don't you want children?"

"Why, yes, but not yet. In a year maybe."

Jacob tried to stop a gurgle of laughter threatening to spill over and out of his mouth, but he controlled himself and his thoughts. "You know we have to have sex if you want to conceive," he reminded her.

"I know that. I'm not stupid! I just don't want to take any chances that I may get pregnant before I'm ready.

I want to have some fun. And you are going to allow me to have what I want because if you don't, I'll tell everyone in Portsmouth that you are being a beast to me, and that you're in love with some common white trash!"

Jacob laid his head on the pillow, tired out and too drained by tonight's events to think straight. He didn't want to touch cold, uninviting flesh any more than she wanted him to touch her. He wouldn't caress her again. He turned his back on her. "We're going home tomorrow, so if you have made plans, cancel them. Stone Plantation needs my attention. As my wife, you will be by my side…like any good Southern woman!"

He lay in the darkness, deliberating that du Pont would not get onto his land, never mind up to his front door. She would have to be dealt with, but for the life of him, he didn't know how the hell he was going to get rid of her.

Chapter Fifty-Seven

After four days in rugged terrain and without bearings, Mercy and Nelson found themselves in deep trouble. They had no idea where they were, they and their horses had no food, snow was falling day and night, and the horses laboured with weakening legs as they waded through it.

They travelled in what seemed a never-ending world of snowy ground, trees, and hidden rocks that had caused Mercy to fall off her horse twice. Sleep was impossible due to the relentless, bitter cold, and they had not come across any shelter in days. The landscape was difficult to gauge because of the vast canvas of fir trees and nothing else. Mercy had at times despaired, for she had absolutely no idea of which direction to take. Everything around them looked the same as it had the day before and the day before that. For all she knew, they had been going in circles. There were no markers or clearings to give them a clear path or a horizon. There was nothing but a ceiling of trees and a ground of crusted ice and snow.

Mercy sat huddled as close to the small fire as possible, urging it to extend her some heat.

Nelson was shivering so much his body shook from head to toe, and his numbed hands found difficulty holding his icy-water-filled tin cup.

Mercy was crying softly, without the strength to scream her frustrations. "We're going to die, Nelson. We can't go on like this. I'm afraid to sleep because I'm sure I won't wake up again," she sobbed and shivered at the same time.

"We's needin' proper shelter. Is January now, January den February. Dem be dead months," Nelson told her through chattering teeth. "We need to hunker down somewhere till spring; that's what we's need do, Miss Mercy."

Mercy agreed with him. Getting to their destination was important, surviving until then was paramount. Speed of foot or horse no longer mattered.

"Nelson, I'm sorry I got us lost. You've had a rotten life, and now you're going to freeze to death because of me. Please forgive me."

"Don't you's be worrying none 'bout me, Miss Mercy. If we does find a town, you's gotta leave me and go find you'self a warm bed."

"No, and don't you dare even to suggest that again!" Mercy told him sharply.

She unfolded the map, shaking in her numbed hands and peered at the writing on it in the shadow of the flickering flames.

Watching her, Nelson asked, "Why's you looking, Miss Mercy, when we's don't know where we at?"

Mercy's chapped lips cracked when she spoke. "I just need to do *something*. But you're right. I haven't got a clue which way we went after Smithfield." She folded the map and threw it in the fire. "If I die first, please bury me deep in the ground. I don't want to be eaten by wild animals. Will you promise me?"

"Ain't no one dying, not you and not me, and dat's a fact," Nelson lied.

"I want to believe you, but we must be miles from a town. We haven't seen lights in the distance or smoke or shelter. I've been a fool. I thought I could do this, but I've never seen land like this."

"Guess dyin' here is better than a hanging."

Mercy sobbed louder "We have to move. We can't stay here tonight. The branches being this heavy will drop piles of snow on us. We'll be buried in the stuff soon! And this bloody fire is useless! The horses will freeze to death, and they're already starving. We can't let those horses die. If they die, we die, and…and I don't want to. I want to see Jacob!" Mercy covered her face with her hands, forgetting Nelson for the moment.

Nelson watched her anguish. She was closer to death than she knew, he thought. They both were. He nodded but said nothing. He went to the horses and rummaged through the bags on the ground. They would have to get rid of most of their load if the horses were to have any chance of surviving. He dumped the pans, plates, and heavy shackles and then suggested that they put on as many extra clothes as would fit, to give added warmth.

Mercy heard the rummaging and joined him. She began digging into the snow with the hatchet that she'd brought, struck now by the realisation that they had packed at du Pont's house as though they were going on a picnic or adventure, when in actual fact they were like the blind leading the blind on a journey through treacherous and unknown territory.

As Mercy dug with numbed hands, she wondered how, for a second time, she could have been so arrogant and stupid. "You're pathetic, Mercy Carver," she chattered to herself. She had been given love with Jacob, friends like Belle, Hendry, and Isaac, and she'd thrown everything away only to find death in some forest, somewhere in Virginia. If she died, it would be her own fault. But if she lived through this, she was going to demand Jacob leave his wife. She had to picture that scene; him saying yes, and both of them loving each other until they died of old age. She wasn't going to die at the age of eighteen like her father had. She wasn't!

She dug through the snow and solid icy ground beneath, cursing herself yet again for making bad decisions, and also for wasting time digging a hole to bury clothes that no one would ever find in this godforsaken land anyway!

Nelson took over the digging. When the hole was deep enough, Mercy grabbed all her clothes that were of no use. The bloodied gown went first, followed by the hooped underskirt, which had long since been battered and hacked to fit inside the bag, and finally the bloomers. She suddenly laughed and then sobbed, until between laughing at the irony, crying with sorrow, and shivering with fear, she looked and felt like a madwoman.

Nelson crossed himself. "C'mon now, Miss Mercy. C'mon, up you's get. This ain't no time for cryin'. Sobbin' ain't gonna help you's keep you strength up."

Mercy tried to stand, but her legs were trembling with cold shivers. "You've become…very bossy," she told him.

Nelson lifted her to her feet and tightened the blanket knot around her chin. He helped her onto the horse, and his own legs shook with her weight.

Mercy dozed on and off, finding her body starting to slide off the horse's back and then righting it up again. As she looked down, trying to protect her face from the wind, she saw the snow jump up at her. It was like a crisp, white cotton sheet. It looked soft and inviting; she felt she could sleep on it and be quite comfortable. She was tired and her muscles were relaxed. She felt that nothing could bother her anymore; nothing at all. Yes, she could sleep quite easily on the ground and wrap that cotton sheet around her…she didn't even feel cold anymore.

Mercy felt no pain when she eventually slid off her horse some time later. She landed on the soft, powdery snow and sighed with contentment. Sleep, she should sleep for a while…

Nelson, slightly in front of Mercy, heard her fall and her horse whinny. He stopped and dismounted, feeling as though he were doing everything in slow motion. His body was shivering in spasms, which made walking in the knee-high snow almost impossible.

He got to Mercy and shook her. There was no response. She seemed to be unconscious. He tried again, calling her name, demanding that she get on her feet.

He thought about lying down beside her as she looked so peaceful. But his instincts told him that if he did that, neither of them would awaken to see a new day.

He took Mercy's gun from her holster. He cocked it and fired it into the air. Mercy roused, and he shouted,

"Move, Miss Mercy! You's gonna die if you's lie there. Get up now!"

Mercy looked up at the black face and sighed. "Leave me alone. I don't care!"

Nelson lifted her, and with all the strength he had left, managed to drape her body across her horse's saddle. He pulled the horse behind him and reached his own horse, but he didn't mount it. Instead, he continued to trudge through the snow, one hand holding on to Mercy's unconscious body and the other his horse's reins.

Time passed in a blur. The steps Nelson took became shorter and shorter. The scenery didn't change, and even if it had, he couldn't distinguish anything under layers of snow and the blackest of nights.

He stopped abruptly and smelt smoke in the air. Leaving the horses and Mercy, he trudged onward again, this time with a more vigorous effort. The smell of smoke was becoming stronger. He could see it clearly now. It was high, not a campfire but a funnel. He choked back a sob and walked another few feet. There, in a clearing, he saw the small cabin, candlelight coming from within, and a chimney stack with smoke billowing out of it.

He turned around and got back to Mercy and the horses as fast as he could, and then led them to the cabin.

Nelson saw no other choice. He had to ask for help for Miss Mercy. He might be shot at, but he would die trying to save her. He reached the door, his whole body shaking with cold, fear, and exhaustion. He thought that they might be trappers…bear trappers. Trappers were hard men. They would shoot him on sight if they had a mind to. He banished the thought and lifted his fist.

A grey-bearded man, hair tied back and balding at his hairline, opened the door before Nelson's fist touched the wood. The man faced him with a rifle pointing at Nelson's chest and suspicion etched on his face. He looked at Nelson, the horses, and the body draped over one of the horse's backs. "What's your business here?" he asked suspiciously. "Who is that?"

A woman joined him at the door and also stared at Nelson from head to toe. The rifle was still pointed, just inches from Nelson's body. No one spoke.

Nelson's shivering body was near to dropping where it stood. He tried to stand upright in the front of the couple. Finally, he mumbled, "Sah, help us...please?"

Again the couple stared at him in silence.

"Please." Nelson murmured with quivering lips. "I'se knows I caint come in…but the woman…she a white woman. She done save my life. Please, masah, ma'am, please warm her up. She be dyin'."

The woman's eyes darted to the body draped over the horse's back. Pulling her thick woollen shawl up and over her head, she then ran out of the house and over to where Mercy lay. She lifted Mercy's head up for a better look and gasped. "Good Lord, Charlie. He's tellin' the truth. We got ourselves a woman here."

Nelson stood aside. He watched Charlie run to the horse and take Mercy in his arms. Charlie trudged the few feet and rushed her straight inside.

The woman looked again at Nelson and said, "Well, what you waitin' for? Get inside afore you freeze to death."

The woman turned to Charlie then and said, "Go get those horses to the barn. Put some dry blankets on them and get them fed."

Charlie nodded and pulled on his jacket, hanging behind the door on a hook. "Be back in a minute," he told the woman, but not without leaving her the rifle first.

The woman ushered Nelson inside.

Mercy felt hands on her. They were undressing her. She tried to rouse herself from sleep. She attempted to open her eyes to see who was touching her. She lifted an arm to defend herself, but it rose and then fell limp by her side. She tried again to open her eyes and this time managed to see a blurred face. It was a woman. She closed her eyes again and felt heat on her skin. Her arms were being pulled out of her jacket sleeves, and she was being covered by something warm. She opened her eyes, this time keeping them open, and saw the woman's face clearly for the first time.

The woman removed Mercy's gloves and began rubbing her hands and fingers. She removed Mercy's boots and socks and put a blanket-covered hot brick by her feet.

Mercy felt a painful tingling sensation, as though blood was rushing to her extremities, giving them life after days of numbness. "Where are we?" she found the strength to whisper.

The woman smiled. "Y'all never mind about that now, child. I'm Corslina. Call me Lina. What's your name?"

Mercy gave her a weak smile. "Mercy…Mercy Carver. Nelson…where's Nelson?"

The woman looked at Nelson and asked, "That'll be you?"

Nelson, wracked with shivering spasms, couldn't sit still, and to make matters worse, his top and bottom teeth were clicking together loudly. "Yes, ma'am. Nelson Stuart."

"There's a blanket on that chair over there. Git out of that jacket and those wet britches, Nelson Stuart, and sit by the fire. Then tell me what the hell you both doing all the way out here on a night like this?"

Lina removed Mercy's hat whilst waiting for the explanation. The hat had knotted tightly under Mercy's chin. The leather thong was caked in ice and hard as a twig.

When the hat came off, Mercy's hair tumbled out in a mass of curls to her waist, and the woman sucked in her breath. "Oh, my," Lina said, astounded. "Why, you're a comely child. Is he a slave?" she asked Mercy. "We don't take kindly to slavery. We do what we need to do with our own, God-given hands. Ain't no call for slavery in our book. Are you a slaver? Are you a bounty hunter?"

"No, I am not!" Mercy told her abruptly, in a hoarse voice. "I'm sorry…I didn't mean to shout. I hate slavery. I found Nelson. Some men were going to kill him. Since then, we've been making our way North, trying to get to a slave-free state, only I'm not too sure which one comes first now."

"He's a runaway then?'" Lina turned to Nelson, ignoring Mercy's answer completely.

Nelson hung his head.

Mercy thought she saw the first sign of trouble.

Lina, who had risen, stirred a pot that hung above the flames in the enormous fireplace that filled almost one wall of the cabin.

Mercy was now fully conscious, albeit drowsy. She watched Lina and then looked around the room. It was cosy. There were curtains on the window, homemade ornaments, multicoloured blankets, two chairs in front of the fire, and a dresser which held plates, cups, and crockery.

Mercy lay on top of a small, narrow bed just under the window. Nelson was sitting in an armchair with a blanket wrapped around him. She saw Nelson's mouth move; he was praying, just as she was, for some of that food in the pot.

She studied Lina's profile. She was quite elderly, although it was difficult to pinpoint her age. She had salt-and-pepper hair, but she was of an athletic build and with a darker skin than most of the Virginian women she'd seen. She had brown eyes and full lips. She probably had been very beautiful in her youth, Mercy thought.

"I reckon you two must be hungry as a bear just woke up from hibernation," Lina said.

Mercy was handed a steaming bowl and a wooden spoon. She stared at the hot meat stew. Looking up at Lina, she thanked her, crying now with sheer relief and pent-up exhaustion. Lina bent over her, placed her hands on either cheek and kissed her on the forehead, making Mercy cry even more.

Lina said tenderly, "You get that inside you, child. That'll get the blood flowing through you."

"Thank you," Mercy whispered again.

Nelson got his bowl next and put it straight to his mouth, draining the hot gravy and not minding that some of it ran down his chin.

As they ate the stew and tore at some bread with their teeth, Lina talked.

"So y'all want to get Nelson here to the North. That's a mighty kind thing you're doing, but you're more likely to get yourselves killed if you go on like you've been doing. Y'all could cross into Pennsylvania, but you've still got a whole bunch of miles to go afore you get there. Y'all ain't never gonna make it in this weather."

Mercy's lips quivered as the cold, hard truth hit her. Lina was right. They wouldn't make it out of this snow-ridden world alive if they left now.

"Please, Lina, can you tell me where we are?"

"We're about ten miles east of Richmond," Lina told her.

"Oh, my God, is that all…Richmond? That place is low down on the map."

Lina laughed. "Low down…you mean South?"

"Yes," Mercy said. "You see I thought we were heading North. I believed we were much further North. But this journey has been taking forever. We just keep going in a line from east to west and back and forth. Oh, no, Nelson, we've still got such a long way to go."

"I reckon you be right, Miss Mercy," Nelson said, still shivering.

"Y'all got family?" Lina asked Mercy.

"No; just some friends in Portsmouth," Mercy sobbed again in between spoonfuls of stew.

Lina looked at the pair of bedraggled travellers and shook her head in dismay.

Charlie stomped back in the room. His hat was thick with snow. Mercy watched him stretch his arm out to shake the snow off it before he closed and barred the door with a thick wooden plank. He removed his boots and put on animal fur slippers, which reached just above his ankles. He took his jacket off and stared with saucer eyes at Mercy, gulping down the stew. "She's a young 'un!" he exclaimed to Lina.

"I know…young and not too bright by the sound of it. She thinks how she's going to walk her horse and a runaway slave through snow and ice all the way to Pennsylvania. Goddamndest fool thing I ever heard. Charlie, this is Mercy Carver, and this here is Nelson Stuart. Mercy's from England. She wants to free Nelson."

"Do you, now? Well, that's mighty interesting to hear, but y'all ain't going nowhere tonight or tomorrow," Charlie said, taking a bowl of stew.

Mercy looked from one to the other and then at Nelson.

"No, sir. Y'all 'll be dead by morning," Charlie continued. "I reckon your best bet is to stay here a while."

"Are you sure we won't impose?" Mercy asked.

"Y'all be imposing if Charlie and me'd have to bury your frozen bodies out there," Lina said.

Charlie smiled at Nelson. "Son, you ever faced a black bear, shot a deer, or trapped a beaver?"

"No, sir."

"You wanna learn? I could do with the help. There ain't many bears around, not this time of year. Most of them be hibernating or birthing, but I still get the odd one early spring, them that come out of their sleep sometimes if they're hungry enough. If you two wanna stick around until we can figure out what to do with you? Well, I'd be appreciative of any help you might wanna give me. These old bones are getting as stiff as pokers in this weather. I got knees that swell up and fingers that caint hardly grip nothing. Y'all sure be doing me a favour."

"I'se a fast learner, sir," Nelson answered.

Mercy said, "I've never seen a bear."

Then you've been mighty lucky. A child like you would ha' been ripped apart in seconds had you come across one. You can thank the Lord they's a sleepin,'" Charlie said.

"Blimey, they sound dangerous. Who buys the bears?" Mercy asked.

"We got a trading station not far from here. Traders come and go all winter. It's real quiet here, but you'd be surprised how many trappers and traders are 'round these parts. Ain't never heard of a young woman dragging a slave around in winter looking for freedom, though. No, sir, that's a new one on me."

Lina turned to Mercy. "Child, you need a good night's rest. Y'all probably sleep the day through tomorrow. We got an extra room you can sleep in, so you won't be disturbed. Nelson, you can sleep right here on this here bed. You're lucky to be alive, both of you, and it's only by God's grace that you still have all your fingers and toes. Looks like they're turning pink now, just like they should."

"I thought I had frostbite," Mercy said.

"Nope. If you had frostbite, might have had to take some of those fingers and toes…you sure are one lucky child."

"Thank you for your kindness," Mercy said.

"Don't thank me yet, child. You've got a lot of talking and explaining to do tomorrow. I'll be wanting to hear the whole story. We're gonna have to figure out how to get you to Pennsylvania without getting you both killed."

"Why are you being so kind?" Mercy asked.

Lina laughed and sat on the bed. "Don't you see what I am?"

Mercy looked into her face. "No. What are you?"

"Why, I'm a nigga', just like Nelson here. Y'all might not notice at first, but that would be on account of me having three parts white blood and one part black. But I am a nigga' child," Lina told her. "And I don't care for Nelson here being caught by no slaver."

Chapter Fifty-Eight

Isaac was deep in thought as he waited for Jacob to change into warm clothes. Just as he had been leaving Hendry and Belle's house, Jacob had insisted on going with him to the train station before Jacob headed back to Stone Plantation. Isaac was pleased. He had much to say to his friend, and the journey together would give him the opportunity to finally make peace after the harsh words spoken on the day Jacob left to marry Elizabeth.

Isaac's decision to go North this morning in such dire weather had been made easier after Sheriff Manning's announcement that the search for Mercy Carver had been officially abandoned in the Portsmouth and Norfolk area. Isaac had originally thought of making his way North in the spring, but had changed his mind after this announcement and also after considering the worsening political crisis that was developing between the Northern and Southern states. This was not a good time to be in the wrong part of the country where the crisis could quickly turn into armed conflict.

He wasn't looking forward to the long journey ahead of him. On main lines, trains could reach a speed of twenty-five to thirty miles an hour, although he doubted that the journey this morning from Portsmouth to Williamsburg would be quick and easy, given the high probability of thick snow on the tracks.

Once he got to Williamsburg, he would change trains and head to Richmond. From Richmond, another train would go as far as Aquia Creek, and then a distance of fifty-five miles would be covered by steamboat in order to reach Washington, DC. From Washington he'd take his time, stopping off in New York for a couple of days before taking the final train to Boston.

He had already decided to break his journey in Richmond. It was as good a place as any to begin his search for Mercy. He would employ people to look for her on the coast and further inland towards the west. He would order them to make their way North for as long as he thought necessary. They would report directly to him in Boston.

The two men sat in the waiting room on the train station's small platform. The train had already arrived from North Carolina and was being readied after a heated debate between the driver and stationmaster on whether it was safe to run it today or not.

Isaac and Jacob sat in silence, unsure of what to say to each other. Isaac, at last, began, "Thanks for coming to the station with me. I appreciate your company."

"I wouldn't have it any other way. I'm going back to the plantation right after I leave you. I wanted to talk to you. I'm glad I got back in time to see you before you left. You were right; I was an ass. I've made the biggest mistake of my life, and I'm regretting it every day."

"You're talking about Elizabeth?" Isaac asked.

"Yep. I should have suffered the consequences and stuck to my decision to call the wedding off. Losing Mercy is far worse than anything the Coulters or anyone else could have thrown at me. They would have gotten over their hurt pride eventually, whereas I will never forgive myself."

Isaac allowed another pause to settle between them. He had been steadfast in his resolve to make an offer to Mercy. For weeks, he'd planned what to say and how to begin a conversation leading to the question. He'd said the words often in his head: *Mercy, come to Boston with me. I want to make you my wife if you'll have me.* He would have done everything in his power to persuade her that he could offer her a good life and that she would come to love him, given time. He would have faced Jacob, damning the consequences, for Jacob had nothing to offer her now, and Isaac did. But Mercy hadn't come back…

He watched Jacob, who was staring into space, deep in thought. He was saddened by Jacob's appearance. His face was gaunt; he looked as though he hadn't slept for weeks, and it had become obvious that he and Elizabeth didn't like each other. During the silence, Isaac wondered what was worse; Jacob loving Mercy, having felt her in his arms and known her love, or Isaac loving her, wanting her, and *imagining* her in his arms.

Isaac broke the silence again. "I take it you had no luck on your travels. Was there nothing? Not a clue or a word from anyone you met?"

Jacob shook his head. "Nope. I wish I had some good news, but Mercy seems to have vanished into thin air. I was so sure she would keep to the coast and use boats. But, God help her, she hardly had time to see my land, never mind study Virginia. Truth is, she could be anywhere by now."

"But if she's not following the coast and sticking to towns with lodgings and supplies, where would she have gone? Surely not west? Not in this weather?"

"I don't know, but it's a possibility. If she wanted to hide, going west would be the safest bet, I reckon. All I know is that I rode and took packet boats for over seventy miles, and somehow Mercy managed to slip by every port, harbour, lodging house, food house, and supply store without someone taking notice of her, but as soon as this damn weather gets milder, I'll be heading on out again."

Isaac looked into Jacob's face with a questioning raised eyebrow. "Jacob, you went on a blind man's trail with no direction to follow and with no information to arm yourself with. You didn't really expect to find her that way, did you?"

"I had to do something! I thought I could catch up with her," Jacob snapped back.

"Hey, hold up. I know, and I would have gone with you if you hadn't been so bullheaded, running off like that. But you left without questioning the one person who could have given you answers. Goddammit, you should have gone to du Pont and beaten the truth out of her before taking off like a bat. Don't tell me you're afraid of her?"

Jacob gave Isaac an icy stare, unwilling now to share news about his visit to her house. "Don't be an ass, Isaac. I know what I'm doing, and I know what's to be done, so don't you go thinking you know what's in my head!"

"I would have gone to du Pont's house, but I guess it wasn't up to me."

"You're right. It's not up to you. Mercy is my responsibility."

"She's not. Your wife is your responsibility," Isaac shot back.

"Do you mean to fight with me? I came here so we could part on good terms. When are you going to get it into your head that Mercy doesn't love you? If she did, you would have found that out on the ship. God knows you fawned over her enough."

"Well, way I see it if she's not here, she ain't in love with you either."

Jacob sighed. Isaac was not the friend he had once known. His obsession with Mercy had ruined any chance of continuing their relationship on an even keel. All trust between them was lost.

"I came here to say goodbye and to remember the good times with you," Jacob repeated. "Let's leave Mercy out of this."

"Yep, you're right. You lost her, and you're a damn fool. Guess I ain't got no more to say neither."

"She's not lost. She'll be back, and when she comes home, I'm leaving Elizabeth. I'll take Mercy anywhere she wants to go."

"I'd appreciate a letter from you if you find Mercy. You can give me that, right?"

Jacob was silent.

"Here's my address in Boston. Use it. We may be at odds now, but in memory of our friendship, I'm asking you to promise me you'll write me if you find her?"

Jacob took the folded piece of paper and put it in his coat pocket. "If I get a second chance with Mercy, I'll leave everything I own to be with her; I will find her, and when I do, don't you go thinking you're going to take her from me. We're friends, but I swear on God's green earth, I will fight to keep her."

"Like your slaves?" Isaac said.

"Yeah, like my slaves. I'll fight Lincoln and the Northern States to keep what's been in my family for generations, and that includes the slaves on my land if that's what you're asking?"

"Jacob, you and I both know that there won't be any more slaves soon. Lincoln won't back down. His policies will stand, and the North will follow him."

"Well, it looks like some of the Southern states have a mind to secede from the Union, and I caint say I blame them. Hell, if Virginia joins them, I'll put on a uniform. I don't like bullies, and that's exactly what Lincoln is."

Both men sighed with relief at the sight of the stationmaster, who strode into the waiting room with his blue cap, white with snow, and a ruddy face longing for warmth. He crossed the room to the log burner in the corner, rubbed his hands together in front of it, and then seemed to remember that he had a job to do. "Train's ready, fokes, so all aboard that's going aboard."

"How's the track looking?" Isaac asked him.

"It ain't looking so good further up that line, but we've sent men out. Might mean you fokes will get stuck a while, but we'll try our best to keep her moving."

Isaac nodded and turned to Jacob. "Well, I guess this is it."

"Yep, this is it, Isaac. We've had some good times, you and I. You've been a good friend."

The men shook hands, looked at each other for a moment, and then Isaac turned and walked towards the train.

Jacob watched his old friend board the train and then left the station with one sure thought in his mind.

Their friendship was over. Coming here had been a mistake. He walked to his carriage, pensive and saddened, took the note out of his pocket and tore it up.

Chapter Fifty Nine

April 1861

April arrived. Gone were the cold, biting winds and relentless snowstorms. Spring rains fell persistently upon the land. It caused riverbanks to slide, dislodging small trees, fallen branches, and bare trunks to slip into the river's path. Some of the soil, rushes, logs, and branches barricaded the natural flow of water in places, causing flooding along the riverside and into the woods, making the terrain just as treacherous as winter days when it was too dangerous to venture farther than the eye could see.

The white landscape surrounding Lina and Charlie's cabin finally changed. Leaves sprouted from branches, bushes flattened by the harsh winter began to straighten and rise in a kaleidoscope of colours, and the smell of spring air was glorious.

The snow during January and February had put any plans to travel northward on hold. However, Mercy had insisted that she be taught about survival in the terrain that had almost killed her. She spent a great deal of time outdoors. She hunted with Charlie and Nelson and proved herself a worthy trapper. Charlie taught her how to follow trails in the snow. He showed her the best way to seek shelter in the very worst of weather, how to set traps for cottontail rabbits, and the techniques used to shoot wild boar. On a couple of occasions lately, she had watched how he hunted and killed a couple of large male black bear as they emerged from hibernation.

She had also spent many days indoors with Lina, who taught her how to cook the local wildlife, and clean and treat rabbit and fox furs. At times the women sat by the fire and talked for hours. Lina was to Mercy, the mother she had never known. Mercy was to Lina, the child she had never borne.

Lina was in her late forties, Mercy learned. She had been born a slave in the state of Mississippi. Her grandmother, also born a slave on the same plantation, had been the master's favourite. She had lain with him when she was just fifteen, and Lina's mother was the result. Lina spoke about her mother with pride and honoured her memory every day. She had been light-skinned and a renowned beauty. She had gained the attention of black and white men alike. However, it had been a neighbouring plantation owner who had taken her virginity by force. Lina had been born, bordering the two races and fitting into neither. The worst day of her life, Lina said, was the day the neighbouring plantation owner, her father, took her mother away.

Lina had never seen her again. Charlie, a friend of her father's, had swept her off her feet and paid for her freedom. They had left their home and moved here, where they had lived for well over twenty years.

Mercy sat up front with Charlie on the bench seat, watching as he casually steered the horses pulling the covered wagon through backwoods trails and across shallow river fords.

Lina and Nelson sat under the circular, canopied roof in the back, hidden from sight, and talked incessantly about the North and the freedom it would bring Nelson.

They had been travelling for just over two days and were heading south-east to the mouth of the Chesapeake Bay Estuary. They would cross at the widest part of the river to Newport News. The distance from the cabin to their final destination was, in Charlie's estimation, a little over eighty miles. However, they had broken their journey the day before in a small hunting cabin occupied by white slave sympathisers.

Mercy and Nelson had not been told the full details of the trip they were to undertake. As each mile passed, they heard the incredible stories of runaway slaves aided by the Underground Railroad. This organisation drew on an extensive network of volunteers, white and black, who spirited fugitive slaves to the North by using waterways, boats, safe houses, and covered wagons that crossed the shallow waters of the Potomac River.

When Lina and Charlie first told Mercy and Nelson of their plans, Mercy had been sceptical. She had already seen the dangers posed by the Chesapeake Bay. But, as Lina pointed out, she had been ignorant of its secrets, one being the hundreds of slaves who had escaped using the very route Mercy had discarded. Lina and Charlie had been adamant that this was the only way to fulfil Nelson's dreams of freedom, and that it had to be now before it was too late.

Seven Southern States had already seceded from the Union, among them, Lina and Charlie's home state of Mississippi. There was talk of war from every mouth in Richmond, as Texas, Florida, Alabama, Louisiana, North Carolina, and South Carolina also disavowed the Union in a display of solidarity against the new president's anti-slavery policies.

Militias were practising drills, uniforms were being produced, arms were being collected, and politicians and leaders were being chosen. In the frenzied atmosphere, Virginia waited and watched, believing that she would secede within days to join her sister slave states.

Mercy knew very little about the politics. However, after she learnt about the possibility that Virginia might also secede, her thoughts turned to Jacob and what this might mean for him, Belle, and Hendry. Jacob was never far from her mind. She still felt his closeness even after all these months apart and had never stopped believing that they would one day be reunited.

As they neared the harbour, Charlie halted the wagon. He and Mercy climbed in the back to sit with Lina and Nelson. Charlie was pensive. Sadness crossed his face as he looked at the others.

"Now I know we've all come to care for each other, but I also reckon this is the last opportunity we might have to get this boy to safety. Nelson, son, I ain't coming with you. I have some very important business to attend to, and so I'm leaving you in Lina's care. My Lina knows these river crossings like the back of her hand. She's helped dozens of slaves to freedom, and I caint imagine you in better company. She's a much better guide than I could ever be.

"Lina will drive the wagon, but you, Nelson, you'll stay tucked away. You'll sit behind these old wooden crates until Lina tells you to come out. You hear? I reckon there ain't much cause to worry cos I'm betting just about every other person you meet will be thinking about our country being ripped apart soon. They surely won't be paying any heed to this wagon or who's in it. The most important thing is to keep you out of sight until Lina meets her first contact."

"Charlie, can't you come with us?" Mercy asked.

"Nope. Like I said, I got business. You just do like Lina tells you, and I'll be back here in six days. I'll meet you in Newport News; Lina knows where."

"I guess this is the last time I'se ever gonna see you," Nelson said, miserably. "You knows I wants to stay with you at the cabin. Best home I'se ever had. I ain't thinking freedom can get any better than what you gived me. How can I done repay you, Mr Charlie?"

"Nelson, if the good Lord is with you and you reach freedom, well, that's payment enough. Just promise me that you'll learn to read and write. Then you can let us know how you're a doing. We're gonna miss you, but you're gonna be free…free, Nelson, and that's what you should be thinking about," Charlie said.

Mercy was afraid to speak. She didn't want Nelson to see her sadness. He had seen enough tears in the last days at the cabin. She had spoken at length to him. She didn't know if he would heed her words, but she hoped that when he got into Pennsylvania, he would remember her words and act upon them.

She had given him enough money to buy himself a new suit of clothes, food, lodgings, and a horse and wagon. She watched his expression now. He was afraid, yet there was a spark of excitement there too. She sat closer to him and held his hand.

"Nelson, remember what I told you. You don't have to be alone. When me and Lina get you where you have to be, I want you to do as I said. Mr Isaac Bernstein is a good man. We are very good friends, him and I. I know he'll be in Boston by now, and I believe he will want to help you. Boston is far to the north. You might not want to go all that way, but I can't bear to think of you being alone in a strange city with no one to help you. Just remember that Isaac's father is the chief surgeon at the Massachusetts General Hospital in Boston. You ask for him at that hospital and give him the letter I gave you, along with the address Lina gave you to write to. You keep that letter and that address safe. If you can't write to us, Mr Isaac will do it for you. I'm sure…no, I know Isaac will find you a job and make sure you have a good life."

"I'se don't have no place else to be, Miss Mercy. I done told you that, so I'se reckon I will go find your Mr Isaac. If you say he be a good man, then I believe in you. Don' you worry none about ole Nelson."

Charlie and Lina had a brief and private discussion. After Charlie had left them, Lina took over the driver's seat and headed straight to the harbour.

Darkness had descended, and the roads were clear. They had about a mile to go until the first harbour, which sat next to a small trading station. Lina smiled at Mercy. "Mercy, this is what I live for…this and my Charlie. I think about every slave I've helped and wonder what they're doing with their lives right now. I imagine my mother being one of them. I often wonder if she's happy, but I doubt it. I was lucky. My Charlie loved me and I loved him, but my mother was used. I reckon she's still slaving away on my father's plantation. He's probably had a whole bunch of children just like me by now. But I'll always love my mother."

"Do you ever think about going to find her?" Mercy asked.

"Yep. Charlie promised to take me this summer, but all those plans we made last year might be thrown out the window on account of what's going on. I ain't never heard so much hatred a spoutin' from men's lips. I done reckon we'll all be shootin' each other soon."

"I love Virginia, Lina. I know it almost killed me, but I love it all the same."

Lina patted Mercy's knee and said, "While we're on the subject of love…I knows you love Jacob Stone. God knows I do. So take some advice from an old woman who knows about being happy with a man. Life is too short to worry about what you are to him. You might not be his legal wife, but if that man loves you, and you love him like you say you do, it don't matter a damn."

"I know, but it seems to matter to everyone else. I want to see him more than anything. I still love him with all my heart, but I have been through so much. How can I go back to Portsmouth, knowing that I will be hated by everyone for being his mistress? He lied to me."

"Well, some might say he lied, others could think he just omitted to tell you some things," Lina suggested.

"It's the same thing. I love him but I feel humiliated. And what if I see Madame du Pont? I want to kill that woman or destroy her life. I need revenge, and that's not good; it's evil. I sometimes think I'll go mad just thinking, thinking and wondering about all the terrible things I want to do to her."

"Child, I believe in fate. It might be good fate or bad fate, but the good Lord knows what we need to be doing and where we need to be when we journey through this life of ours. All I'm a saying is that love is more important than reputation, money, and fear of the unknown. If fate gives you love, you grab it. Love, child, will get you by in just 'bout every rotten situation life throws at you. You got a decision to make, cos there ain't no more time for you to sit around wonderin'."

"I'm scared, Lina. I'm scared *she'll* still be there."

"Don't you go worrying none about that du Pont woman, no more. You hate her all you want. Jacob will protect you."

"You don't know her," Mercy said with bitterness. "She'll kill Jacob too if she has her mind set on it."

"I know enough about her by now to know that you're tough enough to best her. She a bully, but I reckon she ain't got no power left, not after you got rid of that Eddie, you been tellin' me about. You're a strong woman, Mercy. You knows you shoot better than any man. If you see that du Pont woman, you just look her in the eye and you tell her she ain't nothin' to you now. There ain't no use in killin' her, Mercy, but you can best her just by making her feel real small."

In the ensuing silence, Mercy digested Lina's words and thought about fate. She didn't really know the city of Portsmouth. The only memories she had of it were nightmarish flashes of fear. She hated the thought of going back to the street from where Eddie had abducted her, but she was not the same person now. She was passionate about life. She was stronger in body and mind. She was no longer in a strange country, for life in the backwoods and journeys up the rivers were more familiar to her now than anything she'd seen or experienced in the Elephant and Castle. She hadn't lived there. She had existed.

Her joy at discovering new adventures each day had convinced her that her fateful journey had been necessary. Some of it had been horrific, but necessary all the same. She wondered what she would be doing right now had she not crossed the River Thames on that fateful October day. What if she had not ended up in Liverpool? She would never have met Jacob. If Eddie had not abducted her a second time, she would not have met Nelson, Lina, or Charlie. These events had played a pivotal role in her life. She was not afraid anymore. Fate was like a giant, invisible hand that lifted her from place to place so that she could be exactly where she needed to be.

Where she was supposed to be going, or what she was meant to be doing next, she wasn't sure. She knew she loved Jacob. She just didn't know how to get back to him. Portsmouth was where he lived, but she didn't want to set foot in the place. "I hope fate comes to guide me now."

"Fate always guides. You just don't see it doin' its job, is all."

Mercy cast these thoughts aside and asked, "Who will meet us at the harbour?"

"Well, if I'm right, it'll be an old friend of mine. We call him the captain. He's been on the river for fifty years, and there ain't nothin' he don't know. He'll take us across to Newport News; always works at night, the old coot. He's took countless men and women just like Nelson across to the bay. We call it the Chesapeake Station."

"Have you been doing this for a long time?"

"I've been helping the Underground Railroad for going on twenty years. Did I ever tell you the story of old Harriet Tubman?"

"No."

"She's a fine woman; famous in my line of work. Born a slave in Dorchester County, up there in Maryland. She escaped her master, but that woman keeps coming back to the South to help niggers. I met her once. She don't look like much, but she's got more courage than anyone I ever met. We call her Moses, on account of the number of slaves she takes to freedom."

Mercy's eyes brightened with a thought. "Lina, I would like to help you. I want to be involved in the Underground Railroad."

"I don't reckon you'll be good at it, child. On account of you gittin lost every five minutes. Ain't no point in guiding' a slave if you caint figure out where you're a goin' yourself."

Mercy giggled. "That's not fair. Charlie's taught me a lot. I know I can find my way around now."

"Well, don't matter none. I reckon all this comin' and going will stop soon. Ain't no telling now what's gonna happen round these parts if a war breaks out. I reckon runaways all over the South will be looking for a way out, but war means soldiers, and it ain't gonna be so easy to hide a nigger no more."

Chapter Sixty

The harbour was deserted. One packet boat sat alongside, but there were no lanterns glowing, and as far as Mercy could tell, no one was on board. "Nobody is here," she whispered to Lina.

"Oh, he's here, all right. The captain sleeps on the dang boat."

Lina walked up the ramp and stood on deck. A moment later, the figure of a man came out from the shadows. "Captain," Lina said.

"Well, if it ain't my Lina. Where have you been hiding all winter?"

"How d'you do, Cap'n. Me and Charlie been at the cabin. Been a bad winter up there," Lina told him. "I got one for you. He's special. Can you take him?"

The captain took off his hat and scratched his head. "You could have given me notice, Lina. Been a few coming and goings here lately, 'n people are gittin' skittish with all this secession talk. Fokes travellin' north, others runnin' scared. Can you hold him till tomorrow? Give me time to make arrangements?"

"No. He has to go now."

"You coming with him?"

"Yep. We're going all the way up with this one."

"I got a couple of boys onboard. I guess we could. I can take you to Newport News, but you'll have to git him up the Peninsular a ways on land. You might find a boat east of Yorktown but I ain't promising nothin'."

"I just need you to get us across. I'll take it from there."

"Well, Lina, seems to me the whole damn country's going stark ravin' mad. I reckon I might as well join the craziness. I took seven runaways across last week. Spring brings them out like starvin' bears. Bring the wagon on. I'll get my boys up."

The ropes were freed from the docking post. The boat moved slowly and silently in the calm waters. Mercy sat in the wagon with Lina. Nelson was down below the deck, hidden. "Will the captain get into trouble if he's caught hiding Nelson?" Mercy asked.

"He will, child. He'll get a hefty fine 'n could go to jail. He wouldn't be the first."

"That's terrible. Will he leave us when we get to the other side?"

Lina smiled. "He's got to. There might be a boat farther up the bay. We'll head up the Peninsular and hopefully meet it. If it's there, it'll be beached on the shoreline, more than likely. We might be lucky enough to make it up to the narrowest point of the Chesapeake Bay towards the Susquehanna River."

"Then what?"

"Well, then we pray. We'll get Nelson back in the wagon and cross land to the Eastern Shore at the Maryland border. That'll be the hardest part. That's where most slaves git caught, but Nelson's got us for cover. He ain't alone, not like some others afore him."

Lina watched Mercy's eyes grow wide. "Don't you fret none. I ain't aiming on gittin' caught."

After a long night travelling through wetlands, woods, and narrow muddy roads, Lina finally gave Mercy good news. They had reached the Eastern Shore, from where steamships sailed north on a daily basis. Mercy first saw the sea and steamship, as the wagon descended down a dirt track at the side of a shallow hill above the jetty. The ship's lights flickered brightly as a long row of lanterns. On the jetty, Mercy observed the ship's crew loading loose crates through one entrance and passengers through another.

The ship was nothing like the Carrabelle, Mercy noted. Its white two-story decks with windows from bow to stern were impressive. On the top deck, a tall, fat funnel was already smoking, signalling that the ship would set sail soon. Halfway along its length was a giant wheel, for the moment, motionless. Mercy was worried. There were too many people waiting to board, and too many crew members, for her liking.

"It's gonna be tricky," Lina said, thinking as Mercy was. "Not all captains are abolitionists. Some will report a runaway in a heartbeat. We just gotta find a way to get him on board with us. We need to put him in a crate now before we get down to the jetty. If we succeed, the steamship will take us right up the Delaware River into Pennsylvania. That's much better than trying to get there by land. We gotta take the chance, Mercy."

"Lina, if this goes wrong, I will take all the blame. Nelson is my responsibility. I don't want you getting into any trouble," Mercy said.

"Child, we both in this together. Ain't no takin' no blame, one without the other. You should have worn a dress, like I asked. I'm tired of seeing you in britches and wearing that stupid hat. You could charm your way out of anything if you'd just taken my advice and looked like a woman for once."

Mercy touched her hat. It had become a habit. Eddie's hat had meaning. It meant victory in the face of defeat and she needed a victory.

Chapter Sixty-One

The sun was rising. Lina ordered Mercy to remove her hat and allow her hair to flow down her back. Adrenaline pumped through Mercy's body. She had never been this far north. She felt her senses heighten with a mixture of fear and excitement. But she also felt the weight of responsibility on her shoulders.

"Child, all you got to do is distract every man you think might be taking too much notice of my three crates. The men who'll get the crates onboard for us have to be thinking about you and your charms, not about the possibility of a runaway slave who's inside one of them."

Mercy handed her hat to Lina, undid her top three buttons, exposing just the right amount of cleavage to gain the crew's interest. She pinched her cheeks and bit her lip to bring some colour into them. Lina was right; she should have worn a dress.

After securing Nelson in the crate, Lina drove the wagon the rest of the way down the hill. At the jetty, Mercy's job was to find someone willing to look after the horses and wagon until their return later in the day. This was attended to without too much difficulty, for many travellers left behind their horses in the care of men who earned their living at the harbour stables.

The containers sat on the jetty, looking perfectly normal among hundreds of others. Nelson was inside the second crate, marked *Margaret Mallory. Destination: Pennsylvania.* Packed solid around Nelson were furs and skins to stop his body moving when the container was lifted. There was nothing else to do but wait, Mercy thought, standing in line.

She was not overly worried at all now. The crew were not paying much attention to the cargo, save looking briefly at the destinations, marked on the crates' lids.

Mercy chatted to the men pulling the containers, which had been placed on a wooden pallet. As they pulled the ropes attached to the pallet, she insisted they tell her about Pennsylvania. Every few minutes, she produced a silly giggle and patted their arms. She was in the way and was being a bother. She could tell by the impatient expressions on their faces that they couldn't wait to get rid of her. No matter, she thought, continuing to giggle like a silly girl, this was precisely what Lina had ordered her to do, and she was doing it well.

After Nelson and the crate had been stowed, the two women boarded. Standing by the rails, Mercy felt the ship move slowly away from the dock and sighed with relief.

"When Nelson gets out of that crate, he'll be in a slave-free state," Lina said. "It'll be up to you to get him his papers when we get to Chester. I promise you; we won't leave him 'til he's a free man."

The steamship left and made its way up the Delaware River, making landfall just inside the Pennsylvania border. When Lina's crates had been deposited on the jetty, Lina left, returning a short while later with a horse, cart, and driver.

Their destination now was the nearest border town of Chester. After being on the road for ten minutes or so, Lina told the driver to stop. The crate hiding Nelson was opened. Nelson stuck his head out, breathing in fresh air after having only small slits to breathe through inside the crate. He stepped out of the crate and stretched his limbs in the back of the cart. "I ain't never doin' that agin," he told Mercy.

The driver faced Lina and Mercy with an angry scowl. "I didn't sign up for no runaway! What do you two think you're playing at? I ain't taking you no further, so you can git them crates off my cart and take your chances with the law. I want no part in this."

Lina stared the man down. Mercy panicked.

"Sir, I have to insist you take us. We don't have much time to debate this with you," Mercy said.

"You'll git off the cart now," the man ordered again.

Mercy went for her holster, drew her Colt, cocked it, and pointed it at the driver. Dear God, what the hell was she doing? she thought, panicking.

Surprise and anger crossed the driver's face. He stared at the gun and then at Mercy, who was trying her best to look menacing. "What you gonna do with that, little lady?" he asked angrily.

"I'm not going to do anything with it as long as you take us to Chester, where this slave…who is not a runaway, by the way, will get his freedom papers. He's my slave, and I have the papers to prove it."

"If he's your damn slave, why was he in a crate?"

"That's my business, but if you must know, the last time I took him on a ship, we were both thrown off. I didn't want to be left behind this morning. I have a very important appointment, and I need my slave with me."

"Show me his papers."

Mercy took the ownership papers from her breeches pocket and thrust them towards the driver. "I am Mrs Margaret Mallory, and if you can read, you will see that Nelson Stuart belongs to me."

"How do I know you are who you say you are? How do I know he's not on the run?"

"I am no other. This is my name, and I'm proud of it. If he were on the run he'd be running, wouldn't he? He wouldn't be daft enough to stand here beside his rightful owner. Now, are you going to take us or not?"

The driver looked at Mercy and then Lina. "Well, I reckon I ain't gonna argue with no gun. You damn Southern woman are all kinds of crazy. If you were a man, I'd have your hide for sticking a gun in my face. But seeing as how you're just a girl, who more 'an likely caint shoot for shit, I reckon, I'll let this go. I ain't no lover of slavery anyhow."

Chester was a small town. Mercy went straight to a haberdashery with Nelson, whilst Lina went to a store that bought furs and sold supplies to trappers. When Nelson was suitably clothed, Mercy took him to the sheriff and asked where she could get Nelson his legal papers. The sheriff directed her to the courthouse, situated at the end of the street. Her heart was thumping so hard, she could feel it pulsate. This was what she had been waiting for. This was her dream coming true.

After waiting for three hours, the judge arrived. He sat with his feet on his desk. Mercy sat in front of him, Nelson standing hat in hand behind her. The judge looked over the ownership papers and then at Mercy. He looked puzzled.

"Now wait. You came here all the way from Portsmouth Virginia to free your slave?"

"I did, Judge. But this isn't the only reason I'm here. I'm doing some business in your lovely town. My partner and I are selling furs. I needed my Negro to see to the cargo and drive the wagon, so I just thought whilst I was here I'd give him the freedom I promised him a while back. He's getting old and of no use to me now. You see I'm getting married. My new husband has plenty of slaves, so I don't see the point in keeping this one. He's been loyal. Haven't you, Nelson?"

"Yes, Ma'am," Nelson mumbled.

"Well, all right then," the Judge said. "I ain't done this in a while. We don't get much call to free slaves here. Those Southern slavers are too busy tryin' to hold on to their niggers, from what I can tell."

The judge signed the document and read the words written on it to Mercy and Nelson. "Nelson Stuart is hereby granted status as a free man and a citizen of the United States of America."

Tears streamed down Mercy's cheeks as she paid the legal fees.

Outside, they met up with Lina. Nelson held his papers in shaking hands. His eyes were bright and wet. For once, he was lost for words.

Mercy kissed him on the cheek. The time had come for him to find his own way. Lina held Nelson's hands and squeezed his fingers gently.

"You have money. Get as far north as possible," Lina told him. "Do like Miss Mercy said, and take yourself to Boston. You keep them papers real safe and don't you go with any man you don't think you can trust. There are good people, Nelson, but there are also bad men who'll abduct you and sell you in a heartbeat." She kissed him on the cheek and stepped back, releasing his hands. "I'll let you say goodbye to Mercy before she fills the sidewalk with her tears."

Mercy fought back her urge to cry. This was a painful moment, even more so than she had envisaged. "I can still come with you, all the way to Boston," she said hopefully.

"We done talk about this. I'se got to do this alone, else I ain't free. I'se walking in a white man's world now, an' I done need to make my choices, just like you said. You'se got to get to your man. You'se tell him he gotta leave dat wife of his if he done want a good woman like you."

"I will Nelson. Promise me you'll buy a horse or take a coach to Boston. Keep to main roads. Don't take any chances and trust no one. It's over; it's all over. Our journey together is at an end, and I hope now you'll be safe and happy."

"I ain't never gone forget you, Miss Mercy. You been my angel sent from the Lord himself. You'se the bravest woman I'se ever did see. God bless you."

Nelson turned and walked away. Mercy stood, hoping he would turn to smile at her one last time, but he did not. A part of her wished that she could have convinced him to let her go to Boston, right to Isaac's door. But

Nelson was right. This was his journey now. She had plans of her own, and they could not be put off any longer.

She cried and fell into Lina's arms, saddened by her loss, gladdened by their victory, and now ready to face her own future.

"Let's go, child. I sold my furs, and we got a steamship to catch," Lina said.

Mercy was surprised to see the cart driver. She lowered her head in shame, unable to look at him the eyes. "I'm sorry I pointed a gun at you," she apologised, wiping her tears away. "I would never have shot you, you know."

"Well, like I said. You Southern women are all kinds of crazy, but you ain't no crazier than my wife when she's in one of her womanly moods."

Chapter Sixty-Two

Mercy sat in her room and looked out onto the street. She felt tired and was listless. The last few days had been nerve-wracking, but she had accomplished everything she had set out to do. She felt Nelson's loss keenly, yet at the same time, she had never experienced such satisfaction.

Nelson had gone. She would never see him again and felt strangely alone with a grief that could not be contained.

She wore a dress, purchased in Newport News, on their return. She had been much surprised when Lina stated that they would be staying in a boarding house owned by Charlie. She was told to dress for dinner, for Charlie would be back in time to eat with them. Yet she had no desire for company.

The knock on the door startled her. Was it dinnertime already?

She opened the door. Her eyes widened and welled up with tears. Her heart pounded, as she fought for breath and as she lifted her hand to stroke Jacob's face her fingers trembled.

Staring at him, she drank in the vision she'd imagined for so so long. He walked into the room and closed the door, and she fell into his arms. She cried. Jacob's eyes were also shining bright with tears that slipped down his cheeks. Neither spoke. Instead, he kissed her so deeply she thought she might faint with ecstasy.

His mouth left hers and then his lips settled on her forehead. "Don't ever run from me again, my love," he murmured. "Please, don't put me through that hell."

"I'm sorry...oh Jacob, I'm so sorry!"

"Charlie found me at Stone Plantation and told me everything. He brought me to you. I thanked God all the way here. Sweet Jesus, Mercy. Have you not been through enough that you had to take yourself off to the backwoods in the depth of winter? I love you, my darling...my Mercy, I love you. I was a fool...I was a damn fool blinded by duty. But I promise you; I'll never let you down again."

He kissed her with a passion that took Mercy's breath away.

They began to undress each other. They reached the bed and made the most passionate love. It was urgent, ardent, and left them spent and in tears. Mercy felt the absolute joy that had been missing, that feeling of wholeness, of being so close to another person, it was almost as though she were possessed by soul, heart, and mind, as well as body.

She drew her finger across his eyebrows, down his cheeks and along his lip line. "Jacob, we have so much to say to each other, yet I don't know where to begin. Please tell me you love me again. Tell me that no matter what happens, now and in the future, fate will always bring us back together."

Jacob looked adoringly into her eyes. "I love you. I will *always* love you. My darling Mercy, I have nothing to offer you in Portsmouth, but I'm begging you to return with me. We belong together. No matter what happens, no war, no wife, no duty, will ever divide us again. I've spoken to my lawyer. I'm going to annul my marriage...I've already begun the proceedings. I don't care what it costs me or what threats Elizabeth's Pa makes. I will not lose you a second time."

"You should not have married her in the first place," Mercy snapped. "You were weak, Jacob, feeble and selfish. You let me down." She snapped her mouth shut, wishing she hadn't sounded as bitter as sour milk. She had just given herself to him, completely, knowing that he was going to return to his wife. "Is Madame du Pont still living in Portsmouth?" She had to know.

"She is. I wanted to kill her. I almost did. But I believe we might have come to an arrangement. She will never mention your name. She knows that if she does, I will destroy her. She will never get onto my land. Hendry and Belle will see to that. Little by little, we will blacken her reputation, and she will become an outcast. You have my word."

"That's not good enough, Jacob. I want her gone! I can have no future with you or in Virginia with her shadow hanging over us. She is my demon, and I have to rid myself of her. She has to die!"

"Hush darling. You are not a murderer. We'll find a way to get her out of our lives. I promise you. Mercy, did Eddie…did he…?"

"No, I left that house unscathed. Unfortunately, he wasn't as lucky."

Jacob kissed her and then smiled. "My brave and resilient Mercy Carver. You're quite a woman."

"I know how to murder men, that's for sure," she said inadvertently. "Jacob, everyone is talking about war. You will take up arms, won't you?"

Jacob nodded and sighed. "I am already resigned to doing my duty, and when war comes, and the first shots are fired, I will fight. I must. It's my obligation to defend Stone Plantation and my rights."

"Will you hate me if I tell you that I despise slavery? Will *this* issue divide us as it has your States?"

Jacob smiled tenderly. "Nothing will change how I feel for you. I admire your courage and honesty. Your convictions are yours to own. Don't ever let anyone change the way you see the world. I am a slave owner, but you know this and love me all the same. We won't allow it to come between us. Charlie told me Nelson is a good man, and I believe he'd be a dead man had you not rescued him. I'm proud of you under these particular circumstances."

"You're so very wrong. He saved me." Her eyes brightened. "Tell me about Belle and Hendry?"

"They have a daughter. They have named her Grace."

"That's wonderful. I'm happy for them. I wish I could have been there at the birth."

"Belle does too. She and Hendry miss you. They will remain at Stone Plantation if I go off to fight."Jacob paused, looking pensive, and shamefaced. "There is nothing between Elizabeth and me. You have to believe that."

"I do, Jacob. I do, my love," Mercy soothed him. "She doesn't have your heart, for I know it's mine. I felt you follow my every step and every mile. I know you love me, and I also know our destinies are intertwined."

"Elizabeth may leave and go back to her family of her own accord," Jacob told her. "She hates Belle, and she will have no power if Hendry runs the plantation when I'm gone. Mercy, I will be free of her. She has denied me a husband's rights in her bed, and no man on earth will blame me for leaving the marriage. When she leaves, will you go to Stone Plantation and live with Belle and Hendry? When the time comes, will you marry me? Will you be my true wife?"

Mercy's expression was full of conflicting emotions. There was joy in her eyes, worry, and anger.

"Mercy, tell me. Will you have me?"

She kissed him. "I will, perhaps. I'm sorry Jacob, but I must be free of du Pont, and you must be free of Elizabeth, before I go back to Portsmouth or Stone Plantation, or give myself to you forever. I'm staying right here. Will you remain with me for a while? We should talk about all that has passed and about all that may or may not happen in the future.

"Of course I'll stay."

"Mercy smiled. "But when you do leave me, know this: I am yours. I will be here in this town, waiting for you, longing for your return. I will keep myself busy, knowing that you will come back to me. I will never doubt your love, and you must never doubt mine. Eddie, Madame du Pont, and even your marriage did not and cannot defeat us...and, my darling, neither will war."

About the Author

Jana Petken is the author of the multi-award winning epics, The Guardian of Secrets, The Errant Flock, and Mercy Carver Dark Shadows. She is Scottish and presently resides in Spain. She has a military background and has travelled extensively, studying conflicts and the after effects they had on the population. She is a full-time writer but says her hobbies include, walking great distances, and painting in oils.

Contact Jana for updates and information on her other books:

http://www.amazon.com/Jana-Petken/e/B00I2WAUVC/ref=sr_ntt_srch_lnk_1?qid=1444405825&sr=8-1

http://www. janapetkenauthor.com/

https://www.facebook.com/AuthorJanaPetken

@AuthoJana

petkenj@gmail.com

Here's what readers thought of Jana's other books

The Guardian of Secrets

"An epic in every sense, The Guardian of Secrets is War and Peace for a new generation. Packed with emotion and feeling, The Guardian of Secrets details the turbulent decades of the early twentieth century and the tragedy of the Spanish Civil War. Although fiction, this novel reads as reality and as with all her later books, you feel as if the author has travelled back in time and experienced the events for herself."

Blood Moon: The Mercy Carver Series, Book 2

"I am quickly becoming a dedicated Jana Petken fan. After reading "Dark Shadows," book one of the Mercy Carver series, I felt compelled to continue following Mercy's perils and adventures, and book two did not disappoint me. In this sweeping historical tale, Mercy is separated from Jacob, the handsome Southern plantation owner she loves. As the American Civil War breaks out, friends become enemies, and Mercy's fate is to be loved by two men, one a doctor for the Union army, and her dear Jacob, a captain for the Confederates."

The Errant Flock

In true Petken form I was transported back to a very dark time. Poverty, blackmail, oppression, fear and torture were some of the main themes. I literally read this book with a giant knot in my tummy. This author has a true gift.

The Scattered Flock

Jan Petken's flair for sweeping tales is incredible. I read her first book, Guardian of Secrets, many years back and with the Flock trilogy, she doesn't disappoint. Set in Spain during the Inquisition, we live the days through the eyes of our protagonist, David Sanz. Though his story starts in Errant Flock, the first book of the series, the author has ensured that one does not feel lost if you get into the series with the sequel. There is enough background to help you get up to speed.

There are two perspectives to the story, one is that of Dave Sanz and that is the effect of the times on the common man and the hardship they have to endure. The other is through Rafael Perato, one of the ruling class who is on a quest to find out who murdered his brother, The Duke. Along the way, he discovers how deep the intrigues go and how far the corruption extends.

The author brilliantly brings alive the era with her vivid background and complex characters as well as the horror of the inquisition and the futility in the face of such evil. This is one of the times that I wish I had read the first book, before moving on to the second and now I can't wait for the third of the series.

Swearing Allegiance

Jana Petken has done a wonderful job of making the reader feel a part of a difficult & often tragic time in history. The horror of war is mixed with the life and loves of the Carmodys, an Irish family caught between Ireland's fight for independence and World War I. A very worthwhile read.

Coming June 2017, Flock, ***The Gathering of The Damned***

Printed in Great Britain
by Amazon

47030756R00296